PRAISE FOR *ISLES OF THE FORSAKEN*

"In fantasy novels, we hope for many things—vivid and unfamiliar landscapes, complicated and compelling characters, unexpected plot twists, high stakes and huge risks. Gilman delivers all of the above and more. This is a smart and engrossing political novel about imperialism and the clash of cultures in a fascinating new world. The best news? Apparently there will be more. Write like the wind, Gilman!"
—Karen Joy Fowler, Nebula and World Fantasy Award-winning author of
What I Didn't See

"This book is about a people under siege, as well as a commentary on colonialism and invasive wars. . . . It hooked me in from the very beginning."
—herebedragons.com

"The interesting cast of characters did wonders for propelling me onward through the story. . . . An excellent start to a series I know I want to continue with!"
—Bibliotropic

"Vivid world-building, fascinating characters, and a rich, complex story—I love this book!"
—Kij Johnson, Nebula and World Fantasy Award-winning author of
The Fox Woman

"It's beautifully written. It's complex and ambitious in scope. . . . Even better, it's actually about something."
—geekspeakmagazine.com

". . . once all the players in this drama are gathered together it is impossible to turn the pages fast enough to find out what happens next."
—Reading Reality

". . . The good news for Gilman and ChiZine is that I very much want to find out what happens. Can I have the next book now, please?"
—Cheryl's Musings

ISON
OF THE
ISLES

CAROLYN IVES GILMAN

ChiZine Publications

FIRST EDITION

Ison of the Isles © 2012 by Carolyn Ives Gilman
Cover artwork © 2012 by Erik Mohr
Cover design © 2012 by Samantha Beiko
Interior design © 2012 by Danny Evarts
Interior Image © 2012 by Danny Evarts & Tommy Davis
All Rights Reserved.

Library and Archives Canada Cataloguing in Publication

Gilman, Carolyn, 1954-
    Ison of the isles / Carolyn Ives Gilman.

ISBN 978-1-926851-54-9

    I. Title.

PS3613.A358S56 2012   813'.6   C2011-907676-4

CHIZINE PUBLICATIONS
Toronto, Canada
www.chizinepub.com
info@chizinepub.com

Edited and copyedited by Sandra Kasturi
Proofread by Samantha Beiko

 Canada Council   Conseil des Arts
for the Arts   du Canada

We acknowledge the support of the Canada Council for the Arts which last year invested $20.1 million in writing and publishing throughout Canada.

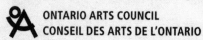 ONTARIO ARTS COUNCIL
CONSEIL DES ARTS DE L'ONTARIO

Published with the generous assistance of the Ontario Arts Council.

PREVIOUSLY, IN
ISLES OF THE FORSAKEN

The Forsaken Islands are scattered like the spray of a breaker off the western coast of the Inning continent. Inhabited by successive waves of peoples, the isolated archipelago is an intricate collage of ancient histories, races, and cultures. Inning is a young nation by comparison, but the Innings are on history's upswing. They have set out to build an empire around their system of government by rule of law, and their principles of reason and justice. *Isles of the Forsaken* begins the story of how Inning invades the Forsakens, setting off a war that tests the deepest beliefs of both nations.

Harg Ismol is a native of the Forsakens who spent seven years in the Inning Navy, rising to the rank of captain. But when he returns home to the island of Yora, he finds that his people, the Adaina, are still living under the thumbs of the enterprising Torna. The Torna are also natives of the Forsakens, but have collaborated with the Innings to gain power. There is even a Torna governor, Tiarch, ruling the isles for Inning. But change is coming; the Innings intend to occupy the isles and spread their system of law to its farthest edges.

Nathaway Talley, the youngest son of a powerful Inning political family, has come to Yora with idealistic intentions of uplifting the natives. He quickly runs afoul of their complex culture when he meets and decides to rescue Spaeth Dobrin, the island's dhotamar.

Spaeth is Lashnura, the oldest and oddest of the races inhabiting the Forsakens. Called the Grey Folk because of their grey skin and hair, the Lashnura play the role of cosmic balance-keepers. In their traditional belief system, the world is a battleground of natural forces called the Mundua and Ashwin. The Lashnura keep the balance between these forces through atonement, by taking on the sufferings of human beings through a curing rite called dhota. The dhotamar gives blood to establish a psychic bond that allows him or her to take on the diseases and injuries of others. But once they have given dhota, Grey Folk can never break the bond to the person who has been cured. Partners in dhota become bandhotai—deeply bound together, psychically, emotionally, and sexually. The Lashnura are saintly figures, but not through their own choice. They are compelled by biological necessity to sacrifice themselves for others.

Spaeth has never given dhota, but is under terrible pressure to do so. Created only seven years ago to be the sexual partner of Goth, the revered dhotamar and shaman of Yora, she has lived a sheltered existence. But Goth has disappeared from Yora, and the arrival of Harg and Nathaway propels Spaeth into the outside world, where she has to reconcile her heritage of compassion with her ardent desire for freedom.

Soon after arriving back, Harg runs afoul of the military occupiers of Yora, and is forced to flee along with Spaeth and their friend Tway. They go to the island of Thimish, where a group of local pirates form the nucleus of a brewing resistance to Inning rule. Harg is drawn into the insurgency, and leads an attack in which the natives capture a fort, three Inning warships, and a group of hostages. The most important hostage is Nathaway Talley.

Before the rebels can follow up on their victory, they learn that the Innings also have an important hostage: the Heir of Gilgen, a Lashnura religious figure who plays an essential role in the leadership system of the isles. In times of crisis, a leader will arise and claim dhota-nur in order to become Ison of the Isles. Dhota-nur is a deep soul-cleansing performed by the Heir of Gilgen. It frees its subject of all the painful memories that cause a person to act out of balance. The captivity of the Heir of Gilgen will prevent an Ison from arising. But more pressing than that, the Heir is Goth, to whom Harg and Spaeth both have complicated emotional ties.

Spaeth's treacherous spirit familiar, Ridwit, manipulates her into leaving for the capital city of Tornabay to find the Heir of Gilgen. Harg follows, bringing Nathaway Talley as a bargaining chip to secure Goth's release. He knows by now that the Innings in Tornabay are commanded by Nathaway's brother, Admiral Corbin Talley, the cultivated but coldblooded head of the Inning Navy. What he does not know is that Talley is at odds with Tiarch, the cunning Torna politician who is the Innings' viceroy. Tiarch's agent, Joffrey, manipulates Harg into meeting with her; but before they can come to terms there is a coup, and Tiarch is ousted from power. She flees with a portion of the Navy that is still loyal to her, and Harg persuades her to join the rebellion against Inning.

Meanwhile, Nathaway escapes from the rebels, but his brother, the Admiral, treats him as a traitor because his letters home have been published and have created sympathy for the natives. Disillusioned, he also escapes from Inning control. Through a series of coincidences he meets Goth, and together they perform a dhota ritual to free Spaeth from the control of the Mundua who have taken over her mind. As a result, Nathaway and Spaeth become joined by a bandhota bond. Goth urges them to flee, and gives Nathaway a mysterious stone pendant that helps them escape. Nathaway makes the fateful decision to abandon his old life and follow Spaeth and the rebels.

ISON OF THE ISLES

THE WINDWARD PASSAGE

When daylight filtered into the *Ripplewill*'s forward cabin, Spaeth stretched out her naked limbs in luxurious comfort. Beside her in the berth, Nathaway Talley was still asleep. A stripe of sunlight lay across his bare shoulder, as if the day were caressing him, as infatuated as she. Gazing at him as he slept, she loved everything about him: the bony angles of his body; the texture of his exotic, pale skin against hers; the way his untrimmed blond bangs fell in his eyes. She loved his smell, she loved his private parts for giving her so much entertainment. With that in mind, she bent down to kiss them awake.

He gave a startled little noise and reached out as if to make sure it was really her being so personal. She straddled him then, and watched as his nearsighted blue eyes focused on her with that look of complete surrender that only one other person had ever given her.

If Spaeth had been a person given to reflection, it might have troubled her that his devotion, while sincere, was not entirely voluntary. She was now the beneficiary of the slavish dhota-bond she had sought so hard to avoid herself. Why Goth had paired them she had no idea, but she accepted it as a gift to her—a strange gift for a man to give his beloved, but one she was quite cheerful to enjoy.

She leaned forward to tickle Nathaway with her hair. "I love having a bandhota," she said. He didn't answer, just reached up to hold her by the arms. A fleeting sadness crossed his face, as if waking brought back the memory of some loss. It reminded her vividly of Goth. Even the green pendant resting against his chest was Goth's. It was as if the Grey Man had created a replica of himself to console her. But Nathaway was much younger and more vigorous. She scooted down to tickle him in a more provocative place.

"Again?" he said, as if astonished at her. But he was joking.

"What do you mean?" she said. "It's been forever."

"At least six hours."

For three days now they had been unable to get enough of each other. The others on the boat were tolerantly amused, but a little agog at the intensity of their libido. Spaeth knew it would fade in time—with her first, since the bond was less lasting on the recipient than on the giver of dhota. She wanted to explore every crevice of him while it was strong.

This time he did it slowly, in time to the rhythmic rocking of the boat, so that it seemed as if she were washed in an ocean of liquid love. She rode the waves as he flowed into her, waking every nerve of her body, making her throb with need.

When they came out on deck, the others cast knowing glances in their direction. It made Spaeth feel cheerful and lucky, but Nathaway wouldn't meet their eyes. She couldn't imagine what his problem was; they all knew he couldn't control himself.

The *Ripplewill* was bounding over the waves like a frisking pony, sending spray flying in rainbow sheets. Even the boat seemed to feel elation at being free of the city. Spaeth made her way to the foredeck, facing west. She was glad to be warmly wrapped in an old coat one of the crewmen had given her, for the northeast wind at her back was piercing.

Tornabay hung like a black haze in the back of Spaeth's memory. She was not proud of the way she had acted there, but self-blame was not a strong part of her nature. In her own mind, she had been lured there by the treachery of the Mundua, then cast into a labyrinth of evils through which she had barely managed to find her way. If it had not been for Goth . . . She tried to drive from her mind what might have happened.

But now she was free. There was a clear sea before her, a strong wind behind, and the Isles all around. She breathed in the mora, like healing oxygen to her starved system. Here there was no suffering to tug at her desires, nothing to own her against her will. She almost felt as if she could drive the *Ripplewill* forward with the wind in her heart.

She took her hands from her pockets and looked at them. They were strong now, the skin a healthy shade of grey. The nails were pearly, purified by the cleansing power of dhota. She clenched them, thinking of Goth. She could still feel his healing touch. Right now, he would be suffering under the brunt of the disease he had taken from her body. He would have to endure that illness alone, with no one to treat him kindly. The ignorant Innings wouldn't even know what ailed him.

Nathaway was making his way forward to join her. He walked stiff-legged, clutching every handhold he could find, constantly off-balance on the canting deck. He needed to relearn everything, she thought—even how to walk.

Soon he was standing precariously beside her. "Where are we?" he said.

Torr had taken them north from Embo to throw off pursuit, since everyone would expect them to go south. They had passed northwest up the strait between Esker and Fosk, called the Windward Passage. "It looks like we're close to the Widewater," she said. "That far island must be Bara. I don't think we need to worry about any Inning boats catching up with us now."

"Then where will we go?"

She frowned, not wanting to think about the future yet. She wanted to enjoy the day.

She stepped to the weather rail and stood looking down into the water. It was a deep green, shot with long sun-shafts. The shadow of her head scuffed across the waves, and the sunbeams all seemed to be radiating from it like a spiky crown. Down there, she thought, lay the realms of the Mundua.

Nathaway joined her. Now his shadow was crowned with light, too. "What do the Innings think lies below the sea?" she asked. "Just more sea?"

"No. The sea has a bottom."

"And what is under the bottom?"

"Rock."

"And under the rock?"

"There is nothing under the rock. That's all the world is, just a ball of rock."

How safe they must feel, she thought. Utterly in control. She looked up to where the thin blue shell of sky hid the realms of the Ashwin. Only the Isles lay in between the ancient antagonists. Her lovely land, saved from unbeing only by the precarious balance of power between the forces, and the balance of suffering and joy that was the peculiar gift of humankind.

Nathaway was still talking. "It's a ball of rock revolving around the sun, you see. As it spins, it turns away from the sun, making day and night. It's tilted on its axis, so the days and nights are longer or shorter depending on which side is tipped toward the sun. That's what creates seasons." He stopped, watching her. "You don't believe me," he said.

Spaeth shrugged. "It's probably true in your land. Not here."

"If it's true, it has to be true everywhere."

To her, every permutation of every truth was possible. The universe was a layer cake of truths, all coexisting.

"Maybe the world *is* a ball of rock," she conceded. "But the lands of the Mundua still lie under the sea."

"Both things can't be true. They contradict each other."

"So do hope and despair, but they both exist."

"That's not the same," he said. "They are things of the mind."

"So are rocks and seasons, in the long run," Spaeth said.

The wind was blowing his hair into his eyes. He brushed it away; it was instantly back. "I can't believe Goth didn't teach you—"

"What? To think like an Inning?"

He frowned. "To use your reason. You have a good mind, Spaeth."

"He probably thought it wouldn't make me happy. It hasn't made you happy." He looked startled at this, but it was true. Ever since she had met him, she had felt an unfulfilled longing in him, as if the world had not quite lived up to his expectations. It was as if he thought the universe ought to behave by certain rules, and he was always disappointed when he found out it didn't. Yet he never revised his expectations—instead, he tried to revise the world to conform to them. It would never occur to an islander to demand that the universe behave.

A wave made the deck of the *Ripplewill* lurch, and Nathaway was flung against her. She caught hold of him to keep him from toppling overside.

"We can't become like you," Spaeth said softly, her arms still strong around him. "We have to find our own way. With mora."

"Magic?" he said sceptically, as if this solved nothing.

"Mora isn't just magic. It's the force that holds everything together. This land is thick with mora. Can't you feel it? Look out there, how the sea is sparkling, winking at us like it knows a joke. *That's* mora."

He didn't answer, just stood looking out at the sea, as if seeing it her way were a challenge to his personal boundaries. As if he couldn't acknowledge the world's personality without questioning his own.

Having an Inning for a lover was going to be hard work, she thought. And then she wondered: had Goth given him to her, or her to him?

At sunset they gathered in the cramped main cabin to settle on their route. Tway was uncharacteristically moody. Before anyone else had a chance to speak she said, "I think we should circle round and go back. We've left three friends stranded in Tornabay with a pack of vengeful Innings on their heels."

Nathaway stirred restlessly, and she turned on him. "Well, it's true."

"If they're in custody already, there is nothing we can do," he said.

"We still have you to dicker with," she said darkly, making Spaeth clutch his arm possessively.

Torr interrupted, "We don't know the Innings have them, or even if they're still in Tornabay. They could all be leagues away by now, heading for the South Chain, and we'd only get ourselves captured going back for them. Harg wouldn't thank us for that. I say we should head to Harbourdown to rendezvous. That's where they'll go."

Glancing at Spaeth, Nathaway said cautiously, "I've got another idea."

They all looked at him, silent with surprise. He went on, "I've been asking myself what we could do that would be really effective. I think we should go to Fluminos."

For a few moments there was silence. Then Tway said, "The Inning capital? What good would that do?"

"It might do a lot of good," Nathaway said. "What's happening here in the Forsaken Islands isn't being controlled from Tornabay. The Navy obeys orders from Fluminos. That's where the occupation is being planned, and where we need to go to stop it. You have to understand how our system works; it's all in the laws and courts. What we need to do is bring suit in the High Court to challenge the occupation."

Spaeth tried to imagine entering another city. The very thought made her mind revolt. No Lashnura was made for it. They were too vulnerable.

Tway was scowling suspiciously at the Inning. "Why are *you* thinking of ways to stop the occupation?" she asked.

For a moment Nathaway looked flustered. He suddenly discovered something interesting in his hands, to avoid meeting any of their eyes. "I . . . I've come to think it's being handled wrong. We're violating our own principles, subverting our own system. We need to pull back, not just for your sake, but for our own. Otherwise, nothing we do here will be really just."

He was admitting he had been wrong. Feeling as doting as if she had created him, Spaeth squeezed his hand. "How many people live in Fluminos?" she asked softly.

"Tens of thousands," he said. "Maybe hundreds, I don't know."

"And how many dhotamars do they have?"

"None."

All those people with no one to love or cure them, lashing out in their pain. The very land would ache under them. No wonder they came here to escape. "I couldn't go there," she said faintly. "I couldn't cure them all."

He was looking at her anxiously. "No one would want you to. You might even like it, Spaeth. I would make sure you were treated well. You could meet my family. You would like my sister."

"I would die," she said.

There was a silence. They could hear the wind outside. Cory, the sailor on watch, was playing his tin whistle out on deck. It made a plaintive, reedy sound. Spaeth shook her head to clear it of thoughts. All of this talk was useless. Nathaway knew as well as she did where they had to go. "Anyway, we must go to Lashnish," she said.

Tway and Torr had heard nothing of this, and they looked as if she were raving. "It's a hundred years since Lashnish was capital of the Isles," Tway said. "Why go there?"

"Because Goth told us to. I don't know why." She looked at Nathaway for corroboration. "He said to go to Lashnish, and find the Isonstone." She looked around at the others. Their faces were lit at odd angles by the lantern that swayed from one of the beams, and the glow from the small cast-iron stove.

"He said that?" Tway asked intently. "To find the Isonstone?"

"Yes."

"Why? What does it mean?" Nathaway interrupted.

There was a short silence. Then, in a low voice, Tway said, "When the Isles are in danger, and the balances need to be set right again, a great leader will arise. He or she must go to Lashnish and strike the Isonstone as a public pledge. If the candidate is fit, then the Heir of Gilgen will answer the summons before the next full moon. There, in sight of all, the Heir of Gilgen performs dhota-nur. The candidate's body and mind are both stripped clean before the people he would lead, so that they can see his soul. An Ison must be freed of all pain, so that nothing controls him."

"That's barbarous," Nathaway said.

"It is our custom," Tway said, "and the only way there can be an Ison." She turned to Spaeth, who shrank back before the stern look in her eyes. "If Goth told you to find the Isonstone, he must have intended to send you in his stead, knowing he could not answer the summons himself. He was passing on his power, and his responsibility as Heir of Gilgen."

"To me?" Spaeth said, quaking.

"You are the closest thing he has to a daughter."

Nathaway caught her hand and held it protectively.

She wanted to escape, to flee, even to Fluminos if that was what it took. What good had it done her to escape the traps of Tornabay, and the grim compulsion of the Black Mask, only to be forced into another sort of slavery? If what Tway said was true, then Spaeth was not free, as she had thought. Somewhere out there was the bandhota she would still be given to. The balances themselves would link her forever to the Ison they chose. Her freedom was like an autumn day, doomed by the imminence of winter. This might be the last choice she would ever make.

She looked at Nathaway, wanting him to take this duty away from her, and knowing he would do it if he could. But that was impossible; both of them were caught in a shadowy current they could not resist.

That night, Spaeth was wakened by the feeling that something was wrong with Nathaway. When she reached out for him, he wasn't beside her in the berth. The boat was moving with a strange, arrhythmic pitching. She sat up, and in the light filtering under the door to the main cabin, dimly made out the glimmer of his pale body, hunched over a pail. He looked marvellously ill.

"It's nothing," he managed to say when she touched him. "Go back to sleep."

But she couldn't lie there with his seasickness permeating her consciousness, so she pulled on some clothes and left to get away. It made her impatient that such a trivial ailment in him could have such a hold on her.

The lantern in the main cabin was swinging at a crazy angle. Tway sat beside the stove, mending a sail. Spaeth went over to warm her hands; the cracks around the stove door gave off a dull yellow glow.

"Where are we?" Spaeth asked.

Tway bit off the end of a thread. "We came out of the lee of Fosk half an hour ago," she said. "The wind's been picking up since then. Torr says it's going to be a regular nor'easter."

Heavy footsteps sounded on the deck above, and the hatch was jerked open. A black roar of wind and spray came in as Torr lowered himself into the relative quiet of the hold.

"We need some help above," he said. Tway rose at once, but Spaeth put a hand on her arm. "Let me go," she said. "I need some fresh air."

"Well, that we can give you," Torr said.

When she emerged onto the open deck, a lashing of cold spray met her. She groped for a handhold in the wind; the canvas smock she had put on pressed against her like a sail. Slowly she made her way back along the lantern-lit deck to the cockpit, where Torr stood at the helm. His eyes were scanning the black sea warily. "We're going to have to take a second reef in the mainsail if you can handle the tiller," he said.

"This is a nasty storm," she said. She meant it literally; it had a malicious mood.

Torr shrugged. "It's a treacherous part of the Widewater, here."

"How far are we from the end of Esker?"

Torr gestured into the blackness. "You tell me."

As the skipper went forward, leaving her alone in the cockpit, Spaeth wondered if they had just escaped the firesnakes of Embo to fall prey to the horned panther. It was Ridwit who ruled the storms, or so the stories said. Would an old friendship have any weight against the wrath of a betrayed god? Spaeth clutched the tiller hard.

Keeping the boat on course proved to be hard work, for the waves and wind were tugging hard. One moment Spaeth would brace herself against the cockpit wall and push with all her strength to keep the tiller straight; the next, the trickster waves would loosen their grip or fling the rudder the opposite way. In the dim lantern light she could see that Torr and the sailors had made their way forward to where the mainsail strained, the boom nearly skidding in the foam to the lee of the leaning boat. Torr waved back at Spaeth. She heaved the tiller over, and the *Ripplewill* veered into the wind. As soon as the sail began to flap loose, Cory lowered the halyard; Torr strained to pull in the swollen, slippery main sheet and bring the boom back over the boat. The sail cracked like a whip in the wind.

It should have been a routine task; they had all done it a thousand times. But just as Galber was leaning out to catch hold of the sail, Spaeth felt the impact of an invisible wave against the hull, and the tiller was wrenched from her hands. The mainsail puffed out with wind; the boom swung violently to starboard, knocking Galber sprawling on the narrow deck. The *Ripplewill* rolled madly and Galber slipped to the edge. Torr lunged after him, one hand still on the main sheet. Then a wave broke clear over the bow and came rushing aft, a furious river of foam. It picked up Torr and Galber like sticks of driftwood and threw them against the low gunwale rail. Spaeth cried out, expecting to see them washed over into the churning sea the next moment. Then a sheet of spray doused the mid-ship lantern and plunged the scene into darkness.

There was nothing she could do. She could not leave the tiller; *Ripplewill's* nose had to be kept into the shifting wind. Cursing, she leaned into her task. A gust threw back her canvas hood. Alert for its mood and strategy, she realized the wind's treachery with the sail had been no accident. Something out there had found them.

A solid shape lurched into the light of the cockpit lantern. It was Torr, supporting Galber. He lowered the seaman onto the floor of the cockpit, looped a rope around his waist, and secured it to a cleat. He turned briefly to Spaeth, thumping her on the back and roaring, "You're doing well," then disappeared forward again.

She realized at once that Galber was badly hurt. At first he smiled back bravely at her, as if to say the sea would have to try harder to get *him*. But gradually the colour left his face. His lips turned grey, and he began to tremble.

Spaeth's instincts were screaming. She fought to keep her thoughts from bending toward him, attracted by the magnetism of his pain. Grimly she gripped the tiller; if she took her hand from it, she would put all their lives in jeopardy. *Concentrate on the wind*, she repeated. *Keep the bow into the wind. Don't look at him. Don't think about him.*

Her self-control was frayed to a thread when Cory appeared, coming aft. He called, "Bear off to larboard, as close to the wind as you can!"

"Cory!" she screamed. Hearing the agony in her voice, he came closer. "Galber's hurt."

Cory glanced at Galber. "Hold on, I'll get help," he said, then disappeared again.

Spaeth nearly screamed in frustration. Galber was fading now, chilled and in shock. Vividly she could feel his mind still fluttering with life, his pain like a sweet bath she could drown in.

Someone was taking the tiller from her hand. She lunged toward Galber, blind now to all but his need.

Tway pulled her back. "We've got to get him below!" she said.

Yes. Spaeth summoned a vestige of control. Galber groaned as Cory and Tway helped him up. It sent a stab of aching pity through her. "It's his shoulder! Be careful of it," she said. They manoeuvred him precariously forward to the main hatch, down the ladder, and at last onto the berth by the stove.

Instantly Spaeth was at his side. "Get me a knife!" she ordered.

Tway's hand on her arm was firm. "Spaeth, no!" she said. "You can't give him dhota."

She was right, of course. Spaeth swallowed back a wild, wordless cry of frustration. If she cured him, she would be bound to him forever, imprisoned in a blissful cage of love. His injury had all the marks of a scheme to turn her from her goal, to divert her so she would never reach Lashnish. She had to be cruel now, and leave him to his suffering. She backed away, the compulsion sharp and piercing in her.

Nathaway was bending over Galber. "You say it's his shoulder?" he asked.

"Yes, the right side," Spaeth said.

"Get me a knife," he said.

They all stared at him, motionless. "To cut away his shirt, damn it!" he said.

Cory handed him a knife. Spaeth groaned at sight of it.

"Get her out of here," Nathaway said sharply. "I can take care of this."

Tway pushed her up the companion ladder, out into the wind.

The slap of cold against her face was calming. With Tway behind, she made her way aft to the cockpit, where Torr stood at the helm. He eyed them curiously. Gradually, as the sharpness of Galber's suffering faded, Spaeth began to realize how close she had come to giving in. And then there could have been no Ison for the Isles.

That had been the purpose, of course. Spaeth stared out into the blackness where the Mundua dwelt. They had thought she was their tool, but now she had slipped in their hands, and was threatening to cut them.

Spaeth looked at Tway through the rain. "They are trying to stop me," she said.

Tway bent close, frowning. "Who?"

"The Mundua. They don't want me to reach Lashnish."

"Then why hurt Galber?"

"To lure me into giving dhota. They're cruel, Tway; they don't care who they hurt, or how badly. You're all in danger."

Ripplewill had steadied under Torr's hand. She was not so far heeled over now, and met the waves head on instead of floundering at their mercy. But the wind was still building, and in the dim light of the stern lantern Spaeth could see whitecaps peppering the sea. Between the patches of foam and spindrift the black water had an ominous, polished look, like metal.

When Cory returned from the cabin, he brought a flask of hot nog to warm them all. But there was chilling news. "The Inning says Galber's got a broken collarbone," he said.

"Then we've all got to pitch in," Torr said, his voice as flat as his understatement.

Cory had brought rope for lifelines. Each of them tied a length around their waist and made the other end fast to a cleat with about ten feet of slack to allow them to move about. Then they settled down to wait.

The cold water seeped into their boots, and the taste of salt crusted the insides of their mouths. In the lulls of wind Spaeth could hear Torr talking softly to his boat. "That's it, *Ripplewill*, into the wave; no, don't jerk that way; it'll swamp you for sure. That's it—stop heeling—there. Brave girl!"

Spaeth rose to stand beside the skipper, hugging herself for warmth. "Can't we turn south and search for a harbour?"

Torr reached under his rain gear and took out a gold Inning watch. He held it in the binnacle to keep the rain off. "An hour past midnight," he said. "I expect we can."

Some spray hit Spaeth's body like a handful of pebbles flung hard. She would feel bruised in the morning, she thought. It seemed eons away.

Cory spoke up. "I think we should stop fighting the storm."

"What do you mean?" Spaeth said.

"Take down the sails and lie ahull. There's nothing downwind of us now but the Widewater, unless we're blown all the way across to the Outer Chain. Open sea's our safest course. We can just hold tight till the Panther's tired herself out."

He didn't know Ridwit. Spaeth felt a gnawing unease at thought of surrendering, letting the wind blow them far from the sheltering isles, where humanity's only anchor lay, into the open wastes. But Torr finally said, "You're right. An island coast is more danger to us now than the sea."

So that decided it. Again Spaeth took the tiller, and the others went forward to strike the mainsail, with Tway taking Galber's place. In order to maintain some control over the craft, Torr had them set a close-reefed mizzen and a tiny forestaysail. Even with these small rags of sail, the *Ripplewill* picked up an alarming speed as she began to run before the wind.

The waves grew with every mile they made into the Widewater. The sea was no longer the familiar plain of day; they had entered a rugged, unknown countryside. Climbing each wave, the *Ripplewill* would slow down; but when she crested the hill of water and the wind caught her, she plunged forward with sickening impetuosity, down the gaping valley, the entire hull shivering with speed. Torr struggled to steer diagonally down the slopes to prevent the boat's speed from burying the bow in the next wave. The crew all peered into the night, keeping watch for rogue waves that might catch the boat abeam and flip her over sideways. Once, they shot up over a crest with more than usual speed; when the wave fell out from underneath, *Ripplewill* plummeted through air before striking the surface again with a jolt that made the bulkheads groan.

"If we're not leaking now," Torr said through his teeth, "then this little lady is built better than I knew." Cory went below to check.

To Spaeth, the entire world seemed animate with anger. A cold anger this time, not the flaming rage of Embo. She could feel it in the black, muscled hills of water around her, in the wind that whipped the spume from their crests. The *Ripplewill* seemed tiny as a chip of wood.

She looked at Torr standing at the helm, his eyebrows bristling with droplets. "Torr, have you ridden out a storm like this before?"

"Don't worry," he said. "We can make it, as long as we only have wind and sea to outwit."

"What else is there?"

For a while he didn't answer. At last he said, "Pariah storms, my uncle used to call them. When the chains on the Mundua and Ashwin start slipping, the winds that blow can make the circles themselves flap like a rotten sail. He always said it was such a storm that ended Alta, long ago, when the wind tore a great rip in reality. He thought a pariah storm would end the Isles, some day. Gloomy fellow, he was."

Like a trickle of chill water down her back, the thought came to Spaeth: Goth's hand was slipping. It had been for months. Something had gone terribly wrong.

Spaeth untied her liferope from its cleat and wrapped the end around her waist. "I'm going forward," she said.

"Why?" Torr demanded.

"I have to be alone. Don't anyone follow me."

He scowled at her, but "Mind your step," was all he said.

She held onto the gunwale rail as she went forward, now climbing a steep slope, now slipping forward down one. She passed the mizzen and the mainmast, and came to the foredeck, washed in spray. Here the motion of the boat seemed even greater, her speed dizzying, for there was nothing between her and the sea.

She clutched the rail hard. "Ridwit!" she shouted. The wind ripped the voice from her mouth. "Ridwit!" she called again.

The moon broke out from the scudding clouds, and for a few moments the churning landscape was lit plain to see. In every direction hunched the black shoulders of monster waves, their tops flaring with spray. Where two waves collided the sea boiled with foam, and spray flurried west before the wind. As the *Ripplewill* plunged into a trough, the great lurching shape of an oncoming wave towered above her, until it seemed the small craft would be buried under the mountain of water.

The wave had eyes, Spaeth was sure of it. "What do you want?" she screamed at it.

The *Ripplewill* rose on the wave's flank, and the giant lumbered on underneath. The wind hissed in Spaeth's ears; she could almost hear words. "You coward!" she shouted. "Does it make you feel big to hurt a few humans who can't even fight you?"

The moon plunged under again, and the world turned black. Spaeth sensed rather than saw the sinuous black shape dashing across the waves beside the boat, keeping even.

"You have grown very keen, my little ally," the wind snarled in her ear.

"I've learned to see through you, traitor! All you've ever done is trick me. You warned me that someone was in alliance with you, and all the time it was me!"

"It was funny, wasn't it?" Ridwit said. "It would have been even more funny if you had killed the Heir of Gilgen."

Spaeth's rage was black as the night. It *was* the night. Its power dwarfed her, mighty enough to shatter worlds. "See?" Ridwit hissed. "You are still better off with me."

"No!" Spaeth cried. She had to resist this time. She had to struggle—for what? For powerlessness? To become a mite raging at the mountains?

She felt her own mouth stretching open as Ridwit laughed. *I must pull free,* Spaeth thought in panic. *I must become who I am.*

"Together, we have the power," Ridwit said. "Let's smash this little boat."

It would crunch in her hand, its puny planks disintegrate to kindling. And all the heartbeats aboard would grow cold and die. The thought wrenched Spaeth's mind off its course.

"Leave us alone!" she screamed. "These humans never did you any harm!"

The water laughed coldly against the hull. "What a weakling they make you. You are just like all the other Grey People: a doting fool for them. You will never have control while you let them enslave you. Give them up."

Spaeth thought of Galber, bearing his pain because she couldn't; of Tway's loyalty, Torr's trustworthiness. And Nathaway, who loved her with such abandon.

Tears filled her eyes as she felt the power drain away, leaving her helpless. She was on her knees now, still clutching the rail, a river of water washing around her legs.

Our only power is pity, she felt Goth say. Spaeth had never felt more helpless. There was cruel laughter on the wind.

"Do you really think you can be the Heir of Gilgen now?" Ridwit said. "After you allied yourself with me? You proved yourself unfit."

"Leave me alone!" Spaeth's voice was drowned in the wind.

Step by step she made her way aft, to join the others huddled there. When she came close, Tway reached out to help her down into the cockpit, and put a warm arm around her.

"Torr! Larboard beam!" Cory shouted. The skipper glanced around and threw his weight against the tiller to bring the boat about. Spaeth turned to see the looming shape of a huge wave bearing down on them.

Torr's manoeuvre came too late. The wave lifted the *Ripplewill* up; a breaker arched above like a gaping mouth edged with teeth of spray. Torr's mouth formed the words, "Hold tight!" and the wave broke. A furious force of water buried them all. Spaeth had grasped a line, and now the deluge tore at her body, knocking the air out of her, pulling until her grip began to slip. All her will was in her hands, forcing them to keep clenched to safety. There was no up or down any more, no air, nothing but the elemental force of water.

Then there was a surface again, a place where water ended and air began. Spaeth gasped in. The wave was receding before them. Torr and Tway had been knocked to the other side of the cockpit, and Cory was nowhere to be seen.

Tway lunged for the tiller; Spaeth crawled through a wash of water to the spot where Cory's liferope was fastened. It was taut; she heaved, but couldn't budge it. "Torr, here!" she shouted. He came to her side, a dripping bear of a man. With slow, powerful movements he began to pull the rope in. Cory's head bobbed above the water a little way to starboard. Hand over hand, against the force of the waves, Torr hauled his crewman in.

When Cory was near enough, Torr cleated the line and leaned over the gunwale to give him a hand. Their fingers almost touched; then the boat lifted up on a wave, carrying them apart. Spaeth could tell Cory was weakening from being dragged behind the boat in the wintry water. Again Torr leaned overside. This time the boat tilted into the sea, and the two men's hands clasped. With a heave of superhuman strength Torr hefted Cory up and over the gunwale. Cory collapsed, gasping and dripping, on the floor of the cockpit.

Nathaway appeared out of the night. "What happened?" he shouted.

"Wave knocked her over," Torr roared. "I mean over flat. The mast was in the sea. But she righted herself, by the horns! She came up again like a top. My little beauty!" He seemed about to throw himself down and kiss the deck.

Instead he thumped Tway on the shoulder till her clothing squished. "It's that keel of Yoran lead!"

"We Yorans usually know which way is up," Tway said.

Torr turned to the Inning. "How is the hold?"

"Wet," Nathaway said.

"You two get down there and help him," Torr said to Cory and Spaeth. Cory tried to protest that he was fit, but Spaeth could tell he was bruised and bone-chilled. "That's an order, Cory," Torr said ominously.

The hold was a dark and swimming chaos. Everything that had not been fastened down had been pitched to the floor, and now floated in a foot of sloshing water. All lights had been extinguished, and the tinder was drenched or lost. Somewhere in the darkness, Galber was groaning in pain.

"Where's the pump, Cory?" Spaeth demanded to distract herself from the sound of Galber's voice.

"Over here." They groped their way aft and set to work, dragging the pump into the centre of the cabin and running a hose out the hatchway. Then each of them took one side of the seesaw pump handle. It remained to be seen whether they could pump faster than the water was leaking in.

Survival became a matter of grim persistence. It was forcing burning muscles to bend yet again and again, until Spaeth lost all track of time and all memory of anything but the fragile shell of wood that kept out the hostile sea.

She was still working in a stupor when Nathaway put his hand on her arm and said, "I'll handle it now. You rest." Spaeth realized with surprise that she could see his face; and what was more, she could see the hold around her—no longer aswim in water, but cluttered by jetsam as if left by a receding tide.

When she emerged onto the open deck, the morning was dawning dull over a pewter sea. The *Ripplewill* still scudded west before an angry gale. When lifted high on the back of a wave, Spaeth could see miles of grey combers surrounding them under a lowering sky. But the light rushed to her head like a strong liquor. They had survived the night. Not by magic, not by power—by sheer stubborn unwillingness to let each other die.

Torr was still at the helm. His face wore an absorbed expression as he scanned the sea, attuned to every nuance of water and wind. From time to time the bow would disappear in a wall of foam, but it always rose again. They could no longer doubt their boat; every movement she made was like part of their own bodies.

The wind shifted north during the day, and turned cold. All their efforts at starting the stove again proved futile. Everything in the boat was drenched, and all they could do was bear the chill and hope for land and shelter ahead.

It was a worn and weary crew that finally raised a cheer when Torr sighted a line of hills on the western horizon. They gathered in the cockpit, peering ahead as the coast rose before them. "It has to be some island of the Outer Chain," Torr said. "We've been blown clear across the Widewater."

The shore was a line of jagged, rocky cliffs, their tops swathed in waterlogged clouds. The sea churned at their bases, spray leaping high against black rock. Even at a distance the booming of the breakers sounded.

They turned south along the coast. At last they spied the roofs of some stone cottages dotting the hill beyond a headland that surely hid a sheltering bay. The cheering sight of smoke rose from chimneys into the rain-soaked sky.

"I am going to sit down in the first fire I see," Tway declared. "I think you could turn me on a spit for an hour, and I'd scarcely thaw."

"I think I'll have to peel these clothes off like an orange rind," Cory said.

Torr said, "Well, I'm going to sleep for two days, and nothing on earth is going to wake me."

They were skirting the headland before they saw what lay in the harbour. Torr jerked the tiller round, making the *Ripplewill* heel sharply in confusion. There, behind the arm of land, rose the tall masts and square rigging of a frigate guarding the bay.

Nathaway looked deadly weary. "The rest of you might slip past an inspection, but they'll notice me," he said. "If they're suspicious, they might detain us. There could easily be a warrant out for my arrest."

Spaeth looked at Torr, then slowly shook her head.

"It's a far piece back to Lashnish," Torr said. But he pushed the tiller over and sent the *Ripplewill* shooting out to sea again. "Let's raise the mainsail, Cory," he said. "If we're going to defy the Panther, we might as well do it like we mean it." He patted the *Ripplewill*'s transom. "Hold tight a little while longer, darling. You can't rest yet."

THE
SLEEPING CITY

Dear Rachel, Nathaway wrote. He was sitting at Torr's desk in the aft cabin, the portion of the *Ripplewill* that had been least damaged by the storm, and easiest to restore to a semblance of order. It had taken them several days to find a friendly harbour, perform some necessary caulking and repairs, and dry out their clothes and bedding. Now they were headed east again with a piercing north wind on their larboard quarter. At first, the deep roll of the swells had made it difficult to write, but Nathaway had caught the rhythm now.

There were already two closely written pages on the desk, in which he had poured out his feelings of betrayal at his sister for having published his previous letters without permission, and a vivid account of the trouble it had gotten him into. Now he had reached the part of the letter where he had to explain where he was and how he had gotten here. He sat staring at the page with the ink drying on his pen, unable to think of any justification that would reconcile his family to what he had done.

He had, in fact, developed a reasoned legal argument for his actions. In it, he had been a victim of unlawful detention by the military authority, and his escape from Inning custody was purely an assertion of his rights against unjust coercion. His flight in no way implied collaboration with enemies of the state. He could almost believe it himself.

But Rachel was a more exacting judge, and would instantly throw out his arguments. His task was complicated by the fact that he had to leave out large portions of the story. He could include his meeting with Goth, but not the pivotal fact that he had participated in a curing ceremony to restore Spaeth to health. He could say how he and Spaeth had escaped the palace, but not what they had seen along the way. He could not suggest how deeply he had become submerged in the strange, sacrificial world of the Lashnura, or his growing respect for their ethics. He would have to weave a carefully detached and factual story. And yet, the facts would never explain why he had abandoned his duty, deserted his country, and disobeyed all legal authority, in order to follow Spaeth into exile. There was no way to portray those actions as anything other than rash and immature at best, treasonous at worst.

No way but one, the portion of the truth he knew Rachel would accept. Suddenly coming to a decision, he wrote fast:

> I can't explain this, Rachel, except to say that I love her and found it impossible to abandon her, even though it meant forsaking my home and duty to my country. Please try to understand, I've never felt anything like this before. She is all I can think of, day and night—not my obligations, not my family, not my home, nothing but her. I am perfectly confident I will feel this way forever—the thought of not feeling this way is just impossible to contemplate. She has completely transformed me. I know what I have given up to be with her—I think of it every day—but there is simply no other choice I could have made.
>
> My greatest fear now is that she will become entangled in this rebellion, not through her own choice, but because of her heritage. Already some of our shipmates regard her as an Heir of Gilgen, as Goth was before her. The Heir of Gilgen, you must know, is obliged to play an important ritual role in the creation of an Ison to lead the Isles. If there is a demand placed on her to anoint such a leader, then she will become his ritual bride through the ceremony of dhota-nur. I cannot think of the possibility without the utmost dread, for if it should happen, I would surely lose her—and that means I would lose everything. I can't think about it; I have to drive it from my mind. After all, it may not happen.
>
> Oh Rachel, what is to become of us? It seems unlikely that we will be allowed to live in peace, with our countries at war. On the one side, the rebels' success is bound up in her decisions. On the other, there will be repercussions for my actions, when Corbin wins—as, of course, he will. We can only live for the moment, hoping the day of reckoning will be postponed, but knowing it must come—to which of us first, we don't

know. It makes the time we have together painfully sweet, like a poison
that must kill us, but which gives us intense happiness in the meantime.
Why could this war not be settled peaceably?

∾

On the next day, the mountainous outline of Roah appeared on the horizon
before them. Its black, steep-shouldered shores rose abruptly from the sea,
crowned with pine and cloaked with mist and endless rain.

There was a sentinel frigate anchored at the entry to Roslip Firth, but as the
Ripplewill approached, it made no move to interfere, and so they passed on into
the narrow inlet that pierced deep into the heart of Roah. Anyone who did not
know it would scarcely have imagined that a city lay at its end. Steep, forested
slopes loomed high on either side. Streaks of white interrupted the black cliff
faces where streams rushed down through gorges, and through the breaks they
could glimpse layer after layer of hill disappearing into the mist, herringboned
with pine. Torn shreds of cloud snagged on the jagged tree-tips. Far above, gulls
hung almost motionless in the wind, wings spread.

The channel jagged right, then left. As they were rounding the final turn,
the westering sun came out from the clouds behind them, illuminating the
scene ahead. Here, the gorge widened out into a broad, deep bay. Above it, on a
west-facing slope of the mountain, rose Lashnish: tier upon pink marble tier,
luminous against the dark pine slopes. From its face a thousand windows gazed
westward, gleaming in the sun like eyes filled with tears. It looked tranquil and
old, absorbed with memories and regrets. The travellers lined the forward rail,
gazing at it, thinking there could be no more beautiful city in the world.

"The Sleeping City they call it," Torr said.

"Why is that?" Nathaway asked.

"It wakes only once every century or so, when an Ison arises to lead the
Isles."

A grand, white marble quay outlined the waterfront, curving round to form
two breakwaters that projected into the bay like open arms, with towering
lamps on either end. At the base of the curve, opposite a broad street that led
uphill, a set of wide ceremonial steps descended under a towering arch into the
water.

Another ship of Tiarch's fleet was moored in the quiet bay, its reflection
unrippled beneath it. Even though there was no sign of curious customs
inspectors here, Torr was cautiously reluctant to bring the *Ripplewill* in to that

graceful marble pier, so they cast anchor in the harbour, and made the jolly boat ready to ferry passengers ashore.

"Should we look for lodgings?" Tway asked, looking to Spaeth and Nathaway.

Neither of them answered at first. At last Nathaway said, "'Find the Isonstone,' that's all Goth said."

"All right, then. You find the Isonstone, I'll find lodgings."

It proved to be no difficult task. The first person they asked, a Torna shopkeeper, gave them directions to the Isonstone. "It's up in the Old Town, in the Pavilion cloister," he said, as if it were a question he was used to answering. "Follow the Stonepath uphill; it'll take you right there. You'd better hurry; they close the gates at sunset."

The Stonepath proved to be the central spine-street of the city that led straight uphill from the harbour, lined on either side with imposing buildings. As Nathaway and Spaeth mounted the hill, the harbour sounds and smells fell away behind them, and the spires of the ancient city rose all around. The mood grew peaceful and quiet, as if suspended in time.

The ancient Altan architecture was better preserved here than in any place Nathaway had ever seen. It had an airy quality, complex with pillared porticoes and lofty arches, made of white marble with grey veins. There were whole blocks of Altan buildings that looked like they had once been ceremonial halls, or administrative centres; but their tall doors were closed now, and no guards stood at their gates. Their windows looked dusty and unused.

As they passed a side street, Spaeth clutched Nathaway's arm. "Nat, look!" she said.

A tall, silver-haired man was leaving a building with a dog on a leash. He looked perfectly unremarkable as he stopped to chat with a woman leaning out a window across the way. "What is it?" Nathaway asked.

"They're Grey Folk, both of them," Spaeth said. "They can live in the open here, as if they were free people."

The farther they climbed, the more grey faces they saw. Spaeth stared at them, entranced and hopeful, but she herself drew few answering stares. Nathaway was another matter. He was aware of eyes following him with puzzled frowns, and suspicious glances from passers-by. It made him feel as if they had passed one of those invisible boundaries that exist in cities, into a protected enclave where he was an intruder.

The Stonepath came to an end in a broad, deserted square. Facing them was a tall building of white marble, friezed with ancient Altan symbols. To Nathaway's eyes it looked like a court, or a college building. The main entrance was between tall, fluted pillars where the copper gates still stood open on the square. Hand in hand, Nathaway and Spaeth walked forward. No one was there to challenge them.

Inside the gateway was an open lawn planted with trees and shrubs, and lined on all four sides with a covered walkway set back behind airy arches. The little enclosed park was very quiet, and had a contemplative air, far removed from the world and its concerns.

At the very centre of the lawn was a marble plinth, and on it stood an ordinary boulder of granite. As they approached, Nathaway saw that its face was pocked where it had been battered in the past by blows from a sledgehammer that stood cradled in a wrought iron stand next to the stone. Some of the spalls were so worn by rain and time that they were just dips in the stone surface. But there was a fresher scar on the left side.

"Perhaps that is Ison Orin's," Spaeth said in a low voice. It seemed irreverent to talk loudly, here.

"How long ago was that?"

"I don't know," she said.

"Sixty-two years," a voice answered. They turned around to find an elderly Grey Man watching them from under the shadow of one of the arches. He was dressed in an ancient, traditional style: a long tabard and leggings, with a short mantle around his shoulders. It reminded Nathaway of the legal robes worn by advocates in court. The man came forward, studying them curiously. He had a short fringe of white hair around his bald head, and was carrying a book.

"Is this the Isonstone?" Nathaway asked.

"Indeed it is," the Grey Man said. He turned to look at it. "Those scars on the stone go back six centuries. They all stood here, the leaders willing to forfeit their self-will for the sake of the Isles. And out in that square is where the Heirs of Gilgen bled to erase all harm from those leaders' hearts."

They regarded it in silence for a while.

"I'm surprised it's not guarded," Nathaway said. "Aren't you afraid someone might seize it? Considering its importance."

The Grey Man frowned piercingly at Nathaway. "There are safeguards you cannot see. Still, I thank you for the warning."

"I didn't mean—"

"We don't get many Inning visitors," the Grey Man observed.

"Really? I should have thought . . . Is it all right? No one told me—"

"Don't worry, it's perfectly all right, if your intentions are good. I am just curious what brings you here."

Nathaway looked to Spaeth, but she seemed shy to answer, so he said, "We were told to come here, by her . . . father, Goth."

"They call him Goran now," she said faintly. "Goran, son of Listor."

There was a short silence. Then the Grey Man said slowly, "Goran is your father?"

Spaeth hesitated. "Not really. He created me."

The man absorbed this a moment, then turned sharp eyes on Nathaway. "And you?"

"I'm . . ." he groped for some explanation of who he was that had any relevance here. "I'm her bandhota," he finally said.

There was a long pause. "I can tell you have a story," the Grey Man said at last. "My name is Auster. Could I offer you some hospitality? A cup of tea, perhaps?"

They readily accepted this invitation. Auster led them across the cloister to a doorway under one of the arches. Inside the building, the quiet, sparsely furnished corridor reminded Nathaway even more strongly of a college. They walked by a group of young Lashnurai dressed like Auster, whose conversation fell silent as they passed.

"What is this place?" Nathaway asked.

"This is the Pavilion," Auster said. "We have a little community here."

"Are you scholars?"

Auster seemed pleased at the description. "Why yes, I suppose you could say that. We are healers, historians, guardians of the stone. We strive to keep our ancient traditions alive."

Nathaway felt as if he had stumbled on a priceless discovery. A seat of ancient learning, here in this secretive city, utterly unknown to the outside world. Perhaps no other Inning had seen this place. Certainly, no other Inning had had the key to it that he did, coming as bandhota to the Heir of Gilgen. He felt elated, awed at his good fortune.

They passed a door standing ajar, through which Nathaway glimpsed bound volumes on shelves, and another where racks of seedlings stood under a window. A third room, lined with cabinets full of tiny drawers, had a medicinal scale on a marble counter that looked like it came from an apothecary shop in Fluminos.

He was burning with questions by the time Auster led them up a staircase and paused before a tall, closed door. The Grey Man knocked on it, listening for some response; then he signalled them to wait. "I want to introduce you to someone," he explained, then disappeared inside.

When they were alone in the hall, Nathaway turned to Spaeth. "This place—this institution—did you know it was here?"

She shook her head. "Goth never mentioned it."

"I wish I could spend a month here," Nathaway said. "It's utterly undiscovered. I could write a treatise."

Before long the door cracked open again and Auster gestured them inside. They stepped into an office whose walls were crowded with artworks—botanical sketches, complex astronomical diagrams, coloured maps—whose antiquity made Nathaway's throat go dry. A tall, austere woman rose from a table spread with ledger books. Her face was strong-featured, with sharp, intelligent eyes, and her coarse grey hair was pulled back in an untidy bun. She looked around sixty.

Auster said, "Allow me to introduce you to Agave, the namenda of our community. I'm sorry, what's your name, my dear?"

"Spaeth," she said. "Spaeth Dobrin."

Agave was studying her face with a fierce intensity. She held out her hands, and after a slight hesitation, Spaeth reached out to clasp them. The older woman's eyes fell for a moment to Spaeth's arm, where the false scar from the attempt to cure Jory made it look as if she had given dhota. "You say you are Goran's daughter?" she said.

"No," Spaeth said. "He made me, seven years ago. From his own flesh. For sex."

Agave dropped Spaeth's hands and stepped involuntarily back. "That is so like him," she said. Her voice was pregnant with anger.

Defensively, Spaeth said, "You don't know him. You can't judge him."

"Oh, but I do know him," Agave said bitterly. "Too well."

"You do?" Now Spaeth's curiosity overcame her resentment. "How?"

Diplomatically, Auster interrupted, "Perhaps we should sit down for a chat. Let me put the kettle on for some tea."

He ushered Spaeth and Nathaway into chairs, but Agave was still too disturbed to sit, and roamed the space between them and the window, her lean face restless with memories.

"I knew him years ago, in his youth," she said. "Oh, he was a charming man then. Handsome, yes, but shallow as a pie pan, promiscuous as a cat. You should have seen him, flirting with the merchants' daughters like some sort of Inning prince. For that's what he was, you know: a weakling corrupted by the Innings."

"No!" Spaeth interrupted. "He knew nothing of the Innings."

Agave turned on her. "You're wrong. He was raised in the Governor's family at Tornabay, back when the Governor was still an Inning, before Tiarch arose. It was clever and cruel of them, to try and corrupt the child who was the very soul of the Isles. The rest of us could only watch, and feel our hearts ache."

"But it didn't work," Spaeth said.

"Didn't it? Then why, when they set him free, didn't he come here to Lashnish, to take up his responsibilities? No, he went off somewhere to soak in his carnal pleasures, while the land cried out in need."

Listening, Nathaway could easily reconstruct the situation in his mind: at the time Agave spoke of, after the battle of Sandhaven, Goth had been a political pawn, prisoner of the people who had killed his father. What could have been more natural than to mimic them? What better way to camouflage himself, than to appear feckless and irresponsible? But he had clearly alienated an orthodox faction of his own people.

"And now," Agave said, "there he is, back in Tornabay, collaborating with the Innings again."

"He is not collaborating," Spaeth said hotly. "He is their prisoner, and it is nearly killing him. I know nothing about what happened years ago, but you are wrong about what is happening now."

"And what do you know about it?" Agave said, her demanding gaze on Spaeth.

"I saw him ten days ago," Spaeth said. "It was when he told us to come here, because he could not."

Agave paused at this, arrested by some thought. She looked at Auster; his eyebrows rose quizzically. "He told you that?" Agave said.

"Yes," Spaeth said. "We were to find the Isonstone."

"Tell me," Agave said slowly, "did he give you anything? Some sort of talisman?"

Spaeth shook her head. "No, nothing."

"What kind of talisman?" Nathaway said suddenly.

Agave seemed to notice him for the first time. "Something ancient," she said. "A token."

"Something like this?" Nathaway pulled at the string around his neck, and brought out the green stone pendant Goth had given him.

The effect on the two Lashnurai was electric. They both gave involuntary exclamations and started toward it. Auster reached out, but pulled back without touching the stone. He looked at Agave, and there was strain in his voice. "Is it the real thing?"

"Bring me a lamp," she said, and he hurried to fetch one. She bent close then, but looked to Nathaway. "May I touch it?"

"Yes, of course," he said.

She took it reverently in her hands as Auster held the lamp close. She examined first one side, then the other, then sighed, returning it to Nathaway. She straightened, looking at Auster.

"What is it?" Nathaway asked.

The Grey Lady's voice was tensely controlled. "It is called the Emerald Tablet," she said. "An ancient artefact of Alta."

He looked at it. "Is it really emerald?"

"That is what the records say." She seemed about to go on, but stopped herself. "Only the Heir of Gilgen may possess it. It has been passed down for generations from one Heir to the next."

Auster's eyes on him were grave. "Son, are you sure he meant to give it to you?"

Self-consciously, Nathaway glanced at Spaeth; she was watching curiously. "I asked him if it was for Spaeth," he said. "He said no, I shouldn't give it away to anyone."

"And you had no idea what it meant?" Auster said.

"No," Nathaway said. "I still don't. Why would he give it to me? Obviously, I'm no Heir of Gilgen."

Once again, Auster and Agave exchanged a look. It seemed as if far more were going on between them than Nathaway could catch. Agave's face was stern with anger. "That fool," she said in a low voice. "The irresponsible fool."

"Now, Agave," Auster said to calm her. "Consider that he may have known something we don't."

"It was a message to us," she said. "One last bit of defiance." She turned her desperate, angry eyes on Nathaway. "What did he know of you?"

"Really, nothing," he said. "We'd barely met."

"And so he gave you this precious thing solely because this girl of his had given dhota for you?"

Nathaway hesitated, not wanting her to misunderstand, but not wanting to set her straight, either. But before he could think of something to say, Spaeth interrupted, "I never gave him dhota."

Auster and Agave both turned to her. "You said you were bandhotai," Auster said.

"Oh, we are," she said, reaching out to take Nathaway's hand. "He gave dhota for me. I would have died otherwise."

A flush of terrible embarrassment heated Nathaway's face. He couldn't meet their eyes. He started to say, "It wasn't really me, Spaeth. It was Goth—"

"Are you denying the bandhota bond?" she said, as if it cut her to the heart.

"No," he said desperately. "Of course not."

Turning to the listening Lashnurai, Spaeth said, "Do you think I couldn't tell who was curing me? Just look at his arm."

Nathaway sat staring at the floor, cooking in his discomfort. Quietly, Auster said, "May we see your arm?"

He was no longer wearing the bandage, but the scar was still ugly and inflamed. When he pushed back his sleeve, he heard Agave suck in her breath.

There was a short silence. Then Auster said, "There is something going on here that we don't understand."

Agave pulled a chair forward and sat down for the first time, facing Nathaway, close enough to touch him. "We need to get to the bottom of this—what's your name?"

"Nathaway Talley," he said.

For once in his life, there was no sign of recognition at the name. "Are you willing to help us, Nathaway?"

"Look," he said weakly, "I really don't care about the Emerald Tablet. If it's so important, you can have it."

She shook her head. "No. The artefact itself is not important. Or at least, not as important as the act of giving it, which is what holds all the meaning."

"Then I'll give it to you."

"Not in your present state of ignorance. That would be no better than throwing it away. Goran gave it to you for a reason, and I have to know what that reason was."

"Well, you can't find out from me."

"Yes, I can," she said. She reached into a leather pouch at her belt, and brought out a stone knife.

"No!" Spaeth cried out, springing from her chair and clutching Nathaway's arm. "He's mine!"

"Don't worry, girl," Agave said, "I'm not going to give dhota. I simply have to see inside him. I promise you, I won't change a thing. There will be no bond."

Spaeth seemed unreconciled by this. "You can't go inside him," she pleaded. "He is private, my own."

Auster moved to her side and put a comforting arm around her shoulder. "We cannot keep our bandhotai to ourselves, my dear," he said gently. "We all have to share them with the world."

"But I've only had him for a week!" she said. There were tears in her eyes.

36

"And you will have him still," Auster said. "This will change nothing between you." He drew her away to her chair. She looked desolate.

"Sit with her, Auster," Agave said.

He sat on the broad arm of her chair, his arm around her shoulder. "Now, you must not touch him while Agave is working," he said.

Nathaway's heart was floundering, caught between his sharp sympathy for Spaeth's pain, and nervous agitation for himself. He looked to Agave, who was watching him closely.

"You will need to help me," she said seriously.

"What—" he started to ask. His mind was swarming with questions, conditions, scenarios, as if he were drafting a contract, seeking certainty. That was what the law gave you, certainty.

"You will have to trust me," Agave said. "You will have to give yourself up, and surrender all your doubts."

She was holding out the knife to him. He took the handle in unsteady hands. "Go ahead," she said. "Just a drop, it's all we need."

He had to exhale twice before his hands were steady enough. Then he turned up his wrist and pricked it with the knife tip till a drop of dark blood flowed out onto the skin. He dipped his finger into it. Then, as he had seen Goth do, he touched it to Agave's forehead, and to his own.

She took both of his hands in hers, holding on strongly. It felt as if she were supporting him. "Don't be concerned," she said softly. "No harm will come to you."

Calmness seemed to flow into him then, and he relaxed, closing his eyes. He felt like the surface of a pool, agitated at first, but gradually becoming smooth and clear. Agave entered him delicately, like a drop of dye dissolving in the water of his mind, suffusing every inch of him, sinking deeper and deeper. He had accepted her presence completely when, deep inside him, he felt her move, reaching out. It triggered a flash of buried emotional memory, and he instinctively clamped down, struggling against her. For a moment he was back in his body, and she was stroking his face, saying "Shhh," to calm him. He realized that he had cried out.

Under her control his heart slowed again, and she carried him back into the pool, sinking, wrapped around him, into the deepest parts of his mind. The next time a memory exploded into his consciousness he was better prepared, though he was still dimly aware of flinching and groaning. After that they came fast, a jolting cascade of experiences he had long forgotten, vomiting out into the open.

They were all the ugly memories, the ones that carried the sharpest emotions—shame, terror, hatred, rage. All the times he had failed to act right, or had allowed his emotions to act for him. Everything he was ashamed of paraded before his eyes, as vivid as the first time he had experienced them. The portrait of himself sickened him, and he longed for her to stop probing, stop exposing him for what he didn't want to be.

But she didn't stop. On and on she went, right through his life, till the pool of his mind had turned dark and turbid with pollution. It felt unclean on his skin.

Long after it had become unendurable, it finally ceased. He was floating again, but far deeper now, so deep there was no surface, and a lucid glow was all around him. The water was crystal clear now, and the light seemed to penetrate every crevice of his being. He floated on it, weightless, unencumbered, and free. All the impurities had washed away, leaving him transparent, more naked than he had ever been. He was nothing but a flow of sensation without any taint of self to block it. He was utterly clear, and all the world showed through him.

When he came back to the room in Lashnish, Agave was still holding his hands, but her head was bowed in exhaustion. He felt battered, and his face was wet with tears. She finally looked up at him, and their eyes met. They said nothing; no words were adequate.

When she let go of his hands and sat back, he knew that she had not been entirely honest about the lack of a dhota-bond. It was not the sharp and sensual bond he felt for Spaeth; but Agave had seen parts of him that no one else had witnessed, and there was an intimacy in that. She rose and kissed him tenderly on the forehead. Her hand rested on his hair for a moment with a maternal warmth. "I am sorry to have made you endure that," she said. "It was very hard for you. It is always harder for a good person than for a bad one. It is impossible to tell beforehand."

She walked away then, and Spaeth came over to Nathaway's side, putting her arms around him. "Oh Nat," she said, "I didn't know she was going to hurt you."

He still felt too drained to talk, but he squeezed her hand.

Auster had gone over to Agave's side, and they were talking softly together. Nathaway couldn't hear their words, only the murmur of their voices. He leaned against Spaeth, feeling secure in her warmth. He wanted to sleep.

Presently Auster and Agave seemed to come to some resolution, and Auster went back to stir up the fire under the teakettle. He was soon pressing a cup of hot tea into Nathaway's hands. "Drink it, my boy," he said. "We need you back with us. We have some decisions to make."

It was strong and stimulating, and Nathaway soon felt alertness tingling back into him. He realized that the windows were completely dark. "How long has it been?" he asked.

"Just a couple of hours," Auster said lightly. "Come with me, I'll show you the lavatory."

It felt good to stand; his muscles were stiff. Auster said nothing of consequence to him while they were alone, but when they returned to Agave's office, the two women were deep in a conversation that broke off when they entered. Spaeth looked reluctant and disturbed.

When they were all seated again, Agave took a long draught of tea and pushed the hair back from her forehead. She looked exhausted; there were dark circles under her eyes. "First," she said, "I must tell you a little more about this talisman you have, the Emerald Tablet.

"Long ago, in the days before history, the Altans were the greatest civilization the world has ever known. They discovered all the underlying geometry of the world. They knew the crystals and the chords of music, and why they are alike. They even knew the harmonies that drive the stars and compose the soul.

"But in the strange last days of Alta, the forces of disorder—those the Adaina call the Mundua and Ashwin—became unbalanced, and nothing the Altans could do would put them right. So they encoded all their knowledge in a single crystal, and created the Lashnura to carry it down through future generations, bit by bit working to restore the ancient harmony that had been disturbed. We are like single notes in a song they composed long ago. The world as it once was is locked in the Tablet, all its parts forming a chord we cannot yet hear."

Nathaway lifted the pendant and looked at it; it seemed far too worn and ordinary for the exalted legend attached to it. "Is the information still there, do you think?" he asked.

"We must hope so," Agave said.

"Could it teach us all the Altans knew?"

She shook her head. "If you mean could we learn to speak their language or rebuild their cities or do their computations, no. Perhaps that kind of knowledge is there, but inaccessible to us. The knowledge it conveys comes in another form. Every Lashnura on earth is driven by implanted instincts that ultimately derive from what is encoded in the Tablet." She hesitated, as if the words came painfully. "If ever we are to be free, we must relearn enough to mend what has been broken."

"Then why isn't the Tablet kept locked away safely?"

"As I said, we can't read it any more. That is what the Heirs of Gilgen are for—to interpret it for us. It does not speak to them in words or knowledge, but through instinct and unconscious acts. They are our only, imperfect access to what lies in the Tablet. Their ultimate purpose, like ours, is to lead the world back to its ancient symmetry. When that has happened, the Grey Folk will have served their purpose and our suffering will no longer be necessary to set the scales right."

Nathaway was silent. He could understand her mythic beliefs, but he could not share them. It seemed as if these dignified people, in their desperation, had resorted to a magical faith. He felt compassion for them, and some admiration, but their eschatology was a delusion.

Misreading him, Agave said, "We are as puzzled as you. But ultimately, you are the only one who can answer the question of why you have it. We want you to stay here and let us help you learn more."

At this, he looked at her hopefully. "Really?" he said. "We could stay here?"

"We would be very pleased at that," Auster said.

It was a priceless opportunity to delve into the knowledge of the Lashnura. Everything about this place intrigued him. The archives alone might solve a thousand mysteries. He looked at Spaeth, scarcely able to conceal his eagerness. She gave him a wan smile.

"I would be honoured to stay," he said. "I've wanted to learn about your people all along. I want to know your history, and your teachings. If you'll have me, I would love to be a student of your ways."

"Good," Agave said, smiling; but it was a smile tinged with pain. Impulsively she reached out and took his hand. "Nathaway," she said, and her yearning for his welfare was plain to see. She took Spaeth's hand then, and placed it in his, enclosing both their hands in hers. "Both of you need to know that there is no power in the Lashnura way. Power is what the Mundua and Ashwin have. For us, there is only surrender and acquiescence. Can you learn that?"

Nathaway and Spaeth looked at each other, and neither of them wanted to answer yes. "I don't know," Nathaway said.

"Well, at least I haven't lied to you," Agave said.

At that moment, the sound of a distant explosion came from outside, rattling the glass in the window. It was soon answered with an even more thundering roar. All of them rose to go to the window and see what was going on. The noise seemed to be coming from the harbour.

"Auster dear, run down and find out what is going on," Agave said.

He turned to the door, but even before he could reach it there was a nervous rap on it. When he opened it, a girl stood there—the first Lashnura child Nathaway had ever seen.

"Namenda Agave," she said, "there is an officer here to see you."

"An officer?" she said sharply.

"Yes, in a uniform."

"Well, show him in."

Nathaway said quickly, "It would be better if Spaeth and I left. We are not particularly anxious for the Navy to know where we are."

"Don't be absurd," Agave said severely. "You are under the protection of the Pavilion now. The Pavilion is inviolate. No one would dare harm you while you are here."

He did not share her sense of invulnerability, and might have argued, except that at that moment, the door opened and Joffrey stepped through it.

He was resplendent in a Native Navy officer's dress uniform, booted and braided with authority, carrying his hat under his arm. Nathaway had never seen him in uniform before; he had known Joffrey only as Tiarch's clandestine agent among the rebels. They had last met when Joffrey had arranged for Nathaway's escape from the *Ripplewill* in Tornabay. The instant he entered the room Joffrey saw Nathaway, and froze.

"Justice Talley," he said tensely. He glanced around, his mind clearly scrambling to account for Nathaway's presence. "Are you here on your brother's behalf?"

"No," Nathaway said. Then, since they were being honest, "Are you?"

"No," Joffrey said. "I am here on Tiarch's behalf."

"Isn't that the same thing?"

"Not any more," Joffrey said.

Only then did Nathaway remember what he had overheard in the hallways of the palace, that there had been a break between Tiarch and the Inning authority. The chaos it had caused was the main reason he and Spaeth had been able to escape.

Joffrey had turned to Agave, and now pressed his hands together before him with the index fingertips touching, and bowed. "Ehir," he said. "Pardon me, my message is from Tiarch to you, Namenda Agave. May we speak privately?"

"Whatever Tiarch has to say is of concern to everyone here," Agave said regally.

Joffrey looked around the room as if memorizing every face. Then he held out a sealed letter to her. "This conveys Tiarch's greetings to you and your revered institution," he said.

Agave took it and broke the seal. "What is going on? What is this firing in the harbour?"

"Don't be concerned about that. It was just our ship saluting the Governor's arrival. I had intended to be here before this, in order to inform you, but I was delayed."

There was a pause while Agave read the letter. At the end she looked up at him. "Are you Vice-Admiral Joffrey?"

He bowed. "Any questions or concerns you may have, I am ready to address. We are eager to have cordial relations with the Pavilion while we are in Lashnish."

"So her letter says. It doesn't say why she has come to Lashnish."

Joffrey smiled thinly. "The answer to that question lies with this gentleman's brother. Ten days ago, Tiarch was removed from office by the Inning authority she had served so long and loyally. What they didn't reckon with was that the militia and much of the Northern Squadron was more loyal to her than to Inning, and they rallied round her. She has come here to make Lashnish her headquarters while she appeals her dismissal to Fluminos."

"Why Lashnish?" Agave said tensely. "What are her intentions?"

Unspoken, but obvious to everyone in the room, was the question, *Has she come here to claim dhota-nur?*

"At the moment, her intentions are to set up an administrative base for her government, the legitimate government of the Forsakens," Joffrey said. "Lashnish is a central location, since Tornabay is now off limits to us."

He hadn't answered the real question, but his bland expression told them he didn't intend to.

Nathaway was still trying to grasp the situation. "The Navy mutinied?" he said, barely believing it.

Turning to him, Joffrey said coolly, "That is doubtless the construction certain parties will put on it. We prefer to think that the Navy stayed loyal when given an illegal order."

So the Navy that had just arrived was not the Navy that Nathaway had been fearing, but a renegade force bent on making Lashnish yet another rebel stronghold. This was all going very badly for Corbin. But by now, Nathaway didn't care. He wanted nothing to do with any of it, and felt some alarm that trouble seemed to be doggedly following his scent. The refuge he had just managed to find was to be plunged into the midst of things. He turned to Agave. "Agave, pardon me for speaking, but you need to stay neutral in this. If you have any power, don't throw it to one side or another; it'll only make you a target."

"The Pavilion never makes judgments," she said, "until we are approached in the proper way. Then we will play our part as we always have done." She turned to Joffrey. "You may tell that to Tiarch."

He inclined his head respectfully. "I will do so. She will doubtless wish to visit you herself, once she is settled here."

"She will be welcome, as are all," Agave said.

Joffrey nodded, then looked appraisingly one last time at Nathaway, and left.

When he was gone there was silence in the room. Outside the window, down by the waterfront, they could hear distant shouts and some celebratory gunfire. It seemed very far away, up here.

Agave turned to look at Auster. Silently, he moved to her side and took her hand. "It is all happening so fast," she said. "We have no time. Just listen to them out there, Auster. Our city is waking."

THE BELLS OF HARBOURDOWN

Just off the rocky coast of Thimish, Harg Ismol was sitting in a place uncomfortably familiar to him, on the horns of a dilemma.

The aft cabin of the warship *Smoke* was still lavishly furnished with the belongings of its absent captain, who had—either through choice or chance—ended up on the Inning side in the mad scramble when Tiarch had sailed from Embo with her navy. When Harg had first inherited the cabin, the sight of the man's perfect mahogany shaving stand, his wine chest, his silver service, and curtains had said only one thing—that this was a warship that had never fired a gun in war. Harg had occupied his share of captains' quarters during his time in the Native Navy, but that had been in the Southern Squadron, a mean and stripped-down fighting force often thrown into the midst of battle. Nothing could have brought home to him how pampered the Northern Squadron had been in comparison like seeing how their captains lived.

But it had not taken him long to detect the symbolism behind all the captain's luxuries, and the indispensable role they played in enhancing authority among the Torna officers. And that was where his dilemma lay. He was trying to figure out what to wear for his triumphal return to Harbourdown. If he appeared in the spectacular Vice-Admiral's uniform hanging before him, as he had every right to do, it would alienate the Adaina companions he had left behind less than a month before. All that official lace and plumery would say only one thing to them—Tiarch's-man. It would look as if he had crossed over, become co-opted by the enemy.

On the other hand, if he didn't wear it, it would have an effect on the Torna officers of the three warships that comprised his little squadron. Despite his rock-solid Navy credentials, they regarded him with scepticism, still convinced he had been promoted over them solely for being Adaina. They followed him in obedience to Tiarch's orders, but every second he was being appraised.

So he left on the civilian trousers and white shirt he was wearing, and put on the uniform jacket over them, leaving off the waistcoat and stock, but keeping the crimson sash. He hesitated over the epaulettes, but kept them in the end to remind the Tornas of his rank. He pulled on the boots, but under his trousers. The hat was far too showy, out of the question, so he left it off. In the end he tipped the shaving mirror to try and survey whether he had produced the proper look of deliberate informality.

There was a knock on the door, and Harg called, "Come in." When he turned, Captain Jearl was standing there in full dress, every detail precisely according to regulation. When he saw Harg, he stepped in and closed the door.

"Is that how you're going to appear?" Jearl said, his voice noncommittal.

Inwardly, Harg winced, but he said, "Trust me, Jearl, it's necessary. You'll understand when we get there." He had to make it seem to Harbourdown like he was bringing in the three warships, not like they were bringing him in.

Jearl said nothing, as usual. The thin, grey-haired officer had the useful gift of reticence. He thus avoided offending, but as a result Harg never knew quite where he stood. The man had been a commander under Tiarch for twelve years, and knew more of Inning naval tactics and training than anyone in the fleet. If he resented having an Adaina upstart put over him, he had never shown a flicker of it; but then, he had not shown much of anything but reserved courtesy.

"Shall we go up on deck?" Harg said.

"If you please, Admiral." Jearl held the door open for him.

The oddness of Harg's position was the result of a week of hurried bargaining aboard Tiarch's flagship, as her fleet had retreated from Tornabay. Considering that he had brought nothing to the table but the promise of Adaina alliance, he had come off surprisingly well. To give him the authority he wanted, she had appointed him one of two Vice-Admirals over her fleet, the other one being Joffrey. Harg's promotion had supplanted dozens of Torna officers who had served her for decades, and she had given him the power to promote Adaina officers to any ships he was able to capture. Now all he had to do was persuade the Adaina that the deal was to their advantage as well as his.

While they were bargaining, Tiarch had argued that, whatever his formal rank, his command ought to be limited to the ships already captured by the Adaina at Harbourdown. But then the news had come in about Holby Dorn.

The messenger had arrived as he was sitting down to dine at Tiarch's table along with four or five of her top captains. The conversation had turned to grave silence as the messenger related the story. Dorn and his pirate fleet had sailed north to brazenly raid the prosperous town of Torbert, southernmost port of the Inner Chain. But this time the Adaina marauders had not contented themselves with plunder. With an organized ferocity they had never shown before, they had gone house to house, rounding up male Torna inhabitants and herding them into a warehouse on the wharf. Then they had surrounded the makeshift prison with gunmen, and set it on fire.

Harg had been the only Adaina at the table as the news was delivered, and he saw the Torna faces around him hardening with hatred. It was exactly the effect Dorn had wanted to provoke: to divide the races and prevent any such alliance as the one Harg had been labouring to achieve. At that moment, there was nothing he could do but express revulsion and outrage as loudly as anyone in the room. But all the while he was aware, as they appeared not to be, that Tiarch and her navy were the very people who had driven the Adaina to the brink of such vicious retribution. At the same time, he had felt the horrible truth that it was now his problem to solve.

When he had been able to get Tiarch alone, he had made the case that she needed to let the Adaina take care of Dorn. Otherwise, he argued, it would devolve into an endless revenge cycle, Torna against Adaina. "The Innings are the enemy," he had said. "We can't get distracted killing each other." She had accepted the argument, and that was when he had gotten the three ships to command, with the understanding that his first mission was to pacify his own people.

Before they could appear on deck, Harg and Jearl had to wait for the deck officer to initiate a ceremony involving whistles, bells, parades, and commands. Jearl was a stickler for propriety, and all the naval rituals were punctiliously performed on his ship. It struck Harg as a little antiquated; the Northern Squadron was still mimicking a pre-war Inning Navy, before the transformations wrought on it by Admiral Talley. But he said nothing. The formality was important to them, and not to be meddled with lightly.

Once on deck, they found that the squadron was nearing the entry to Harbourdown Bay, with the *Smoke* in the lead. "You sent the cutter ahead?" Harg asked. He had not wanted his own people to mistake the warships for an enemy and sail out to attack.

"Yes, sir," Jearl answered.

"Shall we give them a salute?"

"I had anticipated that."

Jearl gave the order for the gunnery crews to assemble, and Harg watched from the quarterdeck as they cast loose their cannons and took up their tompions, admiring their organization and training. The common sailors were mostly Adaina, but they obeyed their Torna gun captains with a willing efficiency that gave Harg hope for the blended Navy he wanted to create. "They're very well trained," he said to Jearl.

Jearl's deep-lined face didn't move at the compliment. "They're on their best behaviour because you're watching," he said. It was the first intimation Harg had had that Jearl noticed the effect an Adaina admiral had on an Adaina crew.

As they cleared the headland, the bay and town became visible, and Harg scanned the ships at anchor. All four of the captured Navy vessels were there—*Windemon*, *Pimpernel*, *Spinneret*, and the majestic *Ison Orin*. With surprise, he recognized a fifth one as the armed sloop from Yora. Barko had been out collecting, it seemed. The thought of being able to confront a captured Captain Quintock filled Harg with evil glee.

As the *Smoke* entered the bay, she fired a rolling salvo, magnificently precise in its timing, that echoed back from the cliffs and the dark walls of the Redoubt above the town. In answer, the ships at anchor began to fire—a chaotic, haphazard barrage that made up in enthusiasm what it lacked in discipline. Jearl made no comment, for which Harg was grateful.

A six-oared skiff set out from the *Ison Orin* even before the *Smoke* cast anchor, with Barko Durban perched in the stern, grinning hideously enough to scare the fish away. Harg waved to him from the quarterdeck, even if it was beneath the dignity of an admiral. As the skiff pulled up beneath the warship's side, catching onto the main chains with a boathook, Barko yelled up, "Hey Harg! Can't you go anywhere without warships following you home? Keep this up, and we'll need a bigger harbour!"

Soon he was up on deck, looking more piratical than ever, having acquired a gold earring to add to his raptor nose and predatory squint. When Harg introduced him to Captain Jearl, there was a moment when he felt the discontinuities were beyond ironing out; but Jearl took it in stride, or at least with no more than the usual reserve.

"The townsfolk have prepared a little welcome for you all," Barko told them, "but they're wondering if the sailors are all going to have shore leave at once."

Harg said, "Jearl, get together with the other captains and work out a schedule for leave, one ship at a time. The town's too small for all of them."

Jearl merely nodded, but Barko gave Harg a sideways glance, reacting to the easy way he issued orders to a man whose power over them would have been absolute three months ago.

"I was hoping the *Ripplewill* might have made it back," Harg said.

Barko shook his head. "We thought you might know something of her."

"We got separated in Tornabay. So you haven't heard anything from Torr? Calpe? Gill?"

"Nothing."

"I see the *Vagabond*'s not here either," Harg said, having scanned the harbour for Holby Dorn's boat.

"I gave Dorn to understand that he wasn't very welcome here any more," Barko said.

"You've heard what he's been up to?"

"Yes." Barko, to his credit, looked uncomfortable. "I need to talk to you about that, Harg."

So there was more to the story. Harg wanted to hear it, but the subject was too grim for the moment. "When we get ashore. Jearl, pass the word to the other captains. We'll meet on the town dock as soon as they can get there." He turned to leave in Barko's skiff, but was delayed by a short leave-taking ceremony, approvingly observed by the Adaina seamen on deck.

"Vice-Admiral, eh?" Barko said to him when they were in the skiff alone.

Not sure of his footing, Harg said, "I needed some public acknowledgment from Tiarch that she was with us."

"So who's the admiral?"

Trust Barko to get right to the point. He knew perfectly well that the only admiral over Tiarch's navy was Tiarch herself. Which meant, technically, that Harg was following her orders. "We need them, Barko," Harg said. "The chance was too good to pass up. It was like a navy was being handed to me, free."

"Well, the Tornas in town are happy about it," Barko said.

"What about the Adainas?"

"Depends on who you ask. You need to step carefully, Harg."

For a moment, Harg felt miles out of his depth in these treacherous political waters. Blowing things up he was an expert at. Putting things together was infinitely harder.

The feeling of inadequacy faded when he stepped onto the town dock and saw the crowd assembled in the market square. A huge cheer went up as he waved at them. The Adaina captains of the other captured ships were already assembled, and he touched hands all around and got the story of how they had captured the sloop from Yora—the handiwork of the fierce young captain of the *Windemon*, a woman named Katri.

A decorated open carriage rolled into the square and pulled up at the end of the dock, but Harg wouldn't budge toward it until the three Torna captains joined them. This event was accompanied by an impressive amount of pomp and regalia. Harg introduced the captains all around—the Tornas dignified and official in their uniforms, the Adainas with an air of rebel outlawry about them. Together they walked down the dock to the waiting carriage, a pasted-together coalition of opposites with the seams already showing.

But that seemed not to matter to the crowd. As the officers climbed into the carriage and set out on a slow circuit around the square, all the bells in town began to ring. Big, deep bells tolled; bright brass bells jangled; boat bells, harbour bells, and hand bells clanged. The music cascaded down from the roofs and windows, washing over them all. Then the big guns far up in the fort joined in, booming in joy, a thundering bass to the treble of the bells. The cheers sounded like breakers on the shore.

Harg felt utterly engulfed in love. It was like sunlight soaking into his limbs, warming him, making him light and buoyant. He wanted to stretch his arms out wide enough to embrace all of Harbourdown, to give them back what they were giving him.

The carriage circled the market square once, then set out down some of the nearby streets, and returned at last to the square, pulling up at Rosenry's, the tavern that had become the improvised assembly-house of the rebellion. On the steps, Majlis Callow and the other prominent merchants of the town were waiting to welcome them all. After some short speeches, they all went in to the back room, where a feast was waiting. Tankards and lobster broke the ice, and soon Tiarch's officers, insurgent leaders, and merchants were all laughing and drinking together.

As Harg looked around the room in a golden haze of beer and conviviality, the problems seemed surmountable. The Tornas officers' protectiveness of their rules and status, the Adainas' lack of training, the differences in custom, all of it seemed resolvable. He found Barko and Jearl standing on either side of him, and said, "You see, this is what we need. A navy that's a genuine combination. We've got to show the Innings we can collaborate, all of us together."

"Sounds like a toast to me," Barko said.

And so Harg called out for quiet and proposed the toast, "All of us together." Everyone raised their glasses and repeated, "All of us together!"

Later, he and Barko went out to smoke a pipe on the porch of the inn. A rain squall had passed while they had been inside, and now a reckless wind was rocking the harbour boats, making their masts swing like pendulums. The square was empty.

"So what's this news about Dorn?" Harg said. "Has he done something I don't know about?"

Barko took a long, thoughtful pull on his clay pipe before answering. "It's not so much what he's done as what he's saying, and how it's changing people's opinions."

"What's he saying?"

"You can probably guess. He's calling us all collaborators. He was questioning our motives even before the news arrived that you had joined Tiarch."

"I didn't join Tiarch!" Harg said sharply. "She joined me."

"Either way. Dorn says he's the only true Adaina leader, the only one who never served the Innings, never truckled with the Torna. He says he was fighting back while you were sucking your thumb, and now he's still fighting back while you're sucking up."

"Asshole," Harg said darkly.

"It makes sense to a lot of people."

It made sense because there was a kernel of truth in it. It also spoke to the deep resentments built up through the years of Torna power and Adaina subjection. It appealed to the base parts of people's natures.

"Look, I respect Dorn for what he did in past," Harg said. "But it got him nowhere. His real problem is that there's a new leadership with better ideas, who want to do what it takes to win."

Barko shrugged. "All the same, I wouldn't go into the Adaina section of town alone at night, if I were you."

This shook Harg to the bone. "Really? Is it that bad?"

"There are people who have been whipping themselves up into a frenzy over this. It's like you opened the lid, and everything's exploding out. With Dorn questioning your motives, it could get really nasty."

Uppermost in Harg's mind was a feeling of betrayal. He had just fooled himself into believing he was loved, and now, like every other time in his life, he found it wasn't true.

Right under that was exasperation at the short-sightedness of it. People cared more about airing their grievances than about solving them. "Damn it," he said. "Why can't they just leave me alone and let me win for them?"

There was a long silence. When Harg finally looked over, Barko was watching him appraisingly. "We do have a system for dealing with this," he said. "A system that would wipe out all doubt about your motives."

He was talking about dhota-nur. Harg looked away, his jaw set.

Barko went on, "It's making people pretty nervous that Tiarch is in Lashnish with the Isonstone, and you're here."

"Tiarch can have the damned Isonstone, and welcome to it," Harg said.

"You're in the minority on that."

"Well, my vote is the only one that matters."

Barko was shaking his head. "I don't get it, Harg. You're already doing all the work an Ison would do. Why not have the legitimacy?"

Harg had never talked to anyone about this, not even Tway. For a while he stared out into the harbour, at the magnificent fleet assembled there. Reluctantly, he said, "Do you know what dhota-nur is?"

"It's getting rid of all the bad memories, all the mistakes, all the crap that collects in your life and controls you," Barko said. "Why would you not want that?"

In a low voice Harg said, "Take away all the bad memories from my life, and there wouldn't be anything left of me. That's all I am—just a collection of mistakes and rotten motives. If a dhotamar made me into a good person, I wouldn't be myself any more."

"You're too hard on yourself, Harg," Barko said.

"I'm not apologizing. If I didn't have any regrets or grudges, I don't know if I'd want to get up in the morning, much less do what it takes to be Ison. We don't need a good man to lead us, Barko. We need someone mean and cunning. Dhota-nur wouldn't make me a better commander. It's too much like . . . mental castration."

"Oh." For a moment, Barko was shocked into silence by this image. "Well."

They stood awkwardly, not looking at each other. At last Barko said, "Ison Orin went through dhota-nur, and it didn't neutralize him."

"He *lost*, Barko," Harg said.

"So you're saying all these centuries the Grey Folk have been wrong about what makes a good leader?"

"Don't ask me what the Grey Folk think."

Barko eyed him sideways. "Would it be different if the Heir of Gilgen weren't your kmora-father?"

Harg felt something inside him tense at mention of Goth. Since failing to rescue him, Harg had felt an overlay of guilt on top of all the other feelings. It felt, irrationally, as if he hadn't tried hard enough. As if, on some level, he hadn't really wanted Goth to be free. "What-ifs don't matter," he said.

Barko fell silent. As they stood there, Harg's thoughts strayed back to his childhood—a time when random, unpredictable things had constantly happened to him, and everyone in his life had proved unreliable, Goth most of all. By age twelve he had known that the only person he could ever really trust was himself. To lose any control over himself was like letting go of a life preserver in a cold ocean. It was, simply, a matter of survival.

The door behind them banged open and Katri sauntered out. "What are you two doing out here?" she said. "Everyone was asking where you were."

Shaking off his mood, Harg turned to go back inside. "Come on, Barko," he said, "there's still beer left."

❧

When the warship *Smoke* cleared the headlands of Ekra, there was nothing but the north wind and the steely waves of the Widewater ahead. Unprotected now by the island's forested hills, she heeled over and surged ahead, the water boiling under her bow. The clouds seemed almost low enough to snag and tear on her masthead.

Harg braced himself against the *Smoke*'s quarterdeck rail, glorying in the sudden pitch of the deck under his feet. It felt good to get the details blown out of his brain, to be actually *doing* something. A stinging spate of wind-blown spray struck his face, and he grinned. The ship had too much sail on for safety, but he loved the sensation of the straining oak muscles beneath his feet.

Ahead and behind sailed the long, staggered line of his fleet. The ships ahead were already taking in sail; the ones behind were still in the lee of Ekra. It was a grand sight, all of them together. Seven tall warships: it was a fleet to go to a man's head and make him cocky, if he was so inclined.

Captain Jearl approached across the quarterdeck, and Harg forced his face back into a proper military impassiveness. The ship's crew was mounting the ratlines to reef the sails. Each seemed to know his or her job; their movements were smoothly synchronized. Harg was about to praise their training when he saw the captain frowning critically at some imprecision, invisible to him, and he decided to stay quiet.

Smoke's first lieutenant, Jonci Garlow, joined them on the quarterdeck. She was the most radical of the innovations Harg had thrust upon the unwilling Torna officers in the past two weeks. It had caused one of his few outright arguments with Jearl. He had finally persuaded the captain that they needed to train up some Adaina officers by having them serve under men of superior knowledge of Navy discipline and procedures. Jonci had seemed like a good choice for the experiment. She had spent a lifetime commanding ships, mostly merchant vessels out of Harbourdown, where merchantmen often had to fight to keep their cargoes. Her cool competence had impressed Harg, and so far she had taken her fastidious captain's directions with tact. Harg badly wanted her to succeed.

She squinted off toward the northern horizon, where a dark streak of squall was heading toward them. She wore her dark, grey-shot hair pulled back and tied in a scarf, but it always looked windblown anyway. "Weather's not with us," she said. "The Mundua are hunting."

"They can't swallow ships this big," Harg said. "We'd get stuck in their throats."

The frown on her sharp face told him she wasn't convinced. Reaching inside her uniform coat, she brought out a packet of dreamweed. She walked across to the lee rail and stood there, the wind whipping her hair about, while she cast a handful of weed onto the waves. Harg realized the crew on deck was watching her—the Adaina with anxious approval, the Torna with amused contempt. He clenched his teeth, knowing she had just lost face with half the crew; yet if he stopped her, he would lose the trust of the other half.

Jearl was standing erect at his side, looking straight ahead.

Down in the ship's waist, a grizzled brown seaman took out a dreamweed packet of his own and walked to the gunwale. Harg could see half a dozen others ready to do the same. "Get back to your post!" the Torna boatswain snapped at the sailor. The man stopped, glowering. Then he looked up at Harg, as if waiting for him to intervene. Harg stared back, rocklike. "Do you want a whipping?" the boatswain shouted. "Get back!"

At last the sailor glanced skyward, pocketed his weed, and turned back, muttering.

"You can see the problem," Jearl said, his eyes still on the horizon ahead.

"We all have to bend a bit," Harg answered.

Except for the *Smoke*, the ships from Tiarch's fleet were still commanded by the Torna officers who had come with them, while the ones from Harbourdown were Adaina-led. Originally, Harg had wanted to mix the officers on all the ships, but in the end he had given in to the vehement objections of both parties. The Tornas had argued that it would subvert their discipline, the Adainas that it would undermine their authority. Neither side wanted to take orders from the other. In the end Harg had decided to wait until the divisions were smoothed over by action.

The ship's bow plunged, and spray leaped over the forecastle. Some of the sailors whooped as the chill water soaked them. They were good seamen, the Adaina; unused as they were to the big ships, they had taken to the techniques instantly. The discipline was another thing. Yet they had to learn it.

The last of the line of ships had cleared Killy Head. Now the fleet was truly on open sea. Ahead, the lead ship was flying signal flags. Harg squinted at them, but waited for the signal lieutenant, spyglass under one arm, to come up and report. The young Torna officer saluted the air somewhere between himself and Jearl. "*Wavedancer* reports sighting the target off the larboard bow, sir."

"Wear round in formation," Harg said. The lieutenant saluted and left to give the signal.

As soon as the signal was up, they saw the *Wavedancer* shift course to a southwesterly heading. The second ship waited till it reached the spot where *Wavedancer* had changed course, then followed like a soldier on parade. But the third came about too soon, ruining the clean orderliness of the line.

"Lieutenant!" Harg said. "Signal the *Spinneret* to get back in line."

Spinneret was Dev's ship—one of Barko's pirate recruits. He had seemed a resourceful captain, ready to take a risk. But not, apparently, a stickler for proper procedures.

Harg glanced surreptitiously at Jearl's erect figure. He had started out impressed by the man's knowledge, but now he realized it was almost all book-learned, from old training manuals that still reflected the days when the Innings had used their ships as if they were moveable forts that could be moored alongside targets and used to batter them to bits. The Northern Squadron had seldom attacked anything on the move. Instead, they depended on their mere presence to scare off adversaries. For a peacekeeping force, it had worked. For a fighting one, Harg knew it wouldn't. Not against the Southern Squadron, at any rate.

It was the *Smoke*'s turn to come about. Jonci gave the orders in a crisp, calm voice, and the crew brought the ship about with a quick precision. The sails filled again on their new course, riding with the waves. The yawing of the deck was much less giddy now. "Make ready to attack," Jearl said.

"Gun crews on deck!" Jonci called out. As the order was relayed below, a stream of young men and women poured out onto deck, one knot of them whooping and tussling with each other in high spirits. The gunnery master bellowed at them, and they assembled, ten to a gun, and set about releasing the trucks, attaching tackle lines, and making ready to load.

Harg watched with interest, for guns were something he knew intimately. The ones aboard the *Smoke* were impressively modern for such a backwater as the Forsakens: seven feet of solid cast iron barrel, they were mounted on rolling trucks so they could recoil inboard, with tackles secured to the carriage to run the guns in for loading and out again to fire.

Now he could see the target ahead—a raft of old barrels with a mast, which they had towed out earlier and set to drift with a sea anchor. It bobbed and wallowed in the waves. "Ports up!" Jonci ordered, and all through the ship there was a deep rattle as the gunports lifted. Jearl scowled, and Harg knew it was because the ports hadn't gone up precisely at the same second.

"There's too much sea to use the lowest guns," Jearl said crossly, glancing over his shoulder at the approaching squall.

"The Innings won't let us choose good weather," Harg said.

The first boat was almost upon the target. "Lieutenant! Signal to fire at will," Harg said.

The signal flag was no sooner up the mast than they saw a puff of smoke erupt from the *Wavedancer*'s side. A few seconds later a ragged report reached them. There seemed to be no effect on the target.

Wavedancer sailed on. One by one, as the ships came even with the target, they took their turn firing on it. Harg watched carefully for each puff of smoke and its timing.

Smoke's gunner went down the larboard battery, checking the priming on each gun. Jonci ordered, "Run the guns out!" The crews heaved at their tackles till the black snouts of their weapons protruded from the side of the ship.

On such a rough sea, the aim would be more a matter of the ship's heading and roll than of any adjustments to the guns. As the target neared, Harg felt an old itch of excitement. He glanced back to make sure the steersman was alert, then reminded himself it was Jearl's business, not his.

Each gun captain had a piece of slow match smouldering, waiting for the command to hold it to the touchhole. The target seemed very far away, but with these guns, four hundred yards was point-blank range; it would do no good to get closer.

As they drew even with the target, everyone fell silent. Then, as *Smoke* began to lift on a wave, the gunner shouted, "Fire!"

The main deck battery gave a deafening bellow and the huge cannons recoiled back on their breeching-ropes. Half a second later, the gun deck battery fired. The ship rocked with the force of the explosion. The gun crews peered through the clouds of smoke to see what effect their salvo had had.

"Reload, rot you!" the gunner shouted. The crews turned back to their duties. Wet sponges hissed, thrust down the hot throats of the cannons.

From the quarterdeck Harg could see what most of the crew couldn't—that the entire salvo had gone sailing harmlessly past the target into the sea. As he watched the men methodically sponging, loading, ramming, and wadding, he said to Jearl, "They need practice. If they can't move more quickly than that, the Innings will be aboard us between shots."

"Yes, sir," Jearl said noncommittally.

"During the war, we aimed to refire our guns within a minute's time if we could."

"I have heard two minutes mentioned as a goal."

"When the other ship's firing on you, two minutes might as well be a day. If we tangle with the Southern Squadron, and they can get off two shots for every one of ours, we'll be in trouble."

"Yes, sir."

Harg couldn't help getting the impression that to Jearl, the prospect of actually meeting the Southern Squadron in battle was more theoretical than real. He raised his voice so that Jonci and the signal lieutenant could both hear. "All right, we're going to come about and bear down on the target again, and this time we're going to get off *two* shots before we're past. And we're going to make them hit."

A gust of wind painted dark streaks across the sea, and raindrops began to spot the deck. Harg ignored it, watching as the line of ships came ponderously about. They had to tack twice, close-hauled against the unpredictable wind, in order to come on the target again. The pace was irritatingly slow.

By the time the fleet was in position to attack again, the rain was falling in sheets. Harg paced back and forth, trying to keep an eye on the other ships through walls of wind-driven rain. Jearl stood immobile, streams of water running from his hat.

The flag went up to signal the attack, and ahead the *Wavedancer* made the last course change to bring her down on the target. The raft was hard to spot this time—now hidden, now revealed by the building waves. Jonci's voice cut through the drumming of rain on the deck as the port battery made ready to fire.

"Sacred horns!" Harg swore, peering ahead. "What's *Windemon* up to?"

One of the ships had broken from the line, already made ragged by wind and waves, and seemed to be shaking out the reefs in its sails to overhaul the ship ahead.

"Lieutenant! Signal *Windemon* to resume position," Harg snapped. Inwardly, he cursed Katri, *Windemon*'s captain. She had the daring defiance of a pirate, and her Adaina crew loved her for it.

If Katri saw the signal, she paid no heed. *Windemon* and *Spinneret* drew abreast; now Dev was putting on sail as if it were a race. As they neared the target the two ships parted, one on each side, with barely 500 yards between them. They fired simultaneously. Even the laconic Jearl gave a startled exclamation. Splinters flew, and the mast on the target twisted, swayed, then came crashing down into the sea. A cheer went up from the *Smoke*'s crew.

Harg clenched his teeth. That little show of bravado would cost him dearly. All the effort he had spent defending his Adaina captains to the sceptical Tornas had gone flying into the wind with one rash, undisciplined move. He wanted to throttle Katri.

The way back to Harbourdown was grey with a drenching downpour. As soon as the ships nosed into the harbour, Harg said, "Signal all ships' captains to assemble on the flagship. I'll see them in the aft cabin."

They were already arguing when they came in. Katri and Dev were together, displaying a smug defiance that set Harg's teeth on edge. The Torna captains were sourly disgruntled.

"If it's each ship for itself, we might as well be a pack of animals," one of them was saying.

"What I can't stand is commanders who don't think for themselves," Katri shot back. "Some people can't pee without permission."

"You're out of line, Katri," Harg snapped. "You've been out of line all day."

"Damn right I have," she flared back. "This sailing around like we were soldiers on parade—anyone who's been in a fight can tell you, it's not how to win. You've got to swarm your enemy, intimidate him."

Jearl's face was stiff and expressionless. "What you did was against all the rules of naval combat," he said in a dry, clipped tone.

"Whose rules?" Katri said impatiently. "The rules of the people we're fighting, that's whose! Well I've got a rule for you. If it's two to one, the enemy's twice as busy as you."

"If you attack from both sides, you're as likely to hit your ally as the enemy," Jearl said.

Harg caught the quick glance Katri and Dev gave each other, and instantly understood. "Did you hit each other?" he demanded.

"Only a little hole," Dev said. "Easily patched."

"You might not be so lucky in a real battle," Jearl said.

In a rebellious undertone Katri said, "What do you know about real battles?"

"What was that?" Harg said.

"Nothing," Katri answered.

"It *was* something. Listen here, Katri. The issue isn't who was right. The issue is, you had orders and you disobeyed them. You're not a pirate any more, and you can't just take it on yourself to decide our battle tactics." He paused, hating what he was going to have to say. "You're relieved of your command until further notice, Katri. Your first lieutenant will be in charge of the *Windemon* till I decide what to do."

Katri stood staring at him, her mouth set in an angry line. Dev was scowling darkly, arms crossed. The Torna officers were utterly quiet. The silence stretched painfully; then Katri turned and strode out.

For a moment Harg thought Dev was going to follow her. Harg said, "We can't fight a war never knowing who's going to be behind us when we attack, or whether they'll follow orders. We can't be negotiating strategy and deciding tactics by vote. To beat the Innings, we have to use the weapons of the Innings: discipline and order. Otherwise, we might as well sink all those ships out there in the harbour, and save the Innings the trouble."

Dev was still scowling, but he didn't move. Harg turned to the Torna officers, who were staring at him with a surprised respect. "Now, the other big problem I saw today was gunnery. I want all gun crews to be able to reload and fire again in less than two minutes. Drill them till they can do it."

The ride ashore in the gig was silent. All Harg could think was that Katri was right. He would make her wait a fortnight, but he would reinstate her, because she had more instinct for a fight than the rest of them combined. He needed that pirate cleverness and initiative, and the Tornas needed it too, if they could only see it. And they would, in time. That was the problem—it took time to mould a functioning force out of a mismatched collection of martinets and rebels.

When he stepped onto the dock, an aide was already waiting for him with news. While they had been out, a merchant vessel had arrived from Tornabay, having dodged the blockade. "There was someone on board who wants to see you," the aide said. "He is waiting in your office."

Harg had been looking forward to a pint at Rosenry's, and he headed toward the Customs House in a bad mood. But when he entered his headquarters and the newcomer rose to meet him, everything else disappeared. It was Gill.

They hadn't seen each other since that confused night in Tornabay, when all of Harg's plans had fallen apart and they had had to scatter and flee. Harg was across the room in a few strides, and engulfed Gill in a bear hug. "By the root, am I glad to see you! Tell me what's happened. Where's the *Ripplewill*? Where are the others?"

Gill was smiling. "Hello, Harg," he said. He looked windblown and weary. "I got here as soon as I could."

"Where have you been?"

"I've been in Tornabay, hiding out. They never got close enough that night to get a good look at me; they were too busy going after you."

"What about Torr? Tway?"

"By the time I made it to the harbour, there was no sign of *Ripplewill*. She must have gotten away in the night. I couldn't find Tway. But Harg—they captured Calpe."

He desperately didn't want to hear this. "What have they done? Tried her?"

"No. You're not going to like this."

"What?"

"One of the Innings in the palace there, a fellow named Provost Minicleer, keeps a kind of harem, a collection of women to serve his pleasures. He took a fancy to her. She's his personal prisoner."

The thought of Calpe—his fierce, beautiful lieutenant—served up as a native delicacy for some Inning lecher's consumption made Harg wither inside. "Is there any chance of rescuing her?" he asked.

"Not now," Gill said. "Tornabay's swarming with troops. The Southern Squadron finally arrived."

This news had been inevitable, but even so it had a doomsday sound. "Tell me," Harg said intently. "Ships, men, anything you know."

"They've got thirty-nine ships—fourteen warships, ten frigates, the rest sloops and supply boats."

Harg calculated rapidly. "That means over six thousand men."

"More than that. They were short when they got to Tornabay, so a lot of the crews were raised by press gangs. They just about swept the streets clear."

"When are they setting out?"

"A squadron has probably set out already. They hadn't intended to move so soon, but when the news about Holby Dorn came in, the outcry in Tornabay was so loud, Admiral Talley was just about forced to act. He promised to send a squadron against Dorn, under Commodore Tenniel. He'll follow soon himself, with the rest of the fleet."

"Where's this squadron heading?"

Gill shrugged. "Wherever Dorn is. You probably know that better than they do."

Harg shook his head. "Dorn's a free agent, more's the pity. But he's served a good purpose now, getting them to split their forces." His mind was flying. He could never have taken on the whole fleet with just seven warships; but an isolated squadron on police duty, expecting nothing more than pirates, was a bait too good to pass up. Tiarch would be livid; his remit was to deal with Dorn, nothing more. But sometimes opportunity just trumped orders.

An echo of his own words about discipline and orders came back to him briefly, but he thrust it from his mind, and clapped Gill on the back. "You're a hero, Gill. I'm going to get Rosenry to give you a good meal and a good night's sleep so you can leave with us tomorrow."

"Leave? For where?"

"We're going to go hunt us some Innings."

A BEAUTIFUL WAY TO DIE

The dawn was holding its breath as Harg swung himself up onto the *Smoke*'s main deck from the -gig. His order for silence had held; from the seven ships anchored behind Mariveg Head not a sound rose but the occasional creak of rigging and the tap of blocks against the yards as the swell rolled under them. The clammy fog still hung thick, but it now had the sickly yellow hue that meant there was clear sky somewhere above. The rigging drooped listlessly in the still air.

The captains were already assembled on the quarterdeck, waiting for him. He paused till Jearl and Gill had followed him up from the gig, then spoke, softly.

"Pont City is about five miles south of us, across a strait and down the coast. It lies on a bay open to the west." He cupped his left hand to show them. "The bay is almost closed off by a long sand spit that comes down from the north, here where my thumb is. Dorn's fleet is hiding inside the bay, and the townspeople have stretched a log boom across the ship channel in the bay mouth. The Inning fleet is anchored outside the bay, in a line along the sand spit. They can't shell the harbour or the city from where they are; they're probably just waiting for daylight to demolish the boom and move into the bay. We've got to make sure they don't get that far."

He looked around at their faces, all grave and intent. So far so good. "They've got nine ships anchored about 150 yards apart in a line stretching north-south.

On the north they're sheltered by a little sand point. They've put their biggest ships at the south end of the line, nearest the bay mouth."

"What kind of firepower do they have?" one of the Torna captains asked.

"That's the bad news. We're probably outgunned." He glanced at Jearl. In reality, there was no "probably" about it. One of the enemy mounted sixty-four guns; the islanders had no ordnance to match that.

It was ten days since they had set out from Harbourdown to cut off the Inning squadron, and this was the first they had seen of it. They had sailed first to Torbert, Holby Dorn's last known location, on the assumption that the Inning fleet would stop there; but there had been no sign of them. The terrorized citizens of Torbert, after an initial panic at the arrival of an armed fleet, had begged them to stay and defend the town; but Harg had no ships to spare. The Inner Chain was awash in panicky rumours, but at last some solid news had arrived: Dorn's pirates had attacked a merchant convoy on the Middle Sea. True to his new style, he had bloodily slain all the Tornas aboard, then fled with his booty toward Pont. And so Harg's fleet had stood out to sea while the citizens of Torbert lined the wharves, frantic to see their defenders go.

Earlier that summer, the rebellious town of Pont, inspired by Harbourdown's example, had overrun a small Inning garrison and declared its independence. It was not clear to Harg whether they actually supported Dorn, or just had no way to expel him from their harbour once he took refuge there. The consequences would be the same for them either way, since the Innings would not make fine distinctions: Pont would share Dorn's fate, unless something prevented it.

Last evening, while his warships hid behind Mariveg Head, Harg had watched from the hill as the Innings sailed by. Nine vast floating fortresses, wall upon wall of iron and oak. The low, pink sunlight had made the tiered sails look like thunderclouds sweeping across the water. Now he understood better the seeming recklessness with which Talley had split his forces. The single squadron anchored for the night outside Pont Bay was more than a match for the rebels' whole fleet.

Harg glanced around. The deck of *Smoke* was cleared for action; the gun tackles were unlashed, the rammers and sponges laid out, the crews assembled at their stations. Tubs of water and sand stood about, the one ready to put out fires, the other for scattering on the deck if it should become slippery with blood. Above, the topsails stirred restlessly in a waking wind. Harg felt its breath on his cheek; the wind was north. The plan that had been a vague hunch in his mind as he had peered across the water at the Inning squadron suddenly crystallized.

He scanned the circle of faces. His captains looked tense and grim. He would need a different mood for his plan. He grinned at them craftily.

"We're going to give them a little surprise," he said. "If I know my Innings, they won't slip anchor when they spot us. They'll expect us to take them on in line of battle, one ship apiece, and duel it out like gentlemen, because that's what Rothurs would do. We're not going to act like Rothurs; we're going to mob the windward end of their line and leave the lee ships to watch the show. Their biggest ships won't be able to beat upwind to help their friends—at least, not until too late."

One of the Torna captains protested, "There won't be space alongside their line for more than one of us per ship."

"We're going to attack them from both sides."

Now he really had their attention. He went on quickly: "They've got to be moored far enough from shoal water to swing round on their anchors; so there has to be room enough for a ship to cut between them and moor to their inshore side."

"Inside point-blank range," one of the captains said faintly.

"Right. We can unnerve them that way, and do some real damage." He didn't need to mention that the reverse was also true.

Another said, "Our ships will be trapped between the Inning line and land. It won't be easy to withdraw."

"We're not going to withdraw," Harg said.

He glanced around the circle. He could anticipate a hundred other objections: What if the wind changed? What if they struck each other? "We'll have to aim low and carefully. I'll lead the inshore squad in *Windemon*; Jearl will take the seaward side in *Smoke*. Who will join me? Barko?"

The lean pirate was grinning with glee. "I'm with you, Harg. They'll never expect this. It's completely mad. They won't even have loaded their inshore guns."

Not about to be outdone by Barko, Dev said, "I'll go, too."

"All right," Harg said. That would put the biggest risks on the Adaina ships, but that didn't surprise him. He turned to the Tornas. "Now, I want your ships on the outside to moor no more than 200 yards from the enemy."

Jearl was frowning at him. It was closer than any of the Torna officers had been trained to go. A few of them exchanged glances.

"We're going to make them think they fell into a nest of firesnakes," Harg said, voice low and fierce. "They will never have seen anything like this."

They had begun to catch his drift, even some of his fire. He said, "All right, go back and warn your people we're going to be striking quick and hard. They're going to have to fight like the Ashwin. If we win, we'll have revenge for Sandhaven." He got seven tense smiles.

He touched hands with each of them as they turned to descend the gangway and return to their ships. He could almost feel their emotions transmitted through their palms. Once, when he felt the slightest faintness he said quietly, "I'm trusting you, Gall; the rest of us are dead if anyone fails." Gall's grip tightened in his hand.

Last of all, he touched Jearl's hand. "If anything happens to me, you're in charge," he said. Jearl nodded gravely. Then Harg turned to Jonci, whom he had promoted to temporarily replace Katri aboard the *Windemon*. "Let's go."

When they arrived at Jonci's ship, he asked, "Has everyone had breakfast?"

"Everyone but you, Harg," Jonci said.

"Right." Food was the last thing he wanted. He felt impossibly keyed up. The world around him seemed unnaturally distinct. The decisions were made, everything was ready.

And then the wind died. Harg paced the deck in an agony, glancing up every few seconds as if he could will the wind back into being. Jonci stood stoically by the wheel; the crew had all settled back to wait. In the breathless quiet a thousand details were occurring to Harg; he had to force himself not to pester Jonci with questions.

"The sea teaches you patience," Jonci observed to Gill as Harg passed them. "It's got its own time for everything. It's no use thinking we can choose."

Harg forced himself to stop moving, though staying still took more effort. Jonci was right; he was acting like an Inning, thinking time was at his command.

Ten minutes later the sails stirred. The fog was lifting; the masts now cast faint shadows across the deck. Still Harg didn't move. Another gust came, and the crew began to look up and stir. Harg forced himself to wait, impassive, until he was sure there was a steady breeze. At last he said, "All right, let's weigh."

The *Windemon* was third in line as they came in sight of Pont Bay. Dev's *Spinneret* was in the lead. The Inning ships were still anchored where Harg had left them at dawn, noses pointed north into the wind.

"They've seen us by now," Jonci said at his side. "Are they moving?" If the Innings headed out to sea to fight where they could manoeuvre, it would be a very different battle.

"They won't," Harg said. "They'll think they're safer where they are."

He was right. All along the Inning line the gunports were opening like rows of black teeth, but they made no move toward their sails. Ahead, the

Spinneret was rounding the small spit of land that protected the Innings on the north, *Wavedancer* in her wake. As the second ship cut a few yards inland from *Spinneret's* course, she shuddered; her masts bent forward and the sails belled out as she was brought to a sudden halt. She was aground on an unseen shoal.

"Ashes!" Harg said, wincing as he watched the *Wavedancer* pivot around on her bow, driven broadside on the shoal.

"Well, now we know where the shallows are," Jonci said.

"That's an expensive buoy," Harg muttered.

Dev's crew were whooping like the wild pirates they were as they swept down on the Inning line. One of the Inning ships let loose a broadside while the *Spinneret* was still out of range, wasting their shot. Harg smiled grimly; it was exactly the kind of move he'd been haranguing his own officers about. He knew how these Inning ships were going to fight.

Spinneret headed straight for the gap between the first and second ships; seeing where Dev was bound, Jonci set course toward the second and third. As they passed the second ship, there was a puff of smoke, then a booming report; Harg felt *Windemon* shudder underfoot as a ball crashed into her side. A shower of splinters went up where another one had hit the gunwale just abreast of the line of gunners.

"Hold your fire!" Jonci's voice came calmly. Harg felt a surge of elation. Gods, but his captains were good.

They were in between the two ships, passing barely fifty yards from the carved and gilded stern of the ship that had fired on them when the *Windemon* let loose her port batteries. There was a deafening concussion, and the guns recoiled inboard. Instantly the gun crews were swarming around the cannons. A few moments later the starboard battery thundered a volley on the ship that would be their main opponent; with a grim amusement Harg noted that the name *Discipline*, painted on her bow, had been defaced with shot. As they emerged on the other side, barely inching into the unknown waters, he was pleased to see that Barko had been right; the *Discipline's* crew was still scrambling to load the inshore batteries. He could imagine the consternation on their decks.

"Now's our chance!" Harg shouted out. "Let's fry the bastards!"

The stern anchor cable roared overside, and when the wind swung the *Windemon* parallel to her opponent, the bow anchor followed. Harg went to the taffrail to see where the rest of the fleet was. There was another roar, and he was momentarily blinded by a cloud of eye-stinging, throat-burning smoke from the quarterdeck guns. Blinking away his tears, he saw that the rest of the fleet, slowed by having to skirt the foundering *Wavedancer*, was still out in the bay, bearing down on the Inning line. "Can they see our signals?" Harg said to Gill, who stood at his side. Then, "Never mind, send one up anyway. Say, '200 yards.'"

"They won't need to see that one," Gill said, turning to summon the signal lieutenant.

The next moment the *Discipline* fired the 22 cannons of her starboard battery. There was a whistling rain of iron, a swift, deadly tattoo of hits, and a scream. For an instant a stunned silence fell over *Windemon*, broken only by a sobbing moan from the main deck. They had never been fired on before, Harg thought; they didn't know what it felt like. Then Jonci's calm, capable voice was ordering the wounded taken below. Harg forced himself to the quarterdeck rail to look at the legless man being carried down the companionway, a trail of blood following. His only thought was that the rhythm couldn't be broken; the crew couldn't be allowed to think, or they would all be dead. Their only hope was to fire faster and fiercer than the enemy.

"Pay them back for that one!" Harg shouted. "We've got her to ourselves a few minutes; let's win before the others come."

Someone gave a defiant pirate yell; Harg blessed him, whoever he was. The gunners jumped back to their tasks, their shock not over but put aside.

Soon *Windemon's* deck was an inferno. The line of cannons crouched black and angry all down the deck; they roared, bucking back on their breeching ropes, only to be tackled, tamed, and muzzled again. Their black smoke turned the day dark and the air acrid. Soon the *Discipline* was invisible past the sooty billows; the only evidence she was even there was the screaming hail of fire that tore up the rails and planking, sent cut rigging thumping to the deck, and showered deadly splinters through the unnatural gloom.

Behind them, the *Spinneret* was stinging her opponent like a tenacious wasp, but Harg could see she was being badly mauled. As the broadsides kept coming, a jagged hole was torn in her side where two gunports were battered into one; a grisly trickle of blood ran out and down the hull. As Harg watched, her foremast shook, then twisted, splintered, and slowly fell, taking a tangle of rigging with it. Now *Spinneret* was crippled; there would be no escape for Dev.

Harg motioned Gill to follow him, and set out for the foredeck to spy out the action ahead. As he walked the length of the deck he shouted out encouragement, though he couldn't any longer hear his own voice. He knew that the gun crews were in a strange trance of routine motion: swab, load, ram, prime, run out, train, cock, fire, again. When he passed, their sooty faces grinned at him with a weird elation, like damned souls that didn't yet know they were in hell.

Ahead, he could see that the *Ison Orin* and *Pimpernel* had their opponent in a ship sandwich and were battering it mercilessly. The last five Inning ships were still riding at anchor, unopposed and useless. No, not quite useless—one was firing a mortar into the melee. "Idiots," Harg said. In these close quarters they were as likely to hit their own ships as their enemy.

When he returned to the quarterdeck, Jonci appeared at his side. "The *Discipline*'s fire has slowed a lot since *Smoke* came up on her larboard side," she said. "We must be doing some damage."

"We've got them sweating in their pretty uniforms," Harg said. He felt a surge of fierce glee. He clapped her on the back. "By the horns, we're in the right place today, Jonci! This is where we were meant to be. Your crew—"

His words were cut off by a hot blast of wind past his ear. The concussion knocked him sideways, and he staggered into Gill. Jonci was no longer beside him. He looked around for her, and finally saw her, writhing like a smashed bug, halfway across the deck. Her right arm and shoulder were missing.

Gill was clutching his arm. "Harg, are you all right?"

His skin was tingling strangely; he had to gasp for breath. *Don't think*, he told himself. *Don't even try.*

"Get the captain below!" he ordered. "Who's her lieutenant?"

"Me, sir," a white-faced young man said. Too young, Harg thought with a wild stab of remorse. For an instant he wanted to shout, *Go home! Get out of here!*

"Have the gunners step up their fire. Tell them they're turning the battle."

"Yes, sir."

"Look, Harg!" Gill pointed ahead. The next Inning ship in line had been dismasted. Now a stray shot had severed her anchor cable and she was floating downwind, trailing a mess of rigging in the water. For an instant it looked like she was going to foul Barko's ship, but the wind carried her past it, toward shore.

One enemy out of action. "We'll finish her off later," Harg said. "Signal our ships to move on to the next in line. No, wait."

Something was happening toward the downwind end of the Inning line. The five ships, the big ones with no opponents, were raising sail. Harg squinted through the smoke-haze to see their course. Beneath his feet the deck vibrated with the redoubled effort of the gunners; his teeth felt like they were shaking out of their sockets. He guessed the Innings were going to try to tack upwind and come down on the line of fighting ships from the side. His mind was working ferociously, graphing out their course, the timing, the best way to meet the attack. Then the five ships veered downwind.

"They're running away!" Gill exclaimed in disbelief.

"The bastards!" Harg said. He wished he could see the faces on the *Discipline*'s deck, when they saw their best ships abandoning them.

Escaping. Harg cursed at how slowly his mind was working. He couldn't let them get away. They would still be a danger to be tracked down and attacked, perhaps under less favourable circumstances. But the battle he had started was not yet won.

For an instant Harg weighed a near-sure, but incomplete, victory against the chance of winning or losing it all. He glanced at the *Windemon*'s rigging to evaluate the damage, then roared, "Lieutenant!"

Jonci's first lieutenant came up. "What's the state of your ship?" Harg asked.

"We've got some holes below water line. She's taking on water. The lower gun deck is bad; three guns out of commission . . ."

"The rigging, man. Can she sail?" Harg asked impatiently.

"Give me ten minutes to repair—"

"No. Get her under whatever sail you can, and repair as we go. We're following those ships." Harg turned to Gill. "Hoist a signal for *Ison Orin* and *Pimpernel* to pursue the enemy. The rest can finish up here under Jearl's command."

"We can't catch them," Gill said.

"We can't if we don't try!"

When the *Windemon* pulled ahead through the gap in the line left by the grounded Inning vessel, and her guns fell silent, Harg felt he must surely have gone deaf, so quiet it seemed. He was astonished to note it was almost noon; they had been pounding the *Discipline* for two hours. For the life of him he couldn't account for the time.

With the fore and mizzen sails set, there was a momentary lull in activity on deck. Harg picked his way across the wreckage. The planking was grooved and pocked where shot had glanced, and littered with smashed wood and fallen rope. One gun whose barrel had burst was still smoking, having blown up its own gunport. Here and there exhausted gunners sprawled against the gun trucks. Harg paused by one who sat, knees drawn up and head buried in his arms as if to block out all the world. The sight reminded Harg of himself, once. How many years ago had it been, that first battle when he had thought his senses permanently unhinged? Only six years. It seemed much longer.

The wounded and dead had not yet been taken below, merely dragged aside in the rush and piled like lumber between the gangways. Harg skirted the area, wishing his deafness had lasted so he would not have to hear the voices.

"Go see how Jonci is," he said to Gill.

Gill looked at him oddly. "She's dead."

"Oh," Harg said.

When he mounted the quarterdeck again he could see the line of battle behind them. The northernmost ship in the Inning line still lay anchored, unopposed since the start, but trapped between the battle and the sandbar, her broadsides useless, unable to move without running onto her own allies. *Spinneret*, *Smoke*, and *Lark* were still duelling it out with their opponents. The departure of three rebel ships seemed to have heartened the defenders, and the lagging pace of the salvos had picked up again. Harg guessed it would not last long, if Jearl kept pressing them. It was something in the body language of the Inning ships; it spoke to some sixth sense of their hopelessness at being trapped, abandoned by their friends, in the storm of a ferocious attack.

"Harg, look," Gill said. "*Wavedancer* got free."

He was right; the rising tide had evidently lifted her from the shoal, and now she was sailing in to join the fight. "Quick, signal her to join us," Harg said. It was a godsend—a fresh ship, as if dropped from the sky. The odds were still long against them, but it helped.

Then he noticed activity at the harbour's mouth. Two rowboats were out there, pulling aside the boom, and a cluster of sails was billowing out behind.

"Ha! Dorn's coming out to join the fun," Harg said.

"It's about time," Gill scowled.

Harg trained his spyglass on the leading ships of Dorn's fleet, to see which way they would turn—to help Jearl polish off the ships already under attack, or, as he hoped, to join him in pursuit of the others. But as he watched in disbelief, they set course due west.

"The rotting cowards!" Harg said. The pirates had seen their chance, and were fleeing the scene of the engagement.

The hopes of every man on deck had risen at the prospect of reinforcement, and now they were staring after the pirate fleet with betrayal in their faces. Harg collapsed his spyglass with a click. "So much for solidarity," he said in disgust.

He turned to scan the sea ahead. The Inning ships had a formidable head start. Under normal circumstances, Harg's ships would have been faster; but with damaged rigging and hulls their small advantage was gone. For an instant he thought of calling off the chase and turning back to finish off the battle he could win.

"Sir," the lookout called, "they're only under topsails."

Harg frowned and squinted into the distance to confirm this inexplicable news. To escape pursuit, they ought to be crowding on sail for dear life.

"Do you suppose they haven't seen us?" Gill said.

Harg suspected something grimmer. They weren't fleeing at all; it was only a ruse to draw away part of the islander fleet to a distance where they could turn and overwhelm it. And Harg had taken the bait.

"I wonder how they knew what I'd do," Harg said.

"What do you mean?" Gill hadn't yet figured it out. Harg glanced at the four ships with him. The *Ison Orin* was strongest, but looked badly damaged; the *Pimpernel* was just barely a warship; the *Wavedancer*, far behind them, was only a frigate. They would be outgunned, facing undamaged ships and fresh crews. The Innings must be laughing up their sleeves.

"Lieutenant!" Harg called. The *Windemon*'s new commander—Harg still couldn't remember his name—had emerged from the companionway, looking grim and harried.

"We've got to get *Windemon* in shape," Harg told him. "We're going to be in battle again soon."

The man's voice had a shrill, overstressed edge. "I've got forty wounded in the cockpit, and thirteen dead. We're leaking like a sieve; there's four feet of water in the well, and making fast. The lower gun deck's like a knacker's yard—"

"Stop whining at me!" Harg exploded. "I don't want your complaints, I want something *done!*" He realized his own voice was edging up the scale, and forced his jaw shut. This wasn't good; they sounded like fishwives.

But his outburst had actually calmed the young officer, given him a focus for his anger. "Aye aye, *sir*," he said icily, and turned away.

For an instant Harg felt his weariness. His nerves were tight as stays. He sank down on the signal chest rather faster than he'd intended. He took out his pipe to steady himself. "Have that youngster over there fetch us something to eat," he said to Gill, trying to sound unconcerned.

When he had eaten and smoked, he looked out again over the deck, and it seemed like a different ship. The *Windemon*'s weary crew had gotten all her sails up and pulling, and the rhythmic thump of the pumps sounded from below, at work reducing the water in her bilge. The ship was straining forward before the north wind, wounded but game, as if eager to meet the almost certain death ahead.

Gill lowered his spyglass with a low whistle. He had been studying the enemy. "Are we going to take on that three-decker?" he asked.

"Don't worry," Harg said with a false lightness; "it's not how many guns they have, it's how many hits they get."

"You've got a plan, don't you?"

He said it with perfect trust. In his tone there was not a shade of doubt that somehow Harg would pull them through. That trust was everywhere, in the glances the crew cast in Harg's direction as they worked. They could see that he was leading them into a bloodbath, and they still trusted him.

Harg glanced upward to hide his thoughts. Clouds had rolled in from the north, and the sky was overcast and angry. Above their main top a seagull was gliding, an escort from the Ashwin. Looking at it, Harg suddenly had a rock-sure premonition that he was going to die.

Oddly, the foreknowledge had a settling effect on his mind. The anguish of others' deaths faded before the fact of his own. Seized with a mad serenity, he smiled down on the main deck bustling with his loyal, doomed crew, and felt already the bond of death drawing him tight to them. He had to be cruel; there was no choice. It was necessary to betray the individuals in order to bring to life the greater being they formed collectively. Now Harg could feel that being, almost as if his nerves were tied into it. Every eye in the squadron was his eye, every ear his ear. Its sails were his limbs. It was his instrument, subsuming his individuality till even his own death made no difference.

"Yes," he said to Gill, at last answering his question. "I've got a plan. Fight like devils."

He had entered a new state of complete concentration. "Signal the other ships to fall back within hailing distance," he said. Soon they would be drawing within firing range; being upwind, it was the rebels' choice when and how to attack.

When the *Ison Orin* was close, he leaned over the gunwale, hands cupped around his mouth, and shouted, "Time for a reel! Pick a partner and dance! We get the big one."

The people who lined *Ison Orin*'s gunwales shouted comments and eager catcalls; the *Windemon*'s gunners, roused to the occasion, hooted back raucously. Soon an epidemic of high spirits, fuelled by an unacknowledged panic, had spread to all four ships.

"Hoist the signal to form line of battle," Harg said.

"Harg," Gill said quietly, "Jonci's lieutenant. He's already in a panic, and we haven't fired a shot. He's demoralizing the crew. You've got to do something."

The man was clearly in line to take over; if Harg put someone else in his place, it would be a crushing slight. But this was no time to be thinking of hurt feelings.

"Lieutenant!" Harg said. The young man came up. "You've done a good job getting the ship ready. I'm going to need you in charge of the main battery below. I'll take over Jonci's duties here."

No explanation, no excuse; it was just a fact. The lieutenant flushed, saluted without a word, and turned to go below.

"Well, that was easy," Gill said.

Easy for him to say. Harg clasped his hands behind his back to keep from fidgeting. He had never intended to command the ship himself. He squinted out over *Windemon*, trying to think of some strategic advantage.

"Hoff!" he shouted at the marine sergeant, who hurried forward. "Station some men in the tops with rifles to shoot down on their decks. Take along some baskets of grenades as well. Line all the yards with men."

"Yes, sir." Soon there was a flurry of activity.

The Innings were making no attempt to manoeuvre round and seize the advantage of the windward position. They just kept on course to the southwest, as if waiting to see if the rebels would be foolish enough to attack.

The wind had picked up, and the bow was crashing into the waves. "That's right," Harg looked up to where the Ashwin watched. "Send us some sea."

"You want to fight in a storm?" Gill asked.

"They won't be able to open their bottom gunports if the sea's high," he pointed out. "We'll be more evenly matched."

They were coming into firing range. "Ready your guns," Harg told the gun master, and quickly there came the thunder of cannons rolling back on their wheels to be loaded. *Windemon* was swooping down on the Innings like a white-winged bird of prey. The ropes were singing, the spray leaping from their path. "Gods, what a beautiful way to die," Harg said.

Soon, *Windemon* had matched pace with the *Conqueror*, the big warship that Harg had picked for a partner. As they glided in tandem over the waves, *Windemon*'s guns erupted; seconds later, *Conqueror* answered. The air shrieked with shot and the sound of wood cracking and splitting. This time there was no shocked pause; the crews were serving the guns in a demoniacal fury, laughing and yelling through the sulphurous murk. *Windemon*'s deck heaved as the next salvo went off. Then the answering grape was buzzing through the air like a cloud of hornets. Fountains of water leaped over the gunwales from cannonballs that landed short.

Harg knew it could not go on long like this. Gun for gun, the *Windemon* could not hold up. He glanced aft. The rebel attack had begun to break up the Inning line. It was time to try an old pirate trick on them. "Back the topsails," he ordered. "Ready, starboard battery."

The hands seized the braces and swung the yards round till the sails, instead of pulling forward, pressed back against the masts, checking the *Windemon*'s forward movement. She dropped astern of the *Conqueror*. Harg watched till the perfect moment, then shouted, "Now! Come about!" The quartermaster spun the helm to port. Again the yards swung, catching the wind. *Windemon* veered across *Conqueror*'s wake, and as they passed the big ship's unprotected stern the starboard battery roared into it. The windows of the captain's luxurious cabin shattered inward.

"He'll be eating glass tonight!" someone shouted.

The *Conqueror*, reacting belatedly, was wearing round to match the *Windemon*'s new course and bring her port batteries to bear. Or what should have been her port batteries. As the big ship lumbered round, Harg could see the gunports popping up raggedly, the men scrambling to load. For the second time that day the Innings had assumed their foe would stay predictably on one side. "Get another round into them before they're ready!" Harg implored his gunners. They were already sponging and ramming like madmen.

The *Windemon* was on the lee side now, which gave her an advantage; with both ships heeled over, the *Conqueror*'s guns were angled downward, and her lower battery useless, while the *Windemon*'s guns were perfectly angled. Soon the deck was a crowded maze of smoking, red-hot cannons recoiling back on their haunches. The firing was a constant roar. Harg saw one of the powder monkeys take a shot as she was measuring a cannon charge into its flannel bag; the explosion etched the sight of her flying limbs on his retina, bright with a grisly beauty. For a few moments, the whole scene was orange with the belching breath of the guns. Then a rending crash and a horrible chorus of screams rose from the deck below.

A messenger lad appeared out of the main hatch. "Sir," he said shrilly, "Lieutenant Garret says to tell you half his starboard guns are gone and there's a nasty fire below."

Harg nodded, more stunned than calm, though it looked the same. "Tell Garret I'm sure he's doing a good job." The lad raced off, and Harg turned to Gill. "Go see if he needs help."

The *Windemon* couldn't take much more of this. If Harg didn't think of something else soon, the rigging would be so shot away there would be no manoeuvring her. To buy some time and confusion, he gave the order to back the topsails, then to fill; but the Innings were catching on to him now, and soon matched *Windemon*'s erratic speed. "Rot them!" Harg muttered. All they wanted was to stand back and blast his ship into scantlings. He had to keep them reacting, he had to keep the initiative.

Again he ordered the quartermaster to come about across the bigger ship's stern. At first it seemed the Innings wouldn't react until too late. The *Windemon* was crossing only yards from the *Conqueror*'s stern when the big ship slowed, her tall aftercastle looming close. Harg saw they were going to collide. Ranks of uniformed marines lined *Conqueror*'s taffrail, bayonets set and muskets levelled.

"Prepare to fend off boarders!" he shouted.

All along *Windemon*'s deck the gunners and seamen seized up cutlasses, pikes, and pistols. They were only an exhausted rabble facing those drilled troopers. Harg knew what the first musket volley would do to them.

With a lurch and a squeal of rubbing timbers, the *Conqueror*'s stern hit *Windemon*'s larboard quarter. Grapnels flew out to hook the gunwales together. For an instant the soldiers held their fire as an Inning officer's voice called out, "*Windemon*, do you surrender?"

Later, the stories said that Harg's reply was stirring and heroic. What he actually yelled back was, "Up your ass!"

On the last word a volley of muskets exploded. Harg ducked, expecting a whir of bullets around his ears; but the soldiers on the *Conqueror* were falling back, breaking ranks in confusion. Only then did he realize the volley had come from above him. The men he had stationed on the yards, forgotten, had taken the troopers by surprise.

With a banshee howl, the *Windemon*'s crew surged forward. At last the Innings' troopers got off a ragged volley. Then a rain of grenades landed on the *Conqueror*'s deck, and the soldiers' line broke apart. The pirates were ready to surge forward over the bulwarks, but Harg shouted, "Not yet! Get back to your guns!"

The two ships were still caught at the stern like the blades of a giant scissors. If left, the wind would pivot them together, the blades closing in a death lock.

A boy was hacking at the grapnel ropes with an axe. "Leave those!" Harg ordered. "Run, get some of our grapnels. Now we've got them, we're not going to let them go!" He turned to the quarterdeck gunners nearby. "Aim at the masts. Use chain shot. Bring them down." Then he was shouting down to the main deck gun master, "Clear their deck. Use grape and canister. Don't leave anyone alive to board us." He waved his hat to the men in the yards. "Keep up your fire! Take their yards if you can!"

With infinite pleasure he felt the concussion as the lower deck guns began to fire. He blessed Garret, or Gill, or whoever was down there rallying the crew amid the carnage and fire. Then the *Conqueror*'s guns answered with a furious bellow, so close their tongues of flame licked *Windemon*'s sides.

Slowly, the scissor blades closed. The riggings meshed, the hulls jarred up against one another.

The messenger from the lower deck appeared at Harg's side, his eyebrows singed. "They're muzzle to muzzle down there," he shouted. "Our guns are poking into their gunports." Black smoke was billowing from the hatches.

"Keep firing," Harg said. "Don't let them board."

On the weather deck, a gap had opened where *Conqueror*'s shots had disabled three of the main deck guns. Harg vaulted down into the confusion, spreading a flurry of orders around him. He set one gun crew to clearing away the debris, and led another group starboard to haul one of the unemployed cannons across the deck. "Clear a path, there!" he shouted, noticing only in a detached way that the obstructions in their way were bodies—some dead, some still living. The men leaned into their task, heaving at the heavy carriage while their feet slipped on blood. The deck timbers groaned and sagged under the weight. Bits of burning sail dropped on their shoulders.

At last they manoeuvred the cannon into the gap and hooked it to the ring-bolts of the old, shattered one. A sleet of grape showered around them, and they all ducked for the deck. One shot knocked Harg's hat from his head. He picked it up; for an instant the situation seemed unaccountably funny. He fanned his face and said, "Hot weather we're having." His companions laughed with an edge of hysteria.

Just then a shout and a despairing wail went up; the whack and splinter of a new salvo sounded, this time from the unengaged side. Harg leaped up to see an Inning frigate on their starboard quarter, guns grinning blackly. Desperately he looked around for his other ships, trying to see who had let this one loose, who might come to *Windemon*'s rescue. The next instant he knew there was nothing he could do about it, not even return their fire. He didn't have enough crew left to man both batteries. "Ignore them!" he shouted. "Fry our own fish!"

He reached the quarterdeck again. Gill appeared at his side, his face sooty and streaked. "We'll have to abandon the lower guns, Harg," he said. "They're just about knocked to scrap iron anyway. The whole ship's side is one huge hole, and the stanchions are blasted away. There's almost nothing holding up the deck." As he spoke there was a blast from the *Conqueror*'s lower deck guns, and the shell sailed unimpeded out *Windemon*'s opposite side. Harg had to stifle a laugh at sight of the Innings firing right through his ship.

There was another mangling blast from the frigate on their unprotected side. "Rot them!" Harg said. It was all he could say.

Garret was coming up the gangway through the smoke, his face white with panic.

"They've hit one of our pumps. We're going to sink," he said shrilly. "We've got to surrender."

"He's right, Harg," Gill said. "We took on too much. It's time to call it quits."

For an instant Harg felt wrapped in heavy coils of failure. He couldn't move, he couldn't think. He couldn't even say the words he needed to say. His gaze strayed upward. The snipers, unseen amid the rigging, had succeeded in clambering across the interlocked yards into the tops of the *Conqueror*, and were shooting down on the decks of the enemy. As he watched, one of them tossed a lit grenade right down the *Conqueror's* main hatch. A huge, bright explosion rocketed out of the big ship's depths. By some impossible luck, the bomb had hit some piled-up charges. Men and smoke poured from their companionway, only to be met by a shower of grape from *Windemon's* last remaining guns.

"Ready to board!" Harg shouted. "We've got them now!"

The *Windemon's* battered crew seized up their weapons. One of them caught a main yard brace and swung over onto the enemy's deck. Others climbed the bulwarks.

"Cease fire! Cease fire!" a voice called from the *Conqueror's* deck.

"Do you surrender?" Harg yelled. He climbed up on a gun carriage to see three Inning officers huddled in a knot of Torna subordinates, in desperate conference. Bright flames were licking out of their companionway.

"Yes, damn you! We surrender!" a voice cried at last.

For an instant Harg stood motionless, unable to believe it. He glanced over his shoulder and saw that the frigate that had been firing on them had finally been engaged by one of his other ships, and was now turning tail to flee. Then he believed it.

"Come with me, Gill!" Harg said, and leaped across onto the *Conqueror's* deck. In a moment he was facing the Inning commander and his haggard officers. "Your pistol, please," Harg said peremptorily. The Inning handed it over in silence, and Harg stuck it in his sash. "Take these men prisoner, Gill," Harg said, then turned to survey the scene from his new quarterdeck.

A lull of desperate exhaustion had descended over the two ships. The corpses could scarcely be told from the living, all sunk flaccid against bulkhead and mast. An eerie hush replaced the constant roar of guns, and for the first time in hours Harg breathed fresh air. He looked up at the tangle of rigging, outlined like tree branches against the sky, and it occurred to him that he had not died.

Everywhere the once-graceful ships were mangled and smoking. When the wind paused, the stench of blood and burned flesh rose. As his normal self began to return, Harg's head throbbed, and he leaned over the ship's rail, mouth filling with saliva, sure he was going to vomit in his moment of victory.

"Sir? You have orders for us?"

Three of his men were standing by. Throat aching with the effort to hold down his sickness, Harg turned to them. "Yes, take a party to disarm the prisoners, then set them to work fighting that fire. If you need help on the pumps, set the prisoners to work."

He had to stop there; he had used up all his spare energy. The men were watching him with an awed, hesitant friendship, and for an instant he felt an intense, almost mystic bond with them. "We cheated the odds, didn't we?" he said with a faint smile. He could have said anything; it didn't matter. What mattered was the moment.

They left him. The setting sun had pierced a hole in the west, and lit the undersides of the storm clouds. A lone seagull circled the *Conqueror*'s mast, then headed west as if to lead them into that sunfire. Harg took out a pistol and aimed it, wanting to shoot the damned bird out of the sky.

He never pulled the trigger.

THE LAWS OF WAR

The waterfront of Lashnish had been transformed by the invasion of Tiarch's fleet. No longer did the marble pier embrace the inner harbour in serene symmetry; it was crowded with boats and noisy drayage jostling between the warehouses, shipyards, barracks, and magazines of a busy garrison town. Recruits had been flocking in, and housing along the waterfront was bursting with transients and hopeful contractors wanting to supply everything from lumber to tar to dried peas.

High above the noise and confusion, the Old City still rose, crowned by the pillared face of the Pavilion. From the doorway of his headquarters on the corner of Promenade and Stonepath, Vice-Admiral Joffrey scowled up at the monument to ancient Lashnura power, so oblivious to the bustle at its feet. He was waiting for the conveyance he had ordered to take him up to Tiarch's palace-in-exile. Ordinarily he would have walked, but today it was windy and raining, and the steep, stone-paved street was a rushing streambed.

When he looked downhill across the wharf, he could see his grand fleet crowding the inner harbour. He felt a fierce, possessive pride in his fourteen ships. Touching the letter in his pocket, he resolved that no force on earth was going to pry his fleet away from him, whatever the outcome of this rebellion. He had not studied in the Corbin Talley school of strategy for nothing. Sometimes, the student even surpassed the master.

The cab rolled up and Joffrey crossed to the curb, the disrespectful wind flinging rain into his face. The driver didn't need to ask where he was bound; he shuttled between the Navy offices and the Governor's residence two or three times a day. It was inconvenient, but Tiarch had her reasons for staying aloof. When she had come to Lashnish, she had chosen to establish herself in an old stone mansion as close as possible to the Pavilion, where the symbolism would hang heavy around her. The main entrance to her residence lay on the Isonsquare, the broad plaza in front of the Pavilion, barely forty paces from the Stone itself.

Tiarch's doorman greeted Joffrey respectfully, and stood by to take his coat and hat. One of the Governor's secretaries, coming down the narrow stairs, glanced at the tall clock in the hallway, for Joffrey was early. "I need to speak with her before our meeting," he said.

"I'll go see if she is free," the secretary said.

Joffrey followed the woman upstairs and stood in the quiet, carpeted hallway till the door clicked open and the secretary gestured him in.

Tiarch was sitting by a roaring fire in the high-ceilinged room overlooking the Isonsquare. The rain blew against the tall windows, and the heavy drapes moved in the draft. Joffrey came over to stand by the fire.

"Coffee?" Tiarch offered; a pot and three cups stood on a table beside her chair.

"No, thank you," Joffrey said.

"What's on your mind, Joffrey?"

He stared at his boots for a moment, coming to a decision he had been debating all morning. "A boat came in from the South Chain this morning, with a reply from Harg."

One of the Governor's eyebrows went up. "I take it he was not on the boat."

"No. He declines to come here as you requested, because he feels his presence is required in the South Chain. The main force of the Fourth Fleet has set out from Tornabay, and he wants to be there to receive them."

In fact, Harg's letter to Tiarch was in Joffrey's pocket, but he had decided not to give it to her, even though he had resealed it so that only a practiced eye could tell it had been opened. The problem was that it was written in far too reasonable a tone, giving convincing strategic justifications for the man's intransigence. Joffrey suspected that it had actually been written by Jearl, or one of the other Torna officers. Apart from being entirely too literate for Harg, it lacked that antagonizing Adaina bluntness. It might actually convince Tiarch that the man was right.

Now, the Governor's fingers were drumming on the arm of her chair in irritation. Knowing what she was thinking, Joffrey followed up, "As a matter of fact, Harg requests that you will send the rest of the fleet to join him in Harbourdown, in order to put up a more effective resistance. He also has a variety of demands, mostly for gunpowder and money to pay contractors."

He knew that the last thing Tiarch wanted was for Harg to take on Admiral Talley. The wholly unauthorized aggression against the Innings at Pont, which was being celebrated all over as a great victory for the islanders, had effectively closed off most avenues for diplomacy. The nationalists in Fluminos would be howling for vengeance now. If only Harg could have managed to lose, a magnanimous compromise might still have been possible. As it was, he had thrown all of their futures in jeopardy.

"What am I going to do with this man?" Tiarch mused.

"Well, if you send him any more ships, his fleet will outnumber yours."

She gave him a sharp glance, from which he knew that she also had foreseen this danger. She had created a monster by giving him the little support she had.

"Is it true that Talley's fleet has finally set out?" she asked.

"Apparently, yes." Joffrey paused.

"Well?" Tiarch demanded, noting his hesitation.

"There is some rather odd news about that. He has taken the Heir of Gilgen along, as a prisoner in his flagship."

Tiarch was silent as she worked out what this might mean. "Damn him," she said at last. "He has figured out how the Heir of Gilgen can profit him."

"Just like his brother," Joffrey added.

They both glanced automatically to the window, where the Pavilion stood, bastion of Lashnura power and learning, already infiltrated by an Inning agent. And, as long as Namenda Agave refused to heed all warnings, there was nothing the mighty Tiarch and all her fleet could do about it.

"Damn these Talleys," Tiarch said. "They are cleverer than they have any right to be. They know that the way to control the Isles is to control the Lashnura."

Joffrey actually felt a grudging respect. He had not spotted Nathaway as an operative, despite being trained at counterespionage. He rarely made mistakes like that. It showed that the master still had something to teach the student.

There was a soft knock on the door, and the secretary looked in. "Your guest has arrived, Governor," she said.

"Show him up," Tiarch said.

Joffrey went to the window to look down on the vehicle that had brought the eminent visitor to Tiarch's door. He noted with satisfaction that his advice had been followed; it was a plain black carriage devoid of ostentation, suited to the confidential nature of the transaction.

Only four or five people in Lashnish were supposed to know the identity of Tiarch's guest. The fact that the news was not running wild all over town was a credit to the discretion of Tiarch's staff. The man even now mounting the steps was a legate from the Monarch of Rothur.

The man who entered the room was lean, dark, and immaculately dressed. His close-trimmed black beard, shaved away in a ram's-horn spiral down his cheeks, was a mask hiding any expression he might have had. Tiarch rose to greet him; he bowed low in Rothur style, showing his small skullcap.

"Welcome to my humble residence, Legate Svitchak," Tiarch said. "I regret that we cannot receive you with the same hospitality I could have shown in Tornabay."

"No matter, respected lady," the Rothur answered smoothly in accented Inning. "We fully understand your circumstances."

"Allow me to introduce Vice-Admiral Joffrey, head of my Navy."

"Ah, sir," the Rothur said warmly. "I convey the congratulations of my Monarch for your admirable victories."

"Thank you, Legate," Joffrey said.

"You may not realize, but we in Rothur are great lovers of irony," Svitchak said, smiling. "It has given us the keenest pleasure to watch the Inning Navy bitten by the very dog they trained."

The metaphor gave Joffrey some secret pleasure himself.

"We have some experience with this man of yours, Harg Ismol," the Rothur continued. "There was a time when we would have gladly hanged him, if we could have caught him. Now we will have to reconsider."

"Please do," Joffrey said, "at least until we're done with him."

Svitchak laughed. "I see you are an ironist yourself. We shall get along, I can tell."

Two servants entered the room with fresh coffee and pastries, and Tiarch ushered Legate Svitchak to a warm seat before the fire, casting a glance over her shoulder at Joffrey. He gave her a bland smile.

They spent some time getting acquainted—speaking of the Rothur's journey, his impressions of Lashnish, anecdotes of their families at home. Svitchak took the opportunity to present Tiarch with a gift from the Monarch, a bottle of rare and valuable liqueur.

"The Monarch particularly wished me to tell you, Governor, how sympathetic the whole Rothur nation is to your cause. We have known for many years that the Innings wish to rule the continent, and we regret deeply that you have become the victims of their imperialist ambitions."

"It gives me consolation to know that the Monarch sees our misfortune in that light," Tiarch said.

"We believe that Inning actions here reveal a larger geopolitical goal. Since we stopped their aggressions to the south—" (Joffrey felt a touch of the aforementioned irony at this interpretation of the recent war) "—they have shifted their attentions to the north. We believe their strategic goal is to build up a navy that will enable them to dominate shipping and threaten cities all up and down the coast. Naturally, such a thing is of concern to us."

Tiarch said, "Yet if we should lose, Inning would have not only the pine forest resources of the Forsakens, but also our shipbuilding and nautical expertise."

"The risk is very evident to us," the Rothur said. "Unfortunately, as you can imagine, our country is weary of war. I fear the Monarch would find little support for a course of action that would embroil us again."

"We can do our own fighting," Joffrey said.

"Yes, you have demonstrated that, if I may say so." Svitchak's teeth gleamed white in his beard. "But the Forsakens are a small country with few people and fewer resources. Moreover, you have—pardon me for saying it—a reputation for fractious divisions. Do the people of the Isles share your ambition? What do the villagers of the South Chain, or the tribes of the Outer Chain, say? Are they all prepared to pay the price of war? You have taken on a fearful enemy. It will be a heavy price."

There was a short silence. Then Tiarch said, "The gracious support of your Monarch would help to unify us, by convincing even the doubters that we could prevail."

Svitchak smiled. "It is kind of you to say so, but I suspect the party our support would have an effect on is the Innings."

"That is still useful to us," Tiarch said.

"I do not doubt that. But my Monarch needs to look ahead, to who will rule the Isles once this is over. If it is to be Tiarch, then we are satisfied with the outcome. But we fear the Adaina will not follow Governor Tiarch through the sufferings of a long war. There is no name they will follow, except the name of Ison. Who, we ask ourselves, is to be Ison? Will it be Tiarch, or someone less acceptable to us?"

This time the silence was long, as Tiarch picked up her coffee cup and took a deliberate sip from it. When she put it down, she said, "That's a question I cannot answer now."

"But it is a crucial question, you see."

"Yes, I can see that," Tiarch said.

The conversation shifted to less troubling matters. At length the legate rose. "I know you have an engagement for dinner, so I will leave you now. You know our feelings and concerns."

When the Rothur was gone, Tiarch walked pensively over to the window, and stood looking out on the Isonsquare, where for six hundred years the leaders of the Isles had passed through dhota-nur. Joffrey came to her side.

"Why don't you do it?" he asked.

"You flatter my vanity," Tiarch smiled. "I thought of it once, actually."

He studied her. "Then why . . .?"

"Do you know what an Ison is, Joffrey?"

"Of course I do."

"No, I don't think you do. An Ison is a tool of the Lashnura. A person who has been tamed and moulded by the Grey Folk, a mind manipulated by dhota-nur, a heart bent into a Lashnura shape."

"I cannot imagine you becoming a tool of anyone," Joffrey said.

"Neither can I. That's why I'm not going to do it."

She turned back toward the fire, taking up the poker to stir it to life again. When she had it blazing, she faced Joffrey as if she had come to a decision. "Joffrey, I want to send you on a sensitive errand, one only you can perform."

"Yes?" he said cautiously.

"First, I want you to take ten of those ships down in the harbour and deliver them to Harg."

He said nothing, but his whole being was tense with rebellion.

"Then I want you to continue on to Fluminos, to open some direct communication with the High Court."

He weighed this plan. It had certain attractions to him—access to a world of imperial power politics beyond the ken of most islanders, if he played it right. A diplomatic errand would give him contacts no military appointment could equal. But the trade-off, apparently, was ceding control of his navy to Harg Ismol. The thought had a bitter taste.

"Why me?" he said.

"You have friends in Fluminos, you lived there once. There are not many islanders who have the connections you do. Or know as much about dealing with the Innings."

"They might not be interested in talking," he said. "They might just throw me in jail. Or hang me, in lieu of Harg Ismol."

"I didn't say it was without danger. But you will know how to sound them out. You will know the channels through which we can approach them. I can give you some names and introductions, but it will be up to you to make the best of them."

"What about the Rothur alliance?" Joffrey asked.

Sardonically, she said, "For now, it might be best if the Innings and Rothurs don't know we are talking to them both."

Another reason she needed him. Weaving a web of diplomatic duplicity took a certain complexity of mind. He gave her a half-smile to match his half-agreement.

"I knew I could count on you," she said.

৯

Goth was wandering down the throat of a frozen amethyst wave when he felt the tug of reality calling him back. He pushed the call to the back of his mind; it smelt of time and physicality. He did not want to return.

Every day he was piercing farther into the circles achra opened to him. At first the drug had only given him respite from the ulcerous pain of separation from his bandhotai. But soon he had found that he could use it to vault free of this circle where ghosts always followed him, tugging at his limbs to bring him back.

For weeks a recurring vision had appeared to him, but only from afar. At first, he had taken it for a floating mountain of ice, glowing glacier-bright across a dark sea. It was jagged with multiple spires and pinnacles, and from time to time the sun glanced off its face, as if it were made of mica. It had taken two slivers of the drug to come close enough to set foot beneath its cliffs of polished ice, sculpted by rushing meltwater into enigmatic shapes. For a long time he had wandered amid the puzzling geometry of its translucent pilasters and rippling friezes, till at last he had realized that it was a deserted city around him, if a city could have been made of spun glass. It teased his brain with its almost-presence, as if it were only potentially there.

Three slivers it had taken to wander amid the echoing glory of spiral halls and intricately branching rooms. He discovered that the city was a world in miniature, a densely coded architecture of everything. At first the jewelled maze had overloaded him, left his mind quivering with intense sensation. Every keyhole was a theorem regressing to infinity, every leaf a lifetime.

In the moments when, inevitably, he returned to the circle where he was a prisoner, he wondered whether the dream were just a hall of mirrors reflecting back his own mind. There was no way to find out but to return.

Once a week—more frequently, in recent days—the soldiers would fetch him to dine or talk with Admiral Talley. Those conversations seemed surreal in a way the crystal city had ceased to. Something was needed from him, he knew; but what and by whom, he could not fathom.

That was what they wanted now. Already he could feel his limp spine, his sluggish organs in their bag of skin. Someone was rocking him to and fro—no, the whole room was rocking. He was on the ship. Each thought fell like a slow drip of water into his consciousness.

Presently, brisk hands were chafing his skin, helping him sit. He observed as they coaxed his body into standing, then as they washed and shaved it. He felt a detached amusement to see his arms and legs manoeuvring themselves into the intricate folds of Inning clothing. In a mirror he glimpsed the gaunt shadow of someone he remembered once having been.

Admiral Talley was working at his desk in the great cabin of the warship. It was late afternoon, but so overcast that two oil lamps were burning over the Admiral's desk. When he looked up, their light cast shadows on his alert face. But Goth didn't need the light; he was seeing with an uncanny clarity.

"I'm sorry to have interrupted your pleasure," Talley said sardonically. His eyes travelled up and down Goth's body, appraising him critically. "I wish you would have some self-restraint in regards to the achra. You are deteriorating into a pathetic addict."

"I am only what you have made of me," Goth said. The Admiral was keyed up, his unease like a sharp camphor scent in the air. Goth knew this man well by now.

"When I gave it to you, I did not expect you to take to it so enthusiastically. The objective was not to destroy you." He laid his pen down in its silver tray and sat back. The only refreshment on his own desk was a glass of lime water, part of the strict regimen that was his personal discipline.

"What does it do for you, the achra?" he asked.

He didn't expect a serious answer, but Goth found he wanted to talk about it. It had become the most important thing in his life. "I thought at first it would give me freedom," he said. "I thought that was what I wanted—to roam the circles free of all the human bonds that tied me down, to pierce farther than I had ever gone before. But now I think I was wrong. Those bonds were my sustenance, my past. I drew life from union with those I cured. To be free of them is a sterile release. No, I want them with me still, but not ruling me as before. I want to be simultaneously with and apart from them, engaged and detached. Does that make any sense?"

The look on Talley's face was one of old frustration. Somehow, Goth had once again thwarted his desires.

"What do you want from me?" Goth asked.

The Admiral looked away, shaking his head. When he looked back, his stare was fixed and unreadable. "At the moment, if you can possibly focus, I need your advice on a strategic issue."

They never spoke of military matters. Goth said, "I cannot help you. I know nothing of strategy."

Talley's sparse smile looked like a pencil line. "I'll teach you some, then. The first law of warfare is, know your enemy. I need some insight into Harg Ismol."

No one had uttered that name in Goth's presence since he had left Yora. He had expected never to hear it again. His ears buzzed with the shock of hearing it from Corbin Talley. Through suddenly awkward lips, he said, "What has he done?"

With a humourless laugh, Talley said, "What *hasn't* he done? Humiliated the Inning nation, and me in particular. Captured our ships, conquered our forts, routed our best commanders, well nigh united the Torna and Adaina against us."

Not wanting to believe it, Goth whispered, "No."

"Oh, yes."

"Someone must stop him," Goth said.

"I am trying my hardest."

That was not what Goth had meant. He searched the Inning's face for some understanding. "Why is he fighting you?"

"I had thought perhaps you could answer that."

Slowly, Goth shook his head. "I have not seen him in seven years. I didn't know he was back in the Isles, or even alive. We're utter strangers, now."

With a restless gesture, Talley said, "I would not ask you this in company, but we are at war, and I cannot afford to be delicate. Where do matters stand between you and him?"

Goth was silent, not out of reticence, but because he was perplexed by the question. How *did* he stand with Harg? He had been asking himself that question for almost thirty years, and was no closer to an answer.

"Come, come," said Talley impatiently. "Is there animus or affection?"

Groping for something to say, Goth finally managed, "We are not bandhotai."

"From my information, you are something rather more intimate than that," the Admiral said.

Goth stared at him, uncomprehending. There *was* nothing more intimate than bandhotai. He had mentioned it to indicate that they weren't close. "What are you talking about?" he said.

"It's common knowledge that he is your illegitimate son."

Thrown into confusion, Goth said, "Then common knowledge is wrong. Where did you hear that?"

"From the most improbable source," Talley smiled ironically. "The *Fluminos Intelligencer*. Via an unimpeachable correspondent on Yora."

"Then your newspaper is in error."

"Well, let me ask it this way, if you will forgive the indelicacy. Did you sleep with his mother?"

"Yes, of course," Goth admitted a little reluctantly. "We were bandhotai."

"And she became pregnant after that?"

"Yes."

"Well, you see, in Inning we call that a father."

"In the Isles, we don't. Immet Ismol was the man who acknowledged the child, and agreed to raise it. I never agreed to any of that."

"Ah. Well, in Inning we just call that a father who is not living up to his responsibilities."

Stiffly, Goth replied, "We have different customs."

"Well then, let me hazard a guess. Would it be accurate to say there is no love lost between you and Harg Ismol?"

There was a long pause as Goth considered the question. At last he said, in a muffled voice, "No. That would not be accurate." There were very few things he was certain about when it came to Harg, but this was one of them. There was love all right—guilt-ridden, ambivalent, reproachful, demanding, impossible to satisfy—but it was love.

Memories were flooding his mind, vivid as a vision. She had been so passionate, so recklessly human. They had loved each other like people on the edge of madness for months, till all the village buzzed. They had crept out to meet on the hills when she was large with pregnancy. Lying there on the sand, he had pressed his cheek against her naked belly to feel the child kick inside, both of them laughing.

And after her death, how hard it had been to see her child growing more like her every day. Everything about the boy had drawn him—most of all the pain just under the surface, given away in a thousand unconscious signals. Goth had longed fiercely to enter that mind and soothe it, especially since he was the source of so much of its trouble.

"I couldn't have a child," he said, almost to himself. "It was too dangerous. Any child of mine would have been a pawn, a tool, just as I have been, as I am now. I could not create a living soul, just to resign it to suffering. What I did was necessary to protect him."

He looked up; Talley was watching him with a strangely complicated expression. "And I suppose it never occurred to you that he would want any say in the matter?" the Inning said.

"I could have solved it all," Goth answered. "I could have made him content with his life, if only I could have given him dhota. But he would never accept it from me. It was the only thing he could control, the only way he had to reject me back, to hurt me as I had hurt him. I only wish . . ." His voice trailed off.

Softly, Talley said, "You wish?"

"I wish I knew if he has forgiven me."

Talley said nothing. He simply sat watching until at last Goth became aware of him. "I'm sorry," Goth said, shaking his head. "This is not what you needed to know."

Shrugging, Talley said, "How simple the world would be if we had no fathers." And Goth realized he had not been thinking of Harg at all.

Looking out the stern window, Goth longed for the soothing bite of achra under his skin. When he returned to the mosaic halls of ice, he would remember none of this. There would be no responsibilities, no old mistakes to pursue him.

And yet, if Harg was walking the world unhealed, driven by old wounds, he would have to be stopped. Otherwise he would dash himself to bits against the unyielding wall of Inning power, and quite possibly take half the Isles with him. Goth felt an awful premonition. He had created this monster himself, out of his own folly and fear.

"You have to release me," he said, standing unsteadily. "I must do something about this."

"Sit down," Talley said with a trace of impatience. "As long as they haven't got you, there can be no Ison. Do you think I'm going to let you perform some barbarous sacrifice so this madman can become a god to all the Forsakens?"

"Is that what they are saying?" It was an arresting thought—half appalling, half appealing. It was almost impossible to imagine—and yet, it might be more dangerous to leave things as they were.

"Would you do it?" Talley was watching him appraisingly.

"He would never ask. Not from me."

"Not even to have the adulation of all the Isles?"

"Adulation means nothing to a true Ison. The Isons do not act from pain, or ambition, or any inner compulsion. They act only for the Isles. That is why people follow and trust them. Only the unhealed act from personal motives. That is why we do not allow them to have power. An unhealed person with power can be terribly dangerous. Like Harg. Like you."

A frown glanced across Talley's face, sharp as a knife. "What a pernicious system, to bind your leaders' hands so."

"It is no different than yours. You are bound by the law."

"Only if one believes in it."

"But you do," Goth said seriously.

For a moment Goth saw a furtive flicker of introspection in the Admiral's eyes. Then the frost was back, opaquing the windows of the man's mind. "I believe in success," he said. "I believe in what works, by whatever means."

Talley rose. "Come here. I want to show you something about leadership."

He led the way up on deck. Goth followed, squinting and shading his eyes even in the cloudy gloom. As the Admiral came on deck there was a flurry of brisk salutes. Talley nodded absently at them, and led the way aft.

The ship was anchored with a fleet of others in a broad harbour protected on the west by a long spit of sand. In the back of the bay a town lay—or what had once been a town. It was now a smoking rubble.

Talley called for a spyglass and handed it to Goth. "Here, look more closely," he said.

Goth scanned the scene. It had once been built of whitewashed brick and red tile roofs. Scarcely a building was left standing now. Goth could pick out a few figures moving about in the ruins. On the beach a row of corpses was lined up like cordwood.

"Did you do this?" Goth asked.

"Yes," Talley said dispassionately. "Two days of bombardment from the sea. Then we landed a force to finish them off."

"Why?"

"It was once the town of Pont. They assisted Harg Ismol, allowed him to refit his ships here. We informed them of the consequences, then carried them out."

On the headland to the south, the ruins of an ancient Altan fortress lay guarding the entry to the harbour. An Inning flag now flew from it. On its tumbledown walls, outlined against the sky, was a forest of spikes. Goth trained the spyglass on them, then recoiled. On each spike was an impaled body, guarding the harbour entrance in a ghastly vigil.

"Rebels," Talley explained. "The local resistance. Most of them are still alive."

There were dozens of them. An act of cruelty this enormous had a terrible power, a power that echoed down through history.

"You are shifting the balances," Goth said softly. "It will take centuries to shift them back."

Talley's face had no expression at all. "I mean to make the price of rebellion too high to pay," he said. "It is the quickest way to cut this conflict off— to make it ugly beyond their imaginations. I have nothing to lose; I can raze every town and burn every field in the South Chain. I can make this place a smoking waste. You see, it doesn't matter how many battles Harg Ismol wins; he can win a thousand, and I will still win the war. Because he is shackled by wanting to save something. All I need to do is destroy."

His eyes were bright now. "Inexorably. Like a law of nature. That is justice."

Goth turned away from the sight. "I want to go back to my cabin," he said.

"Can't face what you have brought about?"

"This is not my doing."

"You could stop it. Just call on them all to lay down their arms. Publicly repudiate Harg Ismol, and this would be over."

So that was what Talley wanted. Goth found himself looking into the icy depths of the Admiral's eyes. Ice so cold it burned. "Betrayal," Goth said, almost under his breath.

In a neutral tone, Talley said, "Sometimes it is necessary to betray a man, in order to save a nation."

With a deep anger, Goth said, "You cannot put your guilt off on me."

"That wasn't my intention. I intend only to give you the choice to stop me."

Goth pointed a wavering hand at the spike-lined hill. "That is *your* choice, not mine. *You* chose to do that."

With a faint, remote smile, Talley said, "It was what the laws of war demanded. My nation wishes me to conquer the Forsakens, and I do as my nation asks. Do you still think your rebels can win this war?"

Goth had not known before, but now he was sure of it. He was about to say so when he realized that what he and Talley meant by "the war" were probably two different things.

"If you mean the war of guns and ships and armies," he said, "they probably cannot."

"Is there another one?"

"Yes, of course. The inner war, the war of balances."

"Of ideologies, you mean? Whoever wins the war of force will win that one as well. History is written by the victors."

It was not what Goth had meant. He gazed at the hillside, tried to count the spikes, lost count. The thought of so much pain made him lightheaded. The world blurred into unreality.

"Those people there," he said, "they are winning the war. They will enter your soul, and all your people's souls. They will always be with you now. The more you hurt them, the closer you will be bound. Some day you will not be able to look at yourselves without seeing them."

Talley gazed across the harbour with a fierce detachment. "Can't you get it through your head that I don't believe in your balances, or your atonement? They have no power over me. And you have no power, either."

Goth laughed. He would not have done it, except he felt the drug leaving his system; he stood at the edge of the blank madness of desire, and it made him reckless. "But I do," he said. "I am your victim. Every person becomes his victim."

"I have merely given you your heart's desire," Talley said. His voice was light; but the drug had made Goth's senses unnaturally keen, and he heard the provocation underneath. For some reason Talley wanted Goth to break down and condemn him, to stand on high moral ground.

"May I go now?" Goth said.

Talley looked at Goth as if they were the only ones in the world. The edges of Goth's vision were blanking out; he could see only Talley's face, at once very near and very far away.

"You are escaping me, aren't you?" Talley said.

"More every day," Goth said. "Whatever you want from me, you had better get it soon."

"Damn you!" Talley said, very quietly. "I want you not to be a good man."

Abruptly, he turned to the marine captain who stood nearby and ordered, "Take him back below. Tonight, give him no achra. I want him to survive long enough to see me break the back of this rebellion."

Goth nearly cried out in agony at the thought of no achra; but his throat had gone dry, and no sound would come out. He began to tremble as they led him back to prison.

6
STORM OVER VILL

In a secluded inlet on the north coast of Vill, a silent army was coming ashore. Harg watched the ant-swarm of activity from the deck of the *Windemon*. It was a scene of controlled chaos. Four ships lay at anchor in the bay, disgorging their loads of men and equipment in a calculated rush. The water was crowded with rowboats, the beach a milling mass. Nearby, there were tense, hushed orders from the shiphands controlling the ropes of a cannon swaying in a hammock from the improvised crane of the *Windemon*'s main yard. Ropes and muscles taut, they slowly lowered the iron barrel into the cutter waiting below.

Barko appeared at his side. "Everything ready?" Harg asked.

"As ready as it can be," Barko said. He grinned in exhilaration, looking even nastier than usual.

Harg clasped his friend's hand. "Good luck." Then, on an impulse, he hugged Barko close. "Be careful," he said.

"I will. See you in Villamish." Barko turned toward the waiting gig.

Harg wished he were going, too—or that he were sending someone less valuable to him. Barko's party would have the riskiest, and most important, job. But the plans were long since settled, and he owed Barko the opportunity. Even so, he watched the gig leave with a feeling of misgiving. The knowledge of battle ahead waited like an ulcer in his stomach that could only be cured by living through it.

So far, the plan was going like clockwork. The day before, they had been miles away at Bindlequay, waiting for the wind to change. At sunset a dark wall of cloud had appeared on the western horizon and the wind had shifted strongly to the northwest. They had set out under cover of darkness. All night and all day they had sailed south, well away from land, trying to avoid being sighted.

They had made landfall at Dohr, and met there with the scouts from Vill, who had the information they needed. The Inning fleet was still at anchor in Villamish Bay, resting after the hard labour of bombarding and burning the defenceless town. The local resistance knew the number of troops and armaments Talley had stationed in the fort. They provided a map of the island. Everything Harg had wanted. All they needed now was for an avenging fleet to swoop down on the Innings and trap them in harbour.

And then news had arrived that almost stopped the attack cold. An express boat from Lashnish caught up with them, carrying the news that Vice-Admiral Joffrey was on the way with ten more ships. If they could wait till he arrived, the two fleets would be more equally matched, the risk less weighted in the Innings' favour. But if they waited, the chance to trap Talley in port might slip away. He might sail off to another isle, to level another town, and the next time they met the circumstances might not be so favourable. Harg had assembled the captains to ask their opinions, but they had deferred to him. In the end, he had decided to go ahead.

Leaving most of his fleet hidden at Dohr under Jearl, Harg had taken four ships and crept stealthily over to the Innings' very back door on Vill. The force they landed would travel overland, hidden by night. By dawn their cannons would be positioned on the ridge north of Villamish harbour, in easy range of the ships sheltered there. Meanwhile, Harg and Jearl would rendezvous and sail round to blockade the Inning fleet in the harbour. With his ships trapped, Corbin Talley would have no choice but to surrender to a force less than half his size. By this time tomorrow, the war might be over.

Gill was coming back on board from his reconnaissance ashore. "Well?" Harg asked him. "Have we been seen?"

"Of course," Gill said. "In a couple of hours, half the Adaina on the island will know we're here. But I don't think they'll give us away. They're hailing us as saviours, especially now word has spread that you're here. After what the Innings did to Villamish, the islanders want revenge. They've heard about Pont, too."

"Any news about Talley's fleet?"

"They say it's still in harbour, just as it has been. In this weather, they won't leave unless they get wind of us." Gill frowned up at the lowering sky.

Night had fallen by the time they landed the last cannon. Signalling by lantern, the ships drew offshore and began to beat north again, away from danger of discovery. Now for a while all they had to do was wait. While Barko's troops spent a hard night hauling cannons over the hills, the officers on ship could eat a leisurely dinner and catch some sleep.

The officers gathered in the after cabin for the evening meal. Harg wore a uniform, in deference to the Torna present; but around his waist he wrapped a scarlet sash with a dirk thrust into it. Katri presided as captain of the *Windemon*, promoted again by Harg after Jonci's death. Everyone present was either a veteran of the Rothur war or had been through the battles at Harbourdown and Pont.

The conversation took a turn toward grisly humour as they reminisced about other battles—ears shot off, ships afire, a man who contrived to strangle himself in the rigging. Listening, Harg could hear the awareness of death in all their voices.

"You think *you've* seen it all," said the gunner's mate, a thickset man with bushy eyebrows. "In Rothur, I had a gun crew that figured out how to skip a ball off the deck of an enemy ship, like a flat stone on water. I was on top of them to quit and aim at the target, till they bounced a ball twice down the deck of a Rothur warship and right into a crowd of officers. The rotting lubbers were so dumbcracked to see a cannonball bounce, they stood staring at it till it knocked them down like ninepins."

The first time Harg had heard the story, the fact that the gun crew was Adaina had been a big part of it. Now everything had shifted. The dividing line was no longer Torna and Adaina, but veteran and non-veteran. They had had to depend on each other, and save each other, too many times now to make fine distinctions. In the end, life and death were the only distinctions that mattered.

When the air was dense with pipe smoke, Katri called for some music, and a fiddler came in, followed by a boy who played the tin whistle. They started out with wild jigs, but soon fell back on the mournful music of the Isles, and everyone sang the words in a growing effusion of sentimentality. Half a dozen lost causes of the past were made noble by music.

It was not yet midnight when Harg felt the rhythm of the ship's motion shift, and he pushed back his chair to go up on deck. Gill and Katri followed to escape the smoke, leaving the rest to sing down their nerves.

"Why do all those songs talk about losing?" Harg said as they closed the cabin door behind them.

"Because up to now the Adaina have never won," Katri said. "It's hard to get used to the feeling."

For the hundredth time Harg was wondering if he should have waited for Joffrey to arrive. He gave a regretful laugh. "Serves us right, for thinking our leaders ought to be good people," he said. *A good man wouldn't lead all these ships into battle*, he thought. He couldn't act with such calculated cruelty, knowing how people were going to die.

When they emerged into the air, a spate of rain was hammering on the deck. The night was pitch black. The dim binnacle lamp seemed like the only light in all the world. "If the Mundua are trying to help, I wish they'd stay out of it," Harg said to Katri.

"The weather won't matter so much once we're in the lee of the island," she said.

"I'm thinking of Barko."

"Oh, right."

There was no way to know if the land force was running into problems, no way to come to their aid, no way to rescue them easily in this weather. He peered south, toward the island, but saw nothing.

"I think we should set out early," Katri said. "It may take us a while to find Jearl in this weather, and there's no danger of our being seen. It's black as Ashte's ass out here."

"Fine. Give the signal." Harg would be just as happy to be moving.

It did not, in fact, take them long to find Jearl; by some happy coincidence they spotted the signal lanterns on the *Smoke*'s mizzen peak barely half an hour later. By then the wind had them all tossing under reefed sails, so Harg decided to run the chance of taking the ships round early to the island's lee side where the town lay. On a normal night, they might have been spotted from Villamish Fort; tonight he guessed there was little chance of it.

Harg had expected to be able to see some lights from the town as they drew down the coast, but all was dark, bombed into oblivion. When they had come even with the spot where he guessed the harbour entrance lay, he gave the signal for the ships to take up their positions in a broad arc about a mile from shore.

"We'll wait for dawn or Barko's signal, whichever comes first," he said. "Then we'll close in."

The waiting frayed his nerves; he couldn't go below despite the cold wind and the spurts of rain. They were caught between risks. If they came within blockade range early, the ships would be exposed to the guns from the fortress.

But if the alarm went up before they were in position, the Inning fleet might slip from the harbour. He couldn't let either thing happen.

"Who's there?" one of Katri's officers demanded in a tense, hushed tone. He was staring out into the blackness of the sea, one of the watchmen beside him. When Harg came up he turned back, shaking his head. "I thought I saw a ship," he said.

Everyone was jumpy, Harg thought. He longed for the boom of Barko's cannon.

In the end, it was the dawn that came first. One moment all was pitchy, the next there was a faint greyness in the eastern sky. Gill emerged onto the main deck, yawning. "Signal the ships to make ready, Gill," Harg said. "We'll move the instant we can see where we are."

He glanced east, then swore softly, for he could see the outline of a ship's rigging already moving against the sky. "Ashes! Who's broken position?" he said.

He was answered by a fiery flash. The air exploded, suddenly alive with hot lead. As if in echo, broadside after broadside went off, all down the line of his ships.

The *Windemon*'s crew was erupting onto deck in a panicky chaos. "To your quarters! Man the guns!" Katri was shouting. The gun crews had barely assembled when a second broadside ripped into them.

"Close up! Form line of battle!" Harg bellowed from the taffrail, desperately hoping the next ship in line would hear and pass it on. He couldn't even see how close his ships were, or where the enemy was. All he could tell was that the fire was coming from the offshore side. The attacking ships weren't acting like some patrol that had blundered into them and decided to open fire. They were sure, coordinated, guided by a ruthlessly efficient plan. Was it possible that the full Inning fleet had sneaked out of the harbour under cover of night, and had come on the rebels from behind?

Two hundred yards away, the orange light from another broadside momentarily lit up the scene, and he glimpsed the *Lark*'s decks milling with confusion. Not one of his ships had yet managed to return fire.

He was swearing a long string of nonsense words. At his side, Gill said, "What do you want us to do?"

Harg forced himself to shut his mouth and think. Think. That was his job. "Count their ships for me as they fire," he said. "I've got to know where they are."

The crash of splintered wood sounded. He glimpsed the masts of a ship passing across their stern, guns smoking. "Rot them!" he said. There were too many of them. It had to be the full fleet.

Katri was looking to him. "You still want us to hold the line?" she asked.

"Do I look crazy?" Harg said. Somehow, Corbin Talley must have been warned. It was the only way he could have known.

"Gill, signal to withdraw," Harg said.

"Withdraw?" Gill looked as though he hadn't thought the word was in Harg's vocabulary.

"It's an old pirate trick," Harg said.

A cannon boomed, and the bulwarks near them exploded in a shower of splinters. Something hit Harg's face with the force of a boxer's fist and sent him careening back onto the deck.

For a few seconds, every nerve in Harg's body seemed to be rerouted; he was aware of nothing but excruciating agony in his right eye. Each time he tried to blink or jerk away from it, the pain skewered him again, drove deeper.

He was on his back, lying on the deck. Gill was at his side, trying to pry his hand away from his face. Harg fought him, crazed with pain. At last Gill won. "Blessed Ashte!" he said. "You men—come here quick! Take him down to the aft cabin."

It occurred to Harg that he had been killed. No, this hurt too much for death. He gripped Gill's hand. It was the nearest thing. "Don't worry, Harg, you'll be all right," Gill said in his ear.

Harg wanted to laugh, to say it was a lie, but his throat wasn't working. Then someone was picking him up; he was floating through the air, downward. He was supposed to pass out now, he thought; but tonight nothing was going the way it was supposed to. All around him people were shouting, moving furniture. Then he was laid on a cot. He couldn't open his eyes, or the pain came back.

They pried his hand away again; it was sticky with blood. "Gods, that's awful," someone said. Harg tried to raise his hand again, to feel what was wrong, but someone stopped him.

At last he managed to get some words out. "Just patch me up so I can go back on deck," he said hoarsely. "Just make me last till we're out of here. After that, it doesn't matter."

Someone pressed a pipe stem to his mouth, and he smelled the dreamweed. "Here, smoke this," Gill said. Then, to someone else, "We have to get that splinter out."

There followed what seemed like an endless round of consultations. The dreamweed was making Harg relaxed and dizzy. The room seemed terribly cold; he was shivering. Someone was knocking on the door. A cannon ball, he thought, and laughed silently. A whole crowd of cannon balls at the door, waiting to tumble in on him if he answered. It was no more than he deserved. How had Talley found out?

"He's unconscious now," someone said.

"No, I'm not," Harg answered. His face felt like someone was ramming a bayonet into it. "What's happening? Who's giving orders?"

"Keep smoking," Gill said.

There was something he had to warn them about, something no one had thought of. That was his job, to think. "Barko!" he said. "What about Barko?"

"Get on that side," someone said. "Hold him down."

Another voice muttered, "This is going to be useless if it's gone into his brain, you know."

"You godless rotting mutineer," Harg said. "I'll court-martial you for that."

Gill said, "All right, Harg. Brace yourself, this is going to hurt."

Gill had a way with understatement. It felt like they were ripping his eye out with a fishhook, and half his face with it. He choked trying to scream. This, *this* was where he was supposed to pass out. Bleeding Ashte, why couldn't he pass out? Then they were dabbing his face with a sponge, and he was gasping as if he'd just run a race. Blood was flowing into his ear and down his neck as if someone had turned on a spigot. He wanted to swear, but couldn't think of any word eloquent enough.

They were bandaging his head, trapping the fire inside. He opened his left eye, found he could still see. Gill was handing him another pipe. "Here, go to sleep."

Harg reached up to feel his right eye. It was covered with bandages.

"It won't be doing you much good any more," Gill said. "You'll have to wear a patch."

That news gave Harg a hollow feeling. "And Holby Dorn thought I'd never make a pirate," he said dully.

"Well, you've shown him."

Harg realized he couldn't hear gunfire any more. "Have we gotten away?" he asked.

"Yes, about an hour ago."

Then he *had* been unconscious. It was a disorienting feeling. Gill said, "They're chasing us, of course. But Katri's pretty clever. These pirates are good at running away."

"And our other ships?"

"We had to break into two groups. One headed north, one south."

"But we didn't scatter?"

"No."

Harg felt a grim satisfaction at that. Once again, his captains had proved how good they were. "They deserve a better commander than me," he said bitterly. He knew it was all over for him. He was finished—a beaten, mutilated wreck.

"What more could you have done?"

"I led them into an ambush, Gill!"

Gill was silent a few seconds. "Well, you know what everyone is saying about that. We were betrayed. Talley must have been warned."

It was tempting to believe it, to think this was all the doing of some shadowy traitor. But Harg knew who the real traitor was—himself. He hadn't been smart enough, or careful enough. Talley had proved the superiority of Inning tactics.

When Harg woke a few hours later the boat was pitching wildly. He was parched and unbelievably sore. He sat up in the swaying berth and saw with disgust that the sheets he had been lying on and the shirt he was wearing were both soaked with blood, now drying black around the edges. He stripped off the shirt; though the cabin was frigid, his body felt like a furnace. When he found a canteen of water he drank, then wetted the tail of his shirt and mopped the crusty blood from his neck and shoulder.

The aft window of the cabin had been blown apart; glass littered the floor, crunching under his boots when he rose. Someone had tacked an oilcloth over the hole; it now sucked in and out with a cracking sound, strained by the wind. He nearly lost his balance searching for another shirt; only by hanging onto a beam did he make it safely back to the bed. There, he shrugged on his uniform coat against the chill.

When he came into the wardroom, the sole person there was Lieutenant Barret, who sprang up looking like he saw a ghost. Harg made his way, weaving a little, to where a barrel of water was strapped to a beam. He turned the spigot, letting it run into his mouth. It tasted marvellously good.

"Go fetch me some weather gear," he ordered Barret. He wanted to prove that he wasn't finished yet.

It took a grim effort to climb the companionway ladder. When he emerged onto the open deck he stood for a few moments, clutching the lintel for support, the wind pressing against him. Around him lay a grey, windswept terrain of rugged waves. The *Windemon* was hove to with only staysails on. As he watched, a mountain of water as high as the yard-arm bore down on the ship. She climbed it; the bow disappeared under the breaking wave-top, and a shower of windblown spray stung Harg's face.

He mounted to the quarterdeck in search of Katri. She was standing by the wheel, looking as though she relished the weather. Fit and vigorous. Harg tried not to flinch at her gaze. He felt maimed and hideous.

"I didn't expect to see you walking for a week, after what they told me," Katri said.

"I hear you did better without me than with," he said. He was acutely aware that he had left the battle at the crucial moment.

"That's right," Katri nodded. These pirates were so sensitive. He scanned around for a sign of the other ships, but could see nothing.

"Where are we?"

"Somewhere south and east of Vill," Katri said.

"And the Innings? Our fleet?"

Katri shrugged. "There's no one in charge now but the Mundua and Ashwin. The Innings were hard behind us down the coast of Vill. We were going to try to head east through the channel when this storm hit. That was the end of any thought of fighting."

"Is the fleet scattered, then?" Harg asked.

"Who knows? At least whatever happened to us, happened to the Innings as well."

So Katri had done all there was to do. There was nothing for Harg to do but return below and wait. Wait, and try to imagine where the pieces might fall.

"Harg," she said. He turned back. "Too bad about your eye," she said.

"Yes," he answered dully. He was about to turn away when he noticed she was looking him up and down with a frank appraisal.

"Don't worry," she said. "There's plenty of you left. As far as I'm concerned, at any rate. If you're ever interested."

It was crude, it was insubordinate, but it was just what he needed to hear.

The pieces fell more quickly than he had expected. It was late afternoon, and he was drifting in and out of a drowsy stupor, when Gill came in to let him know that the storm was breaking.

He had already decided what they were to do. First, search for as many other ships as they could assemble. Then, head back to Vill to look for Barko and the land party. When he said this, Gill looked as if he had expected as much. No one needed to mention how risky it would be.

Harg had to force himself to make his way up on deck to gauge the weather.

It felt like someone was pressing a burning coal into his eye socket, and under the uniform coat his shirt was soaked with sweat. It took all his concentration to get up the companionway without giving in to vertigo.

The fresh air momentarily revived him. The clouds were torn and ragged, scudding past overhead. The wind and waves were still strong. To the west a silver band on the sea showed where the sun was breaking through.

"Ship ho!" cried the lookout.

"Where away?" Katri called.

"Off our port bow."

Harg joined Katri, who was peering through her spyglass. "Can you tell whose ship?" he asked.

She shook her head. "She's an Inning Navy ship, but so are we. There's something wrong with her rigging." She handed him the spyglass. He automatically raised it to the wrong eye, then corrected self-consciously. Katri was right; the ship's foremast was down amid a tangle of rigging. Weakened by battle, perhaps, and snapped by the storm.

"We'd better come to her aid," he said.

"Top yards up!" Katri called. "Man the braces!"

There was a quick reaction when the other ship spied the *Windemon* under sail. Watching through the spyglass, Harg realized they were trying to put up a combination of sails that would get the ship under control without the lost foresails.

There was an excited shout from the lookout. "It's an Inning ship, captain! I can see their flags now."

"Flags?" Harg called, wondering at the plural.

"Yes, they've got a blue pennant on the mainmast."

A shock of excitement went through Harg's body; for an instant he forgot every ache he had. "It's their flagship!" he said. "By the root, Katri, the gods have sent us a gift. Corbin Talley's on that ship, and it's crippled, and it's ours!"

He felt alive again. The humiliation, the defeat, were all gone. Everything was reversed by this one wild chance. *Windemon* alone could lop off the head of the Inning invasion.

He gave Katri an incandescent grin. "You know what to do?"

She smiled back crookedly. "Just watch me."

Quickly she shouted out the orders for the *Windemon* to change course in order to come down on the Innings' stern. Soon the deck was swarming with gunners again. Loading and running out the guns was tough and tricky work with the deck pitching. One moment they would be hauling on the tackle up a steep slope; the next, the cannons would be flung forward, straining at their ropes. But word had spread about who they were attacking, and the crews worked in high spirits.

Katri wasted no time making her intentions clear. Passing diagonally across the Innings' stern, the *Windemon* let loose a blistering broadside. "Come about!" Katri called; the sailors sprang to the braces and *Windemon* wore round to cross the Innings' wake again, this time with the starboard battery ablaze. In their crippled condition, the Innings could do nothing to manoeuvre away or bring their guns to bear. *Windemon* could keep sailing zigzag behind the bigger ship until her guns had made kindling of it.

The Innings were desperately firing their two little stern-chasers. They made a brittle pop! pop! against the thunder of the *Windemon*'s broadsides. Katri's gunners were laughing with malicious glee at the sport of it. "It's like shooting at a turtle," Harg said to Gill, then roared furiously at the nearest gun captain, "Stop wasting your shot, man! Watch the waves. Fire on the upswing."

They were getting the rhythm of it, and each broadside caused more damage. "They've got to surrender," Gill said.

There was a glimpse of white on the Inning ship's poop deck. "Is it a flag?" Harg asked.

"No," said Gill, peering through his spyglass. "Look, Harg: this is strange."

An Inning officer in a blue uniform and white waistcoat was pushing another figure before him, toward the battered stern of the ship. For a moment all Harg's attention was on the Inning, but it was not Corbin Talley. Then his gaze turned to the prisoner. Tall but stooping, grey-skinned—there was no question he was Lashnura. He was naked except for a loincloth, his hands tied before him. The cold wind blew his white hair back from his face. There was something desperately familiar about him.

For a minute Harg lost sight of the pair as the *Windemon* came about to bear back down on the Innings. When he had crossed the deck and could see again, the two were standing at the taffrail, directly in the line of fire; they couldn't help but be hit. Harg's mouth was dry and papery; he wanted to raise his spyglass to see the Lashnura prisoner, but didn't dare.

"Harg!" Gill said at his side. "It's Goth! It's the Heir of Gilgen."

The words travelled down the side of the ship as if driven by the wind. Katri called, "Hold your fire!" Harg felt like his head was in a vise; he wanted to look away, and couldn't. The Inning was fastening Goth's bound hands to a line hanging from the spanker gaff above them; at his signal a sailor heaved on the line, lifting the old man till he dangled from his wrists, toes barely brushing the deck, twisting in the wind. His ribcage stood out clearly as he struggled to breathe.

Something inside Harg was screaming. It sounded like an anguished child. Somehow, Corbin Talley had found this oldest, deepest wound in him. He had found the one person on earth Harg loved more than victory. Goth, who had brought him to life and then discarded him. Harg had spent half a lifetime trying to touch that man. And now fate had put him here, helpless, as if to say, *He is yours. Kill him and win, spare him and give your homeland over to all you hate.*

Windemon passed across the Inning stern without a shot fired. The Innings would know now the consternation they had thrown into the rebels. Most of them would think it was blind superstition protecting them; they wouldn't know. Harg thought of the swift victory that had been his minutes ago. He couldn't take his eyes from the form dangling at the Innings' stern. It was part of him there, strung up like a side of beef, helpless and humiliated. He wrenched his gaze away and said, "Katri, come about. Get ready to resume fire."

Katri stood staring at him, the wind blowing strands of dark hair into her face. "We'll kill him if we do."

"I know that!" Harg said. There was a fist inside his chest, squeezing. He concentrated on not feeling it, not listening. He had to act for all the Isles now. Not for himself. It was a test.

"Do as I say!" he said. A look crossed her face that told him she thought he had a plan; she trusted him. She didn't know this was one of those either-or moments, when a decision had to be made, black or white.

Windemon settled on her new course. It seemed like she was travelling down a tunnel; all reality had closed in to trap Harg, to cut off the alternatives. He was clutching the quarterdeck rail desperately. "Fire when you're in range," he said. His voice sounded far away.

"Hold your fire!" Katri's voice cut across his.

He turned on her. Anger flared up white-hot in him. "Are you countermanding my order?"

She said, "That's the Heir of Gilgen, Harg. We can't fire on him. What's wrong with you?"

"Have you forgotten which of us is in command here?" he said. The rage was blinding him, swirling dizzily through his head. "Now carry out my orders!"

She hesitated a moment, puzzlement and distress at war in her face. Then she said, "No. Your orders are against mora."

"You're relieved of your command," he said. He looked around, saw two soldiers watching, aghast. "You two, take her below."

Windemon was abreast the Inning ship, and every face on board was staring at him, frozen. "Look to your guns, rot you!" he shouted. "Fire!"

The tableau broke; they turned back to their guns. Too hesitantly, too slowly. The ships parted; not a gun went off.

"Come about!" Harg ordered. The sailors obeyed slowly; he felt it was only his will forcing them forward.

Gill was at his side. "Harg, stop and think a second."

"Be quiet or I'll arrest you, too," Harg said.

Far to the west, the setting sun had broken free of the clouds and now it flooded the scene with a vivid red light. There were gasps from the crew, for the light had turned the water crimson. It looked like they were sailing across a sea of blood.

Harg saw it all with hallucinatory vividness. There was blood everywhere; it was dripping from the sails, it had soaked the deck. He felt it swimming like tears in his ruined eye, dripping from his chin. All the blood he had ever spilled, come back to drown him. Nature itself had mutinied against him.

Ahead on the Inning stern, Goth's body glowed in the gory light. The Inning stood beside him, gesturing them to back off, to withdraw. There was a long, ugly knife in his hand. The threat was unmistakable.

Harg wanted to blast that scene from his mind, to burn it away forever. "Fire!" he shouted at the gunners. But they were afraid of something larger than him now. Harg seized a smouldering match from the hands of the gunner nearest him and pushed the man away, intending to fire the gun himself.

Then hands were pulling him back. The blood was choking him, darkness was closing in. It was too late; the nightmare had won.

MARK OF THE MUNDUA

There was a smell of rotting flesh. They had put him in the morgue with the corpses, Harg thought. Why had no one given him a decent burial? Did he have to tell them everything?

Goth was bending over him. There was a crow on his shoulder. There had been crows on the spars, he thought—why had he not noticed them? The bird's eyes glittered with malicious intelligence. *I can have you*, it seemed to say.

"Will you let me cure you?" Goth said, reaching out a cool grey hand to touch Harg's flaming face. But it wasn't Goth; it was a strange dhotamar, his face suffused with longing. He wanted to enter Harg's soul and possess him, to gently bend him to the Lashnura will.

"Get away!" Harg said. His voice was a hoarse croak, like a crow's. "Don't touch me."

"Let me help you," the Grey Man pleaded. "I can take away the pain."

The thought made Harg want to weep in longing. Over the long days, the pain had ground him down to a nub. He had no strength left to bear it. But he knew the dhotamar would take away more than that. To be free of pain, Harg would have to surrender all the scar tissue that made him what he was. He wouldn't be the same person afterwards. "Go blow smoke," he said through clenched teeth.

The Grey Man drew back, his eyes filling with tears. "I can't do anything unless he is willing. He must help to cure himself. It's how dhota works."

"*Now* will you listen to me?" another voice broke in. It was Joffrey's. Harg knew he was hallucinating again.

"All right," Gill said. "We'll do it your way, then."

An Inning bent over him, peering into his face.

"That eye will have to go," the Inning said. "It's poisoning his system."

Panic brought Harg awake. Couldn't they see? He only had one eye now; if they took it, he would be blind. He struggled to sit up.

"What's going on?" he demanded. As he said it, he realized he had been asking that question for days now, and people had been answering it, and he couldn't remember a word they had said.

Gill came forward. "We've got to get you well, Harg. The surgeon wants to operate."

The thought gave Harg a horrible, queasy feeling. "An Inning?" he said. What were they trying to do to him?

"Listen, Harg," Gill said in a low voice. "Try to understand this time. The surgeon is one of the Inning prisoners from Pont. We've offered him his freedom if he cures you. He's already done you some good; your fever is way down. Joffrey says their doctors are bound by some sort of rules where they can't harm patients, even their enemies. Maybe it's one of their laws."

Harg didn't dare say a word, but there was a clammy terror in his guts at the thought of a surgeon's knife cutting away his dead eye. All the bravery he had ever learned had been leached away; now he was down to a shivering core of cowardice.

As if he could see it all, Gill said, "Don't worry, Harg. The surgeon's got drugs; he says you'll never feel a thing."

Harg was almost ashamed of the relief he felt.

The surgeon had an air of dispassionate, military efficiency. Feeling faint-headed, Harg watched him set out an array of ghoulish instruments on white linen. Then the Inning produced a bottle of small, milky slivers. "Your arm, please," he said.

Joffrey looked in the door just as the doctor pushed one of the slivers under Harg's skin. Harg's last clear thought was how indecipherable Joffrey's expression was.

There were flashes of lucidity in his memory, like a trail of crumbs leading back. He tried to follow them. There had been sunlight, and another boat, and birds on the yard-arms. Flocks of birds gathered, watching him. There was an oil lamp swinging above him; he had watched it for hours, hypnotized. Then he had held a perfectly sensible conversation with someone he didn't recognize, but who seemed to recognize him. And the guns were going off—no, the guns *weren't* going off, and that was the problem. All the time there was a feeling of urgency that he get back in control. Things were out of control.

Finally the trail led, like a fuse, to the memory where it all started, the one that had repeated in his mind, agonizingly, for days. He held a long-bladed knife. It had been sharpened and resharpened till its blade was thin; he had used it so many times. He pushed the point through the skin of Goth's chest; then, sawing back and forth, cut a long gash just under the ribs. He thrust his hand into the raw-edged hole, there among the warm organs, the blood running down his arm. He thrust upward through slippery things till he found the heart, beating, and squeezed it till Goth screamed.

"Blessed Ashte!" he gasped, sitting bolt upright, his own heart racing. "Did I kill him?"

Tway rose from a seat nearby. They weren't in *Windemon*'s cabin; this place was much smaller. Tway's face looked strained, as if she hadn't slept in days. "Harg," she said, "you didn't kill anyone. You've got to stop talking about it."

Harg knew she had told him this before, too. But the memory was there, so clear. "Is he alive, then?" Harg asked.

"As far as we know," Tway said wearily.

An alternate version was trickling into Harg's mind. He couldn't reconcile them. It occurred to him that perhaps one was true, and one was *true*. He closed his eye, feeling overloaded, exhausted. No wonder they all wanted to gouge out his eyes. He put a hand up to feel his face; it was tightly bandaged.

"We didn't capture Talley's ship, did we?" he said dully.

"No."

"The war would be over now if we had."

"Maybe."

"It would be, Tway. With Talley prisoner, we could have negotiated. Now a lot of people are going to die." He looked up through a haze at her familiar face. She looked a little thinner, but still had that Yoran look, like someone who would always know where the land lay, no matter how far to sea life might blow her. He said, "It was like a riddle. If you could prevent terrible carnage and save your country by killing the person you love most, would you do it?"

Only it wasn't that simple, or that noble. No, somewhere in him there was a part that had wanted to use that knife for years.

She was looking down at him with such an expression of compassion that it finally occurred to him that she was really there.

"Tway," he said. "What are you doing here?" He tried to think when he had last seen her. In Tornabay, on that terrible night, and not since. "I was worried for you. Where have you been?"

She took his hand, and squeezed it. "In Lashnish. I came as soon as I heard you were in trouble. I'll always come if you're in trouble, Harg."

Gripping her hand, he raised it to his mouth and kissed her knuckles. She was his oldest, most faithful friend. He lay back against the pillows, unable to let go of her hand. "Where are we?" he asked. The cabin looked familiar, but he couldn't place it.

"We're on the *Ripplewill*, heading for Lashnish."

It was the last answer he had expected. "Lashnish?" he said. "What for?"

She sat down beside him. Her face was grave. She reached out to feel his forehead, then said, "If I tell you what's happening, will you remember this time?"

"Yes," he said.

"We had to get you away from the Navy, to some place where you couldn't come to any harm. Or cause it."

He sat up, certain now that something serious had happened. "Who's in charge?" he demanded.

"Of the Navy? Joffrey."

He gave an inarticulate sound of protest.

"Look, Harg, he may not be a great hero, but at least he's prudent and sane." As opposed to me, Harg thought bitterly.

"And it's a rotting lucky thing he came along when he did," she said.

"Did he get to Vill in time to rescue the land party?" Harg asked.

Tway shook her head. "I'm sorry, Harg."

"What happened?"

"They were captured. Probably even before your ships were attacked."

There was a twisting feeling in Harg's gut. "Barko?" he said.

"Executed," Tway answered.

Harg looked away. He could see Barko's face so clearly, hear his voice, his sense of humour. To think of him executed like a hundred others by people who didn't even know him—it was unjust, unworthy of the world. Harg had relied on Barko for so much, trusted him so implicitly. It had almost been like having a brother.

In a tensely controlled voice, Harg said, "So what *has* Joffrey done?"

"Retreated. Pulled back to regroup."

It was the opposite of what Harg would have done. He would have pressed on, hunted down Corbin Talley with a ferocious implacability. He would have done anything it took to catch the man, then killed him gladly with his own bare hands. For a moment, murderous fantasies flooded his brain. How would he do it? With a knife? A garrotte around that patrician throat? A pistol shot to the eye would be just. Or hang him from the yard of his own ship till the life was choked out of him, and the crows pecked at his eyes.

His mouth was dry. He realized that Tway was gazing at him in alarm. Something must have showed in his face. He took a long, shaky breath. "Why are we going to Lashnish?" he said. "Why not Harbourdown?"

Gently, she said, "We were at Harbourdown for a while. That's where the Inning doctor treated you. But we had to leave. It wasn't safe for you."

"What do you mean?" Harbourdown was his haven, his adopted home, Barko's home. The place on earth that loved him most.

Tway took his hand between both of hers, and pressed it. "Harg, you have no idea what trouble you're in. The story of what happened aboard your ship has spread everywhere. There's not a fishwife in all the Isles who hasn't heard that you ordered your crew to kill the Heir of Gilgen. If Katri hadn't disobeyed, your life wouldn't be worth the air you're breathing."

It was all wrong, all backwards. The story was true on the surface, but deeply false underneath. He started to say, "But if I had—"

"Oh, there's plenty of ifs," Tway broke in. "If it hadn't been Goth. If you'd just had a pint or two more blood in your brain at the time. It all would have been different, *if*. But that doesn't matter to anyone else, you see. All they hear is, you tried to kill the Heir of Gilgen. And that means you're doing the work of the Mundua and Ashwin."

He couldn't believe her. She was exaggerating to justify what they were doing—putting Joffrey in charge of the Navy, spiriting him away to a place where he could be put under the thumbs of the Lashnura. It was the Grey Folk behind this. They had sent his oldest friend to lure him back so they could correct the insult to their power.

He threw aside the covers and swung his legs out of the bed. Tway said, "What are you doing?"

"I'm going up on deck," he said grimly. "We're not going to Lashnish."

He tried to stand, and almost immediately had to sit again. His legs were weaker than they had ever been, his balance was gone. Fighting a wave of vertigo, he tried again, and failed. Tway just sat watching him as frustration and embarrassment at his helplessness took over. Even his own body was betraying him.

"The crew won't take orders from you anyway, Harg," she said at last. "No one will. Torr was the only captain in Harbourdown who would even consent to take you, and his crew are just as scared of you as everyone else. They didn't want to have a tool of the Mundua on their boat."

He stared at her, appalled that she would say such a thing of him. A human who collaborated with the Mundua and Ashwin was an object of loathing and fear, fit only to be destroyed without pity. "Tway," he said seriously, "I've made no bargains with the Mundua and Ashwin. You know me. I'm telling the truth."

Her expression softened, but her voice was still firm. "I don't think you intend to work for them. You don't even realize how the pain has built up over the years and given them a way to manipulate you. They're sneaky, Harg. They creep into our hearts without our even knowing it, and start to control us. When it happens to ordinary people, they just make their families or villages miserable. But you're not an ordinary person. When you start making decisions out of pain, it's a danger to us all. The Mundua and Ashwin don't need to do anything, you're doing it all for them. You're a force of disorder all by yourself."

She was the person most loyal to him in all the world, and even she mistrusted him. It felt like nothing was solid underneath him. Not only was his strength gone, and his eye, and Barko; so was everyone's belief in who he was.

It was only days ago, it seemed, that a whole fleet of ships would have followed him past the edge of this circle. And now, not even his best friend trusted him. The suddenness of the reversal made him realize, bitterly, that no one had been following *him*; they had all been following his shadow, cast larger than life by the light of his victories.

Tway reached out and put a hand on his arm as he sat motionless. She said, "It breaks my heart to see you like this, Harg. You've got to let your friends help you, don't you see? You've got to admit you need it."

All the weight of his past had settled on him at once. He couldn't hold his head up any more. He sank back on the bed, staring wordlessly at the beams above him, wondering why they had bothered to save his life.

When they came in to Lashnish four days later, Harg was up on the foredeck to catch his first glimpse of the fabled Sleeping City. He had never been here before, and as the *Ripplewill* passed down the deep, pine-curtained inlet, it felt as if he were drifting backwards in time, to some moment isolated from change and the concerns of the world. When at last the city appeared before them, cascading down the mountainside, tiered like a frozen waterfall, he felt uplifted by its ancient grandeur. This was his heritage too, he thought, as surely as the humble Adaina villages of the South Chain. This place of soaring architecture was something his ancestors had done, and it was worth saving, worth fighting to defend. He looked over at Tway, standing beside him, but she wasn't looking at the city; she was looking at him. He reached out and squeezed her hand.

He had woken that morning with some of his optimism revived along with his strength. He had decided not to write off his life until he had had a chance to talk to Tiarch, and hear her diagnosis of the situation. It was hard to believe that he couldn't still salvage something.

When Tway had changed the bandages on his face, he had even steeled himself to look in the mirror for the first time, and it had almost killed his spirits. His face was horribly disfigured by the wound, the empty eye socket still inflamed and raw. He had quickly asked her to cover it up again. It was not that he had ever thought of himself as handsome, but at least his own body had always been familiar to him. He had trusted it, and liked it; it had never let him down. Now it felt like he was walking around in someone else's face, someone scarred and hideous. The kind of person fit to be branded as a pariah.

Torr and his crew didn't want to go ashore, so Gill, Tway, and Harg unshipped the jolly boat and got in, with Gill rowing. He brought them to land at the base of the broad ceremonial staircase that rose from the water's edge to the marble promenade that lined the waterfront. As they climbed the steps, Harg looked up at the archway towering over them, thinking for an awestruck moment that all the great Isons through history must have entered this very way into their capital city.

The quayside street was crowded with peddlers, sailors, children, fishwives, longshoremen, all jostling past, some staring curiously at his bandaged eye and weather-beaten uniform coat. A Navy man standing on the doorstep of a corner building across the street was staring at him, and for a moment Harg feared he was going to call out; but he only turned to say something to a companion standing inside, pointing the stem of his pipe at Harg.

"Let's go straight to Tiarch's palace," Harg said to Tway.

"It's up this street," she said, and led the way.

It soon became obvious that he had been recognized, and that word was spreading of his presence. As they headed up the Stonepath, people emerged from shops and doorways to stare superstitiously at them, and when Harg glanced back over his shoulder, he saw that quite a few of them were following. Alert now, he scanned for a sign of police, but there was not a uniform in sight. He forced himself to remember his old way of walking, before he had been disfigured, before he had doubted their support.

"This is not good," Tway said at his side.

"Just ignore them," Harg answered.

But they were getting harder to ignore. Farther up the street, a block was lined with a knot of young men who broke into cheers and whistles when Harg came in sight. There was something belligerent in their voices. He realized that they were all Torna, and the cheers were aimed not so much at him as at the Adaina who scowled silently from across the street. All the ingredients for a riot were there.

The crowd was getting denser as the street swept uphill between buildings. Harg saw again some faces he had already passed; people were circling around by the side streets to overtake them, swelling the crowd. They were getting noisier and angrier, as well—at each other, at him. Harg kept walking grimly, winded by the unaccustomed exercise. It had been a mistake to come ashore; he had not understood the city's mood, or how volatile it was. Now there was nothing to do but go on. The Isonsquare where Tiarch's headquarters lay was only a block ahead. Then half a block. He had to get there before the wave broke.

As yet, no one had dared confront him. But on the very edge of the Isonsquare that changed. An ancient Adaina woman in a shawl stepped forward to block Harg's path. As he tried to sidestep her, she cried shrilly, "Get out of this city! We don't want servants of the Mundua here. This is sacred ground, where we honour our Grey Folk."

Harg wanted to ignore her, but too many were listening. "I honour your Grey Folk as well, mother," he said. "I've got no quarrel with them."

She pointed a finger at his eye. "That's your punishment," she said loudly. "Mora has branded you so all can see what you are."

"I got this fighting for your sake," he said. "If it's a brand, it's an honourable one."

"It's the mark of the Mundua!" she cried.

She was grandstanding for the crowd. Swallowing his anger, Harg pushed on. But as they passed, someone jostled Gill belligerently. Harg heard the scuffle behind him and instantly turned and snapped, "Stop that." The men drew back, but a wad of spittle landed at Harg's feet. He didn't bother to look for its source, but merely turned and walked on.

Still there was no sign of any police. By now, Tiarch could not possibly be unaware of Harg's presence on her very doorstep. He could scarcely believe she would not let her soldiers protect him.

When he emerged into the Isonsquare, his heart sank to see that Tiarch's doors were shut, her shutters closed, against the crowd. His arm around Tway, he pushed through to the steps leading up to Tiarch's door and mounted them. When he tried the knob, the door was locked. He pounded on it; there was no reply.

When he turned around, he saw that the crowd that had followed him up the street nearly filled the Isonsquare. He could feel their dangerous mood like an electric force: touch it, and it would discharge.

Gill was standing with Tway at the bottom of the steps. "Harg, we've got to get out of here," he said.

There was nowhere to go. All around the square, the only open door was the one into the Pavilion cloister.

A missile sailed out of the crowd and hit him hard on the shoulder. With the pain, anger surged into Harg's brain.

"The Innings would laugh if they could see you now!" he shouted, clutching his smarting shoulder. "What a victory for them to see the kind of thanks I get for walking the road to death for you. Out on the seas, they can't beat us. But you—you can do what they can't, and how they'd love you for it! You idiots, the Innings are your enemies, not me!"

A deep man's voice boomed angrily out of the crowd, "The Innings aren't tools of the Mundua and Ashwin!"

Harg pinned the speaker with his eye. "If the Innings win, you'll have no Heir of Gilgen," he said. There was a surge of noise at the name. Harg plunged on: "You'll have no Ison, and no dhotamars, and in the end no words even to tell your grandchildren what they once were."

There was an incoherent roar from the crowd. Harg knew he was not calming them down. But now he was started he couldn't stop. He heard some cries of "Murderer!" and wheeled around to answer them. "What you don't know is that we could have won the war that day," he said. "We could all be safe now. Only that one man's life stood between us and victory. And because we didn't sacrifice him—because I let him live!—we may all die now, and our memory will vanish, and our islands will be scoured by invaders. You're throwing stones at me for having set the Isles above any one man's life. But no one's life is more important than our country's—not mine, not yours, not the Heir of Gilgen's."

113

"The Heir of Gilgen *is* the Isles!" a woman cried out. A roar of assent passed like surf through the crowd.

"No!" Harg shouted back. "*You* are the Isles. Every one of you. *You* are what we're out there fighting for."

For a few moments there was no reply. Then the man with the big voice yelled, "A man who goes against mora can betray us as well!"

The anger in Harg's head sounded like wind in the rigging. "How dare you say you know where mora lies? What makes you wiser than we who have been out there facing Inning guns? We have been giving our hands and limbs and lives for you. The Innings got my eye, and my best friend's life. Do you dare stand there safe and tell us we've gone against mora? I'll give you this answer: what we've been doing is dhota. Even if our skins aren't grey. We've been giving dhota for all of you, and all of the Isles, and we thought you were our bandhotai, to cherish us for what we did."

He paused, looking out, wishing he could catch every eye in the crowd. "What chance do we have of our hands and legs growing back? Do you think this eye of mine will ever see again? No, I'm just a plain Adaina like you. But we're giving dhota all the same—and I'll tell you this: it's a dhota so big that all the balances are going to bend, and what no one thought could be is going to happen. The skies and seas themselves are going to help us, and we're going to beat the Innings. Not because of the Lashnura, but because *our* suffering counts!"

For several heartbeats there was utter silence in the square. Harg stood still, a little stunned at himself. He looked out over a thousand faces turned to him; in an instant of clarity he sensed it: he almost had their love. And suddenly he wanted it more than he had ever wanted anything.

Then the instant passed. Several people started yelling at once—belligerent voices, breaking the hush. Harg stood there, letting the epithets fall around him. As the hecklers' courage grew, so did their number. Before long, a whole section of the crowd was chanting at him.

They didn't want to free themselves. They didn't want the hard work, or the suffering. They wanted someone to follow, someone to revere. And Harg could never be that person, as long as he was just one of them. The Adaina would never trust themselves to lead.

"All right!" he shouted bitterly. "All right, I'll do it your way!"

He turned to the Pavilion's open gate and started down the steps. Ahead of him the crowd parted, clearing a way. Blindly he walked on through them, through the gate, into the little garden inside. When he reached the stone, he seized the ancient hammer from its wrought iron stand and swung it over his head, bringing it down on the Isonstone in a bone-jarring blow. A huge chip split off and flew into the air.

"There!" Harg turned to face the multitude that had followed him in. "Are you satisfied now?"

There was such complete silence that Harg could hear the voices of the seagulls on the slate roofs, and the fall of an acorn on the grass nearby. Then, the doors of the Pavilion opened and five tall, grey figures entered the garden. The crowd pulled back, leaving Harg standing alone facing them. Slowly they approached him across the lawn until they stood before him.

He had to stiffen his knees to keep them from buckling. He had just faced down a murderous mob, but the fear he felt now went deeper. His hands were shaking; he clenched them at his sides.

The Grey Lady in the middle, a gaunt older woman, said, "Harg Ismol?"

"Yes," he answered faintly.

"Come with us. We have been expecting you," she said.

THE SUMMONS OF THE STONE

The days were dwindling noticeably now, as the brief summer of this northern land gave way to fall. Nathaway could not help but think of the warm autumn days that would be unfolding in Fluminos. The sidewalk cafes would be crowded, and the street musicians would be installed on their accustomed corners. The shops would be decorating their windows for the fall festivals, and the city's heartbeat would be quickening into a thrumming rush. This was the first holiday season he would not be able to go home.

Lashnish, as usual, was veiled in rain. As he walked downhill away from the Pavilion, Nathaway could feel the city's haunted, trancelike mood clinging all around him. It seemed to dwell in the sublime symmetry of the Altan buildings, with their almost musical shapes of harmony and order. He couldn't read these misty streets the way he could his home town's. The complexity here was not on the surface, but deeply buried in its past of lost greatness, its diminished present, its visionary hopes for the future.

The commercial district by the harbour—what he thought of as the Torna neighbourhood—was far more crowded and lively. The events of the past few days had had a galvanizing effect here. As word had spread, visitors had been pouring into the city, taxing its already strained ability to house them all. The mood of controversy and speculation reminded Nathaway of elections at home. There was the same sense that a historic shift was about to occur. But Nathaway could not share in this mood, either. When he tried to think of all the potential outcomes of the situation, there was not a single one that seemed acceptable to him.

His first two errands were at the tobacconist and tavern—not for himself, but for Harg. When he entered the tavern, there was a political discussion going on at the bar.

"I'll bet you a bottle the Heir of Gilgen won't come," said a burly Torna dressed in sailor's clothes. "Would you come to the aid of someone who tried to blow you up?"

"The Grey Folk don't think like us," a shaggy-haired Adaina man retorted. "The worse we act, the more they love us. As long as we ask for cure, they forgive it all."

"But what if he doesn't?" the Torna pressed. "What if he won't grant dhota-nur?"

"Well then," the Adaina said reluctantly, "I guess we'll know that all those victories were really the work of the Mundua and Ashwin."

And then, Nathaway thought grimly, *it would probably turn from a coronation into a stoning.* He felt deeply dissatisfied at the barbarity of it.

The bartender had finally spied Nathaway. When she came over, the two men turned to stare, as people often did, and Nathaway was forced to purchase the bottle of rotgut he had come for in a suspicious silence.

When he emerged, Nathaway looked for the Tiarch's-man who had followed him down the hill from the Pavilion, and saw him waiting across the street. Nathaway couldn't help wondering what would happen if someone threatened to waylay him—would the agent come to his aid, or take notes and report back to Tiarch? Or join in?

His next stop was at the stationer's, for paper and pens—and there, to his intense joy, the proprietor produced a letter that had come in for him from Fluminos. As he prepared to open it, he saw that it had been clumsily resealed. Irritated, he glanced at the shopkeeper he had just paid, but the motherly woman was looking perfectly innocent.

The letter included several newspaper clippings that he set aside, eager to read what Rachel had to say.

> *Dear Nat,*
>
> *You can imagine the mixed feelings your last letter produced here in Holton Street—joy that you were safe, great concern at the terribly compromised position you are in. There is a wide difference of opinion here as to your situation. Mother was principally dismayed by your*

immoderate expressions of attachment to the native girl, and implores you to think ahead and use precaution before doing anything you might regret having to explain on your return here. J [she meant the Judge, their father] is more concerned about your legal situation. He thinks you may have to face some serious charges, and wishes me to say that defending you would be very difficult in the present mood of the country. Whatever you do, Nat, don't get any more involved in this conflict. Even if your deepest convictions seem to be challenged, do nothing that could be misconstrued.

He felt a sense of futility at his parents' advice. The time for precaution with Spaeth was long since gone, and he could scarcely get more deeply involved in the political situation. The fact that his father had actually sent a second-hand message, at some risk, showed that the situation was even more grave than he had imagined. He hoped that the prying eyes who had read the letter were not Inning.

Since you spent so much time flinging accusations at me for the public exposure of your letters, I feel compelled to defend myself. Dearest Nat, you simply don't understand the power of your own story. You do not realize what a poignant romance it is, pitting patriotism against love, all caught up in the cruel compulsion of a needless war. But I assure you, the public does see it that way—for you should know that your letters were avidly read and widely commented on for their compassion and disinterested appraisal of the situation. People are constantly asking me, in great concern, how you are doing and when your story will resume. The fact that it has taken an even more dramatic turn is all the more reason for it to be a public story, and why I would not be doing you any favours to withhold it.

It struck him that her second paragraph had just contradicted her first. She was simultaneously warning him back and egging him on. He shook his head in frustration.

"From a lady, is it?" the woman behind the counter asked him.

"My sister," Nathaway replied.

"Oh, I see." She clearly didn't.

The news from the Forsakens is all anyone is talking about here.

118

The defeat of our Navy at Pont was a severe blow to our pride. You can imagine what the opposition is saying—calling for Corbin's resignation and the reversal of the Navy reforms, attacking the Court for being too lenient with the natives, demanding a swift retribution. The humourists are portraying our Navy as buffoons hoodwinked into surrendering to a pack of feathered savages in dinghies. The press is quite vicious toward the islanders. I will enclose some clippings. Yours is really the only voice not calling for blood. If it were not for you, we would never dream that there might be some reason behind the revolt, or that the names we hear vilified belong to actual people—another reason I implore you not to stop writing.

He glanced at the clippings she had sent, and was shocked, not just by the tone, but by the sheer inaccuracy. It seemed as if every vile slander they could think of had filled the place of facts. He frowned, sensing why she had sent them. She would know his indignation would compel him to find out the real facts and send them to her.

The rest of her letter was full of questions and lists of things she wanted to know. The only significant news from home was obscurely ominous. Due to some threat Rachel was vague about, the city had decided to install iron gates on all the entrances to the Courthouse Square, to be closed when circumstances demanded it.

They have decided to include Holton Street within the gated zone, since our house lies on it. None of us is happy about it, but the world has become such a strange place it seems preferable to the alternative.

He folded the letter, feeling unsettled.

His last errand, at the optician's, was one he had been looking forward to impatiently. The pair of replacement glasses he had ordered had finally arrived from Tornabay. It had been months since he had lost the last pair, back in Harbourdown, and he felt like he had been seeing the world through a haze ever since.

The optician, whose main business was actually navigational instruments, was an obsequious Torna impressed at having such an eminent Inning customer. He brought out the wire-rimmed spectacles and fitted them on Nathaway's face, then held up a mirror so Nathaway could see himself. The glasses looked oddly out of place on his face. His wavy blond hair was so long now that he was wearing it tied back in a ribbon. He had abandoned his Inning clothes, and was dressed all in loose-fitting grey, like a Lashnura. He no longer looked like the sort of person to wear glasses.

He stumbled on the shop steps when leaving, his depth perception thrown off. Everything around him had harsh, clear edges now, a sharpness he found disconcerting. Telling himself that he just needed to get used to it again, he headed back uphill with his packages.

When he reached the Isonsquare, there was a commotion going on, and he came to a halt. Several wagonloads of lumber had been delivered, and a crew of workmen was busy constructing tiered seating to accommodate the crowds expected for the ceremony in two days' time. In the centre of the square, another crew was working on a raised stage.

The feeling of dissatisfaction returned, redoubled. What earthly purpose could this barbarous public ordeal serve? What did it have to do with leadership? From his own experience, Nathaway guessed that dhota-nur would feel like being mentally dismembered. And he had only gone through an attenuated version of it.

It all seemed so sharply defined when he thought about it that way. But then he reached up and took off the glasses, and the Isonsquare returned to the way he had seen it before—all the edges blurring into one another, a realm of shifting ambiguities. When he looked only at the surfaces his glasses made so clear, the borders between barbarism and civility were easy to discern. But looking at it as the Grey Folk did, as part of a perilous world that could only be balanced through the power of atonement, nothing was simple any more. Suffering not only had a kind of holiness; it could uplift whole nations, and shift them into new paths.

Troubled, he hesitated with the glasses in his hand, undecided whether to put them on again. At last he folded them and put them in his pocket, then crossed the Isonsquare to the Pavilion gate.

The gate still stood open, for there was a steady stream of people who came to see the Isonstone; but the entry was guarded around the clock by a sort of volunteer Adaina militia that seemed to have sprung up for the purpose. As Nathaway passed the man on duty, he nodded and received no response. They had never shown the slightest interest in his comings and goings, nor those of the resident Grey Folk. He concluded they were there only for Harg's benefit— either to protect him or to prevent him losing his nerve and absconding.

Once inside the cloister Nathaway paused and walked over to the Isonstone. He felt a need to work his thoughts out, so he went over to a secluded bench sheltered from the rain underneath the overhanging roof. There, he opened the package from the stationer's and took out some paper, pen, and ink.

> *Dear Rachel,* (he wrote)
>
> *Some very dramatic events have taken place in Lashnish over the past week, and I now find myself with a rather painful choice to make. You tell me not to become involved as if it were something within my control; but I am in a position where not doing something will drag me in just as deeply as doing it.*

He then told the story of Harg's arrival in town and the events that led up to the claim of dhota-nur, which Nathaway and Spaeth had watched together from a window of the Pavilion. He tried to recapture the drama of the moment as he had seen it, but was dissatisfied with his efforts.

> *I wish I had the ability to describe to you the electrifying effect Harg's words and bearing had on the crowd that day. Or the effect he has had since then on the Grey Folk here in the Pavilion, who were poised to be prejudiced against him. The clippings you sent are terribly unfair to him. They portray him as a rough, swaggering brute. Nothing could be more untrue. Physically, he is rather small; but he easily dominates a roomful of larger men, not by being loud or overbearing, but by a kind of focused intensity. He has an uncanny ability to size up people and discern the best qualities in them—a trait that makes him quite magnetic, for who doesn't want to be appreciated for his or her best abilities? Everyone feels magnified when they are around Harg, able to achieve things inconceivable otherwise. In short, he is a very dangerous person—not from any malice or intent, but simply from his natural genius at moulding people into what they dream of being, rather than what they really are.*
>
> *The chain of events he set in motion that day by striking the Isonstone is full of peril. You may wonder why, if a man can become leader of the Isles simply by hitting a stone with a hammer, people are not constantly doing it. In fact, it is very rare because of the grave consequences. First, the Heir of Gilgen must arrive to judge the candidate fit for dhota-nur—something everyone here seems perfectly sanguine about, even though they know the Heir to be a prisoner of our Navy somewhere in the South Chain. Presumably he can free himself by some sort of magical means. Only when that hurdle has been passed can the truly important part commence: the dhota-nur, a healing ceremony so arduous it has*

been known to kill the participants. This will all seem very barbarous to you, but take my word, it is justified by a philosophy that makes perfect internal sense, and only falters when it is viewed from outside, by our standards.

My own role in this came about by accident. While in Tornabay, you will recall that I met the Heir of Gilgen, and he gave me a token called the Emerald Tablet which, it turns out, has a long history and plays an important part in the ceremony of dhota-nur. If Goth arrives here in the next three days (which seems impossible to me), he will doubtless reclaim it and all will be well. But in the far more likely event that he does not come, all eyes will then turn to Spaeth, his daughter and rightful heir. If she takes on the mantle of her ancestors and performs the ceremony, it will be at terrible risk—but more than that, if she succeeds, then she will become the Onan, bandhota to the Ison, his inseparable companion and bride. From that day forward she will live only for him. They will be bound by what the Grey Folk consider the strongest bond that can exist between two people.

By now I suppose you can see my dilemma. There is nothing on earth I want more than to prevent her from having to do this thing; and yet, if she does not, in the eyes of the mob here it will expose Harg as a tool of chaos, and he will have to be done away with. I know what you are thinking, that this would surely be the best outcome for Inning. Why should I not rejoice at a solution that would eliminate our most formidable adversary? Well, first, because Harg is my friend. And second, I have become convinced that, in the larger scheme, our nation might actually benefit from him becoming Ison. He is a person of stature; he would give the Isles a voice, and a mind. This may not make sense. I have to admit, it is more of an instinct than a reasoned conclusion.

After days of hinting, Agave finally asked me point-blank whether I would give the Tablet to Spaeth. Knowing what I do now, I refused. Since the ceremony cannot go forward legitimately without it, this would seem to save her from the obligation, and seal Harg's fate. The Lashnura are not happy with me, since they know my decision was made for selfish reasons. But, Rachel, I cannot help myself. When I look at her, and think how lucky we are to have found each other, it makes me want to share my happiness with the whole human race, because surely there is enough to spare. Why should our happiness have to be bought with the suffering of someone else, especially someone who doesn't deserve it? Why should *being true to one person have to involve betraying another? I know how I have to choose, but what I fear is that it will taint our lives with guilt, and poison our happiness.*

It felt good to have finally gotten it down. His thoughts felt clarified, but no easier. He put away the letter to finish later on, for it had taken him a long time and he was now late for his visit to Harg.

Immemorial custom was now governing all the Pavilion's actions. Harg was being lodged in a comfortable room overlooking the Isonsquare, waiting for the day prescribed—and, given Harg's temperament, quickly going crazy from inaction. The Grey Folk found it very difficult to be in his presence, because he fairly radiated pain—physical pain, mental pain, moral pain, all mixed so toxically that even Nathaway could feel it. But because it didn't have the almost sexual attraction for him that it did for the Lashnura, he had become their intermediary and Harg's only visitor. It was an odd reversal of their roles in Harbourdown.

When Nathaway entered the room, Harg was standing at the window that overlooked the Isonsquare, peering out. "What are they doing out there?" he asked. "I can't see."

Nathaway didn't want to answer, but didn't want to lie, either. "They're constructing bleachers," he said.

Harg turned away from the window, looking ill with apprehension. His reaction made Nathaway regret his own involvement, even as witness.

"Here's your liquor," Nathaway said, putting it on the table. "Don't drink it all at once." From the looks of the man, it was a real possibility.

The horrible injury had left Harg looking much thinner and more drawn than before. But what was truly wearing him down was the constant knowledge of the reckoning he had brought on himself. It was preying on his mind at all hours, keeping him from the rest he so obviously needed.

By way of distraction, Nathaway said, "Do you want to see what the Fluminos papers are saying about you?"

"I'm in the Fluminos papers?" Harg said as if he disbelieved it.

"Don't celebrate yet." Nathaway took out one of the clippings. "It says here that during the battle of Pont you took your pistol and killed a twelve-year-old child on your own ship, because she wasn't fetching powder fast enough."

Harg was staring at him. "But that's not true," he said.

"Of course it's not. We're talking about the Fluminos press. Really, Harg, you can be so naive."

He tossed the rest of the clippings on the table. Harg fingered through them, and picked up one illustrated by a woodcut of a fierce, swarthy giant wearing a sash bristling with dirks and pistols, his foot on the neck of a captured woman. "That's you," Nathaway said.

Harg studied the drawing, then looked up. "Do people believe this?"

"Unfortunately, yes."

"Innings are so naive."

Nathaway was actually glad to hear Harg fight back. He said, "Listen, Harg, it makes me as angry as you to think that this garbage is all the public at home gets. It's not to anyone's advantage. How can people make rational decisions about public affairs when misinformation is all they get? I've been wondering, would you help me write up a more accurate account? I'm sure they'd publish it."

The fact that Harg was anything but naive was confirmed by the next thing he said. "Would you let Auster sit in?"

Auster could read, and would be able to check what Nathaway wrote down. "Of course," Nathaway said.

Apparently, the assent was all Harg had been looking for, since he began to tell the story almost at once. Nathaway had to tell him to wait while he assembled his paper and pens.

Talking seemed to calm Harg's nerves. He told the story well, with the precision of memory that Nathaway had begun to attribute to his never having learned to rely on writing. From time to time Nathaway interrupted to ask about something that would be opaque to an Inning audience, but most of the time he simply took it down as it fell from Harg's mouth.

By the time they finished it was dark outside the window, but the workmen in the square had lit a bonfire and were still hammering and sawing by its light. The sounds filtered in through the windows. Nathaway, watching Harg's face, saw the moment when he became aware of it again.

"I wish I could tell you the rest of it," Harg said. "I wish I could get my whole life down before I forget what it meant to me."

He was assuming the dhota-nur was actually going to take place. And perhaps it would, Nathaway told himself. Perhaps Goth would arrive, and all would be well. Feeling awkward, he said, "Harg, do you want me to be there? Would it help?"

Harg shook his head. "No," he said. "I don't want you there. I don't want anyone there."

"You're not going to get that wish," Nathaway said.

The strain on Harg's face was hard to watch. Nathaway suddenly doubted the decision he thought he had made.

"Listen, Harg, I know a little about what it's going to be like," he said haltingly. "When I first got here, Agave did something similar to me."

"What have you ever done to be cured of?" Harg said, looking at him.

"It seemed like a lot."

Harg said quietly, "Have you ever killed a man?"

"No."

"Have you ever made a decision that killed your best friend?"

"No, but—"

"I'm such damaged goods," Harg said. "I'm not the right one for this. It should have been someone better than me."

Nathaway hadn't put his glasses back on, but it seemed like he was seeing very clearly—not just the surfaces, but below them, to the blurred reasons that made things happen. "Harg, that's exactly why you *are* the right person," he said. "The world is so out of balance that a better person's sacrifice wouldn't be enough. It's not really about you at all, it's about the sickness of the Isles, and of my country too. This war is like a fever that needs to be cured, and someone must do that for his land, regardless of his own will or desires."

Harg was watching him, transfixed. "What makes you think I can do it?" he said.

"You've got a better chance than anyone else. And it's not because you're a good man, it's because you're flawed, like the rest of us—because it will be harder for you than for someone blameless."

The moment of certainty faded, and Nathaway wondered how he had known to say those things. But they seemed to have settled Harg's mind somewhat. He still sat staring into the future, but now he looked different—not at peace, but reconciled to his duty.

Nathaway rose. "I've got to go," he said. "I'll leave this transcript here, shall I? You can get Auster to read it over to you."

"No, take it," Harg said. "It's fine. I hope it does some good."

Nathaway hesitated a moment, then gathered it up. "It will, I'm sure." Awkwardly, he added, "Thanks for trusting me."

Harg was watching him as if he were a perfect enigma. About to leave, Nathaway turned back and blurted out, "Harg, I'm glad I met you. You have more courage than anyone I know."

His conscience was hurting unbearably as he left the room.

In the room directly above Harg's, the windows had a better view of the bonfire in the Isonsquare, but Spaeth was not looking out at it. She was crouched on the bed gazing at her fingernails in the light of the bedside lamp. Dark half-circles were growing at the bases. Nathaway had commented on it that morning, unaware what it meant. The Black Mask was returning, too soon.

She had been determined to handle it better this time. But it seemed like the Ashwin and Mundua were already ahead of her, prowling and voracious at the edges of events. How could they not be? Goth had given them a chance they had been waiting for centuries to seize.

Spaeth had known it since the day she and Nathaway had arrived in Lashnish like a rock through the window, shattering the immemorial order of the Pavilion's world. On that first night, Agave had turned to her with anguish in her eyes and said, "Was he sane? Did he know what he was doing?" Meaning Goth.

The Grey Folk of the Pavilion had denied it at first, then fought it, then struggled to understand it. But Goth's wordless message to them was unmistakable: it was time for the Lashnura to lay aside their ancient role, and cease to be what they were. They had served their purpose, and now other hands needed to take up the joy and duty of healing the Isles.

If all Goth had done was send the message, it would have been upheaval enough. But he had backed it up with an action that would break the world wide open. Harg could not be Ison, and neither could anyone else. The Lashnura had forsaken their ancient pact. The Emerald Tablet of Gilgen, and all it symbolized, no longer belonged to them. There would be chaos when it was revealed, and the Isles would collapse like something boneless—but into whose hands: the Innings' or the gods'?

"You can solve this," Agave had told her. "The stone is your right, your heritage. Take it back, and correct this mistake." Since then, Auster and Agave had argued, persuaded, pressured, and pleaded with her. But it was not a mistake, and they knew it—it was Goth's choice. To do as they wished, she would have to go against her creator, her bandhota, and her love. The choice had seemed clear, if not easy.

And then Harg had struck the stone. Watching, Spaeth had known with solid certainty that Goth never would have given away the Emerald Tablet if he had known it would cost Harg his life. The balances, the line of Gilgen, the ancient authority of the Lashnura—all of them were abstractions. Harg was real.

She closed her hands into fists, hiding the nails. "Goth, please come back," she whispered. But even as she said it, she knew it would come down to her.

～

The day of the investiture dawned sunny but chill. In the morning there was frost on the stones that quickly melted as the sun touched it. People started gathering in the Isonsquare at daybreak, to get good seats. By now, the tiered bleachers were set up all around the square. From his window, Harg could see the section roped off for Tiarch and her retinue. They said she was bringing an envoy from the Monarch of Rothur to witness.

His nerves felt jumpy and restless. His breakfast still stood untouched on the table; his stomach was too unsettled to eat it.

"What's the delay?" he said to Namenda Agave. She was standing by the door, as far away from him as she could get and still be in the same room. She had come to bring him some clothes to wear and a few last-minute instructions. When he looked at her, he glimpsed the now-familiar expression of barely-suppressed longing that all the Grey Folk in the Pavilion seemed to have.

She hesitated over his question. For days he had had a feeling that there was something the Lashnurai weren't telling him. They seemed incapable of straightforward answers or explanations. "We must give Goran as much time as possible to arrive," she said.

"I keep telling you, he won't come." The certainty had been growing like a cold lump in his gut. At first he had dared to hope, and dread, that this time it would be different. But as the days had passed without any sign of him, Harg had had to accept that Goth had not changed. He had never inconvenienced himself for Harg's sake before, and he would not do it now.

Misunderstanding, Agave said, "If he is still Heir of Gilgen, no Inning can stop him. The forces of mora themselves will free him."

It was the first time she had put it that way, and he pounced on her words. "*If* he is Heir of Gilgen? What does that mean?"

"We will know by the end of today."

Harg could not fathom these people. The suspicion that something complex and shadowy was going on behind the scenes returned with redoubled force. "Namenda, I have a right to know what is going on," he said.

Her voice was harsh with tension. "We will all know by the end of the day."

She laid the clothes she was carrying on a chair. "You must wear these when we come to fetch you out into the square. When the ceremony starts, you will have to remove all but the breechclout."

"Why?" he said rebelliously.

She answered, "An Ison is not like other leaders, who may hide their characters and purposes from their people. An Ison must be transparent as glass, so the people may know his soul, and all that lies in it. That is the purpose of dhota-nur. The candidate's body and mind are revealed before the people he would lead, so that they can see into him, and judge him fit."

Harg felt sick with dread.

"Dhota-nur is a cleansing," she went on. "Afterwards, you will be changed. I cannot guarantee that you will even wish to be Ison any more."

"I don't now," he said.

For a few moments she was silent; then, in a low tone, said: "I know. That is one reason we all believe this needs to go forward."

He hadn't known that there was any doubt of it going forward, any possibility of stopping it. But before he could ask, she turned to leave. He thought of calling after her, demanding an explanation, but knew it would be fruitless.

When she was gone, he went over to look at the clothes she had brought. They were loose, wrap-around body cloaks made of grey silk, in layers that could each be removed in one dramatic motion. He would look like a sham Grey Man in them—which was doubtless the purpose, to gild him with the Lashnura nimbus, to show that he was to be reshaped in their image. Fine as the raiment was, he could not imagine wearing it without feeling like a blatant fraud.

Restlessly he paced over to the other window, the one looking out on the cloister and the Isonstone. There was a line of people waiting to pass by it, as there had been for days now. Harg watched as a father lifted his child up to touch the scar where the stone had been chipped. He had heard that pieces of the chip were selling for exaggerated prices in the city. A risky investment, he thought. After today they might be worthless.

In the past six hundred years, sixteen men and women had struck the stone and become Ison, and four more had tried and perished. He wondered what they had felt. Had they been filled with the great missions before them, too full for doubt? Had their nobility of soul sustained them? Or had they all been as abject as he?

By early afternoon the Isonsquare was packed, the bleachers full, and still no one came to fetch him. The day dragged by, the sun skimmed the western hills, and the crowd grew restless, for everyone in the Isles knew the ceremony had to start before sundown. Harg paced his room in a state of tension that grew more corrosive with each minute.

The square had fallen into shadow but the sunlight still lit the tops of the buildings when Harg could stand it no more. Leaving his room, he went downstairs to the main door that opened onto the cloister. A cluster of young Lashnurai were in the hallway around it, talking tensely. No one in authority was present. As Harg arrived, there was a thunderous pounding on the door. Outside it, men's voices were raised demandingly. One of the Lashnurai peered out a window and said in a strained voice, "It's a troop of armed men."

Just then, Agave arrived. "Bar the door," she ordered. "They must not come in here."

"Stop," Harg countermanded. He turned to Agave, feeling calm for the first time all day. "Don't trouble yourself, Namenda. I'll handle it."

"You!" she said. "It's you they're after."

"Which is why I'm best to handle it," Harg said.

"No. It's not safe—"

Harg didn't wait to hear her argument. He went over to the door and stepped out.

There were perhaps twenty men gathered outside the door. They were Adaina, armed with clubs and cutlasses. They stood there dumbfounded to see him in front of them. Harg followed his first impulse. He laughed.

"Quite an army you've got here for hunting a one-eyed bird like me," he said. "Maybe you'd better haul up some cannons. Did you think I was going to fly away?"

The men lowered their weapons. "Not now you're not," one of them said.

"Not now, not ever," Harg said. "Why, what would I do? Sneak off into hiding while you and the Innings race to find me first? How am I going to hide with this kind of a face?" His voice veered between wry and bitter.

The men were all looking to the one who appeared to be their leader. He glanced around as if to reassure himself they hadn't behaved like fools. "Your time's almost up," he said. "There's no Heir of Gilgen here."

"Yes, I've noticed that," Harg said. "Listen, put away your weapons before someone gets hurt. I'll go wherever you want, and wait with you till the sun sets."

"Out into the Isonsquare," the leader commanded.

"Whatever you want."

They fell in, surrounding him in a tight knot, and started marching out through the gate into the tight-packed crowd. There was a roar of anticipation when people saw Harg appear, and the men around him had to push and jostle their way forward to the wooden dais set up in the centre of the square. When they reached it, they formed a cordon around the steps that led up to the platform. Unwilling to climb them before the time came, Harg sat down on the third step.

From here he could see down the Stonepath to the harbour, where the sun was still hovering above the horizon. It would be about half an hour till evening came.

He felt strangely detached, even relieved that there would be no more choices for him to make. From the number of weapons he could see, it appeared that a good share of the audience had come expecting to see him unmasked as a tool of the Mundua and Ashwin.

"Were the bookmakers taking bets on this?" he asked the man nearest him. It was a stupid question, as the man's expression let him know. "What were the odds, do you know?"

"They were about even till noon, then they started running against."

"Did any of you make a wager?"

They mostly wouldn't look at him, but one dark, heavyset man scowled belligerently. "I did," he said. "I bet against. No one could have beat the Innings without unholy help."

"Oh, it just seems that way till you know how we did it," Harg said. "They're really not that hard to beat." So he started telling them stories to pass the time. He tried to keep the tone light, as if it had all been nick-of-time victories and pluck over power. As he talked, he kept one eye on his audience and the other on the sinking sun.

As the edge of the sun's disk touched the horizon, a gust of wind blew in off the sea. Some men came forward to light a pile of wood that had been set up for a bonfire, their torches streaming out in the wind. "Looks like they're planning on a barbecue," Harg said with a grim smile. He felt a quiver of nervousness in his chest. As the fire flared up, the faces of the surrounding buildings shifted in the flamelight, and the windows winked. Harg looked over at Tiarch's house. The shutters were all closed, the rooms dark. She was not seated in the spot reserved for her on the stands, either. Tiarch had withdrawn from this battle, just as the Lashnurai had. He was on his own now. As he always had been.

The thought passed through Harg's mind of how like Goth it was to decide everything simply by not being here when he was needed.

He stood up. He had only meant to stretch his legs, but everyone took it for a signal. The guard closed in around him, and a stir passed through the crowd, as the people carrying bludgeons pushed to the fore, and the ones with children began to leave.

Over by the Pavilion gate, there was a stir. Some people were shouting to hold off. Then the crowd parted and in the waning light Harg saw a column of tall, grey-clad figures emerge from the gate, coming across the square, Namenda Agave at their head. The Adaina melted back before the Lashnura.

Where a moment before, armed men had circled him, now a picket of shadowy grey figures took up position.

"What are you here for?" he said to Agave.

In a ringing voice pitched for all the multitude to hear, she answered, "Harg Ismol, we have come to summon you to dhota-nur."

As she said the last word, the sun slipped below the horizon.

❧

Half an hour before sunset, Spaeth had been forced to take matters into her own hands.

When she entered the room she and Nathaway shared, carrying a closed tin canister, he was standing at the window looking out on the Isonsquare. She put the canister on the bedside table, then went over to him, putting her arms around him from behind and resting her head against his shoulder. His whole body was strung tight, rejecting what was going on.

He took her hands in his and raised them to his mouth to kiss them. "Let's leave here," he said. "Let's go back to Fluminos. I don't care if they arrest me; it's better just to get it over with. I can't stand being here any more, not if . . ." He didn't finish, but they both knew what was going to happen in the Isonsquare at sunset if no one intervened. His sense of injustice was so strong, it was corroding him from inside. He was responsible for the miscarriage, but it wasn't in his power to correct it.

"Come away from the window," she said. "You're just torturing yourself."

He let her lead him over to the bed, where he sat on the edge. "Lie down," she said.

"No. I can't."

"All right." She knelt on the bed behind him to massage his tense shoulders.

He was being pulled apart, his Inningness separating from whatever it was in him that Goth had seen and judged fit to waken. She had watched him carefully over the past few weeks, trying to discern it. At times, he seemed no different—just as stubborn and obtuse, just as *Inning* as ever. But in other ways he was wearing well, like a shoe that had pinched a little at first, and was now beginning to fit her perfectly.

The thought gave her a pang of regret. They had become so good together. He was bound to her like a float to a net; he would always be there to buoy her, to lift her head above the water. This time, she felt perfectly confident she would not be abandoned. She trusted him to the roots of her being.

And now, she had to betray him.

He was relaxing a little as she kneaded his back, so she began to rub his tight jaw muscles and neck. At last he consented to lie back on the bed, and she rubbed his temples soothingly. His eyes drifted shut, so she reached over to open the tin canister Auster had given her and took out the sharp-smelling piece of cloth inside. She leaned forward to kiss him lingeringly on the lips, then clamped the cloth down firmly over his nose and mouth.

His eyes came open and he clutched at her arm, but he didn't struggle or try to resist. The drug worked fast, as Auster had promised. His last expression was one of such pained disappointment that Spaeth's resolve wavered; but then his eyes lost focus and his muscles relaxed as consciousness left him.

She kept the cloth on his face for several seconds to make sure he would not waken, then returned it to the canister. She unbuttoned his shirt and took the green pendant from where it rested against his chest, slipping it over his head and placing it around her own neck. For a moment she sat, steeling herself for the next step. A sound from the crowd in the Isonsquare outside called her back. The sun was almost setting.

Locking the room behind her, she raced down the steps to the door. Agave was waiting there, surrounded by students and staff. "Do you have it?" she asked tensely.

Spaeth showed her the tablet. "Yes. He finally gave it to me." She said it so no one would know that a conspiracy was unfolding. On Agave's part, it was a conspiracy to preserve the power of the Lashnura. On Spaeth's, it was simpler: to save Harg, even if she had to do it with a desperate deception.

Agave led the way out. Across the cloister they all passed, through the Pavilion gate. Ahead, the Isonsquare was a shifting sea of windblown torches. Rising in its centre was an empty stage, luridly lit by a roaring bonfire. At first it seemed as if the press of the crowd would block their way, but the people parted and a path appeared to the steps of the wooden platform. It was like walking down a long tunnel of faces.

They arrived. In a ringing voice, Agave spoke the ritual words and stepped aside for Spaeth. Swept forward by her own impetuous momentum, Spaeth seized Harg by the hand, mounted the steps, and led him up on the stage. As they came into view of all, a sound passed through the crowd: not so much a cheer as a huge collective sigh. It was like a wind blowing, lifting her. The platform made her feel raised very high up above the crowd. The sound was different here, somehow muffled. She could see them all, the whole firelit mass of faces, turned to her. It never entered her mind that they would not adore her.

"I am Spaeth Dobrin," she announced, and her voice echoed from the faces of the buildings. "Goran, son of Listor, created me. I am of his flesh. I have come to you bearing the Emerald Tablet of Gilgen."

She held it up then, turning in a circle so all of them could see it dangling from her hand. The sound that rose then was like thunder, battering against them, reverberating off the front of the Pavilion. For a moment it seemed as if the building itself spoke, and Spaeth listened with a sudden apprehension that it would expose her as a fraud and a thief. She looked up at the window where the real Heir of Gilgen lay unconscious on the bed. But the sound died to a mutter without an accusation.

"I have come here tonight because the balances of the world are in peril," she went on. "Someone must act to set them right. I call upon you all to witness dhota-nur."

In the noise that followed her words, she turned to really look at Harg for the first time. Up to now, Agave had not allowed her to see him, and she was shocked by the change. It was not just the eye patch and the livid scar seaming his cheek. His whole mora had matured, grown deeper, as if all the pain of the Isles had come to dwell in his body, in his scarred face. She still felt the sharp stir of attraction he had woken in her before; but now it was mixed with a dawning fear that this was more than she could handle.

Agave had come up onto the platform, carrying a bundle, and now grasped her arm to steady her. "Remember what I told you," the Grey Lady whispered in Spaeth's ear. "Don't take on too much. Do what you can, but save some strength for the end; it is the most dangerous part. Remember, if it comes to the worst, it is better he should suffer than you. You will not feel that way once you are in him, but keep saying it to yourself."

The reminder helped Spaeth steady her resolve. It was not really dhota-nur she had come for; it was a sham to convince the crowd. She needed to do only enough to bind him to her. Had anyone ever undertaken such a dangerous bluff as this?

Without another word, Agave unwrapped the worn red velvet casing and held out a black glass knife. "It is the one your grandfather used," she said. "We took it from the reliquary this afternoon." Her eyes strayed to Harg, then pulled away. He looked tense as an over-tight spring.

As Spaeth took the knife, she heard the crowd stir. But before using it, she turned to Harg. "You will need to take off your coat and shirt," she said.

He didn't move. Agave said to him, "Remember what I told you. You no longer belong to yourself. You belong to the people of the Isles. Your body has become a symbol of that sacred bond, and symbols must be seen. Tonight, all the Isles will come to dwell in you, and what you feel, so will they."

He still didn't obey. Spaeth realized then that it wasn't defiance; he was frozen into immobility. Whether it was terror, a fog of mind, or sheer indecision, she couldn't tell—but regardless, she needed to jolt him out of it. Tucking the knife into her belt, she went up to him, right into the radiant field of his mora, till it raised the prickling hairs on her arms and face. Then she dared to touch him.

She had intended only to run her finger along his ruined cheek, but the intensity of the sensation almost overwhelmed her senses. Before she knew it, she was pressing her lips against the reamed skin as if she could draw the pain out of him that way. Her heart was beating light and fast. She wanted him for herself more than anything in the world. She had always wanted him.

Laying her cheek against his, she whispered in his ear, "Harg, I will need your help. Dhota must be performed by the cured as much as by the curer."

He didn't answer, but she could feel him gather himself together. She helped him unbutton his shirt and jacket, and remove them, and then his pants and shoes, until he stood naked except for his shorts. He was shivering, but she knew it was not the cold wind.

"Kneel down," she said.

"Spaeth, I can't do this," he said seriously.

"Yes, you can," she said. "You have to. Kneel down."

She pressed down on his shoulder, and he knelt abruptly, as if his legs had given way. She took out the knife again. It was so sharp it slid into her vein with scarcely a prick. The blood welled out eagerly, wanting what she wanted. She knelt facing him. Dipping her finger in her blood, she touched it to his forehead and temples, then below each ear, to his throat, then to the centre of his chest, above the heart. As the blood touched his skin it turned instantly from wine-red to clear, disappearing as it sank into him.

While the blood was working on his mind, loosening his defences, she took the Emerald Tablet from around her neck and put it around his, so that it lay against his heart, as it had lain against Goth's for so many years.

"Do you recognize this?" she whispered to him.

"It's Goth's," he said.

Another quaver passed through him. The blood had linked their minds enough that she knew he was reacting to the knowledge that he was now wearing something of Goth's. She put her hand over it, pressing it against his warm skin. "It will collect all the pain you are carrying around," she said. "You must will your pain into the stone."

The blood was taking effect. His mora was almost visible to her now. It glowed ruddy like the reflection of firelight on smoke, flickering with dangerous, unruly power. It sent thrills chasing through her body. She would be the first, the only dhotamar to have him. Finally, after all these years of denying Goth, and denying her, he had been brought to his knees, to the end of his defiant, independent existence.

Her mind reached out, but when it touched him, a shock of energy coursed through her. It flung her away, and the next thing she knew she was crouching on the board floor, thrown back several feet by the force of his mental blow.

The watching crowd was murmuring; they had never heard of anything like this. She breathed deeply to calm the pang of thwarted desire. Harg was sitting back on his heels. "Harg, you have to let me in," she said.

"I told you, I can't do it," he said desperately.

It hadn't been deliberate, just a reflex. She picked up the knife and made another cut in her arm, then touched the blood to his face and chest again. His pupils were already dilated from the first dose, and his skin was clammy with cold sweat. She put her hands on his shoulders and said, "Breathe along with me. Concentrate on your breath."

Together they breathed, together they fell into the blood-trance. This time she saw a pattern in his mora, a rhythm. Like a child skipping rope, she waited for the perfect spot in the cycle, then leaped in. For an intense, exhilarating moment all his fierce energy flowed through her. Then he was fighting again; but this time she yielded, rippling like seaweed in the current. Unable to grasp her, he grew exhausted and fell quiet, breathing hard. She floated inside him, doing nothing.

She could see into him now, better than he saw himself. Everywhere she looked there were old wounds, scars barely healed. They were woven into his being, as if he had created himself out of broken things.

Scarcely daring to breathe, she reached out to touch his withered eye socket. He caught her wrist. "I can give you back your sight," she said. "I can erase all this."

He swallowed hard. Already, she knew, he had begun to reconfigure himself around it, to create a new Harg who was half-blind and loathsome, a person he almost hated, yet couldn't escape. "If I give you that, will you let me be?" he asked.

"Give it to me first," she said, "and then I'll answer."

She knew she would never be able to stop after such a partial cure. He knew it, too, and shook his head.

"It's not your choice," she said. "An Ison must be free of his past. You are Ison, and so you must."

She touched his eye, and he went rigid. He was reliving the moment when he had lost it, feeling again all he had felt then. Soothingly Spaeth stroked his back, whispering words of comfort, till his grip on the pain loosened, and she was there to ease it gently away from him, to let it flow into the stone, then into her. The healing bond began to form between them, knitting them together as if into a single being.

When he had given the wound away, she saw what lay below it—a mangled scar of guilt and shame. She reached out for it, but again Harg stopped her. "Not that," he said.

"Yes," she answered, "that one too."

It was like prying his fingers from around it, but at last he let go, flinching as it all flowed through him again, then into her. She stroked his face, covering it with kisses. She had to relax him. She had to make him willing to let her go deeper, down to the most secret, private parts of his mind. And yet she already wondered how much of this battle they could bear. He was like a person who had set all his own broken bones, and set them crooked, but to have them straight must break them all again.

On she went, opening door after hidden door, going places in him he had never wanted to set foot again. She felt the three floggings that had left his back a rubbled mess of scar tissue. The moment when Jory's brain had been blown away. The insane cruelties Harg himself had committed in revenge. There were hundreds of scars, each one a thread woven into him that she had to wrench from the pattern till it lay raw and bleeding, then knot it into her own heart, till they were woven together at a thousand places.

As time went on, he weakened. His heart was beating far too hard, and he was drenched in sweat. When he stopped fighting, she became worried that she had gone too far; and yet she still could not help going on.

A dim light was shining in her eyes, telling her it was time to stop. She blinked, then realized it was the dawn lighting the sky past the rooftops of Lashnish. They had been at it all night.

Harg was slumped in her arms, his head resting on her shoulder. She shook him gently and he roused. His face looked a decade older than the night before. She loved him tenderly for every hurt he had ever suffered. But she had not yet cured him.

She took the stone from his chest, and put the cord around her own neck. Nearby, the crowd stirred. She realized, vaguely, that there were still hundreds of people around them who had sat watching the whole night through.

Spaeth reached for the knife. She had to cut him loose now, free him from his past.

"All your hurts are half in me now, half in you," she said. "With this knife I will cut you free. All the pain will be mine then, and it will trouble you no more."

She bared her arm. "Come close," she whispered to Harg. "Don't leave me now."

She clenched her teeth and sawed across her arm with the knife. Blood spurted out, falling to the floor. Instantly she realized that something was wrong. She felt only her own pain. She whirled around to look at Harg. His face was a sheet of sweat. He was still holding onto it all. "Let go!" she screamed at him.

"I can't," he said.

"You have to, or all of this is for nothing!" She felt hysteria rising in her throat.

"I *can't!*"

The bond hadn't yet broken; she felt like her body was lashed to his. There was still hope. Somehow she had to calm him, help him to surrender. But her mind was a battle of exhaustion and fear—fear that she had failed after all.

People were crowding around them, thinking it was all over. Someone reached between her and Harg and she screamed a curse. Hands took her wrist to bandage the cut; voices tried to calm her, thinking she was only maddened by his pain. She had to get away, to be alone with him. "Harg, come closer," she cried out.

Someone helped her to her feet, but it was not Harg. She tried to fight them all off, afraid the dhota bond would break. Then Harg was touching her again.

She wrapped her arms around him. "Don't leave me," she said.

He didn't answer. Instead, he picked her up and carried her down from the platform and across the square, through the noisy, turbulent crowd. All around was confusion and frenzy; people were pelting them with flowers. Spaeth tried desperately to ignore it all, to concentrate on the dhota bond, clutching it like a lifeline.

At last there was quiet. She was lying on a bed, and Harg was sitting beside her. She put her arms around him, pulling him against her. She could feel his heart beating against her chest. Her hunger for him was desperate. "Now," she whispered. "Now you can give it all to me."

His face was a mask of tension. "Spaeth," he said. "It's my self you want. I can't give you my self."

She stroked his scarred back, trying to make him relax. The intensity of her love was maddening. "All that pain isn't you," she said.

"Yes, it is," he said. "That's what I am."

"No. There is another you underneath it all. You need to let him free. It's *that* Harg that is Ison."

For an instant she thought his grip was loosening; but he pushed her grimly away, then rose unsteadily to his feet. As if pulling against a strong force, he made his way to the door. Spaeth could feel the bonds between them stretching, as if her skin were being pulled away from her body. He stood at the door for a moment, breathing hard; then he opened it and went through. The bonds stretched and stretched, till the pain was unendurable. Spaeth screamed, but he kept on going.

There were voices around her, people trying to soothe her. She was doubled over in torture, the part of her that was him a blazing mass of raw, ripped-open nerves.

For the second time in her life, dhota had failed.

THE BOUNDARIES OF FORGIVENESS

Outside the Pavilion gate, the city was in a state of exalted relief. The long night spent standing as witnesses had worked a metamorphosis on the people of Lashnish. It had been an ordeal for all. Hour after hour they had watched as their Ison suffered and was purified for them, healed in their stead. Now they all felt a tender affinity for him, as if they owned him, as if his body were theirs as well. They collected in the Isonsquare, touching the bloodstained stage, milling around under the Pavilion windows, hoping to catch a sight of him, wanting to express their feeling of kinship, the way they had shared his experience.

Only the Pavilion was quiet, its gates closed against joy, its corridors hushed with secrets.

Nathaway had gotten as far as the cloister before running out of resolution. He hadn't been able to cross the boundary into the world of hopeful ignorance.

When he had woken on his bed with a splitting headache, it had been night outside, but the light from the bonfire and torches in the Isonsquare had led him to the window. In one glance he had seen it all, and his hand had gone to his chest, where the Emerald Tablet should have been hanging against his heart. Appalled at Spaeth's betrayal, he went to the door, but it was locked, and his pounding drew no response. The Pavilion was deserted; he could have set his room on fire and no one would have noticed. There was nothing he could do but go back to the window and watch.

It had been a strangely compelling drama, considering that nothing visible had happened. The tension and sensuality of the two entwined bodies glued his unwilling gaze to the firelit stage. At times they seemed to be wrestling with each other, at other times supporting each other through some unfathomable pain. The sexual energy of their embrace had seared itself into Nathaway's eyes. They were sharing a kind of intimacy he would never know. It would have been mesmerizing if only they had been two strangers, or any people he loved less than he loved these two. As it was, he had rebelled at the sight, and couldn't look away.

It was morning, and the ceremony had ended, when a panic-stricken young Lashnura woman had come to his door to let him out. "You must come, sir, something terrible has happened," she said. It seemed to Nathaway that something terrible had been happening all night, but he allowed her to lead him, morose and unwilling, down the stairs to Harg's room, where a hushed conference was going on outside the door. When Agave saw him, guilt and anxiety flooded her face. She reached out to grasp his hand, a sign of her distress. Lashnurai almost never touched anyone but each other.

"Ehir, you must help us, help her," Agave said. She opened the door. When he hung back, she said, "Go in."

Reluctantly, he stepped alone into the bedroom where all the city thought the Ison and the Onan were consummating their newly forged bond. Spaeth was kneeling on the bed, hands over her face, a picture of desolation. Of Harg there was no trace.

When she heard the door open, she looked up in feverish hope; then, seeing it was only Nathaway, she gave a wrenching cry of disappointment. He turned to leave.

"Nat, come back," she cried out. "Don't leave, please don't leave me."

He stopped, his hand on the doorknob. His feeling of betrayal was almost evenly balanced by sharp sympathy at her pain. She had chosen another man over him; was it not just that she should suffer the consequences? Betrayal was balanced by betrayal now; they were even. Then she said his name again in such a desperate tone that compassion tipped the scale, and he went to her side. Hungrily she caught onto him, pressing her body against his. He could smell the sweat on her skin and clothes, her own and her new lover's mingled. Blind with instinct, she kissed him on the mouth. Then, with a cry of frustration, she pushed him away, as if it sickened her to touch anyone but the man she needed.

In the next moment, she seized his hand. "Nat, we're bandhotai, you have to help me," she said. Her hair was in wild disarray, her eyes red and desperate.

"You have to get him to come to me. He'll die if he doesn't. We'll both die. You have to help us."

His self-respect was wounded, but not dead. "I'm not going to be your pimp," he said, pulling his hand away from hers. This time, he ignored her pleas and left the room, shutting the door behind him. To the strained and expectant faces in the hallway he said, "Damn you all to hell."

He left then, intending to go down to the harbour and find a boat that would take him away from Lashnish, back home, anywhere but here. He had gotten no farther than the Pavilion gate when the sight of the reverent crowd outside had stopped him cold, and he had retreated to his secluded bench in the cloister to stare at the ground and feel burningly sorry for himself.

He didn't hear or see anyone approaching until Auster sat down on the bench beside him. He glanced at the Grey Man, then away. He didn't want to talk.

"We made a terrible mistake last night," Auster said quietly.

"We?" Nathaway said the word bitterly.

"We Grey Folk. Not you. We should have listened to you. We should have trusted Goran's judgment."

Nathaway wasn't sure what this meant, but he let it drop. "What went wrong?" he asked in a toneless voice.

"We're not sure. She wasn't the person who should have performed the cure. She didn't have the maturity, the force of will. All she had were passion and devotion, and they betrayed her. She risked too much, and failed. Now, two people have been terribly damaged. No, three." He laid a hand lightly on Nathaway's, where it rested on the bench.

Nathaway straightened up, as if to show his resolution. "I'm leaving," he said.

"Don't," Auster said.

"I never should have come to the Forsakens. Everything I've touched here has gone wrong. Now, all I want is to go home."

Once, when he had first come to the Isles, he had thought he knew who he was and where he was going. But the ideas of justice and law that had lit him then with such a pure flame of commitment, now dissolved when he tried to take a stand on them, as if his entire moral landscape had been made of mist.

Auster was silent for a while, and when he spoke, it seemed like he was changing the subject. "You know, we Lashnurai have played a part in the rise of all the great civilizations of this land, and yet none of them has been ours. For centuries we have propelled other races to greatness. We have stood behind all the famous leaders, feeding them strength and resolution. And yet, we have accomplished nothing on our own." He looked sideways at Nathaway then. "It may be you are like us. You are bound up with two people who cannot be what they need to be without you. They can never return to you all that you must give to them. It is a hard position to be in. You can only meet it with serenity, by giving yourself up. We Grey Folk have a saying: *Strength is in surrender.*"

He reached into his pocket then, and brought out something. For a moment his hand closed over it, as if reluctant to let it go. Then he held it out to Nathaway. It was the Emerald Tablet. "This is yours, I think."

Nathaway took it. He turned it over once, looking at it, then slipped the cord over his head. It made him think of Goth, who had set all of this in motion. *Give yourself up*, Auster said. Perhaps that was what Goth had meant him to do. To give up all power, all control, all self-regard, till he became a mere vessel, transparent to the world. Did Goth have any idea how difficult it would be?

In his heart, he didn't really want to go back home, back to comfort and complacency. He had travelled too far for that. The Forsakens had ensnared him now, in their net of ambiguities and contradictions. The Isles had invaded him, embattled him. He had caught them like a disease. Or a seduction.

Harg poured a pitcher of cold water over his head and stood dripping into the basin. He was surprised the water didn't hiss and steam. His body felt like a glowing ingot, and his mind was racing down an endless flume of thoughts. Three times he had fallen exhausted onto the bed, only to wake from dreams where he was running for his life through burning streets.

It was his eyeballs that were aflame now—both the real and phantom ones. He looked in the mirror, and flinched away. The scar had grown worse, reinfected by dhota gone wrong. Even old bruises from the war had awakened, like cankers buried in his body, festering.

Outside in the city, he knew he had become Ison Harg. Already the room around him was cluttered with relics he had inherited with the title. There was a tarnished metal cup with a pointed bottom that wouldn't stand up, a glass-and-enamel phial with a lock of hair preserved in liquid, a flaking shell disk. All were so ancient no one knew what they were or what they signified. Every Ison had owned them, he was told. So must he.

And people had been bringing him gifts. Fruitcakes, wood carvings, skis, scrimshaw, embroidery, hats. He wanted none of it, but couldn't turn it down.

Every gift was woven through with unwanted expectations. Their love would bind him as surely as dhota. And if they ever discovered he was a fraud, his name would be another word for treachery.

There was a knock on his door. Tiarch had been sending messengers over to mend fences with him, now that she was risking nothing by it. Through the door he growled, "Piss off."

A familiar voice said, "Don't you talk to me like that, Harg Ismol."

It was Tway. Harg groped for the patch to tie over his eye, then pulled some pants on. Odd, he thought, that he had wanted to hide his face first.

He was still searching for a clean shirt when she knocked again. "I'm not dressed," he said irritably.

"I think my heart can take it," Tway's voice answered.

He undid the bolt, and she came in. The sight of her was like the smell of spring rain: earthy, rooted in childhood memories. Feeling anchored as he hadn't for days, he hugged her close. It made him feel like Harg again.

"Harg, it's so good to see you," she said, then pulled back to study him. "How are you?"

"No worse than three weeks ago," he said. It was a confession: three weeks ago he had been a wreck, and now he was supposed to be cured.

"I wish you could go out into the streets with me," she said. "The city is ready to float away with joy. They love you, Harg. They would sail into the other circles for you."

He turned away, unable to keep up the charade in front of her. She knew him too well; she would see through it.

"You don't have to hide," she said quietly. "I know something went wrong."

It should have released some of the tension, but it didn't. "Who told you?" he said. "The Grey Folk?"

"Not them," she said acerbically. "They didn't even want to let me see you. They're guarding you like cats around a fresh kill."

He gave a humourless laugh. "You've got that right."

"Nathaway Talley told me."

"Perfect." Of all people to know his most personal secret, an Inning. The brother of his worst enemy, the lover of his bandhota. "Who else knows?"

"No one. The Grey Folk, him, and me."

"Tiarch?"

"No. But Harg, what are you thinking? You can't hide it. You should see yourself. Just looking at you makes me hurt." She came up to him and stroked his arm soothingly. He put his hand over hers. What an underrated thing kindness was, he thought. His nerves could almost relax in her presence. Almost.

"What happened?" she asked.

He didn't want to talk about it, so he shrugged to belittle it. "Spaeth and I just botched it. Both of us together, but mostly me."

"But we watched, all night—"

"Yes," he said, the memory vivid. Spaeth had not been gentle with him; she had been too close to the edge herself. Now his mind felt like a desecrated graveyard, all the buried things dug up and toppled from their coffins onto the trampled ground, stinking. "All night, for nothing."

"Oh Harg," she whispered, "you poor man."

He didn't answer, because a newly disinterred memory had just erupted into the forefront of his mind: the time in Drumlin, shortly after Jory's injury, when he had led a landing party to destroy a Rothur powder magazine. They had never reached their objective, and had settled for burning a crowded hospital instead. Out in the street, by the light of the flaming building, Harg had hacked off a Rothur man's head with a cutlass. His lieutenants had had to drag him away from the bloody remains. On that night, he had turned into a frenzied animal, all for Inning.

"Harg," Tway said at his elbow. He started as if he had been shot. For a horrified moment he thought she might have seen what he had been thinking.

Firmly, Tway said, "You have to do something about this."

She was right, he had to get control. He drew a shaky breath.

"Harg, the dhota-nur didn't fail," Tway said. There was an air of certainty about her. "Neither of you botched it; you just didn't finish. There is one more step to take, and it's not too late. You need to go to Spaeth and do it now."

For an instant, his sleepless brain yearned for the sweet oblivion of Spaeth's touch. All he had to do was go to her, and he would have the life he had glimpsed, a life without remembered pain.

No. That was just what the Grey Folk wanted. They needed him pacified, so he could be their tool. They wanted the Adaina back as they always had been, bedazzled by Lashnura sacrifice and goodness, under their thumbs.

A fevered thought came to him that Tway was not here for his sake; she was here to lure him back to Spaeth, so the Grey Folk could finish what they had started. They had turned his oldest friend into their accomplice.

"Her Inning will be happy to comfort her," he said. He picked up a shirt and started to pull it on with quick, jerky movements. It stuck to his back; he was covered with sweat.

"Nathaway's not the one she wants now," Tway said. "It's not right for you to keep yourself from her. They can die, you know."

It felt so familiar, this manipulation. "I can tell she's Goth's kin," Harg said. "She suffers so convincingly." Soon everyone would be sure he was utterly in the wrong.

"This isn't about Goth," Tway said. "This is about you."

"What is this, the Auntie Patrol?" he said. "We're not on Yora any more, Tway. My life isn't your concern."

"Yes, it is," she said. "It always has been."

"Well, get unconcerned then," he said. When he saw her face, he knew he had hurt her, as he hurt everyone around him, everyone who cared. It made him blazingly angry at himself. "Get away from me!" he said. "Go on back to Yora. Go marry some fisherman and have a dozen babies, and get fat and placid. That's the world you're meant for. Not this one."

Her face was white. "All right," she said. "If that's the way you feel."

It wasn't, but he couldn't say so.

She turned to the door without another word. It was the last he would see of her, he thought. He had severed himself from the past. He had to go forward now, into a world where no one would forgive him.

He could hear the echo of guns in his brain.

When Harg entered Tiarch's office, he found Captain Dev there, incongruously seated on a spider-legged chair. Tiarch rose at once, but Harg deliberately turned to Dev first, reaching out to grasp his arm firmly in greeting. They hadn't seen each other since Vill. But instead of the old camaraderie, the look in Dev's eyes was part awe, part unease, as if Harg had traitorously metamorphosed into a thing of mystery. It made Harg feel like a visitor in his own body.

He turned to Tiarch then, fixing her with a smouldering stare.

She was unintimidated. "Nice of you to join us, Harg," she said.

"Nice of you to let me in this time," he retorted. "Have you decided you can risk supporting me now?"

"It seems to me you've done just fine without my support," she said.

"You mean I've done what you always wanted."

"What all the world wanted, Harg."

An irrational frustration rose up from the volatile place where all his emotions had gone. She acted as if he were still just Harg, and not Ison. Her lack of awe belittled what he had been through. "Well, from now on keep out of my business," he said.

"I wish I could. Unfortunately, your business is everyone's business now."

Dev's eyes were flicking from one to the other of them, uneasy to hear them quarrelling. In a kindlier tone, Tiarch said, "Sit down, Harg. You're obviously not recovered yet. Can I offer you some food? Coffee?"

He sank into a chair. He hadn't come intending to pick a fight with her. His nerves were on a hair trigger. He stared at the floor, appalled at the magnitude of the deception he had undertaken.

As she was pouring him coffee, he looked at Dev and said, "What are you doing here, Dev?"

The captain shifted uneasily. "Vice-Admiral Joffrey sent me with dispatches."

It seemed an odd way to use one of the two best fighting captains in the fleet. "Why, what's going on?"

"Start over, Captain Dev," said Tiarch. "From the beginning."

The news from the South Chain was appalling. The Inning fleet had left Vill in ruins. They had stripped the countryside, burned the fishing boats. Hundreds of Adaina captives—men, women, and children—had been rounded up into Torna merchant boats and shipped off to be sold as slaves in the Inning dependency of Hrakh. When the Navy set sail for Crent, they had not bothered to leave Vill defended. There had been nothing left worth defending, only crows and hungry dogs.

There were no military objectives on Crent; Talley seemed bent on nothing but destruction. Everything that made the island habitable went up in flames or perished. The animals they slaughtered and left lying in the farmyards; the crops and homes they burned, the towns they sacked. And in the midst of their labours they took time to spread terror. There were brutal tales of torture and rape.

As Dev spoke, Harg could smell the smoke and fear, and feel the lick of flames on skin. He had seen such things before. He had even done them; Talley would know that. He would know the nightmares such deeds left behind. The cruelty was a taunting message. A letter from Inning: for every bullet fired, another innocent person will perish. For every battle, an island. This is justice.

Tiarch said, "The news will spread like wildfire now. The entire South Chain will be in terror."

"People are already fleeing," Dev said. "No one knows where the Innings will turn next. There is no safety anywhere."

It was a good enough strategy, Harg thought coldly, if you had the stomach for it. The Innings had nothing to lose by depopulating the Isles. As the terror spread, resistance would disintegrate. Unless something could be done to protect the South Chain, there would be no local support—nothing but two armies fighting over a wasteland. And the Adaina would already have lost what they were fighting for.

Talley has found our soft underbelly, Harg thought. He could see himself now, chasing the Inning fleet from island to island, always a day too late to prevent another atrocity. Soon it would begin to seem as if he were causing the carnage, by failing to stop it. Time was on the Innings' side. Time, rumour, and ruthlessness.

"What's Joffrey doing?" Harg asked.

"Nothing, yet," Dev said. He glanced at Tiarch, clearly unwilling to speak his mind. Harg thought he knew now why Dev had been sent back to Lashnish. He had a mutinous air.

"The Innings know where we are," Dev said. "They aren't interested in fighting us. All they want is to leave the South Chain in ruins."

Tiarch was toying with a pen. At last she said, "Corbin Talley is a monster."

Harg could feel Dev watching him impatiently, full of expectations. Still he said nothing. At last Dev could hold it in no longer. "Harg—Ison—you have to come back and take over. The Navy needs you. The South Chain needs you. You have to stop these butchers, and bring back mora to the land."

Harg looked at Tiarch. She was watching him with a sad smile that said as clearly as words, *Better you than me*. It occurred to him that this was why she had wanted an Ison: someone to take on all the impossible expectations, so she could concentrate on the possible ones.

A hero could have held up under all the hopes, but he wasn't a hero. He was just a damaged human being trying to do his best.

At last he said, "Talley's trying to provoke us. He either wants us to attack recklessly, or to get bogged down defending the South Chain till we run out of support and supplies."

"Well, we can't just stand by," Dev said.

"That's what he's counting on us to say. Talley would be pleased to pieces if we threw ourselves at him in a rage."

Tiarch was watching him carefully. In a neutral voice, she said, "The problem is, we can't win a protracted war. We haven't got the resources."

"We've got mora on our side," Dev said. "We've got the balances."

"The balances don't pay the bills," Tiarch said.

Dev rose in disgust. "I don't have to listen to this Torna talk. There are Torna armies out there raping Adaina women and shipping Adaina kids away into slavery. And you're talking about the *bills*?"

Harg said sharply, "Stop it, Dev. We can't turn on each other. We've got to stick together, and do what Talley doesn't expect."

He looked up and found they were both watching him. "Which is?" Tiarch said.

They expected him to have a solution. Out of all the wreckage in his brain, he was supposed to dredge up a brilliant plan. He had to bluff somehow, or they would discover what a fraud he was. But in the instant he hesitated, he realized he didn't need to bluff; he knew what they would have to do. It was as if he had always known it, in the back of his mind. It was a plan that would take a cool callousness worthy of Corbin Talley.

"Our problem in the South Chain is that Talley has put us on the defensive," he said. "We can't win a defensive war, so we need to turn the tables and seize the initiative again. That means hitting where he's most vulnerable, where he has to respond."

"Yes?" said Tiarch. "And where is that?"

"Tornabay," Harg said.

Both of them were frowning. Harg plunged on, working it out even as he spoke. "Tornabay is his base, his centre of power. All his supplies and support come from there. If we cut him off, he'll be strangled. He knows that, so he can't let us do it."

Tiarch was looking more and more disturbed. "Harg, I don't think you realize how much of *our* support comes from Tornabay. You think the money for all this is coming from the Outlands? No, we have friends among the city merchants."

"All the better," Harg said. "That means we can count on support there."

"Cities that are attacked are destroyed. Cities that are captured are sacked. We ruin Tornabay, and we ruin our support. By the rock, we ruin the Forsakens, because Tornabay is their heart."

"That's why we've got to have it."

Dev broke in. "Pardon me for asking, but what about the South Chain?"

This was the hard part. The part a good man could not have done. Harg steeled himself and said, "We don't have the forces to defend the South Chain. We'll have to pull back."

For a moment Dev was silent, staring at him. "Sacrifice them, you mean. Let them die."

Harg forced himself to meet Dev's gaze. "Do you want to try and save them, or do you want to win?"

"You call that winning?" Dev said.

Inwardly Harg flinched, but he took care to look unmoved. "If Talley sees us going for Tornabay, there's a good chance we can draw him away from the South Chain. Maybe even get him to split his force."

"And there's a good chance he'll just go on burning and flaying Adainas for the sport."

"We could chase him through the South Chain forever. If we defend one island, he has only to go to the next. We can't attack his whole fleet; we haven't got the force. We could win a thousand skirmishes, and still be no closer to victory. But if we take Tornabay, we control the whole Inner Chain. He won't dare let that happen."

Tiarch was looking thoughtful. "But *can* you take Tornabay?"

"Leave that part to me."

Dev rose. The air of rebellion emanating from him reminded Harg of himself, once. "It seems to me the Innings have already won in this room." His eyes bored into Harg. "It's a good plan, all right. Nice and strategic. Talley would be proud to have thought of it. He'd be proud to know he's made you into such an Inning, Harg."

He turned to the door. Despite his anger, his shoulders slumped in defeat. Harg rose to go after him. "Dev," he said, "come back. We want the same thing."

"Do we?" Dev turned. It was no longer just anger in his face; it was biting disappointment. "I want to save my home and my people. What do you want?"

He didn't wait for an answer, just left and slammed the door behind him. Harg was at the door, about to jerk it open, when he stopped, one hand on the knob, the other against the frame, unable to go on.

The silence gathered accusingly around him. At last Tiarch said behind him, "It's a good military plan, Harg."

Her sentence seemed unfinished, so he finished it for her: "Every other way, it stinks."

She didn't answer, so he turned around and said, "That's what you were going to say, isn't it?"

"Well, Dev isn't the only one who is going to feel betrayed. You need to prepare yourself for that."

Harg thought of Crent, then forced it from his mind. He didn't dare let himself think of it. There was no time now for revenge or remorse. They were luxuries he couldn't allow himself. "The only way to beat these Innings is to use their own cunning against them," he said.

That was it. All he had to do was win. Afterwards, everyone would forget how he had done it.

Yet he wondered if souls grew back once you lost them.

ॐ

When Goth came out on deck, the night was sparkling. He watched the sky like a child, feeling that he stood on a beach at the edge of space. A vast teeming sea surrounded the small island of the world. He wished he could step off into the edge of its waves.

He mounted the companion ladder to the quarterdeck slowly. Everything was more of an effort now. Perhaps it was age, or perhaps it was achra.

The drug's effects had changed. Instead of unlocking other circles for him, it was now leading him more deeply into this one. Paradoxically, it was teaching him not to see things deeply but to see them *lightly*—to rest his mind like a feather on the world, unsnagged by any source of pain or attachment. He was gaining insight not by escaping, but by staying exactly where he was, by being more intensely *there* than ever before. He had become acutely aware of the processes of his mind and body, of the flow of his senses across the surface of the world. He now found deep pleasure in the simplest things: a candle, the smell of wool, the feel of a thought in his mind, silence.

Corbin Talley was standing, as usual, at the stern rail, straight as a plumb line. He did not turn when Goth came up onto the quarterdeck and sat in the canvas chair habitually placed there for him so he could keep the Admiral company. Goth watched him, outlined against the smudge of white that was the galaxy.

Goth said, "The ancients used to say that the farther you look into space, the younger it becomes. If you could see to the very edge, you would see the birth of all things. The beginning is present at every moment, pushing outward like a tide on the beach of nothing. We live in the midst of a continual creation."

The Admiral turned to look at him. There were lamps hung on the mizzen spars and by the wheel, and Goth could see his face clearly.

"Have you looked at yourself in a mirror recently?" Talley said.

"No," Goth answered.

"There are times when the light seems to go right through you; I sometimes think you are turning into smoke."

"It must be the achra."

"You are taking more of it than I have ever known a person to survive. It will kill you, you know."

"Are you warning me away from it?" Goth asked, faintly amused at the irony.

"I wish you would cut down."

"I cannot. You know that. It's why you gave it to me."

Talley gave a quick, displeased frown. "I gave you one dose. The rest has been your own choice."

The gesture of pain had been extremely subtle, but it set off the old, instinctive reaction. For a moment Goth was blinded by yearning. Tears sprang to his eyes. It had been growing on him lately, this desire to give dhota one last time. Even as he gained control over all the other bonds, this one was conquering him.

"What's the matter?" Talley asked sharply.

"Nothing." He couldn't give in. It had taken all the power of achra to allow him to transcend the other bonds, however briefly. A new one would make it all fruitless. Especially *this* new one.

Talley sat in the chair beside Goth's, looking intentionally at ease.

Beyond the ship's stern, the shoulder of Bellmorrow Head could be seen, and the smouldering ruins of the town below it. There had been a stone building on the headland, where the townspeople had fled for safety at sight of the Inning fleet. Its dead shell now stood blackened and smoky against the stars. They said the bones lay three feet deep inside.

Goth could not even remember how many ruined towns he had seen by now. Talley always brought him out to witness the devastation, watching with that calculating expression, as if daring him to forgive *this*. It was the sort of thing Harg had done as a child, on a very different scale. Constantly challenging, constantly trying to find the limits of Goth's charity. It was different with Talley; it was not love he wanted. Goth wasn't sure what the man wanted. He only knew he was as helpless to deal with it now as he had been then.

A lieutenant came up to them and saluted the Admiral. "The casualty list, sir," he said, holding out a sheaf of papers.

"Thank you, lieutenant." Talley took the papers, then sat reading the closely written list by lamplight. It went on for pages.

"Surely you didn't lose that many men," Goth said.

"Oh no, we lost no one. This is the list of natives."

"You keep track of them, do you?"

"Yes. Names of all the ones executed, correct numbers at the least for the civilians."

There was silence for a while as he sat perusing the names. At last Goth said, "I should think you would prefer not to know."

Talley set the papers on the small folding table between them, putting the lantern on them to prevent the slight breeze from blowing them away. "That would be to slaughter them mindlessly, as if it didn't matter. Killing is never a meaningless act, you know. Especially not this much of it."

"I am surprised to hear you say it," Goth said quietly.

"Are you? I thought we knew each other by now. I make them compile the list, and I read it, because it is a kind of moral discipline. I will send it back to the Navy office for the same reason. If ever we were to become unaware of our actions, we would have the scruples of savages."

Goth sat silent, wondering what it was about the act of counting the victims that made killing them more scrupulous. Before he could say anything, Talley rose again from his chair and paced away across the deck. He was often restless like this nowadays, constantly in motion. It was hard to watch.

When he came back, Goth asked, "Aren't you afraid of being blamed?"

Talley gave a cynical shrug. "Blame is like the uniform. You assume it with the office." Then, as if feeling he had been too glib, he frowned. "A leader must be capable of facing the consequences of his actions. To be worthy of the role, he has to look honestly and unsparingly at reality, and be a match for it. He must face necessary evils without flinching, wade through horror without changing course."

"You will be a moral cripple in the end," Goth said. "You will loathe yourself. Perhaps you already do."

"No, actually." Talley gave a brittle smile. "I don't loathe myself at all. I do occasionally loathe the things I am forced to do, in order to bring about good results. Rapine and carnage are not to my taste. Thank God I have people to do that part."

Goth winced. "Your people are probably glad to have you as well, to remove the responsibility from their shoulders."

"Oh, yes, no doubt. And there are lofty men back in Fluminos who are glad they have me, to give the orders that would stain their reputations if they owned up to them. We are all just tools, my dear saint. Axes sometimes harm people, but that doesn't make an axe bad. I am just a tool my nation uses to make odious but necessary decisions. At some point they may come to regard me as too tainted to use any more, but I doubt it. Men who can do distasteful things so the country can feel pure are too useful."

His tone was light, but the bitterness was sharp enough to cut.

"You are very different from your brother," Goth observed.

"Who, Nathaway?" He gave a slight, dismissive laugh. "Well, I was the eldest, he was the youngest. We had different family roles. His was to stand on stages looking adorable. Mine was to get brutalized and shot at so my father could claim some vicarious military credentials."

He seemed about to stop there, but then went on. "I was thirteen years old when my father sent me away to the Navy. His opponents were accusing him of being soft on support for the military, you see, and he had to demonstrate his toughness. He intended my career to figure in speeches, not battles. That was my whole purpose, you see. But it didn't turn out that way."

"So your father sacrificed you to the empire," Goth said.

Talley gave him a sharp glance, as if realizing he had revealed too much.

"And ever since, you have punished yourself by taking on the empire's guilt. You can't continue forever, you know. Sooner or later, the accumulation of it will crush your will to keep acting."

"Ah, well. If so, I will just join a long list of people who have given their lives for their countries."

"It's not your life in danger."

Talley gave him an ironic smile. "You think I have a soul? You, of all people?"

The longing had returned, sharper than ever. It was an aching compulsion this time; it took all Goth's attention to force it back. When he said nothing, Talley sat again, restlessly drumming his fingers. Goth watched the profile of his face—so cool and cultivated, hiding such a blazing anger at the world.

"You can't make me stop forgiving you," Goth said softly. "I have no choice. It's how we were created. It would be physically impossible for me not to love someone . . ." He paused, realizing how reckless the admission was, and how helpless he was to stop it. ". . . someone in as much pain as you."

Talley looked like an ice sculpture of a man. For a long time he said nothing. Then, at last: "I am virtually certain I did not hear that."

It was a warning. It meant, *Stay away. Do not reveal your vulnerability, or I will be forced to use it against you.*

But it was too late for caution. "I have wanted to give you dhota ever since I saw you," Goth said. "In all my life I have only known one other person who needed it as badly. You are my last, my worst, temptation."

A shiver passed through Goth's body. Talley was looking at him distantly. "What is it, a kind of lust?" he said.

Goth clenched his trembling hands to help him get control. "It's very like lust," he answered. "But more like love."

"You get pleasure out of it, do you? This dhota?"

"Oh, yes! But we pay. It's like the achra, only we get addicted to the people we cure. I thought the achra was freeing me. But you see how weak I am." He gave a strangled laugh. "My downfall seems to be the people who least want me."

Talley rose and paced away again. For a moment Goth thought he was going to leave. But he turned back and stood, his hands clasped behind him.

"Who was the other person?" he said.

"I think you can guess that."

He gave a slight nod. "I am beginning to find that there are a good many things I resent Harg Ismol for. You are one of them. I can see I will have to destroy him in front of you before I can claim to have won."

This time, Goth couldn't hide his flinch.

"Is that something you could not forgive?" Talley said, a smile frozen on his face. "Have I found the boundaries of your sainthood?" He snapped erect then, and said, "We have two more islands to deal with here. Then we will set out for Yora."

"Yora! Why?"

"Because it is Harg Ismol's home," Talley said. "And I want to drive him mad."

He bade Goth a courteous good night then, and went below.

Goth was left with only the stars for company. They twinkled at him maliciously out of the sky.

FIRE IN THE MOUNTAIN

Dear Rachel,

A fortnight ago, news began to arrive here in Lashnish about the actions of our Navy in the South Chain. I was reluctant to believe it at first. The reports seemed exaggerated, like the rumour and distortion of war. But in the past week, refugees have been arriving here, bringing such disturbing eyewitness accounts that I have been forced to believe them.

Rachel, what is going on? We are a decent, fair-minded people. Who has authorized this effusion of blood? It is beyond my comprehension what policy is being served by the wholesale depopulation of the South Chain. When did butchery, rape, and slavery become tools of statecraft? I would understand severe justice against the rebels, but islanders are being executed in droves, without even a mock trial, without evidence or defence, while the most barbarous behaviour in our own forces is allowed to rage on unchecked. If the intention is to create deep hatred of Inning and contempt for law, then the Navy is serving its purposes admirably. If the intention is to strengthen Harg Ismol's appeal, and make everyone look to him as a saviour, it is also succeeding. But if we ever wish to govern this place, or spread civilization among these abused and dispossessed people, then I am at a loss to understand how the Navy's ferocity can be justified.

As you can imagine, the actions of our fleet have made my position here far more precarious. The news has raised the most frightening *emotions in the city. It is no longer safe for me to go out without a Lashnura escort. Nor is it possible any longer for me to leave. Quite apart from my unwillingness to abandon Spaeth, I am aware of certain things that they cannot afford to have revealed, and which I cannot even hint to you, or this letter would never reach you. Tiarch is convinced that I am a spy, and while I believe Harg would not harm me, things have been unpleasantly tense between him and me.*

And so I watch, and wait. The events around me have taken on an unreal quality, as people make plans, absorbed in all their rivalries and revelries, while the end of all they know approaches slowly from the south.

If you had gotten to know Lashnish, as I did, before the investiture of the Ison, you would barely recognize it as the same place today. We have become a frontier town, besieged by every opportunist, well-wisher, fundamentalist, charlatan, and refugee in the Isles. The political avalanche set off by the rise of an Ison is beyond anyone's power to control. Everyone here is improvising. There is no recipe to follow.

The Palace and the Pavilion, which adjoin each other, both facing the Isonsquare, have become rival centres of power, vying for control of what the Ison and the Onan represent. Tiarch, who still controls much of the Navy and the apparatus of state, understands the role of opulence, public appearance, and graft. Her palace is continually crowded with people seeking favours, contracts, and posts. She handles it with a wily opportunism, as the Ison's de facto *prime minister. We have all been grateful for her well-disciplined Torna militia patrolling the streets, but of course that only adds to her power.*

Agave, on the other hand, understands the role of reverence, aloofness, mystery, and belief. She is the shadow minister, the Onan's spokesperson, the invisible power. This is possible because there is a spirit of religious revival sweeping the land. The teachings of the Grey Folk, real and imagined, are being proclaimed as an antidote to the godless immorality of Inning. The appearance of support from the Lashnura justifies any enterprise, no matter how suspect. Since many of the Grey Folk have lived lives of isolation, they are susceptible to manipulation by the unscrupulous and deluded. All manner of faith healers and fundamentalists have sprung up.

This volatile mix is glued together only by the public's infatuation with two people who have been taken completely unawares by being thrust so suddenly into the most public roles. A life where they cannot stir without being mobbed, observed, and commented on is utterly unnatural to them both. But their awkwardness and discomfort only endears them to the crowd. I believe both of them could grow into their new roles, but no one seems disposed to give them a chance. There is too much power to be seized.

In fact, the people don't really want sober governance from their new leaders. In their desperate need to shake off bondage and poverty, they want inspiration and salvation, spectacle and symbolism. At Tiarch's instigation, we have had parades, performances, banquets, and receptions to distract the populace and sort out the invited from the uninvited. Those who grumble about the expense at a time of war are regarded as sulky and envious.

Harg is besieged by contradictory expectations. People want him to be as grand and opulent as any Torna, but also plain and populist. They want him to be resolutely Adaina, but guided by the Lashnura in all things. The Adaina expect a shower of jobs, largesse, favours, powers. They also expect scrupulous honesty.

He has finally announced that he is leaving Lashnish to return to the fleet—but where they may be bound is a closely guarded secret. Naturally, I am not privy to their councils of war. But it does appear as if they are scraping together every ship available for some major action. Everyone is perfectly confident that Harg will save the Forsakens, and all the might of the Inning Navy will be no match for him.

Meanwhile, there is a terrible darkness approaching. I watch a thousand comings and goings from the window of my room, and I want to shout out warnings, but it would only make me absurd. They all believe that they are at the beginning of something—a newborn nation, a time of hope and ambition. They think that they are busy building something great and good. This is exactly what we wanted from them, once. We wanted them to hope and plan, just as they are doing, but now we have become the wall that blocks them from the future they have chosen. Their new world is ending, not beginning, and we are the reason.

Rachel, what have we become? I still love my country, especially here where its nature seems most contested. I want to stand up for what we really are, not what empire and arrogance have made of us. It is painful to see us as the brutal heel descending on these people's hopes.

I do so hope that I am wrong.

A deep rumble came through the fog. Harg felt it in his boots almost as clearly as he heard it. He glanced uneasily uphill, in the direction of Mount Embo's summit, and thought he saw a flicker of orange light through the mist.

"How close are we to the crater?" he asked the man who was leading him, a native Emban.

"A couple of miles, maybe," the man said.

Close enough to wipe them all out, if the mountain chose. Harg squinted through the mist, wondering if the rumble had been a warning or a greeting. The men in the party ahead would be wondering the same. It was a good thing he had brought mainly Torna troops on this expedition. Adainas would be panicking at this sign of the Mundua's presence, seeing firesnakes in the fog. Tornas would not see firesnakes. Not even if they were there.

It wasn't why he had chosen Tornas for this risky venture. If all went as planned, natives of Tornabay would be the first to enter the conquered city, and it would be easier to prevent them going out of control in their own home. They would have a stake in saving it.

Everyone had told him that Tornabay was unapproachable by land. To its south lay farmland, but no landing spot for ships except at Croom, where the Innings had recently fortified the cliffs to repel invaders. To the north lay rough, mountainous forest. And at the city's back, to the west, glowered the protective bulk of Mount Embo. Tornabay's defenders had no reason to worry that any attacker could cross the roadless lava fields and come upon them from the west.

And so that was what Harg had decided to do. His ships had landed in the tiny west-coast community of Inlet. They had unloaded the artillery and mules first, and sent them off to get a head start on the rough route across the island. Harg had stayed to see the rest of the men and equipment unloaded, then set out to catch up with the vanguard, leaving Drome Garlow in charge of the rear.

In the planning, he had worried that the landing force would be discovered in time for the Innings to send out a sally and catch them on the mountain. He had never considered that the mountain itself might attack.

It was several hours past dawn now. Harg and his guide had come to the edge of the pine forest, where the road ended. Ahead lay the first of three lava fields they would have to cross: a jumbled terrain of twisted black rock from some century-old eruption. The mist had a yellow cast, and smelled of sulphur.

It was easy to see the path the artillery had taken. The cannon barrels, lashed to sledges and heavy carts, were being dragged forward by brute force, with sandbag bridges and timber skids to ease them over the roughest parts.

Now broken rock, splintered wood, and burst sandbags littered the way. Harg and his guide followed the trail, scrambling up and down over snakes of ropy rock that coiled underfoot and bit into their boots.

Farther into the waste, black shapes began to loom over the path—old lava piled into twisted towers, dammed by some obstacle. Harg felt his neck prickle as the path skirted one rock that seemed to be leaning forward to scan him. Echoes of Embo's muttering came from several directions at once.

The path plunged into a cleft like a valley formed by a stream of stone. As they proceeded, the streambed became deeper, till high ridges towered on either side. Only the path they were on looked passable.

When they overtook the advance party, the men were sitting in exhausted little clumps amid the rocks. The mules were corralled in a huge pothole, their heads hanging dejectedly. The sight of Harg stirred the men, and the shouted news travelled on ahead.

The Torna captain Harg had put in charge, a stubble-headed bear of a man named Brixt, came hurrying up.

"The men are spooked," Brixt muttered to Harg. "We've been in this rotting fog since dawn, and it's hard on them, not knowing where they are."

"It's not their job to know where they are," Harg said. "That's why we've got scouts."

"That's not what I mean," Brixt said. "They were starting to ask for some proof we were still in our own circle."

So the Tornas were not as immune to such fears as he had supposed.

"Well, I'm proof," Harg said. "I've just walked up from Inlet. And pretty soon the rear detachment will be catching up with you too, if you don't get moving."

Brixt told him the problem then. The path had led them into a cul-de-sac; the way was blocked by a hill of lava ahead. They were just discussing whether to go back or try to scale the ridge.

Harg felt a coal of impatience burning inside him. "Where were your scouts? Didn't they check out your path?"

Brixt's face turned stony and defensive. "They did, sir. But in this fog . . . well, the scout says the landscape changed since he came through. It's shifting all around us."

"Blood and ashes! You accepted that excuse?"

There was a series of booming explosions from the mountain. It sounded for all the world like laughter.

"Yes, sir, I did," Brixt said stiffly.

Harg took a deep breath to calm his nerves. He had to appear steady and in control. With Brixt following, he walked on down the path. When he came to the front of the stalled line, he saw the problem: a tall, knotted cliff blocking the way. A group of men was standing there arguing about it. The engineers, such as they were. When Harg came up they fell silent.

"So who has a solution to this?" Harg said, scanning them.

They all began to speak at once, till Harg ordered them quiet and extracted, one by one, their answers.

There were three solutions: build a causeway, rig a makeshift crane, or turn back. The causeway would take explosives, the crane would take timber, turning back would take time.

"We can't use explosives," Harg said. "It would give away our position."

"The Innings probably know we're here already," Brixt said.

"But they can't know where. Not in this fog. Ashes! We hardly know where we are ourselves."

"But we don't have any timbers," one of the soldiers said.

Harg wondered what the man was talking about. "It's barely a mile back to the forest. Go fetch some."

They all looked at him in astonishment. "A mile?" Brixt said. "We've only come a *mile*?"

"It wasn't any more when I walked it," Harg said.

They looked dumbfounded, then depressed. "I'll send some men back, then," Brixt said.

"No, wait. What will it gain us?" Harg asked. "What's beyond this ridge?"

The scout was a fox-faced Adaina man whose eyes were mere slits. He was squatting on the slope, his wrists on his knees, knobby hands dangling.

"Stand up!" Harg ordered him. The man gave him a long glance, then obeyed.

"The path beyond is clear enough now," he said. "It would be. The mountain wants us to climb the ridge. Don't ask me why."

Harg would have rebuked him for demoralizing everyone, but it would only waste time. "Show me," he said.

The scout turned and led him, climbing zigzag, up the ridge. At the top the mist seemed thicker, and Harg coughed when he got a lungful of fumes. For a moment they made his head spin.

"The ridge goes on like this for another mile or so," the scout said.

Harg walked along it for a few yards. It was like the back of a giant snake, winding through the tumbled landscape. The going was not exactly smooth, but it would be better than what they had already been through.

"Which direction?" he asked the scout.

"South and east."

It was perfect. As if it had been built for them.

"There's got to be a better way up onto it," he said.

"Not that I've found."

"Go look again." Harg turned back and scrambled down to where the others were waiting. He said to Brixt, "Send your men for the timbers. If we don't find a better way up in the meantime, it will be worth it."

There was a satisfying flurry of activity as a timber-cutting party, a scouting party, and a carpentering team were organized. The men seemed energized again by the prospect of going forward, not back. Those not detailed to work settled down to catch some sleep.

Harg sat back against a stone, thinking that he too should sleep while he had a chance. He closed his eye and leaned back; but as his body relaxed a hundred worries skittered into his mind.

The timing, as always, was critical. The jaws of the trap had to come together at the same time. Jearl, in charge of the fleet, would at this moment be putting up a good show of menacing the harbour, diverting the Innings' attention toward the sea. And Calpe would be preparing her part of the trap. He could trust her not to act prematurely. She had more cunning than the rest of them combined.

Calpe's help had come as a surprise. Her message had reached him when the fleet had first entered the Inner Chain, brought via the brother of an apprentice to a perfumer who did business with the Palace. She was the last person he had expected to hear from, since he had left her behind to be captured by the Innings. Now she was offering to pass on important information if someone could rendezvous with her at a secluded anchorage up the coast from Tornabay.

Everyone had told Harg it was a ridiculous risk for him to do it personally. They had been right. He was too recognizable, the possibility of a trap was too great, and the trip took him away from the fleet at exactly the wrong point in the preparations. He had done it anyway. Calpe's capture had been his blunder, her captivity his responsibility.

And so he had been waiting in a battered fishing boat, a knit cap pulled low on his forehead, when an Inning pleasure yacht cast anchor nearby. It was a useless-looking thing, decorated with gilded curlicues, its deck cluttered with folding furniture. Harg's boat rowed up to it, pretending to have pearls for sale.

A liveried servant listened to his sales pitch, then allowed him on board and took him below to a cabin so bedraped with curtains and full of pillows that it looked like a giant unmade bed. Calpe was lounging barefoot on a couch with another woman. When she saw Harg her only reaction was a slight widening of the eyes. She rose, stretching. The servant left.

She looked stunningly beautiful. Her face was set in a corona of gold-bleached hair. She wore a long gown of some sheer, clinging fabric that revealed and concealed by turns every movement of muscle, every line of her breasts and thighs. Her arms and neck were bare except for bands of silver. At every movement her garments whispered secrets. She was dressed with consummate art, and yet seemed nearly naked.

But if her body was exposed, her face was another matter. Her thoughts had withdrawn behind the armoured barrier of her beauty.

"Harg," she said in a low voice. "I didn't expect you to come yourself."

He glanced warily at the other woman, who was staring at him with a sweet, vacant smile.

"Don't worry," Calpe said. "She can't talk."

The woman smiled like a child.

"The Innings do it by driving a rod into a particular part of the brain," Calpe said. "They know exactly how."

Harg's revulsion must have shown on his face, for Calpe smiled with a glass-bright exhilaration and said, "They would never do it to me. The Innings love to hear me talk. It's half the fun."

"What *have* they done to you?" Harg said.

"Why, given me power," she answered.

"Over what?"

"Over them," Calpe said, steel-sharp. Then the shaded lids half-dropped over her eyes, and she said, "Over their fantasies."

She turned her head, exposing an exquisite line of throat to him, and said to her companion, "That's right, isn't it, Lilly?"

The woman giggled.

"You probably think I am a prisoner," Calpe said. "It's not true. The palace women are free to leave; we simply choose not to. Some of the women there have followed their officers for years. Two of them are even Innings. No, it's the men who are the prisoners, and we know how to keep them that way."

Harg said roughly, "Whose concubine are you? Or do they share?"

She looked at him with half a smile, not minding his reaction at all—almost savouring it, in fact. "I am Provost Minicleer's," she said. "No one else touches me."

He gave an inarticulate protest.

"The other women didn't know how to handle him," she said. "He likes to cause pain, and to feel it himself. Trying to recapture an experience he had once with a Grey Lady, or so he claims. I fight him off, and swear at him, and make him think he's conquering me."

"You've gotten very clever," Harg said.

"One has to be, in this world."

"In the Innings' world, you mean."

"Well, that's this world."

She stepped closer. A faint scent of perfume came to him. "I even told him about us. It made him crazy, to think I'd been yours. He asked all about you."

It was nearly making Harg crazy, to think she was now the toy of some Inning degenerate. Part of him was still strongly attracted, another part repulsed. She had been so fresh, so free. Now pain glittered from her every pore.

"Come back with me," he said.

Her eyes widened a hair. "Do you think I'm a fool?"

"You said you were free to leave."

"I have worked hard to get where I am. You think I was joking about power. The Innings speak freely to their women, and we speak to each other. They never suspect us of understanding them. We hear of every move before it is made, we know their rivalries and plots. They are in our hands most nights. I can be very useful to you, if you're not too proud to have my help."

She was right; she could be useful. And yet, her help was tainted by the touch of Inning. Like everything pure and young in the Isles.

She was watching him closely. "You think I'm a whore," she said softly. He couldn't answer; to deny it or admit it would have choked him.

"Tell me what you know," his voice grated.

She gave him a complicit, my-corruption-is-yours smile. He wanted to slap her.

The information she had was interesting but not immediately useful. There was conflict within the Inning command, and between the Navy and the civilian authorities—plots and politics he only half understood. But as she spoke, it began to come clear to him what role she might play. It made him feel unclean to suggest it, but he did.

"What a charming idea," she said. "Like something out of an Inning opera."

"Will you do it?"

"Of course. My Ison commands me, and I obey."

The pillowed cabin was making Harg claustrophobic. He was about to leave when Calpe reached out and touched the scar on his face.

"Everyone said you'd been disfigured," she said. "But I thought the dhota-nur would cure it."

"There are some things even dhota can't touch," he said.

"What a pity," she answered. "You were so good-looking."

The feel of her cool fingers was maddening. He wanted to touch her in return, to prove his prior claim on her. He could see she wouldn't prevent him.

The last person who had touched him like that was Spaeth. For an instant he held them together in his mind: one primitive and cleansing as a sea storm, the other alluring and corrupt. At that thought, his lust soured on him, and he turned to go.

The Innings are winning this war, he thought as he climbed back into the fishing boat that had brought him. *Whether we beat them or not.*

❧

He woke feeling stifled. He sat up gasping, then coughed when the filthy air met his lungs. There was a fine black dust all over him.

Brixt was pacing irritably. "I don't know what's keeping them," he said when Harg joined him. "It's been almost four hours."

Harg felt disoriented, for he had no sense of having slept so long. At this rate, they might be trapped in this hellish place for days.

Soon after, the timber-cutters returned. When Brixt rebuked them, the young man he'd put in charge said, "It was more than a mile, sir. It was five miles at least."

Now that he'd been out here a while, Harg believed it.

The carpenters quickly set to work building the frame that would hoist the cannons up the cliff and onto the causeway. Once the pieces were rough cut, the head carpenter—a bald, meticulous man who fussed over all the measurements—set to work, carving out huge mortise-and-tenon joints. Brace by cross-brace, the tower went up. By scavenging metal parts from the harnesses, and wheels and axles from a cannon carriage, they rigged a makeshift pulley and winch. Brixt started muttering that they should have brought a capstan from one of the ships; but by notching a wheel to prevent it rotating backward they improvised a system nearly as good.

When the first cannon barrel swung free of its sledge, dangling in a rope cradle, the timber tower creaked but held. The men on the guide-ropes gave a cheer; Harg nearly snapped at them to hold their exuberance till the task was done. Up and up the iron tube swung into the yellow air. The men atop the cliff guided it over to where another sledge waited ready to draw it away, then shouted for the pulley-men to lower it.

Harg never saw what happened. There was a crack of splintering wood. With a shout, the men jumped away, and the cannon fell, then disappeared. A length of rope snaked after it. Harg blinked, but there was no sign of the cannon. It had vanished.

There were cries of astonishment from up on the ridge. Harg scrambled up till he could see what had happened. A jag-edged hole gaped in the ground where the rock had given way and the cannon and sledge had fallen through.

Harg knelt at the edge of the hole to look down. It was pitch black. "By the rock!" a man at his side said. "It went clear down into the realm of the Naked Bear."

The spot they stood on was hollow, a bubble in the rock. Harg tossed in a pebble; it clattered only ten or fifteen feet down. "Who wants to go down and see if the cannon's salvageable?" he asked.

A curly-haired lad too young to be sensible volunteered. They lowered him down by a rope, lantern in hand.

The first thing he called out was, "It's a cave!" Then, "It's big!" From the way his voice echoed they could tell that.

Harg called, "How's the cannon?" But there was no answer. The lantern light had disappeared. The boy had gone exploring, apparently. Harg swore softly. "Get busy repairing that hoist," he said to the men around him.

Presently, the boy's footsteps sounded from below and the light wavered back into view. "It's a tunnel, sir," he called up, his face raised to the light. "It goes on just about forever, underneath the ridge."

"How's the rotting *cannon*?" Harg said. But already his mind was on other things. If the ridge was hollow, they would be foolish to try to follow it. The slightest weak spot, and more cannons might fall through. They might reach Tornabay without a single field piece.

"The cannon's fine," the boy called up.

Harg stood. The scout was across the hole, watching him from sharp, wild-animal eyes. Ignoring him, Harg climbed up on a nearby boulder to see what he could see of the landscape. A gust of wind had cleared off some of the haze, but it only revealed more of what he had already seen: frowning wrinkles of rock, waiting to trap them.

"What do you know of the Mundua?" a voice said at his elbow. He looked down to see the scout, standing arms akimbo, scanning the landscape as if he had just asked a practical question.

"Nothing," Harg said.

"I wish the Onan were here."

Harg didn't reply. Everyone thought it odd that Spaeth was still back in Lashnish, when she should have been at his side. He knew there was speculation about it, and suspicion. Between that and his unhealed eye, they were beginning to guess the truth. He wouldn't be able to hide it much longer.

"You see," the scout went on, "the Mundua may be trying to help us, or hinder us. I don't know which. The Onan would know. I would say it was too risky to take their help, except that you are Ison. They are not supposed to have any power over you."

Harg didn't miss the uncertain phrasing, but he chose to ignore it. "These lava caves," he said. "How far do they usually run?"

"Sometimes for miles," the scout said resignedly.

"I want you to go down and see where this one goes, and if it's possible to get out at the other end. Pay attention to obstructions and narrow spots. You understand?"

The scout did not like it, but he understood. They lowered him down with another lantern, and he and the boy set off together.

A messenger had arrived with the news that the main contingent of troops had caught up with them. Again Harg felt a twinge of disorientation; it seemed to have taken them far too long. He went to talk over the situation with his two captains. By the time he got back, the scout had returned.

The cave ran for a mile, maybe two, before ending on a gentle slope at the edge of the lava field. There were no obstructions a few men with picks and crowbars couldn't clear. "I didn't expect any," the scout said, eyeing Harg.

Gill had come up with the rear detachment, and now stood at Harg's side, looking down into the black hole the cannon had made. He shivered. "Are you serious, Harg?" he said quietly. "It sounds way too easy to me."

"If the mountain wants to help, I'm not going to turn it down," Harg said.

"You're sure this is help?"

If he said yes, they would all believe him. He was Ison. "Yes," he said.

They set to work hoisting and lowering the cannons and mules through the hole. The men weren't happy with the prospect of going underground, but Harg put on a confident face that convinced them.

Anything that could be carried on two legs, Harg sent to join the main force to pick its way overland. Only the heaviest equipment would go by the tunnel. "We'll beat you to the other end," he called cheerfully to Drome as the overland contingent left. Then he caught hold of the hoist rope, set his foot in the cradle, and signalled the pulley-men to lower him down. Jerkily he sank; the broken rock went past like a black eggshell, and darkness closed over him.

Underground, the cave was bedlam: frightened mules braying and kicking, men shouting, sledges and tangled harness everywhere. The dim lantern light barely touched the rubbled ceiling arching high overhead. Harg saw a preoccupied soldier set a lantern down atop a keg of gunpowder, and yelled out a warning. At this rate, they wouldn't need firesnakes to menace them. They were perfectly capable of wiping themselves out without the Mundua's help.

It took half an hour to get the mess sorted out into an orderly line. They strung reins between the teams of mules to keep them all together, then set out, Harg at the head and Brixt at the rear. Gill walked at Harg's side, and the scout carried a lantern before them.

It was easier going than Harg had dared to hope. The floor was a frozen stream of black stone, rippled in the direction of their travel. It sloped gently downward, a little steeper as they progressed. Harg told himself it was only the slope of the mountainside, but it was hard to keep from feeling that they were going deeper into the earth.

In the blackness, there was no telling how far they had come when the scout paused, his lantern showing a branch in the tunnel ahead. Harg called out for a halt, and all down the line behind they heard the drivers curbing their mules.

"What's wrong?" Harg said to the scout.

The man's sharp face was weirdly lit by the lantern: his chin, the tip of his nose, his eyebrows. "There was no spot like this when I came through," he said.

"There must have been," Harg said, knowing it was untrue. "We can't have gotten off track; there has only been one way."

The scout shrugged nervously. "I can scout them both, but I know what I will find."

"What's that?"

"Any path I take will lead out. Any path *you* take will lead wherever the mountain is trying to get you to go."

Harg felt a fatalistic resignation. "You choose, then."

"That will make no difference."

The two branches looked identical, but a wind was blowing from the left-hand one. Perhaps a wind meant a way outside. "We'll take that one," Harg said.

Before long, the downward slope grew even steeper, and the drivers had to rein back the mules to prevent them from going too fast. The wind picked up till it was whistling past their ears. It was warm.

"I don't like the look of this," Gill said.

"You have a better idea?" Harg asked. Gill was silent.

Would there be a song someday about the Ison Harg who was no Ison, who led an army down into the maw of Mount Embo? Harg wondered how the chorus would go. Something about being eaten by fire, perhaps. He could almost hear it, sung to the tune of "Seven Dead Men on the Beach."

They had gotten some ways ahead of the main party when Harg stopped suddenly. "Shield your light," he told the scout. The man took off his jacket and draped it around the lantern till blackness closed in. Or what should have been blackness. There were faint highlights of orange light on the rock walls ahead.

Indecision gripped Harg. "Do you think we should turn back?" he asked Gill.

The sweat on Gill's face glistened faintly. "Would it gain us anything?" he asked.

No. Even if they reversed course, the tunnel might lead them directly back here, as long as the mountain hadn't yet had its way.

"Give me the lamp," Harg said to the scout. "Go back and tell the rest to wait. I'll go ahead and see if it's safe."

"I'll go with you," Gill said.

Harg paused. "You don't have to, Gill."

"I know."

For a moment, their eyes met in the lamplight. They were alone, and Harg knew he could no longer lead Gill on under false pretences. "I'm a fraud, Gill," he said softly.

"No, you're not," Gill said.

"There's something you don't know. The dhota-nur—"

Gill put a hand on his shoulder. "Harg. It doesn't matter. You're still Ison to me."

Harg wanted to confess everything, to prove his own guilt, but he couldn't bear to lose the look of trust on Gill's face. So he shrugged and said, "Suit yourself."

The air grew warmer with every step down the tunnel. Soon the orange light was visible even over the lamplight.

The tunnel ended suddenly. The walls fell away on either side and they entered a huge chamber, a bubble in the rock. They walked forward across a wide ledge that descended in terraces, like a black beach ending in a drop-off. When they reached the edge, they stopped. Before them lay a deep chimney in the rock. Hundreds of feet below, at the base of the cliff, was the surface of a glowing lake. On the edges, it was crusted over, but farther out it was riddled with cracks through which light glowed. Out in the centre molten rock bubbled, flinging white-hot globs into the air. The heat was intense; Harg felt it beating against his face, the hot wind rushing past him into the chimney that continued on over their heads out of sight.

A firesnake nest. It was no place for humans.

"Why have the Mundua led us here?" Gill said. He had to shout to be heard over the rumbling and the rush of wind.

"I don't know," Harg answered. The heat was waking the wound in his face; it was burning painfully. The sight of the bubbling lava was mesmerizing; he had to drag his eyes away and force himself to scan the room. "There," he said, pointing to an irregular opening in the rock wall opposite them. "Another opening. The tunnel goes on."

"We'll have to skirt this well to get to it."

"Yes. Let's check it out."

He set out along the ledge, hugging the wall. His good eye was watering in the heat; the other one felt as if someone had jammed a glowing coal into the empty socket. He came to a halt, fists gripped tight, unable to see where he was going. "You go first," he said to Gill, waving him on.

He followed as much by feel and sound as by sight. The pain kept tugging at his face, as if to send him off course. He had a sudden, wild thought that if he could only wash his face in the lake below, he could be truly clean.

The chamber around him was glowing, as if the rock crystals were interwoven with light. He stopped, dazzled, for he was seeing from the eye that wasn't there. Slowly, irresistibly, his gaze was drawn toward the well, and his feet followed. Only when Gill caught hold of his arm did he stop, on the very edge of the cliff.

He saw it clearly now. Rising from the shores of the lake below were the foundation stones of great buildings, their tops now buried in the black rock above them. Bright lava lapped at their feet; for an instant, Harg saw the golden flank of a snakelike thing slide through the lake, coiled around the base of a tower.

The mountain's power was rising through his legs. He felt magma flowing in his veins.

"Harg, what's wrong?" Gill shouted into his ear. "What are you looking at?"

Harg pointed. "Do you see that? There was a city here once, Gill. It was buried under the lava."

"No. I can't see it."

"I could do that to Tornabay," Harg said.

There was a pause. "Let's get out of here," Gill said.

"You think I'm joking," Harg said.

"No, I don't." Gill took his arm, trying to draw him away from the lake. With an irrational surge of anger Harg jerked away.

"Don't touch me," he said.

"Harg, how are we going to get the gunpowder past here safely?" Gill said.

The practical question made Harg's mind focus, a gear slipping back into its groove. He looked around. "The heat itself won't set it off, as long as we stay away from the well," he said. "All the same, we'd better send everyone else through first, and bring the gunpowder last."

They were walking again toward the tunnel's continuation. With every step Harg felt the certainty drain out of him. The rocks underfoot were an ugly black excretion. For an instant there, Harg realized, he had actually felt like an Ison. He had known what the real ones were like: strong and sure, not scarred and ugly with old mistakes. His eye was hurting again.

Beyond the great chamber, the tunnel led upward again, and the hot breeze was at their backs. "It leads out," Harg said, sure of it without knowing why.

He sank down on a rock, feeling like a twisted clinker left in the path of onrushing events. "Go back and tell them to come on," he said. "I'll wait here."

Gill was watching him carefully. "Don't go back into the chamber, Harg," he said.

"All right," Harg said, though he barely heard.

Alone, he sat staring at the wall. The pain lancing through his eye made him think of how he lost it, and that made him think of Goth. The only person who had always known him through and through. And the only one who had always been perfectly consistent in his rejection.

All I have to do is win, he thought fiercely. *If I win, they will forget everything else.*

He looked back toward the glowing lava chamber. He no longer doubted which side the mountain was on. It would be on his, if only he dared to command it.

He rose and walked back toward the chamber. In the well, the lake was blinding bright, churning. He gazed with his blind eye into the white-gold heat, and again saw a flash of dazzling scales. Deep in the churning lava, a faceted eye like a gemstone was watching him. The mountain's pulse thundered in his body. For a delirious moment he *was* Mount Embo.

The lake closed over the snake-eye. Harg looked across the chamber and saw the head of his troop emerging tentatively from the other tunnel. He signalled at them, waving them on. They saw him, and urged the terrified mules forward. He knew that they saw victory in him.

When all of them had passed through and were assembled in an orderly line in the tunnel, Harg again took the lead. It was only then he realized that he still could see, with a ghostly double vision, from his missing eye.

෨

The tunnel ended just as the scout had said it did, in a slope of rubble leading down to a pine forest. Harg, Gill, and the scout went ahead to determine where they were. The fog had lifted from the top of the mountain, though it still formed a misty layer below. The sun was setting, and they could see Mount Embo's shadow spread out before them.

"Listen," Gill said.

From far away, the boom of artillery drifted up through the fog. "Jearl must have begun his attack," Harg said. He did not mention the other possibility— that somehow Talley had outwitted them and fallen upon their fleet by surprise. Harg was almost superstitious about the man's ability to counter his moves. "Rot this fog," he said. "From up here we could see what was going on if only it were clear."

They scrambled down the edge of the lava flow, looking for a route on around the mountain. Walking on the carpet of rust-coloured needles beneath the pines seemed almost unnatural after so long in a deformed world of rock. The trees ended when they came to a level clifftop where an outcrop of granite plunged sheer to the mountainside below. When they came to the edge, Gill gave an exclamation of astonishment.

An inshore wind had wakened, and was scattering the fog below them. They were directly above Tornabay.

It was impossible. They should still have been miles away. And yet there it lay, in a wide arc along the bay. Below the cliff they stood on, a rugged spur of mountain jutted out, an old lava ridge that split the city like a wedge. The palace rose from its farthest foot. Lamps were just beginning to show in some of the windows. The wind brought a faint smell of cooking fires.

Harg glanced at the scout to make sure he saw it, too.

"I guess we took a shortcut," Gill said.

Harg said nothing. He felt as if an unlikely contract had been fulfilled.

Down in the harbour, a flock of merchant boats and three Inning warships lay penned. The firing they had heard was coming from the two bay entrances, where Jearl's ships were shelling the forts that guarded the straits.

"Jearl caught three of their ships in harbour," Harg said.

"They probably feel safe there," Gill said.

"Safe and useless." Harg turned to scan the ledge they stood on. It looked as if it had been placed here specifically for the purpose of mounting artillery. The palace was well within range. Even the harbour, in a pinch. They hadn't a prayer of hitting those warships, but they could make them feel uneasy. "Go back and tell Brixt to bring up the guns," he said to Gill. "If we can place and train them before dark, we can start shelling in the morning."

"What about the main detachment?" Gill said. "They must be way behind us."

"We'll give them a little surprise," Harg said. As Gill left, Harg turned to the scout. "Take a message to Drome Garlow for me. Tell him our position, and find how quickly he can send a force to guard our backs." The scout looked like a small animal watching a predator go by, knowing the prey would be something far larger than himself.

The unexpected news that they were close to their goal spurred the troops to new efforts. But despite much strain and hurry, the sun was down before the guns were in place and their crews ready to set to work. Harg stood on the cliff edge watching as, across the rocky ridge between them, the palace guards lit torches along the walls. "That's right, mark it for us," Harg said.

"Haven't they noticed us?" Brixt growled beside him.

Harg shrugged. "Maybe the light is in their eyes."

Or maybe, he thought uneasily, they knew something he didn't. He suddenly felt very exposed, out here ahead of the main force. It would be so easy for the Innings to send out a party to dislodge them from this perch. "Has that scout come back?" he asked.

"Not yet," Brixt said.

"Shall we fire some test rounds, sir?" a gun captain asked.

It would be a good idea to get their aim while there was still a trace of light to see what they were hitting. But it would reveal their position and set off a cascade of events that would be hard to control or predict. Harg turned and looked behind them. The western sky was inflamed a livid red. Against it, the mountain was a black silhouette, waiting. A wisp of steam rose from its top.

"We'd better wait till we hear from the main force," he said. "You have sentries patrolling, Brixt?"

"Yes, sir."

"Good. No fires or lights. There's no point in advertising where we are yet."

They waited in silence as night deepened over the valley of the Em. The quarter moon was just rising beyond Fosk when a stir in the rear of the company made Harg jump up. Brixt was coming toward him, and the scout was at his side.

"They're still miles away," Brixt said.

The scout told the story. Drome Garlow's force was camped for the night in a meadow between two fingers of lava flow. The terrain had been nearly impassable, and the troops were exhausted. Drome estimated that it would take them till noon the next day to catch up.

"He could barely believe we're here," the scout said. "If you could see what lies between us, you'd doubt it, too."

So there was no army at his back after all. Mentally, Harg tallied up what he had. Twenty guns and their crews, about two hundred men. Assorted drovers and packers, fifty more. A pathetic sum, if they were attacked. No, he corrected himself mentally—*when* they were attacked. Night might protect them now, but in the morning they would be exposed.

He felt the mountain's presence, insistent in his brain. He didn't need an army to conquer Tornabay. All he had to do was point his finger, and a torrent of fire would flow down on the city, entombing it in glowing rock. Or perhaps, if he wanted, the mountain would torment it over the ages, like that other city he had seen, still preserved in its agony. After Tornabay was only a smoking rubble he could stand over it, lord of all the wasteland, and even the Innings would have to fear him.

We can do it ourselves, he had once said. *With our own hands. No help from gods, no guidance from the Lashnura.* He looked around at the men waiting for his order. They probably had families down there. That was why he had chosen them. This was their home.

"Get the men to the guns, Brixt," he said. "When the moon is halfway up the sky, we're going to start firing."

Brixt's eyebrows bushed out and he seemed about to say something, but Harg silenced him with a glance. *Don't ask me anything*, he thought. *Don't make me admit I am just using them up while they are still mine to use.*

As the gun crews made ready, Harg sent Gill with some soldiers to form a ring of sentinels around them, and guard the way back to the tunnel. When the first cannon bellowed out orange flame, everyone peered through the night to see where the ball would hit. There was no sign.

"Well, make your best guess," Harg said to the gunners. They were almost sure to hit the surrounding city, aiming blind like this; but Harg no longer cared. Terror was the important thing now.

He paced up and down the line of guns as they erupted into the night.

Their jarring power filled him with a mad exhilaration. He wanted to turn and shout at the mountain, *This is my fire. This is my havoc. I can turn this city to ash without you.*

Out beyond the harbour, Jearl had seen the attack and joined in. Harg could see the occasional flash of a broadside from one of the ships, aimed at the forts on the headland. A bright spark of fire was showing in the city at the palace's feet, the only evidence that the bombardment was having any effect.

Harg shouted encouragement at the gunners, to keep them firing and create the most destruction they could in the time allowed them. Every moment he expected one of the sentries to come running up with the news that the counterattack was upon them.

It didn't come. Hour after hour they kept on, with no reaction from the enemy. Only once did they see a flash of answering fire from the palace walls, and the gunners paused to see where the shells would hit; but Harg called out, "They can't touch us. We're too far above them; they can't raise their guns high enough." And it proved to be true.

Fires now twinkled out from a dozen different locations in the city, red and yellow stars. It was strangely beautiful. Watching it, Harg felt as if time had looped around and placed him back in Drumlin. He could almost feel Jory at his side. "What are you doing, taking a nap?" he yelled at the nearest gun crew, who had paused in exhaustion. They moved mechanically to resume working.

When day came, the city was shrouded with smoke. Whole blocks of buildings were ablaze; others had been gutted in the night. The fire was still spreading. Harg watched it. They would remember him now.

"Ison, come here!" Brixt called from the cliff edge. "Look at this." The Inning flag above the palace slowly begin to sink.

"What's going on?" Harg said, unable to believe what he was seeing.

Training his spyglass on the palace walls, he saw the nearest gate begin to open. "Cease fire!" he said. The cannons had almost stopped already. The crews were all at the cliff edge, watching as a mob of people issued from the gate into the square far below. They seemed to be celebrating.

Harg called for a messenger to run down and find out what was going on.

It didn't take long. "The Adaina rose up in the night," the messenger panted out. "When they heard us bombarding, they came streaming into the palace through the cellars, and overwhelmed the soldiers. They're calling for you to enter the city now." His voice dropped. "You'd better come quickly. It's turning ugly. The mobs have been sacking Torna shops. Those fires you see aren't all our work."

Harg gave the orders for a guard to remain with the guns, and assembled the rest to accompany him.

They were met at the edge of the city by a riotous crowd of raggedly dressed, lank-haired people with a feverish glow to their thin faces. They looked like ovens stoked so high with fire that their metal had begun to glow. All around them, the air was combustible with vengeance.

The crowds grew thicker and noisier as they neared the Gallowmarket gate into the palace. Almost all Harg saw was brown Adaina faces, wild with victory. Ahead, some young men were climbing the lampposts, while others carried booty from some smashed shop windows, oblivious to the soldiers approaching. The smell of smoke was heavy in the air.

When they entered the Gallowmarket, the mob pressed in, jostling so close to the ranks of soldiers that they could scarcely keep their places. The people were chanting, "Ison! Ison!" Some were waving sabres.

Brixt's face was tense with anxiety. They were a small troop of armed Tornas in a crowd of vengeful Adaina. "We've got to get through to the gate before they lynch us all," he said.

Or before some panicked soldier fires, thought Harg. He pushed to the front and shouted, "Clear a way! Let us through!"

Slowly they edged forward toward the palace gate. As they reached it, a hush fell over the crowd. A woman had appeared alone under the arched stone opening. She was dazzlingly beautiful, but radiated such menace that no one dared to come close. With the eyes of all the crowd on her, she held up a butcher knife in a hand gory with blood to the elbow. The triumph in her face flamed so bright it almost seemed to light the black underside of the clouds. The watching crowd gave an audible gasp.

Harg felt the fire climbing his legs. Before him, Calpe was coiled with firesnakes. He could do nothing but walk toward her across the empty pavement, his limbs worked by some other power. The yearning and terror of all who saw her beat on his back.

When they met, she took his hand and held it to her heart. "Ison," she said, "You are my lord, and I give you this city." Then she turned and led him over the threshold of the palace, under the gate. Behind, he heard a roar as of the sea.

Inside, the palace had been sacked. Curtains were ripped from the broken windows, the muddied floors were bare of rugs. Here and there people were still at work prying mirrors from the walls and lugging off the heavier furniture. Calpe led him through a hallway whose carved plaster ceiling now gaped open to the sky, and into a warren of wood-panelled rooms. She stopped at a door where two dead Torna guards lay, one with his guts spilling out onto the parquet. It was now guarded by a pockmarked man with a sabre who eyed her hungrily as he stepped aside to let them through.

The room inside was untouched. A thick red carpet yielded like flesh under Harg's boots. A huge gilded bed with a canopy dominated the room. "Your enemy," Calpe said, pointing with the knife toward the bed.

An Inning was lying there naked, spread-eagled, wrists and ankles chained to the bedposts. In the soft flesh of his upper arm were two marks where the slivers of achra had gone in hours before. He now had the hollow-eyed look of someone whose ecstasy had worn away.

Harg stood over him, looking down. "Who is he?" he said.

"Provost Minicleer." Calpe snaked an arm around Harg's waist and stood looking down at the prisoner.

The Inning jerked at the manacles fastening him to the bed. His face was flushed; the rest of his body was very pale, very smooth, almost hairless. "You treacherous whore!" he spat at Calpe.

Calpe whispered in Harg's ear, "Let's make love right here, in front of him."

The thought made Harg's loins throb. He looked up to find Gill standing in the doorway, looking sickened. "Go find someone to take charge of this prisoner, Gill," he said.

"No!" Calpe's voice was so intense that Harg turned to her, silent. She went to the foot of the bed, one hand on either bedpost, looking down on Minicleer with a glittering hatred. "Ison, give me this man. It's all I ask for giving you Tornabay."

Harg felt the firesnakes squeezing him, tight as shackles. "What do you want with him?" he said.

She said slowly, "I want him roasted over a fire, so slowly we can carve off pieces of his flesh and make him eat them."

At sight of her, Harg felt every old wound in his body open anew. Everything Inning had ever done to him was answering her, *Yes. Yes, we will watch him die together, and then make love on his bed while the city around us burns.* He reached out and clasped her bloodstained hand across the bed. He loathed himself. He was just the sort of person to say yes to her.

"He's yours," he said.

Her bloody fingers twined through his. "And I am yours," she said.

Calpe took a set of keys from her girdle and began unlocking the Inning's manacles. She called a name, and two unkempt men smelling of sweat crowded through the door to seize him. Harg left the room, feeling a wave of nausea.

What is happening to us? he thought. *What are we turning into?*

A soldier was coming down the hallway toward him. "Brixt is looking for you, sir," he said.

"Has he secured the palace?" Harg asked.

"Yes, sir. We've closed the gates and are trying to clear the rabble out now. We found some Inning officers and their lackeys locked in the basement."

"Take me to Brixt."

The captain was on the palace wall, overlooking the Gallowmarket gate. Harg leaned against the wall, looking out over the city. Smoke was rising everywhere. The Gallowmarket pavement was littered with glass from broken shop windows. A clump of rioters raced by.

"There are wild bands looting all over the city," Brixt said. "They're after Torna shops, Torna homes."

Harg said nothing. There was nothing he could do about it. He didn't have enough soldiers, and the ones he had were the wrong race. "Is the palace secure?" he asked.

"It will be soon."

"Good. Man all the gates. We can only sit tight and wait till Drome gets here." He paused. "You've done well, Brixt."

The captain was eyeing him. "What about the city?" he said. "There are law-abiding people out there."

Harg looked out at it. "This is the Innings' doing, and Tiarch's."

But it was he who had swept down like wildfire on Tornabay, and loosed all the pent-up energies of vengeance. It was only just, after what the Innings had done to the South Chain. He could make it twice as horrible, and still not match them.

His feeling of sickness returned, and he leaned against the parapet, covered with cold sweat. Behind him, he heard Gill say, "I wish Spaeth were here."

It would do no good, Harg thought. *Not even a Lashnura could forgive me now.*

There were riotous voices in the courtyard below. He turned and saw a ragtag mob leading Minicleer across the courtyard to the gate. He was still naked and barefoot, his wrists shackled behind him. They were tugging him forward by a rope around his neck.

"Stop!" Harg shouted, and the mob came to a halt. Harg came down the stairs to the courtyard and walked slowly across the flagstones toward Minicleer. He stopped mere inches away, looking at the Inning's face. It was stripped clean of everything but pure, primal terror.

"Ask me for your life," Harg said.

Minicleer said nothing. Even now, stripped and inches from a death too horrible to think of, he couldn't beg for mercy. Not from an Adaina.

Harg gestured over some soldiers from the guard at the gate. "Take him down and put him with the other Innings," he said curtly. "Don't let anyone at him."

There was a cry of rage from the mob. Calpe stepped forward, her face feral. "You promised me!" she said.

"I changed my mind," Harg answered.

There was a scuffle, and the soldiers had to lower their bayonets to force the mob away. Other soldiers came running up to surround the rabble and drive them toward the gate. They were screaming curses at Harg as he turned to climb the stair to the wall, where Brixt and Gill were still watching. He couldn't meet their eyes.

11
BOXING WITH THE WIND

Spaeth didn't move when Nathaway came into the room. She didn't move when he sat down on the edge of the bed she lay in. She did not want to be roused into the aching vacuum of the world.

She had scarcely stirred for a week. The lethargy had been growing on her slowly, as her senses shut down one by one to relieve her of the constant pain. She was sleeping fifteen or sixteen hours a day now, and the time awake was hazy and muffled. The only vivid things in life were her dreams, where she and Harg were merged like conjoined twins; his blood flowed in her body, his nerves ran all through her, and she felt full of him beyond bearing. Then she would wake, and the void would return. Awake, she was nothing but a walking, breathing cavity.

There was still a bond between them. She had been hanging onto it stubbornly, tenaciously, knowing that whatever she had to bear, he did as well. It was a contest of wills, which of them could hold out longest. It had already gone on longer than she would have thought possible. How could he still be walking the world, functioning, not feeling it?

Nathaway brushed some strands of hair from her face. Her bandhota. He had been so tender with her, so loyal, so forgiving. She wished she could have repaid him better. Now she turned to him and said, "Is there any news?" He would know what she meant: news from Tornabay, news of *him*.

Nathaway shook his head. "No news," he said.

She turned away. The bed she lay in had been Harg's, and it was still alive with his presence. When she touched her cheek to the pillow, it was his face. When she ran her fingers through the fringe on the bedspread, it was his hair. She could feel him burning against her, tantalizingly close, agonizingly withheld.

"Spaeth, get up and come down to the harbour with me," Nathaway said.

He had been trying to distract her for weeks. At first she had allowed him to drag her along on his visits to the harbour, where the refugees from the South Chain were camping. He had been spending his days with them, helping to distribute rations and clothing, setting up tents, even digging latrines, as if in penance for his race. Everyone in Lashnish thought he was a little crazy.

She didn't like going to the refugee camp. The sight of it only maddened her with a hunger that none of the people there could fulfill. She could have given dhota to them all, and still be empty in the end. She closed her eyes.

"You'll just get weak if you lie here," he said. "You've got to get up and move around."

He thought it was something she could overcome by discipline and force of will. How like an Inning. They thought they controlled everything, and were responsible for everything.

There is no power for us but in surrender, Goth's voice said in her memory. She had always thought it might be true for him, but not for her. That night in the Isonsquare, she had thought the destiny of all the Lashnura lay in her hands, and she could change it. Now she knew: the broad sweep of events would never be her arena. She was to be trapped forever in internal spaces, in personal wars.

She was drifting away again when Nathaway threw back the covers, seized her under the arms, and dragged her into a sitting position. She groaned in protest, but he only began pulling stockings on her feet. He tried to thread her arm into a jacket over her nightshirt till she finally said, "Leave me alone, rot you."

"Will you dress yourself?" he asked.

He wasn't going to let her rest. "Yes," she said.

It took her a long time, since every movement pushed her farther into the world. Her legs were weak. She brushed her hair out of her face, and found it was lank and oily. When she hobbled across to the chair by the mirror, the face that looked out at her was starved and sunken-eyed, like a victim of famine.

Nathaway had a donkey cart waiting at the door. Spaeth drew her hood over her head, hoping to avoid recognition. Everyone in Lashnish wanted something from her, and she had nothing to give.

It was raining, as it had been doing more or less constantly for weeks. It was not cold, but the grey buildings were so bleak that Spaeth shivered. Nathaway put his arm around her. She leaned against him. His body was warm, comfortable, familiar. Her thoughts strayed to memories of how she had enjoyed him on the trip to Lashnish. They had not been able to sleep together since the night of dhota-nur. She knew how hard on him it must be, and yet he never reproached her or complained.

When they came in sight of the shore, Spaeth drew in a breath. The refugee camp had grown. It started on the edge of the outlying warehouse district, and stretched a mile or two farther on down the shore. It was a makeshift city of driftwood shanties and waterlogged canvas tents. The smoke from a thousand campfires rose into the overhanging clouds.

There was a rutted track running through the camp, and the donkey cart splashed on down it. Some Adaina children came rushing out to meet them, running alongside and holding out their hands for money. Their hair was plastered to their foreheads with rain. Spaeth glimpsed the faces of gaunt mothers peering out from inside their hovels.

"I don't want to see this," she said. "I want to go back."

"It won't go away just because you're not looking," Nathaway said.

"But I can't do anything about it."

"That's what everyone says. That's why the problem never gets solved."

They went on in silence. The camp was organized into enclaves, each from a separate island, for even here the common enemy had not wiped out old divisions. As they passed deeper into the camp, they seemed to be fording streams of smells: sewage, rotting fish guts, smoke. When they passed through the tent-village of people from Bute, Spaeth momentarily locked eyes with a ragged girl who stood watching their cart pass with a look of black anger. Half of her right leg was missing.

"There are gangs of young boys who go round terrorizing the rest and stealing food," Nathaway said. "Each island seems to have a faction of them that wars with the others."

"Where are their families?" Spaeth asked.

"They'd probably like to know that themselves."

Far down the shore they came to a part of the camp that was newer and ruder than the rest. Here there were no wood shanties and few tents; the people were living under overturned boats and scavenged scraps of canvas. Nathaway pulled the donkey to a stop.

Spaeth climbed down stiffly. When she touched ground, the mud oozed over her shoes. Nathaway approached an old lighter propped on its side, a canvas awning stretched from its raised gunwale to the ground. Before he reached it, the canvas flap rose and Tway stepped out.

She looked strained and weary. "It's no good," she said to Nathaway.

"You mean—?"

"The baby died."

Nathaway stood looking helplessly angry. Tway said, "They're almost out of fuel here. Can you find some?"

"I can try." He turned dejectedly back to the cart.

Tway saw Spaeth, and made a shooing motion with her hands. "Go on, go back, Spaeth. There's nothing you can do here." She turned back to the propped-up boat. Stepping around Nathaway, Spaeth followed her.

Three people were sitting cross-legged around a smoky fire inside. They looked up when she entered, and Spaeth recognized Wilne, Gill's wife, and her two children.

"Wilne! What are you doing here?" Spaeth said. A terrible thought struck her. "Have the Innings been to Yora?"

Wilne shook her head slowly. Her face was streaked with either rain or tears, and her voice sounded like rocks grinding together. "We left ahead of them. It was easy to see that they were heading there. They would scarcely let it be, since all the trouble started there."

She coughed, then went on. "We went first to Thimish, but those pirates wouldn't have us. Ekra wasn't safe, so Strobe found us a boat that would take us here."

"Can't you find better lodgings than this?"

"We came too late; the city is full. People want too much money for rooms."

Spaeth looked to Tway. "Can't you find them something?"

"I'd have to find lodgings for Tish and Argen and Pilt and Gimp and all the rest, then," she said. "There are hundreds of people living like this, Spaeth."

Spaeth saw then that Wilne held a cloth-wrapped bundle on her lap. It looked very like a baby. Wilne saw her gaze and shrugged, drawing aside the cloth to reveal a tiny, waxy face. "She died an hour ago," Wilne said. "Her name was Pira. Gill never even got to see her."

The two children were crouched silently behind Wilne. The older one was drawing something with a stick in the dirt. She glanced up at her mother's wooden face with an expression that seemed too old for her. As if she saw her own future there.

"I didn't know," Spaeth whispered. "I could have saved her."

"There are hundreds more like her, Grey Lady," Wilne said. "You can't save them all."

There was a long silence.

Spaeth had to get away. She felt like the breath was being pressed from her body.

"Where is Mother Tish?" she said.

Tway gave her a warning glance. "You don't want to see her, Spaeth."

"Yes, I do."

They found Tish and Argen together, sitting on the ground by a fire under a makeshift canvas shelter. Spaeth was shocked to see the change in Argen. He had always been the strictest and angriest of the elders; the children had feared him. Now he seemed shrunken—merely an emaciated, frightened old man. His jaw was covered with an unshaved grey stubble, and the outline of his skull showed under his skin. He sat there chewing slowly, dazed.

Tish had lost some of her teeth, and her face was creased more deeply, but she recognized Spaeth instantly. Her eyes were sharp, devoid of deference or fear. "So you've come back to us, have you?" she said. "Ready to take a bandhota yet?"

"I have one now," Spaeth said.

"So I hear. It looks like he's left you no happier than the rest of us."

Tway said angrily to Spaeth, "She blames Harg for all of this. Even though it was the Innings who did it."

"The Innings were friendly, once," Tish said.

"Now we see what was under their friendship."

Tish regarded them both, then shook her head. "You foolish young people. Challenging the Innings was like taunting the wildcat or provoking the gale. There's an old saying the sailors have: 'If you cannot tame the wind, let it take you where it will.' If we had let ourselves be blown before the Innings' wind, we might have survived. But no, you warmongers wanted to stand in their path as they moved out to conquer. You wouldn't bend before them, in order not to break. You have doomed us all."

"The other way, we would have lost our land," Tway said.

"What do you think you see here but people without a land?" Tish said, gesturing around her.

"We'll get it back," Tway said. "Harg will see to that."

"It's too late for me," Tish said. "And not just because I'm old. It's too late for the children, too. Once you've lost everything, there are parts of you that never grow back."

She turned to stir up the fire and throw on another faggot. The rain was pattering hard on the canvas. Watching her, Spaeth had a sudden premonition that it didn't matter whether they won or lost—the nation that had started to fight was gone. The thought disturbed her so that she stood to leave.

"Go on," Tish said, not even glancing at her. "Go fight the wind."

After leaving, Spaeth stood for a few moments outside in the rain and the churned-up mud. There was a vast, unlocalized pain around her. It seemed everywhere—in the ground beneath her, in the smoky air. As if the entire island were aching. No, all the Isles together.

She drew her hood further over her face and walked down to the rocky beach.

Here, apart from the people, she could feel again the breathing of the sea. The mountains that sheltered the bay were shawled in mist. She listened, trying to feel the sleeping island around her. It was not the deep sleep of the drugged, as she had always supposed; it was only a light doze. She wondered what Roah was dreaming about.

A wave batted at her toes with white paws. Spaeth stopped, staring at it. "What do you want?" she said sharply. She had thought the sea would never speak to her again.

The receding wave hissed in the pebbles. "So," it said, "do you have what you wanted?"

What had she wanted?

Once—when last she had listened to the voice that now spoke to her—she had wanted to span the circles—to pass, as it were, into another state of being: to become dangerous. All of that seemed bitterly futile now. She was trapped, like all of her race, in dependence.

"I want things back the way they were," she whispered. "Before any of this happened."

White fangs bit at the rocks. "Silly girl. You could have it. I could help you. I could set you free."

Was that really what she wanted now? To be without lures and entanglements, without longing, without all their precious, poignant humanity?

"Then he would never be cured," she said, her voice barely a whisper.

"Doting fool. He will never be cured anyway. How could you not know that? You made him what he is, you and your precious Goth. You create a being as dangerous as that, then think your good intentions will tame it. Just like Lashnurai. Do you think he cares that you've given up your freedom for him? He's Ison now; it's all he needs from you."

For a moment she wondered if it could be true. Could the forgiveness of dhota be blinding her so badly? She tried to think clearly.

"I have to get back," she said.

A wave pounced over her feet, and clung to her ankles. "No. Think of your land. He has abandoned you, and all of these people as well. No one is going to save them, unless you do."

"This is too big for me," she said, looking down the beach, at all its thousand campfires. "I can't."

"Yes, you can. You just have to think beyond dhota. The world has outgrown it."

Nathaway's donkey cart was returning down the path, a few sticks of wood in the back. When he pulled up, Tway met him and helped carry the wood into Wilne's hovel. As Spaeth came up, Tway was saying, "We've got to find better shelter for them. Can't you talk to Tiarch again?"

"It won't do any good," he said. "There's no money; it's all going to the Navy."

As they rode together back toward the city, Spaeth thought of the Inning fleet bearing down on Yora. Their cruelty would mar it forever. Before they were through, the kind little island that had reared her would be gone. And after that they would go to Thimish, and then Ekra, and then they would be at Lashnish.

She looked out into the harbour. *Ripplewill* was there.

She knew what she had to do.

⌘

There was a series of flashes out of the night. "Give me that signal lamp, Cory," Torr said. The tin shutter clattered as he worked it. There were more flashes from across the waves. "Prepare to take in sail," Torr said.

They saw three lamps flare, outlining the triangle of bowsprit and main yardarms on the other boat. "Bring her alongside, Galber," Torr called back to the sailor at the helm.

When they came in earshot, the challenge came out of the night: "What boat is that?"

"*Ripplewill*," Torr called. "Is that you, Gort? Haven't they hanged you yet?"

"Torr! I thought you'd be in prison by now," the answer came.

"Where's Dorn?" Torr asked.

"Harbourdown," Gort answered. "His whole fleet's there. They'll be glad to see you."

"What are they up to?"

"You'll have to ask him that."

Torr turned to Spaeth. "You want to stop and talk to Dorn?"

Spaeth had told no one her purpose. Now she felt a mix of impatience and dread. "Ask where the Inning fleet is," she said.

Torr relayed the question. "Somewhere between here and Bute," the answer came. "If it's been as calm where they are as it's been here, they're not moving much."

That was Ridwit's doing, Spaeth knew. She had promised to delay them.

"All right, we'll stop and learn Dorn's plans," Spaeth said.

The bay at Harbourdown was a thicket of masts. All the small ships of Dorn's fleet were there: cutters and sloops, here and there a fishing scow with gunports hastily cut in its hull. As they threaded through, the water inky underneath, Spaeth noted with a dark resentment that Dorn had left Yora undefended in order to protect Thimish.

The *Vagabond* was brightly lit, and ships' boats were clustered round her, as if some council were going on. When the *Ripplewill* came alongside, Spaeth threw back her hood so they could see who it was. There was a sudden flurry of activity on deck when they saw her.

As she swung herself up onto the *Vagabond*'s slightly higher deck, Dorn was just emerging from his cabin. He surveyed her with an expression that was part suspicion, part hunger. He waited for her to speak.

"I have come to help you," she said.

A look of slow triumph dawned on his scarred face. "So," he said, "even the Onan couldn't stand it."

The implied criticism of Harg made the blood rush hot to her face. But she only said, "I want no harm to come to Yora."

He gestured for her to follow him below, then lumbered ahead, moving stiffly. It struck her how much he had aged in the past year.

The aft cabin was crowded with the unshaven, wildly dressed captains of his fleet. The smell of stale beer mingled with the fumes of the oil lamps and pipes. Their eyes were all on her, demanding.

Dorn said, "We were going to move out tomorrow, weather willing."

"To attack the Inning fleet?" Spaeth asked.

The pirate gave her a long, appraising look. At last he said, "To do what harm we can."

"They are stronger than you, you know."

Dorn's face was stony. "We don't have much choice. Our Ison doesn't see fit to defend his own people."

Spaeth wanted to gouge his eyes out. She crossed her arms tight to keep them from seeing her shake. "Well, I will bring you help," she said. "Let me go ahead of you, to Yora. There is a place where I need to be."

"What place?" Dorn asked, his eyes narrow.

"The skull of Hannako."

They all knew what she was up to then. Unwilling glances darted between them, half hopeful, half fearful. They had been thieves and plunderers, but none had ever collaborated with the Mundua and Ashwin.

"We have no choice," Spaeth said softly. "We must make use of what allies we can."

"Well," Dorn said, "you are the Heir of Gilgen."

Spaeth felt a sudden, hysterical urge to laugh. She held it back.

"Don't leave Harbourdown till noon," she told them. "Then, come to Yora."

When she clambered back onto the *Ripplewill*'s deck, Torr said, "Well?"

"Take me to Yora," Spaeth said.

ৰ

The Inning fleet had been becalmed for two days and a night, only miles from their goal. At sunset of the second day the ships were spread widely across the glassy ocean, but all still within signalling distance of at least one other ship. By dawn, the flagship *Pragmatic* was by herself. Her sails drooped limply, her masts traced aimless circles in the sky as she wallowed on a near-invisible swell.

And a strange dawn it was, orange as autumn in the east, black as death to the west. The air was close and oppressive. Down in the waist, a clutch of Torna seamen lined the port rail, staring at the cloud bank approaching from beyond Spole, from the untamed ocean. When Goth came on deck, several of them cast glances in his direction that he had rarely seen from a Torna face.

Up on the quarterdeck, Admiral Talley was quizzing Bellack, the Torna sailing master, about their location. His questions fell in a brisk staccato, precise as a snare drum, dispelling the atmosphere of dread that enveloped the rest of the ship.

When at last Talley dismissed Bellack, the man passed Goth on his way to the companion ladder. He paused and said in a low tone, "Do *you* know what that is, Ehir?" He nodded at the west.

Goth shook his head.

Talley came up, and the sailing master left. "Superstitious yokels," the Inning said dismissively. "They're sure some gods or other are after us."

Goth said nothing. He was virtually certain they were right. The only questions in his mind were who had roused the Mundua and the Ashwin, and what he ought to do about it.

It should have been a simple question. Maintaining the balance, and controlling the forces of derangement, had always been the purpose of his existence. But that was in another world, a world that lay ruined in the bone heaps and ashes the Innings had left behind. Everything had become so wildly skewed in this nightmare tour of the South Chain that the gods no longer seemed as dire an evil as mankind did.

As the bank of clouds drew closer they could see silent flashes of lightning illuminating it in patches. There was still not a breath of air, but Bellack ordered the sails furled. Talley called him up to the quarterdeck.

The master glanced apprehensively at the storm. Faraway crows' feet of lightning were flickering between cloud and sea. Goth had rarely seen the Thunderers reveal their presence so plainly. "We won't dare climb the masts once that hits, sir," he said. "We'll be lucky if we're not charred to cinders."

Through his own unease, Goth could not help but think how balanced that would be, in a way: that Corbin Talley's bones should lie charred at the bottom of the sea. It seemed almost to fit the Innings' ideal of justice.

The Admiral glanced up to the towering masthead, and scanned the flat plain of sea all round. Goth wondered if he finally felt at the mercy of a greater power.

"Have we any copper aboard?" he asked.

Bellack stared. "Yes, sir," he answered slowly. "We carry sheets to patch the sheathing on the hull."

"I want you to cut me some long strips, no more than an inch wide. And we'll need something pointed, made of iron. A bayonet should do."

Bellack still stood, trying to comprehend, so Talley said impatiently, "Here, I'll direct the work. Show me where the copper is."

They went below together. Goth watched as the rumour spread around the ship: their Admiral had some Inning magic up his sleeve.

The first outrider clouds hurried overhead, windy smudges on the sky; but at sea level the unnatural stillness prevailed. Goth gazed into the blackness, feathered now with lightning, and tried feeling the exalted calm of surrender. *Let your mind float like a leaf on the surface of this, as well*, he told himself. He knew now that he was going to do nothing. Nothing but strive to face death lightly.

The cloud was looming over them by the time Talley reemerged on deck with his metal instruments. He called for someone to climb up and attach the bayonet to the tip of the mainmast. The sailors looked upward and shrank away, so he picked out an agile young boy who had often amused them by his acrobatics in the rigging, and handed him the spike. "Do it," he said.

The boy glanced up and swallowed, but they could all tell he was more afraid of Talley than the Ashwin. He stuck the bayonet in his belt and went to mount the ratlines.

His form seemed terribly small outlined against the sky. As he reached the topgallant spar, a ball of lightning rolled across the underside of the cloud above like a drop of water clinging to the bottom of a basin. Goth imagined the sky above them as a brimming vat of lightning beginning to leak.

A bolt sizzled down not half a mile off, yellowing the sea till it steamed. The clap of thunder hit like a blow. Now the boy was at the top of the mast, lashing the spike in place. He finished and turned to climb down, but Talley ordered, "Stay there!" He had been directing another group of topmen to nail the copper strips to the mast, overlapping the ends. Now he picked one man out to carry up a strip to the masthead. "Wire it securely to the bayonet," he instructed.

The man was only halfway up when the lightning hit—a mere flick, an almost casual blow. The boy waiting at the peak convulsed and fell backwards, but after several yards his body caught in the rigging, smoking.

Talley glanced up and saw what had happened, but did not react. The man on the topsail spar was staring in horror at his young crewmate dangling in the ropes. He reached out to try and shake him loose.

"Leave it," Talley shouted peremptorily. "Go finish the job." The man moved rigidly to obey. It was as if the seamen had no more will than the parts of a machine, and Talley was their motor.

Soon they had the copper running all the way from the bayonet spike to the deck, then out and down the hull to the sea. The men scrambled down as soon as Talley gave the word, breathless at their own safety. The *Pragmatic* rolled on the swell, armed with her Inning magic, and flying a corpse in her rigging like a flag.

They were in the thick of the thundernest now. The air was black as night, but all around the lightning forked down, reflected in the sea, wreathing them in a deadly garland. The burned air smarted in their noses.

A lightning bolt sheared the sky, aimed straight at them. Everyone on deck ducked, blinded, then stunned by the deafening crash. But there was no crack of splintering wood, and though men were standing by with buckets and sand, no fire blazed up. The lightning had passed harmlessly down the copper strip into the sea.

Talley looked up to inspect his handiwork. "Check the copper for melted spots," he said, and they saw the deck and mast were scorched all around the metal. The men's spirits, which had been so low, brightened at this proof of Inning superiority.

Another bolt came, aimed this time at the foremast; but at the last moment it was deflected toward the mainmast, as if the spike attracted it. The sky bellowed in fury.

The Ashwin were truly angry now, but it was as if Talley's device cast a spell of impotency in a magic radius all around the ship. The men were shouting and mocking the sky now.

Talley came up to stand beside Goth. "How did you know to do that?" Goth asked.

"I read about something like it," Talley said. "It's been tried on steeples ashore."

Goth looked upward. There, beyond the clouds, the Thunderers clashed their brassy wings in impotent rage. It was as if Talley had created another circle around them where no god could reach.

Ridwit snarled, every hair erect. "They have escaped!" she said. Tiny lightning bolts ran across her back.

At her side, Spaeth said bitingly, "What sort of hunter are you? Track them down."

They stood in a night-black landscape of translucent hills that flickered deep in their hearts with light. From where she stood at the Whispering Stones, Spaeth could see a thousand rolling, tumbled hills. The subterranean flashes that lit them were of all different colours: yellow, blue-white, a cloudy, frosted red. The ground she stood on was a transparent sand, like ground-up glass; but when she moved her feet it snapped and sparked with electricity. She suspected that if she were to run her fingers through that sand they would come away bleeding.

Ridwit turned amber eyes on her. "I know where they are. But they are fighting back."

"How?" Spaeth scoffed. "They haven't the knowledge."

"They're not in any of our circles," Ridwit said. "They're in that circle of their own, that Inning circle barred off from all the others. We can't get through while they stay there."

190

"Trick them across the threshold, then."

"How?"

"The way you always do it! Use their fear. Use their guilt. Use anything in them that is uncured. Do it, or you'll get no reward from me."

Ridwit bared her teeth hungrily at that, and turned back to her task.

❧

The mast tops and yardarms were glowing. Fingers of ghostly light reached out into the air, shifting like something alive. The seamen shielded their faces from it.

"Fools!" Talley said, irritated at their ignorance. "It only means the storm is letting up."

And, as before, he was right. Soon there were gaps in the black clouds above, and to the west the sky was light, reflected in the sea.

But it was like no sky or sea they had ever seen. Not the blue and windy roadway they had hoped for. Bulbous, heavy clouds hung above, ruddily lit with a sunset glow, though it should have been plain day. Below, the sea was glossy—a vast, viscous pool of red.

Talley had gone below, leaving Bellack in charge. The master's face was sweaty and flushed as he looked out at the transformed landscape. The sailors around him had fallen silent.

"It's blood," someone said, voicing what they all were thinking. They had seen so much of it in the South Chain. It had drenched them, and now the universe had sent it back to drown them.

"Set the topsails," Bellack ordered his men, then muttered, "Get us out of here."

They mounted the rigging gingerly, though it no longer glowed. Unbidden, two men disentangled the corpse from the rigging and lowered it by rope to the deck.

Her sails filled, but the *Pragmatic* seemed to make little headway through the thick red liquid. "It's clotting around the hull," a sailor called.

"Holy Alta!" Bellack said, his voice thick. The rudder was already handling poorly, as if clogged. The hull seemed to be dragging. "Are we riding any lower?" he asked.

Goth tried to swallow down his revulsion. He knew he could put a stop to this, but he still held back. It was horrible that murderers should drown in the blood of their own victims, but it was the working of a moral universe.

"What is going on?" Corbin Talley's sharp voice broke on the heavy air as he came up on deck. The strange light stained his white waistcoat crimson.

"Blood, sir," Bellack said. "It's coagulating around the hull." Goth could smell it now; it was not just blood, but rotting blood, days old.

Talley glanced around at the faces of the sailors, and seemed to make a quick calculation to change strategy. He began to laugh. "Blood!" he said. "I've heard everything now. Well, let's check and see. You there, fetch me a pail. And you, run and get the porcelain basin and the shaving mirror from my cabin. You, fetch a good clean lamp."

He tied the pail to a rope, then went to the rail where all could see and lowered it overside. The Torna watched, horror-struck, as the full pail rose up the side, dripping red. Unflinching, Talley grasped the bail and poured a shallow layer of the gory liquid into the white porcelain basin. He then had one of the men hold the lamp close, the concave mirror behind it to focus the beam of light.

"There," he said. "That's your blood."

The seawater was swimming with thousands of tiny creatures, smaller than gnats; the light cast their shadows on the porcelain.

"From time to time they bloom by the millions," Talley said. "If I had a microscope, I could show you that their bodies are as bright red as cochineal beetles. But they only float near the surface; a few feet down the water's as clear as ever."

One of the sailors began to laugh at the man beside him. "You said it was blood," he said.

"Well, you believed me," the second man answered.

"But the rudder," Bellack said stubbornly. "The water was thick."

"All in your mind," Talley said. "As are these Adaina gods you fear. Their only power consists of your fright. Now get back to your posts and set course for Yora."

There was a gust of wind then, like a sigh. The *Pragmatic* heeled, creaking. Bellack began to give orders, and the crowd broke apart, teasing each other and joking. Talley glanced at Goth as he passed him.

"You have won," Goth said.

"Won what?" Talley asked.

He didn't even know there had been a battle.

Goth turned away, filled with a tumult of thoughts. The Admiral and his devices had utterly neutralized the Mundua and Ashwin. They simply could not touch him. He was safe, and where he ruled, the world was safe as well.

"I am no longer needed," Goth said aloud to no one. He was an anachronism, a guardian against a peril that no longer had power. With a flight of exhilaration, he thought: *The Lashnura have served their purpose. We can now pass from this world. Our long vigil is over.*

And in the next moment he knew, no. Imbalance had not ceased to exist. It lived within the Innings, within Corbin Talley himself. He turned to look at him, standing so unruffled, so untouched, beside the wheel, and thought: *That is what we must balance. Somehow.*

॰

From the Whispering Stones, Spaeth could see the Inning fleet on the horizon. They were assembled in line, their course due north towards Yora.

The wind whistled lonely in the swordgrass. There were cat-tracks in the sand all around her, but no sign of Ridwit. The gods had slunk off to hide.

Spaeth stared at the distant white dots that were the Inning sails. She willed them away, but knew there was not a power in all the Isles that could stop them now.

It was past noon. She looked to the east. Around Yora's shoulder came a ragtag fleet of brightly painted boats, looking brazen as a flock of barnyard cocks. Spaeth glanced back at the line of floating fortresses to the south. Without the help Holby Dorn was expecting from other circles, he didn't stand a chance.

She had to warn him that she had failed. The *Ripplewill* was waiting in Yorabay, on the west shore. She might still catch the pirates in time.

She raced like wind across the sand hills, then plunged into the ravine that led down to the bay. Deserted houses and gardens flashed past on either side. A dog still guarding an empty yard barked at her. She burst into the clearing where the town dock lay.

And stopped dead. The *Ripplewill* was still moored at the dock, but square in the middle of the harbour entrance an Inning frigate lay anchored, its gunports up and aimed shoreward.

Spaeth wheeled round to disappear back into the woods. Before she could move, three uniformed marines emerged from the door of Strobe's house.

"By the rock!" one of the Tornas said when he laid eyes on her. "One of their grey-skinned tarts!"

She lunged to one side, but one of the soldiers caught her. She dug at his face with her fingernails. He swore and threw her bruisingly hard to the

193

ground. She tried to scramble off, but the other soldier pressed a bayonet against her spine.

"They say you can't be killed, but by the Rock we can hurt you," one of them growled. She froze then, and they jerked her hands behind her. She heard the clink of metal, and its cold bite around her wrists. One on either arm, the soldiers dragged her down the dock toward the *Ripplewill*.

"Cast this bucket off and we'll tow her in," the marine commander ordered. As one of the soldiers pulled Spaeth aboard, he looked her up and down. "Do we have to save her for the Innings?"

"Pity, isn't it?" the commander said.

"Ridwit!" Spaeth whispered, but knew there would be no help there. They were taking her into that Inning circle where the Mundua and Ashwin were impotent.

All afternoon, from the cramped hole they put her in, she heard the sound of distant guns.

THE STRENGTH
OF SURRENDER

The residents of the refugee camp at Lashnish had slowly reached the conclusion that Nathaway, and by extrapolation all Innings, had an unseemly preoccupation with human waste. The disposition of excrement had begun to occupy a good proportion of his waking thoughts. The primitive conditions in the camp had broken down the Adainas' normal inhibitions. Horrid stinking midden heaps grew uncontrollably, and the children squatted anywhere they found themselves, like dogs. The situation was deplorable for anyone but a cholera germ.

One day, fed up with it, he had gone around with a shovel and a pail, picking up feces. It provoked great hilarity. "What are you going to do with it all?" people called out. "Want more?" Even Tway, when she saw him, broke out laughing and said, "Why, if he's not giving orders he's giving off odours."

"I'm glad I'm able to cheer everyone up," he said, a little irritated.

After that day, he earned a nickname: Shitman. It was meant more kindly than it sounded.

In fact, he had begun to understand that the jokes at his expense were not all a mark of hostility. Among themselves, the Adaina were not the sullen, taciturn people they seemed from outside. They communicated through mock-serious banter and baiting. Since Nathaway was not used to being teased, and never knew how to react, it made him an irresistible target.

From time to time it flashed on him how his law-school classmates in

Fluminos would react if they could see him. All that expensive education, all those political connections, for a career shovelling shit and handing out soap. But then he would try to imagine any of his friends forced from their homes, trying to survive and save their families, with half the dignity of the Adaina, and his imagination would fail.

In the evenings, when he would escape the squalor to return to his comfortable room in the Pavilion, he would wonder if the law could ever take root in the Forsakens. The law assumed a world that obeyed fundamental rules of order—a controllable, just world. The Adaina had good reason for their belief that the universe was capriciously hostile. In a strange way, it sustained them as belief in justice never could have done. At least outrage at the unfairness of their plight wasn't added to their other burdens. Nathaway was the only one who felt that.

On the day when he brought Spaeth down to the camp, he returned after taking her back to the Pavilion, and found that her presence had caused a controversy. He came in on an argument in the section of the camp where the refugees from Thole had settled. A bearded man with a sore on his lip was saying loudly, "Where are they all, with their famous compassion, now that we need them? Hiding up in their Pavilion, that's where. What good are they doing up there?"

Tway was facing him, arguing back hotly. "What good do you think they could do here? With all the ills down here, an army of Grey Folk could die and we'd be no better off."

"What makes their lives worth so much more than ours?" the man retorted.

"Didn't you see her?" Tway said. "She can barely walk. That was just from curing one person. One person!"

"That's what they were made for."

Later, when he had a chance to talk to Tway alone, Nathaway said, "I shouldn't have brought her. It raised their expectations."

"No, it just made them selfish," she said, still angry. "They don't have any *right* to Lashnura help. They ought to know that."

How much greater their discontent would be, Nathaway thought, if they felt they had a right to justice.

That evening he gave Tway a ride in the donkey cart back to the city, where she was sharing her rented room with Strobe and two cousins. On the way they stopped to buy some hot meat pies from a stand on Promenade Street, and found the harbour swirling with rumours.

The woman selling the pies was suspicious of Nathaway and wouldn't talk while he was in earshot, so he went back to the cart and stood biding his time while Tway spoke to her. When she came back they set off again, and only then did she say, "Boats have been leaving all day long, bound for the South Chain. Word is that Holby Dorn is massing a force at Harbourdown to take on the Innings."

Looking out at the harbour, Nathaway saw that the two massive Navy warships stationed there to defend Lashnish were still riding at anchor, but the crowd of smaller boats did seem to have thinned out. He noticed that the familiar shape of the *Ripplewill* was missing. "Torr has gone," he said.

Tway shook her head, looking troubled. "I thought he had more sense than that. Dorn doesn't have a chance against the Innings. They should have waited for Harg."

When Nathaway got back to the Pavilion it was nearly dark, but he didn't go at once to Spaeth's room. Instead, he sat by the fire in the common room, writing another letter while his shoes dried on the hearth. It was later than usual before he picked up a lamp and went upstairs to look in on Spaeth. When he entered, he found the bed empty and her grey cloak gone. The room looked unoccupied.

Fifteen minutes of knocking on doors and rousing people out of bed produced only one person who had seen her leaving the building that afternoon, and no one who had seen her return. Nathaway was having difficulty suppressing his panic. Not a single night had they been separated since leaving Tornabay. "We've got to search the building," he said to Agave, who stood in the hallway in a robe, her loose silver hair falling down to her waist.

She nodded, but his senses were very acute, and he could tell she thought it would be fruitless. "Do you know something?" he demanded.

Agave put a sympathetic hand on his arm. "If she is gone, she will have gone to Tornabay, to be with her bandhota."

I am her bandhota, Nathaway wanted to shout. "Why now, after all this time? And why not tell anyone?" Every Lashnura in the Pavilion would have gladly assisted her in preparing for such a journey. He had a different intuition.

"I'm going to the harbour," he said.

She looked about to say something to restrain him, but then saw his desperate mood, and gave up. "Be careful, Nat," was all she said. "She is not in danger from anyone in these isles. You may be."

If what he suspected were true, Agave was very wrong.

Ordinarily, he would not have ventured into the harbour district alone after dark. The streets were deserted, the taverns the only populated spots.

He walked into the first drinking establishment he came to, asking for a ship's captain, any ship's captain.

The burly Torna seaman to whom the bartender pointed him appraised him from head to toe and said, "Are you the Grey Folks' Inning?"

"It doesn't matter," Nathaway said. "I need to hire a boat. Will you take me?"

"Take you where?"

Nathaway hesitated a moment, then spoke his fear aloud. "Thimish."

The man turned back to his drink. "No one's going to Thimish now."

"Do you know another boat that might take me?"

"I'm telling you, they're not letting anyone out of the harbour any more. Tiarch's orders."

When Nathaway emerged from the door of the tavern, he saw by the light of a hazy half-moon that it was true: the two warships had moved to block the exit from the bay. Word of the outlaw activity had finally reached Tiarch, and she had moved to put a stop to it.

Feeling thwarted, he walked back toward the Stonepath. When he reached the corner, he saw a light burning in a second-floor office of the Navy building, so he climbed the steps. The door was locked, but he pounded on it till a young man in uniform peered out a darkened window at him. He signalled urgently, and soon the bolt shot back.

"I need to speak to Vice-Admiral Joffrey," Nathaway said. "At once."

"What shall I say it is about?"

"Tell him . . . tell him it's a warning."

"Wait here," the young man said, letting him into the vestibule. "I'll see if he is free."

He was, of course. When the assistant showed Nathaway into the office, Joffrey rose from his desk with a cautious courtesy. "Justice Talley," he said. "What can I do for you?"

They had seen little of each other since Joffrey had arranged Nathaway's escape in Tornabay, back when they had both been on the Inning side. Then, Joffrey had reminded him of a small animal with sharp teeth; now, though he blended seamlessly in with the surroundings of power, he still looked carnivorous.

"It seems I need your permission to leave Lashnish," Nathaway said.

"And why would you be leaving Lashnish?" Joffrey inquired.

He looked very grave as Nathaway told him of Spaeth's absence, and of his suspicions as to where she had gone. When Joffrey had grasped the situation, he said, "Wait here. I need to do some checking. Please don't speak to anyone while I am gone. We must not let this become public."

Joffrey left the office, and Nathaway sat down to wait. Presently, he heard a door close below, and from the window he saw a figure in a dark coat and hat hurrying down the street. The young assistant came in to offer him some refreshment, then stirred up the fire and adjourned to a post in the hallway just outside the door.

It was a long time before Nathaway was roused from a doze by the sound of a low-toned conversation in the downstairs hall. He shook off his drowsiness and rose just before the door opened quietly and Joffrey's assistant slipped in and drew him over to the window.

"There is a boat moored at the quay just opposite us. You can see the lanterns on her masts from here."

Nathaway nodded. "What's her name?"

"*Grey Lady*. Go straight there, and you'll be met by someone who will get you through the blockade."

"All right. Thank you."

A weaselish dockhand in a knit cap was slouched against a light pole where the *Grey Lady* was moored, and Nathaway almost walked past him before realizing it was Joffrey himself. He came to a halt, astonished at the transformation.

"Go on, get aboard," Joffrey said in a low voice. He untied the mooring lines and followed Nathaway on deck.

"You're coming?" Nathaway said.

Joffrey nodded, but didn't explain himself.

They rode the ebbing tide out of the harbour, passing right between the two warships. Nathaway didn't see the signal, but the guard on the nearer of the two ships saluted as they slipped silently by.

All the next day they beat south against a warm wind blowing out of Rothur. Thimish was not yet visible on the horizon when the sun set. Nathaway joined Joffrey on the foredeck, where he was nervously scanning the horizon with a spyglass.

"They'll be patrolling Rockmeet Straits like hawks," he said.

"Who will?" Nathaway asked grimly.

Joffrey cast him an appraising glance. "Yes, that's the question. Regardless, you ought to stay out of sight."

The remark brought home to Nathaway his predicament: he was equally unwelcome in either camp.

It was the pirates who still controlled the straits by the time the *Grey*

Lady reached them late the next morning. Nathaway listened from below as the captain hailed the patrol boat, posing as a late recruit come to join Holby Dorn's fleet. There was a long, inaudible exchange of news, after which the usual thumps and shouts sounded as the *Grey Lady*'s crew raised the sails again and the boat heeled over.

When Joffrey finally came below, his news was grim. The battle was over. Holby Dorn's little fleet had flung itself against the Inning Navy just south of Yora. It had been a foolish gesture, desperate and brave, and they had been smashed to pieces. Only half a dozen boats had made it back to Thimish, and the islanders were now arming in panic to defend Harbourdown.

"Spaeth. Is there news of Spaeth?" Nathaway said.

Joffrey nodded. "You were right, she was with them. It gave them great hopes, perhaps unwise ones."

"And?"

"The *Ripplewill* wasn't one of the boats that returned."

Nathaway closed his eyes, concentrating as if he could touch her with his mind. Surely, he thought, he would know it if she were dead. He would feel something.

"We can go to Harbourdown," Joffrey said. "There might be more news there."

"No." Nathaway's voice was reckless with fatalism. "What's the use of that? We might as well go straight to where she is. The faster the better."

"You have some plan?" Joffrey was watching him a little sceptically.

"Yes," Nathaway said, but it was a lie. He had no plan, other than to throw himself on Corbin's mercy and enlist the Navy's help in finding Spaeth. He would worry about talking himself out of trouble later. For now, all his reliance was on the essence of reason at the core of the Inning temperament—his faith that, all the facts being known, justice would naturally prevail.

And so they set a course direct for Yora. As Thimish fell behind them, Nathaway was reminded of the first time he had come this way, less than a year before. How naively optimistic he had been then, how confident in his mission. How many broken promises paved the path back to that time.

They saw the smoke before they could see Yora, for it rose into the sky like a black shroud hanging over the corpse of the island. When at last the rounded hill of the Whispering Stones rose ahead, Nathaway saw that it bristled with a new crown—a thicket of tall stakes, each one with a body impaled upon it, standing out against the sky. They covered the crest of the island in uncountable numbers. A cloud of scavenger birds circled overhead. The sight drew his gaze and fixed it, burning into his memory like a branding iron. Yora had been turned into a mass grave, a charnel island. Its soil would forever be tainted by human bone and suffering.

The Inning fleet was moored on the west side, opposite Yorabay, but as the *Grey Lady* rounded the point, Nathaway saw that there was nothing left of the village. The houses were smoking rubble; the grove of trees had been burned or felled for execution stakes. Only a scar of bare soil and ash was left.

Joffrey had given an order to raise some signal flags to the masthead, and a cutter that had been on course to intercept them steered away and let them pass instead. Nathaway dragged his eyes away from the island to see that they were headed for the flagship *Pragmatic*.

When the *Grey Lady* came up alongside, several officers and a collection of marines were standing on the warship's deck. Joffrey turned to Nathaway and said, "Wait here a moment."

It was not until then that it occurred to Nathaway that Tiarch's Vice-Admiral was in more peril than he, and he said, "I won't turn you in."

Joffrey gave him a slight, condescending smile and said, "Don't you worry about me." He caught hold of the rope ladder the warship had let down, and swung himself nimbly up onto the deck, where he exchanged salutes with the officers and fell into conversation with them. Immediately, two marine officers descended onto the *Grey Lady*'s deck to take charge of Nathaway.

They ushered him up onto the flagship, then stood waiting for further orders. Joffrey had disappeared. Scanning the deck, Nathaway was struck by how clean and orderly it was, how free of blood or pain. One would never know that this was the place from which all the orders had issued.

This time, he had no illusions about how cordial his reception would be. It didn't matter; he was not doing this for himself. He would have to hide his personal feelings, and approach his brother diplomatically. He would be conciliatory and persuasive. His pride was not the issue here.

Eventually, a midshipman came up with instructions for the marines to bring him below. When he entered the great cabin, four Inning officers were sitting around a table where they had just finished a meal, drinking wine. Alongside them at the table sat Joffrey—or yet another version of Joffrey. He was still dressed in his dockhand's smock, but his bearing was completely different. He was painted over with a heavy lacquer of Inningness.

When Corbin looked up, he took in Nathaway's long hair and grey clothes with an expression that made Nathaway feel like he had appeared in public naked.

"So," said Corbin, setting down his wine glass, "have you decided to leave off titillating all the pubescent girls in Fluminos with your sexual adventures among the natives?"

In spite of himself, Nathaway felt his face flushing. "I haven't seen a newspaper, if that's what you mean."

"It's been very entertaining. You fancy yourself quite the romantic hero. So what brings you here?"

Steeling himself, Nathaway said, "I didn't come because I expected you to welcome me."

"That's just as well," Corbin said, his left brow arched to show what an understatement it was.

"I'm here because there is a woman—"

"Ah. I should have known."

Firmly, Nathaway went on, "—a woman who was with the pirate fleet, and whom I need to locate."

Corbin turned to one of the Inning officers. "Have we any female captives?"

The man shrugged. "The native boats were infested with females. Regular floating whorehouses. We've executed a few."

"This one would stand out," Nathaway went on stubbornly. "She is Lashnura. Grey skin, silver hair, young, beautiful. Her name is Spaeth Dobrin."

The name obviously rang a bell with Corbin; he glanced at Joffrey.

"The Onan," Joffrey said.

"Of course. Harg Ismol's concubine." He turned a piercing gaze on Nathaway. "And your native paramour as well. I'm curious how you worked that out. Did you share her, like gentlemen, on alternate nights?"

Ignoring him angrily, Nathaway said, "I wanted to make sure you knew she is far more valuable to you alive than dead. In fact, her captivity might be a decisive factor, as long as you don't harm her."

"How gracious of you to offer us strategic advice. But we do actually have other sources of information."

"Yes, I can see that," Nathaway said, casting a look at Joffrey. The look Joffrey gave him back was cool and cultivated, the very mirror of his Admiral's.

With a deliberate control, Corbin rose from his seat at the table and came around to stand facing Nathaway. His expression had changed; now his face looked carved from flint. Nathaway realized that he had been toying with him up to now.

"I hope you did not come here expecting any special consideration."

"No." Nathaway forced himself to meet his brother's gaze.

"Good. Because I find your actions abhorrent. You have betrayed your country, disgraced your family, and degraded your very race."

The intensity of Corbin's personality was still difficult to face. But this time, Nathaway felt something harden inside him in response. Trying to keep his voice measured, he said, "*I* have disgraced Inning? I'm not the one who has made my country's name another word for butchery and slaughter. I have not defiled every idea of justice our civilization is built on. I have not spread terror or stained our name with savagery. Look at yourself, Corbin. You are the one who has betrayed our country."

Corbin's face froze over as Nathaway was speaking. In a soft, dangerous voice, he said, "How easy it must be to have the privilege of principles. It's only because the nation has men like me to make ugly decisions that men like you can walk around pretending to be blameless."

Nathaway didn't answer. He had already said too much, too truthfully. But he didn't look down, either.

At last the Admiral glanced to the door and ordered, "Guard!"

When the two marines entered, he said, "Put him in the hold with the other prisoners. I'll deal with him later."

Corbin had to resort to force, Nathaway thought, because he couldn't win the battle of conviction.

It had not yet occurred to him how effective force could be.

Over the next two weeks, he learned.

The hold of the *Pragmatic* was a dense jam of prisoners, mostly young Adaina men who would, in due course, be sold as slaves or impressed into service in the Navy. The mass of brown bodies was so close that they slept nearly stacked atop one another, and there was no escaping the constant sensation of skin pressed against sweaty skin. The sanitary facilities consisted of two overflowing buckets, but in the dark crush, most prisoners simply used the floor. Dysentery, lice, and skin eruptions were epidemic; the stench, itch, and misery reduced grown men to mere bundles of nerves.

The fleet set out for Thimish after two days. It took three days of nonstop shelling to reduce Harbourdown to submission. The noise of the cannons on the deck above them was deafening. Sleep, difficult before, became impossible.

At last the guns finally fell silent, and it was clear that Harbourdown had fallen. An orgy of executions would follow. When the marines came below to start thinning out the crowd of prisoners, men pushed away, thinking they were being led to death, and three people were crushed and trampled in the panic.

It was another week before they came looking for Nathaway. When he came forward, filthy and insect-bitten, they put irons on his wrists before leading him up through the warren of dark, narrow stairs and passages. He followed in a daze, feeling as if his head weren't quite attached to his body.

Emerging into the fresh air and sunlight on the open deck was like being reborn. Nathaway breathed in and combed his hair away from his face with his fingers. The ship was anchored in Harbourdown Bay. High on the cliff above, the black bulk of the Redoubt loomed. The town below was still standing, though the damage was visible even from here.

A drum roll called his attention back to the warship. When he saw how the deck was set up, his drowsiness left him. Seven Inning captains in full uniform were seated in a row on the edge of the quarterdeck, behind a long, flag-draped table. In the ship's waist a crowded audience of officers and seamen was assembled. He had seen the setup before. It was the immemorial arrangement for a trial at sea.

To the slow beat of the drum, the marines led him forward to where, below the judges' dais, there stood a large, coffin-shaped block of wood with iron manacles bolted to it at each corner next to the floor. Nathaway's muscles froze when he saw it. He faced the judges and said defiantly, "This is uncivilized. You have no authority to do this to me."

Corbin sat in the middle of the judges. The officer on his right glanced at him; the others were gazing stonily forward or down at the papers before them. Corbin said mechanically, "State your name, please."

"My name is Nathaway—*Justice* Nathaway Talley."

"Put him on the block."

The soldiers forced Nathaway to lie on the block, then pulled his ankles to either side and clamped them into the iron manacles. They forced his arms back till they could fasten his wrists at the other end of the block. Last, they fitted an iron collar around his neck and bolted it down to the surface of the wood. When at last they stepped away he lay uncomfortably spread-eagled before his judges, unable even to raise his head. All he could see was the sky and the masts above him.

"Read the charges, please." Corbin's voice sounded like an icy wind across the silent deck.

There were three charges, couched in complicated phrases. Nathaway's mind was in turmoil, but he grasped the main words: espionage, conspiracy, and treason.

His ears pounded. It was almost impossible to think, lying there like a slab of meat. That was the whole purpose of the block—to humiliate intransigent prisoners and break their will, so they could not defy the court or give false testimony. It was a holdover from uncivilized ancient days. He tried to get a grip on his mind.

The bailiff's voice was still reading accusations. *You did escape from lawful detention. You did reveal vital intelligence to the press. You did aid the enemy by giving them counsel, including legal counsel. You did transmit messages vital to enemy plans. You did make public statements against the interests of the Inning nation.* It was all a tissue of innuendoes that a good defence lawyer could have peppered with holes.

"Prisoner, what is your plea?" Corbin's voice said.

"I deny this court's right of jurisdiction over me," Nathaway said to the sky. His voice sounded husky in his own ears.

"This is not a court," Corbin said. "It is a military tribunal."

"I am a civilian," Nathaway said. "I demand to be tried by a jury of my peers. It is the right of every Inning citizen."

"The Forsaken Islands are under martial law," Corbin replied. "You are subject to military justice."

"Then I assert my right to legal counsel," Nathaway said.

"We can answer any legal questions you might have. But first we need your plea."

Nathaway's face had broken out in a sweat. *Don't submit,* he told himself. *Don't let them break you. If they do this to you, they can do it to anyone. Someone has to stop them.* "You have no right to try me," he said.

"How do you plead?"

"I refuse to answer. This is barbarous. I am an Inning citizen."

Corbin's voice came like a swift slap: "You should have thought of that before you committed treason."

Even in his state of confusion, Nathaway realized that the mask of impartial justice had just slipped.

Corbin was back in control of his voice almost as swiftly as he had slipped. "We cannot proceed till you enter a plea. I must warn you, your continued refusal will be held as contempt of court. We can compel your cooperation."

Nathaway clenched his teeth and stayed silent. He could hear the judges conversing with each other in low tones. At last Corbin gave an order, and the soldiers came forward to unshackle him from the block and pull him upright to face the panel.

The judges had all risen to their feet. Corbin said, "Nathaway Talley, you have been found in contempt of court. You are sentenced to receive fifteen lashes on your bare back, to be repeated daily until such time as you submit to the jurisdiction of this tribunal. Officers, please carry out the sentence."

They seized him by the arms and turned him round to watch as a team of seamen cleared an area around the foremast to set up a wooden framework to carry out the punishment. Nathaway watched, uncomprehending. He couldn't believe they were serious. The law was a long, deliberative process, full of opportunities for delay and reflection. This precipitous action was completely foreign to its spirit. He waited for someone to speak up, to intervene.

The drum gave another roll, and to its slow ceremonial cadence, the soldiers led Nathaway forward. A dark-bearded, muscled man was shaking out the whip. It was a cruel-looking instrument with multiple knotted lashes, designed to inflict half a dozen wounds at every blow. The man holding it grinned brutally at the expression of horror on Nathaway's face. It was clear he was looking forward to the novelty of flogging an Inning.

"Take off your shirt," the marine officer said. Nathaway's disbelief was slowly turning to outrage. They expected him to lose his nerve and give in, intimidated by their apparent willingness to execute the sentence. He could feel Corbin's gaze at his back, and a stubborn determination took hold of him. He took off his glasses and handed them to the marine, then pulled his shirt over his head. There was a murmur from the watching Adaina seamen when they saw the green stone pendant around his neck. The marine gestured for him to take it off, but he put his hand over it, saying, "I'd prefer to keep it."

"Suit yourself," the marine shrugged.

Another soldier came forward to fasten his wrists to the frame with leather straps. There was a pause then, as they waited for him to recant. He stood straight, full of pride and defiance, and said nothing. His eyes were fixed on a seagull wheeling overhead.

"Proceed," Corbin said.

The first blow knocked the breath out of him and buckled his knees; he would have fallen forward if he hadn't been fastened up. Before he could quite collect himself, the second blow came, even more ferocious than the first. He had imagined that he would be able to react with stoic nobility, but there was no possibility of control under such a battering. He was an object, not a will.

He tried to count, but lost track as the lashes cut into his skin, raising stinging welts that finally broke and bled. His body was acting on its own, his back arching away from the pain, his lungs gasping and grunting. When it ceased, he was hanging limply from his wrists, and the deck around him was spattered with droplets of blood. As the soldier stepped forward to release him and help him stand, a surge of mad defiance gave him strength to stand and face the judges.

Corbin said, "Prisoner, what is your plea?"

"You have no jurisdiction," Nathaway said hoarsely.

"Take him below," Corbin said dispassionately. "We will reconvene at the same time tomorrow."

The marines took him to the ship's small infirmary. The surgeon was an Inning, and seemed angry as he inspected Nathaway's wounds, but would utter not a word of sympathy. He did at least insist that his patient remain in a berth in the infirmary rather than return to the fetid hold.

The next morning, Nathaway woke almost unable to move. He felt bruised all over, and the slightest motion set off such a fiery pain that his eyes watered and his breath came in gasps. Nevertheless, they came for him again at the same time, marching him up onto the deck to face the seven judges and the witnessing crowd.

"Prisoner, what is your plea?" Corbin addressed him.

"I deny your jurisdiction," Nathaway said. "I obey only the law."

"Very well," Corbin said. "Carry out the sentence."

Nathaway wasn't able to remove his own shirt this time, and the marine had to help him. As they fastened his wrists to the framework again, he was shaking like a leaf, but his mind was grimly focused on not submitting to his body's needs. When the whip struck his back again, his voice cried out, but not to beg or give in.

He spent the rest of the day in a delirium of pain. He had a fever, which the doctor tried to bring down with cold drinks and compresses. Toward sunset, he was roused by the arrival in the infirmary of one of the Inning officers from the panel of judges. The surgeon helped him sit up while the captain stood looking down at him with an expression of angry frustration.

"For God's sake, what do you think you're proving?" the man said.

Nathaway's throat was parched, and his voice was barely a croak. "Someone's got to check him. What he does here today, he'll do back home tomorrow. He's proving that."

"You don't understand," the man said. "His authority is absolute here. There is nothing anyone else can do to help you. You've got to give in."

"He has no authority over me," Nathaway said. "My sovereign is the law."

"You're insane, the both of you," the captain said in frustration. "Take it from me, he's not going to blink first. I know him. He's the stubbornest man alive."

"No, he's not," Nathaway said.

That night was sleepless. Nathaway floated on a lake of pain as the slow moments passed. When dawn was drawing near, he reached a strange state of acquiescence. The individual will inside him relaxed into the embrace of the suffering that was coming with the daylight. In that dark moment he abandoned himself into its power, its inevitability.

There was a serene madness about him when he faced the judges the next morning. Their faces were full of horror and pity; they couldn't meet his eyes. Only Corbin still looked untouched.

"Prisoner, how do you plead?" he asked.

"I deny your jurisdiction," Nathaway said.

The scene before him was disappearing in black spots as they led him to the foremast, and he lost track of his feet once and stumbled. Implacably, they fastened his wrists to the framework once again. The Adainas were watching in something close to reverence. When Corbin gave the signal, the whip struck him, and all the external world disappeared into the pain. Once again he was trapped inside his mutilated body. All he could do was surrender.

He became aware of cessation. His wrists were still bound, he was still before the foremast, but someone had called a halt. Booted footsteps were approaching. He turned his head to see his brother standing next to him, looking into his face.

"For God's sake," Corbin said in a low, intense voice. "Are you prepared to die just to make your point?"

"Are you prepared to kill me just to make yours?" Nathaway said.

Their eyes met for several seconds then, and Nathaway had a hallucinatory vision that he wasn't even the true target of Corbin's anger. He was a substitute for someone else, someone very like Corbin himself. They were so alike.

And then Corbin said, "Take him below."

When they unfastened his wrists, Nathaway's legs collapsed under him. He could no longer stand up, and they had to fetch a stretcher to carry him away.

But he had won.

13
THE LASHNURA SOLUTION

The women had all been crowded onto a single prison ship by the time they came looking for Spaeth. It was the third ship she had been on. The captives in the hold had staked out territories that they defended against interlopers— little spots of deck that they controlled. Spaeth had been one of the last to arrive, so hers was a cramped spot amidship, yielded to her by two Adaina women in deference to her race.

The first time the Tornas came searching through the hold with a lantern, asking for any Lashnura females aboard, the other women helped her cover her hair and smudge her face with dirt to hide her identity. But the second time, the searchers were more thorough. One of them spat on his thumb and rubbed it on her cheek to uncover the colour of her skin. They seized her by the arm then, and propelled her up the gangway till they reached an upper deck. One of the Tornas knocked on a door, then looked in. "We found one, sir," he reported.

They pushed her into the cabin then. Two men were inside, chatting. One of them rose when he saw her. "Yes, that's her," he said with satisfaction. "At last."

It was Tiarch's man, Joffrey, but dressed in an Inning uniform. "Joffrey, have you defected?" she said.

He gave a small, tight smile. "No. I've always been on the same side."

Whatever side was winning, she thought.

He turned to the ship's captain. "Have her delivered to me in the Redoubt by sunset."

"Very well."

They carried her through Harbourdown in an open cart with her wrists and ankles chained, so the people would see her and know their subjugation. But the only emotion she saw in the streets was fury at the Innings' disrespect. She met the onlookers' eyes to encourage them, and to show that she was neither humiliated nor intimidated.

In the courtyard of the Redoubt, they unchained her ankles to walk her into the building where the commandant's office lay, the door guarded by a marine. Joffrey met them on the doorstep, buttoning his uniform coat. He asked the guard, "What mood is he in?" The man shrugged and made a teetering balance motion with his hand. "Well, this will cheer him up," Joffrey said. Briskly, he knocked on the door, and after a second, opened it and went in. The guard gestured Spaeth to follow.

The room inside was one of worn luxury: a badly trampled red carpet, faded drapes, and once-elegant furniture now scarred by hard use. A lean, grey-haired Inning sat alone in one of the chairs, staring into the empty fireplace. He was not wearing a uniform, but was dressed in unassuming civilian clothes covered with a knee-length brocade jacket. When Joffrey cleared his throat and said, "Sir?" he looked up with an indifferent expression.

"Admiral, I told you I found the woman we had been searching for, Onan Spaeth," Joffrey said. "I thought you would like to see her."

Spaeth realized that she was in the presence of a monster. For that was who this man must be—the commander who had instigated such unspeakable slaughter in the South Chain. Her first reaction was shock at the striking resemblance to Nathaway. But when he looked at her, that impression faded. Nathaway's eyes were always expressive, always engaged in what they saw. This man's were remote, detached, and weary. Weary of conquest, weary of dominion, weary even of himself. The evils they had seen were still there, still with him, but as mere data, without moral weight.

Then, as she watched, his shoulders straightened with self-discipline, and it was like a metal door closed between her and his mind.

"Bring her here," he said.

Spaeth didn't want to get any closer, and Joffrey had to push her forward with a hand on the small of her back. The Admiral noticed her reluctance. "Do you fear me?" he asked mildly.

It wasn't fear she felt. It was more like revulsion. But all she said was, "No."

"Perhaps you ought to," he said. "I have a great many reasons to use you harshly."

Despite his words, there was no animosity in his voice. She said, "You don't hate me."

"No."

"How could you harm someone you don't hate?"

He gave her a slight, ironic smile. "It's my job."

She realized she had been thinking as a Lashnura, as if she were in a righteous world, a world of mora. But she was dealing with an Inning no one could touch, not even the Mundua. He was accountable to nothing.

He continued to watch her from behind his gold-rimmed spectacles, his chin resting on his fingers. At last he said to Joffrey, "She *is* quite lovely, isn't she? He wasn't lying about that." He had the detached tone of a connoisseur appraising an artwork. "What do you make of her, Joffrey?"

"Make of her, sir?" Joffrey said cautiously.

"Have you questioned her?"

"No, not yet. What would you like to know?"

With a slight, restless frown, Talley said, "How she did it. No, *why* she did it. I had expected a schemer, a seductress, someone with the wiles to manoeuvre her way into the beds of the most powerful men of two nations. She seems remarkably young and artless for what she's achieved."

Spaeth pressed her lips together, determined not to react.

"My brother was here looking for you, did you know that?" Talley said.

For a moment she felt a stab of alarm. But surely Nathaway would have nothing to fear; he was Inning, and the Admiral's brother. "No," she said, "I didn't know."

"I'm curious why you fastened onto him. Was it for power? Hedging your bets, perhaps, like Joffrey here? Or was he just an irresistible target because he would succumb so easily?"

Her true feelings were too tender to expose before this evil man. With dignity, she said, "We are bandhotai. I love him. He loves me. We always will. Nothing you can do will change that."

He looked unaccountably annoyed at this answer. "You disappoint me," he said. "I had hoped you were more than just an innocent dupe of this ritual whoredom they call dhota."

In spite of herself, Spaeth felt stung. "Dhota has nothing to do with whoredom," she said. "It has to do with love."

"So I have been told," he said. "It's all about love. The great weakness of the Lashnura."

"Love is not our weakness. It is our strength. You can never understand us till you understand that."

"I know the Grey Folk rather better than you think," he said, watching her critically. "You've convinced yourselves you are above common morality. You hide your appetites under a veil of holy compulsion."

"You're wrong," Spaeth said. "We hide nothing."

"It's not sanctity, it's hypocrisy—an excuse to indulge yourselves in weakness. To destroy yourselves, even."

She saw the pain in him then, flashing out bright and brief as a lighthouse beacon. Its intensity took her breath away. She took a step backward, suddenly afraid—not of him, but of herself, of the way her heart was throbbing, her fingers tingling to touch him. She clenched her fists.

He also appeared to have felt something, because he rose from his chair and turned his back to her. When he turned back, his voice was controlled again. "Well, it will all end soon," he said. "Your peculiar morality will give way to Inning law."

Looking to Joffrey, he said, "How do you propose we should use her?"

"Display her," Joffrey said ruthlessly. "Make her captivity public. The Isles must know we hold the Onan, and rule her. Just think, sir, you hold in your hands the thing your two greatest enemies value and desire more than anything in the world. Think how that thought will torment them."

Talley was watching Joffrey with a morbid fascination. There was a short silence, in which the Admiral looked down at his hands, then pensively up and away from them both. "You enjoy being yourself, do you, Joffrey?" he said, as if it were merely a conversation opener.

Joffrey appeared to be trying to guess the right answer. Talley shook his head and said, "Never mind. Put her somewhere safe till I've decided what I want from her. For God's sake clean her up, and give her some decent clothes. Give her the room next to the other Lashnura captive."

"Yes, sir." Joffrey took Spaeth by the arm and started to pull her toward the door. She refused to move.

"Is Goth here?" she said.

The Admiral looked at her reluctantly. "Yes, for the time being," he said.

"May I see him?"

"You want that?"

"Yes. Please. It is important."

"I will consider it," he said.

It was all she was going to get from him now. She allowed Joffrey to lead her out. When they were on the doorstep again, he looked at her appraisingly, as if he had learned more from the interview than he had expected. She looked away, unwilling to see her own reflection in his mind.

He took her into one of the stone buildings that ringed the fort's parade ground, and up to the second floor. They walked down a long hall, past a door with a ribbon and medal hung on it like a marker—the Admiral's bedroom, Spaeth guessed—then past another door and around a corner. At last Joffrey ushered her into a room, then closed and locked the door.

The room was chilly and threadbare in a no-nonsense, military way—just a rope bed, table, and fireplace. There was a window looking out onto the parade ground, and Spaeth crossed to look out of it. It was not barred, but was directly above a door where a guard was stationed.

Over the next day, the room was transformed by the regular arrival of deliveries—first a tin bathtub and firewood, then towels, bedding, toiletries, rugs, clothes, and a dozen other amenities to improve her confinement. She saw nothing of whoever was directing it all.

All the while she was being pampered by unseen hands, the forced inactivity brought back the ache of unhealed wounds inside her, which danger and discomfort had allowed her to ignore. The thought that Goth was close by tantalized her. More than ever now she longed to see him, and ask him what to do. She even harboured a secret hope that he could help her. How gladly he would take on some of this pain.

In the meantime, all she could do to distract herself was watch the constant activity in the yard below. All day long soldiers drilled and crates of supplies were stacked onto wagons for transport down to the ships. There was a sense of gathering power in the Redoubt, as if a huge spring were being wound tight, ratchet tooth by ratchet tooth. The realization came to her that Admiral Talley was done with playing at war. Now he was preparing to end it all with a brutal blow.

It was late afternoon on the third day when she heard a door closing down the hallway, followed by a low-toned conversation. She went to the door to overhear, but could make out no words. At last the exchange ended, and footsteps approached her door. She stepped away as a key rattled in the lock.

When Admiral Talley entered the room, she took another instinctive step back. He closed the door behind him and stood with his back against it, arms crossed. He had seen her recoil, and was nettled by it.

"Have they made you comfortable?" he asked.

"Yes," she answered warily.

"Is there anything you require?"

"Freedom," she said.

"I'll take that to mean no."

She was silent.

He glanced around the room, but his eyes were drawn back to her. For a while he studied her, and she studied him back. There was something restless about him, distracted.

"We're going to be leaving this place in three days," he said at last. "You will be travelling on the *Pragmatic*."

"Where are we going?"

He hesitated a moment, then said, "Lashnish. It's where I always intended to go, and I'm not inclined to change just because Harg Ismol wants to draw me away."

She felt a flare of interest. Harg's name seemed to burn bright and vivid on the air. "Do you have news? What has he done?"

"Captured Tornabay." He said it dismissively, but she knew better. She felt a slow glow of pride. Once again, Harg had humiliated the mighty Inning Navy.

"That pleases you, does it?" Talley said. "Actually, it has very little tactical significance, as long as we don't overreact. The main consequence is that it puts me under some time pressure to end this, before the cutting of our supply line becomes important."

For a moment he was preoccupied with other thoughts and calculations. Half to himself, he said, "I rarely misjudge an opponent as badly as I have misjudged him. I felt so sure he would act out of loyalty and passion, and come after me. Instead, he did just as I would have done. He saw the strategic weakness and acted on it, like an Inning."

He looked up at her. Despite his relaxed tone, his body was tense. "I wish I knew what he is willing to defend."

He was fishing for information. She clamped her lips tight.

"You, perhaps?" he said. "Would he be willing to defend you?"

He was watching her speculatively. At that look, she felt a chill of apprehension—not for herself, but for Harg. For she held his future. If ever he were to be freed from pain, it was she who must do it. She was his only hope for an uncrippled life, and now Corbin Talley controlled her.

Talley had seen something in her face, and now he came forward till he stood close enough to touch her. She fought not to flinch away. His face was complex with conflicting thoughts. He took her hand, holding it in one of his and running the fingers of the other lightly across her smooth grey skin.

She could almost feel the blood on his hands. And yet, with the touch, awareness of him flooded into her. He was not trying to be seductive. No, he honestly assumed she loathed him, and was enduring his touch only through fear. In fact, he would have been bitterly sceptical of any claim to the contrary. In all his adult life, there had only been one profession of love or loyalty he had believed, and that one only reluctantly. It had a terrible hold on him.

"Goth," she whispered.

He stiffened at the name, and let her hand drop. "What?" he said.

"I see him in you," she said.

"No, you don't."

"Yes," she insisted. "You are bound to him."

"Only in the way an executioner is bound to his victim." A flare of self-hatred lit his eyes. "I have destroyed him. It was laughably easy. He was like a foolish, loving dog that takes poison and then licks its killer's hand." He paused, his face hard. "You wanted to see him."

"Yes!"

"All right," he said. "Take a look at him. See what I've made of him."

Abruptly he turned and opened the door for her, then led her down the hall to the next room. He took a key from his pocket and opened the door. "Go in," he said.

She had expected him to follow her in, but he didn't. He closed the door behind her and turned the lock between them. Apparently, this was a scene he did not want to witness.

The room was on a corner of the building with windows facing south and west, lit now by the setting sun. Down the coast, beyond the black mass of Thimish, a piled-up rumple of clouds glowed magenta. She stood by the door, and watched the form silhouetted against the western sky.

He was standing pressed against the window, palms outstretched, as if he might merge with the glass and, like it, welcome in the fading light.

"Goth," Spaeth said. He did not move.

"Goth!" She crossed the room to look into his face.

The sight shocked her. He was emaciated, and his hair had thinned to a mere wisp on his skull. He looked like an ancient relic, so fragile a touch might dissolve him into dust.

His sunken eyes were open, the pupils dilated so wide there was almost no iris left. A radiant smile was on his face. He reached out to cup a sunbeam in his hands. The light gathered there till it formed a tiny sunball. He lifted it to his face to smell it, like a flower. His cradled hands glowed, translucent; the grey filigree of bone showed clearly. Then, with a quick motion, he tossed the light into the air; it flew upward and dissolved.

Spaeth reached out to touch his face, saying his name again. There was no recognition in his eyes.

"It's all so little," he whispered. "Such a great heap of little things."

She barely existed for him any more. Tears stung her eyes: he was her first, most precious love. All that had happened, all the time they had been apart, seemed to have disappeared, leaving her like a child again. She put her arms around him and drew him close, very gentle, for it seemed like his bones might snap with a careless touch. For a moment she feared that the pain of her need would harm him.

Hesitantly, uncertainly, his arms closed around her. "Spaeth?" he said. "Is it you?"

"Yes, it's me," she said.

"I was very far away."

"I could tell."

"I can't stay with you long. I am almost free."

She drew back to look at him. His face looked like a translucent shell before a bright flame inside him. "Free?" she said. "You want to be free of me?"

He drew in a quick breath. "I have hurt you," he said. "I am sorry." But even as he looked at her, the focus of his eyes shifted, and she sensed he was looking at something else, something brighter and more absorbing than she. "I won't be parted from you, you know," he said. "I will be with you. I will be with all my bandhotai—closer to them than ever. No barriers, Spaeth—none at all!" He smiled with a bright elation.

Something was using him as fuel. Spaeth realized that this was what Talley had intended her to see. "What has happened to you, Goth?" she said.

He struggled to concentrate on putting it in words. "You know how many people I have loved in my life. I cherished them each for their own pasts, their own pains. That was what blinded me. It was really the same thing I loved in all of them. But in people the good is finite, bounded by their individuality. There is an infinite aspect of that good. It is immense. Touching it is like being bandhota to all the world. All of it, Spaeth! The trees, the seas, the air. All the thorny people, all their conflicts and confusion. I feel as if my blood has rained over the Isles."

The euphoria made him seem almost more than human for a moment, then left him drained. He wavered, and she caught him. Carefully she led him to a chair, where he sank exhausted. As his head lolled back she glimpsed something on his limp arm and pushed back his sleeve. The skin was pockmarked with tiny cuts, and there were four fresh slivers of achra under his skin. Horrified, she checked his other arm. There were three more slivers in it. There was enough drug in him to kill two people.

She sat back on her heels, staring at him. She had been given an explanation that explained nothing.

It was laughably easy to destroy him, Admiral Talley had said. So this was what he had meant. She saw now that there was a door leading into the adjoining chamber, Talley's chamber. She crossed the room to try it, but it was locked. When she turned back, Goth's eyes were open, following her wearily. This time he looked barely lucid.

"Admiral Talley did this to you, didn't he?" Spaeth said.

Goth smiled faintly. "He comes through that door to watch me, and lecture me. Not long ago he threatened to take the achra away, but he knows by now it would kill me. I have escaped him, you see." He looked a little pleased with himself.

Spaeth felt a dark, consuming rage. A rage at the universe that such people as Corbin Talley should be permitted to exist. She came back to Goth's side. "I will find a way to punish him," she said.

He scarcely seemed to hear. He was still staring at the door, his smile gone. "He has been my hardest test," he said. He closed his eyes and drew an uneven breath. "How I longed to cure him! But it would have captured me again, snared me in individual love."

"Love!" Spaeth nearly spat the word. "How could you love a man like that?" Her rage now encompassed Goth as well. He was as weak as ever.

"Oh, it's very easy," he said. "Wait until you see him."

"I *have* seen him. He makes me feel unclean."

Goth searched her face. "Didn't you see the pain in him?"

"It doesn't matter. We're in an Inning world now," she said. "There is no balance here; mora is unravelling before them. Dhota has no power for them, or meaning."

She had finally roused him to full attention. "No, Spaeth!" he said. "Dhota *does* have power over the Innings. Its power may be different for them than for us. There is no telling how it will manifest itself in the Inning mind. But dhota will emerge again, just as powerful, though transformed. It is the solution."

He had exhausted himself again, and fell back in the chair. Spaeth sat watching him. By now, the western sky was flaming carnelian and rose. The colours played on his ruined face, giving it a false glow of health. He was using up his physical being fast. Her anger transmuted into sharp grief, she knelt beside his chair and put her arms around him, resting her head on his shoulder. She wanted to stay that way forever.

A shudder passed through his frame. "No," he whispered, barely audible. "Don't call me back. I can almost see it."

She forced herself to draw away from him. His eyes were closed, though she could see them moving under the lids. His breathing was fast and shallow. The light was growing on his face.

His eyes snapped open; the dilated pupils made them look almost black. He turned to the window, where the horizon glowed bright with the dying sun. "Look at it!" he said, transfixed by the sight.

"Yes," Spaeth said. "Sunset."

Goth struggled from his chair and approached the window as if something wondrous lay out there. He pressed a hand against the pane. "You see? You see?" he said.

"See what?"

"The world out there. The whole world is permeated with love."

The edge of the sun touched the sea. Excitedly, Goth fumbled at the fastenings of the robe he wore. It dropped around his feet and he stood naked, a mere skeleton, outlined against the window. He pressed against the glass as when Spaeth had first entered.

The sunlight shone through him as through frosted glass; Spaeth could see his bones, and all the milky membranes of his body. As the light fell on him the obstructions in his body seemed to react. One by one they dissolved into clear water, till at last he was transparent as glass, a mere medium of light.

The sun sank below the horizon, and suddenly Goth was there again, opaque as before. He staggered back, then collapsed onto the carpet. When Spaeth got to him he was unconscious. She put an arm under his shoulders and found he was light as a wickerwork image of a man. She picked him up and took him to the bed. He did not stir as she spread blankets over him.

He was far away from her now, she knew. Either lost in drugged delusion or—or what? She was still wondering what she had witnessed when she looked up and found Corbin Talley standing in the doorway that led to his chamber, watching her.

When Spaeth did not speak, he looked at Goth and said in a metallic voice, "He is dying."

She wondered if he had come to enjoy the sight of her pain. She resolved not to let him see it.

"Let me stay with him," she said.

"You can do nothing."

"I can make sure he doesn't die among enemies."

In another person she might have thought the glance he gave her was resentment. But then he shrugged and came forward. "Very well." He held out a small bottle filled with white slivers. "Let him have this when he wakes."

She looked at the bottle with hatred, then up at him. Their eyes clashed.

"He'll die if he doesn't have it," Talley said.

"He'll die if he does."

"Yes. He will die, regardless." His voice was strictly controlled, but there was a complex undertone in it—a trace of helpless outrage? Was he capable of regret for something that had gotten beyond his control?

Reluctantly, Spaeth took the bottle and placed it on the stand beside the bed. She looked back, expecting Talley to be smiling in triumph at having gotten her complicity. But he was not even looking at her. He was staring down at Goth as if something in him were being slowly impaled.

He turned away before Spaeth had more than a glance; but it left her shaken. She had to clench her control tight to keep from calling him back as he left the room, locking the door behind him. She looked down at Goth. There was a slight smile on his face, as if, from wherever he was, he had witnessed what had just happened.

✌

It was late night when sounds from the next room told her that the Admiral had returned. She sat waiting, watching the door, expecting him. But the sounds died away, and she realized he was not going to come.

She rose and went soundlessly to the door. She laid her ear against the wood, but heard nothing. Carefully she tried the knob, but the door was locked.

She stood in the dark room, and every word Goth had said was vivid in her mind. *How I longed to cure him! Didn't you see his pain? Dhota is the solution.*

Goth was deluded, she thought. And yet, as the thought he had placed in her mind crystallized, the tug of instinct grew strong. The answer was so close. Only a locked door away.

She faced the door, trying to still her mind. It was a locked door in this circle, but it could not be in all.

For a long time she thought her mind was too present to let her enter another circle; she needed some dreamweed. All she had was a nonsense phrase

Goth had taught her once; she repeated it over and over to herself, like a chant.

The world slowed. She let herself sink deeper. The chant was spinning in her head, growing, surrounding her. For an instant the carpet felt wet under her feet; then it was just carpet again. She rode her own breath like a wave, then dove.

Something brushed her face. She opened her eyes to a nightlit jungle, dense with foliage. A tiny, coral-eyed snake dripped from a branch above her; she pulled back and found that her limbs were twined round with creepers and vines. She tugged to get free. The creepers broke with little popping sounds, then the stubs snaked forward to wrap around her again. She had to move. Her feet splashed in black water that sent up a vegetable stench.

Where was the doorway? The sweating undergrowth blocked her sight in every direction. She heard a rustle behind her, and whipped around. Two predatory eyes glowed through the forest.

Then she saw the doorway, a threshold of teeth with ivory fangs on either side. She gathered her mind, stepped between the teeth, and dropped like a stone back into her own circle.

She landed with a thud on her knees. She was in a short passageway with the locked door at her back. A faint light filtered in from the room ahead, and for a moment she thought Admiral Talley was still awake. But as she listened, scarcely daring to breathe, not a sound came from the room. Cautiously she crept forward.

It was a curiously spartan room for the commander of all Inning forces in the Forsakens: a bed, a washstand, a desk, and a table where a dim oil lamp glowed. She wondered what sorts of ghosts the light was meant to keep away.

He was lying on his back, the sheet pushed restlessly down. His head was turned to one side and his right arm was raised as if to ward off a blow. His face had an expression of strain even in sleep.

Spaeth crossed silently to the washstand. There she found all she needed: a razor, a basin, and a white cravat. Without a sound she sliced open a vein and let the blood drip into the basin. When she had enough, she bandaged her arm with the cravat, pulling it tight with her teeth.

She brought the basin to his bedside and knelt there, trying to calm her nerves. Looking down on him as he slept, she knew he would prefer her to slit his throat with the razor than to do what she intended.

She dipped her fingers into the blood and, barely breathing, let three drops fall on his temple. The muscles around his eyes contracted slightly, and for a desperate moment she thought he was going to wake. She waited, but nothing more happened. Slowly she let more drops fall, this time below his ear; then on his exposed throat, then on his chest above his heart.

As the blood turned clear and soaked in, she felt his mind drift free of its moorings, relaxed and open. Spaeth had never entered a sleeping mind before; no moral dhotamar would. She made her own mind float, infinitely light, then settled with a mere feather's touch upon him.

Even asleep, even with the blood, he tensed when her mind touched his. She rested there, radiating calm and quiet, till his guard slowly relaxed. Her instinct had been right; awake, he would have resisted this strongly.

She sent his conscious mind deeper and deeper into sleep. His muscles relaxed and his breathing slowed; he had been semi-alert even in slumber. When there was no longer danger of him waking, Spaeth dipped her hand in the blood again and rubbed it on his temples, throat, and wrists. His breathing changed, and she stopped for a moment to sink his mind even deeper into unconsciousness.

She stood then to gather her energy. She was already tired, and the hard part lay ahead. She looked down at his pale body lying there, completely vulnerable, and a thrill of anticipation passed through her. She could not yet see where his wounds were lodged, as she had in Harg; in the dim lamplight his body was perfect, untouched.

Softly, with enormous care, she sat down beside him on the bed. His heart was speeding up, as if some part of him sensed his danger. She rested a hand on his chest, over the heart, to calm it. The feel of his skin increased her yearning to such a pitch that she could wait no longer.

She merged into his sleeping mind as if she were a dream. It was a strange landscape she found there: cold and unyielding to her exploring touch. His conscious mind was an abstract construction, scarcely even connected to his body. There was no entry there for her. She turned away from it, searching for a way further in.

Everything around her was paved over with discipline. She ran her hand lightly up his thigh, hoping it would soften his mind to her; but he only tensed like a steel trap, denying himself pleasure, controlling his instinct.

She rested inside him then, searching for any flaw, any crack in his sterile perfection. She noticed Goth's presence, surrounded by a hard unfeeling shell. And yet there were fresh scars around it. As she began to blend with that portion of him, an aspect of Corbin Talley was suddenly with her, as if to bar her way. She put her arms around him and they sank together into his past.

It rushed into her so suddenly, and so painfully, that every muscle in her went rigid and her mouth opened in a soundless cry. Talley was struggling in her arms, trying to escape; she held him there, forcing him to stay and feel it all.

They were in a new landscape now, one he had barred off and buried. Here he was not the brittle, flawless man he had constructed. He was a child, thirteen years old, proud and intensely private, consigned into a world whose coarseness and brutality was unimaginable to his parents. Nor had they ever suspected, since shame had kept him silent. He had endured months of terror and despair until he had realized he was only going to survive if he made himself harder and more malicious, colder and more cunning than anyone around him.

His body was stiff in her arms. She pressed him close against her, and stroked his sweaty back to calm him. His body no longer seemed perfect. Everywhere there were wounds, hidden in deep recesses, pooling like blood inside him. He was mutilated, shattered—yet somehow miraculously knit back together in the shape of a man.

She led him back into his past. The memories were excruciatingly vivid. She stood in his young body, in a bare room. He despised the man standing over him—an officer, but a corrupt creature with an appetite for sadism. Corbin had vowed not to let the man see him bend in any way. He was silent as two older boys fastened him face down on the wooden block, and silent as the cane came down with a crack against his buttocks. Spaeth jerked as it bit into her skin, stunning the breath out of her. Still he was silent as the cane came down harder and harder. The tears were running down Spaeth's face, but not his. Ten times the cane fell. The pain was intense. Fifteen times. His torturer was not pausing. He realized then that it would just go on and on till he wept and begged. And not a soul in the world would care. Something in him broke then, and he sobbed and debased himself, until the man was satisfied that his pride was broken. Afterwards, the pain of the beating went away, but his loathing for his own abject surrender stayed.

Then the scene changed to the next winter, when he arrived home for the holidays, and his mother came out to meet him, a baby in her arms. He ignored her coldly, and in the following day met every little mark of affection with grim contempt. That night he made himself sit naked in his room, with the windows open on the snowy rooftops, in order to teach himself to feel nothing.

He had learned to live, even to excel, in a world where he had been ostracized as an interloper, suspected and disdained. Never had he been one of the tight club of officers. Only the horrors of the Rothur campaign had made him indispensable, and by then he had learned to use other people, not to expect their liking or loyalty.

Now that he was started, his unconscious mind was eager to break its isolation, to feed her with himself. He pulled her close, and his yearning merged with hers, intensifying. They loved each other like addicts now. He loved her for suffering with him, with years of thwarted passion. She could feel the desperate rush of air in his lungs, the labouring of his heart, and feared she could kill him by going too far. But he was too aroused now to stop.

One last time she sank into him, reaching as deep as she could. She touched something then, so buried the scar tissue around it was almost as old as he. But it was not a wound. With wonder, she saw it was an image of himself that he had exiled from his mind: the person he had once wanted to become. When she touched it, he sat bolt upright in the bed with a strangled cry. She tried to lull him back to sleep, but he was fighting her now, struggling upward to consciousness. He looked at her, and saw who she was, and gave a sound like an animal in torment.

Someone was rapping on the door. "Sir? Are you all right?" the guard called.

Talley tried to struggle out of bed, and upset the basin, splashing blood across the floor. The sound brought the guard into the room. "Holy Alta!" he said, then seized Spaeth's arm and dragged her away. She cried out in agony, for she was bound to Corbin now in a dozen places.

He was doubled over, gagging. Footsteps pounded down the hall. "Fetch the doctor, quick!" the guard shouted, his voice high and panicky. Another soldier arrived at the door and exclaimed in horror, then disappeared, shouting to someone else, "Assassin! She tried to kill the Admiral!"

"Let me go to him!" Spaeth pleaded, struggling. It hurt worse than she had remembered. "Can't you see he's in pain?"

An Inning officer in a nightshirt appeared, and went to Talley's side. "Sir! Are you hurt?"

Talley raised his head. His face looked ashen. He turned to Spaeth as if she had stepped out of a nightmare into his room. "What did you do to me?" he whispered.

"You can be free of it all," she said. "All those things that have hurt you. Let me take the pain away. Please, do it quickly."

"Good God!" the other Inning said. He was staring at the basin of blood.

"It's my blood, not his!" Spaeth said.

The officer said, "Some sort of witchcraft. Get her out of here."

"No!" Spaeth screamed.

"No!" Talley said, almost involuntarily. He struggled to his feet, shaking violently. The other officer snatched up a blanket and wrapped it around him.

"Let me touch him!" Spaeth cried. "Please, I swear I'll do him no harm. He'll go mad if you don't let me cure him."

The others looked to Talley. He was staring at Spaeth as if he were remembering it all now, and recoiling in horror at the violation of his most intimate being. Spaeth felt an icy hand close around her heart.

"There was no other way," she said. "I had to do it, or you would have gone on uncured. But the dhota isn't finished. I can't truly cure you unless you let me."

In a steely voice Talley said, "There is nothing wrong with me."

Spaeth stood motionless, stunned.

"What did she do?" the other Inning said.

"Dreams," Talley answered. "Just dreams."

The doctor arrived at the door, a valise under his arm.

"Get out of here!" Talley shouted furiously. "She didn't do a thing to me." He wheeled around on the guard. "You, get this mess cleaned up. I'll be in my office." He paused, his eyes on Spaeth. "And take her away. Lock her up where she can't get loose. Throw away the goddamned key."

He pushed past them all out the door. Spaeth felt the bonds between them stretching tight, then stretching again, agonizingly. Her legs gave way as the room swam in bright pinwheels. Somewhere out in the hall, she knew, Talley was doubled over in pain himself.

Then rough hands were wrenching her to her feet and forcing her away from him.

THE LAST DEFENCE

From the walls of Tornabay palace, Harg could see the blackened patches where the city had burned, like scabs on the hillside. The riots, and the fires that followed them, had raged worst in the Adaina sections, the steep ramshackle slums where the buildings were only wood. Even now some plumes of smoke rose, though it was probably only people burning off the trash.

It had taken them five days to get control of the city. When the commanders of the three prongs of the attack—Drome, Jearl, and Harg—had finally met in the Gallowmarket, the populace had welcomed them gratefully as an antidote to chaos. On an impulse, Harg had taken an axe and chopped down the grisly stake the Innings had left standing there. It hadn't been a promise, just a venting of black anger. But he had learned since then that every act was symbolic if an Ison did it.

He had had to be half a dozen people in the following weeks. Harg the Adaina hero riding through the streets to assure the poor it wasn't just Tiarch back again; Harg the conciliator meeting with the merchants to assure them it was; Harg the Ison, Harg the fellow soldier—all of them battling to conceal that other Harg, the one the Mundua and Ashwin wanted for their own. So far, that Harg was hidden, except to himself.

By military measures, the expedition had been a success; but it had so far failed in its main objective, drawing the Innings away from the South Chain. Talley had not risen to the bait. That didn't make control of Tornabay useless, but Harg saw now that it would be a bigger drain on resources than he had anticipated, and the benefits would take time to have an effect.

There were voices behind him; he glanced back to see Gill and Jearl talking. With the intuition of inner tension, he knew it was bad news.

"What is it?" he said expressionlessly when they came up.

They exchanged glances, and Gill cleared his throat. "Holby Dorn attacked the Inning fleet just south of Yora."

At first it made no sense. "Attacked them outright?" he asked.

"Yes."

He didn't want to hear any more. "Go on," he said.

"Word is, it was a bloodbath. The *Vagabond* was shot to bits in the battle."

"Did they capture Dorn?" Harg said.

"No. He was riddled with grape shot, they say. Now he's a hero to the whole South Chain."

What a grand, hopeless spectacle of pirate bravado: Dorn leading his fleet to sure death, doubtless with flags flying, rigging singing, guns flaring over the sea. Harg had once thought it would be a beautiful way to die. Now it seemed pointless.

"He only did it because I wouldn't," he said grimly.

No one answered.

Harg said, "Where is Talley now?"

"Harbourdown. He stopped on Yora to execute his prisoners. There's no one left living there any more, they say. The whole island's just a huge mass grave."

Yes, that would fit the pattern.

"And, Harg—" Gill paused reluctantly. "We think Spaeth was with Dorn's fleet."

A coldness stabbed him. "Dead?" he said.

"We don't know. It could be."

If she was dead, his only hope of release was gone, and he would have to live with firesnakes in his brain forever. It was just, in a way.

In a stiff voice Harg said, "Jearl, you're in charge here. I'm going back."

He turned toward the stair leading down from the battlement. He saw every grain in the stone, and the way the brass door handle of his chamber was rubbed shiny in the spot where his thumb pressed. Then he was sitting on his bed, his arms crossed on his knees, studying the threads of the carpet under his feet. First, Talley had shot away his eye. Now, piece by piece, he was shooting away every other part of him. His home, his friends, every memory, every thing he cared for. Soon he would be nothing but missing parts.

༄

The fort on the headland off Tornabay's harbour fired a salute as the *Windemon* passed it. Harg watched the young men on the foredeck as they touched the linstock to the brass cannon they had just filled dangerously full of powder, and it gave a colossal bang. They swore in satisfaction.

He leaned over the gunwale, watching the white water froth past the bow. It was almost a year since he and Jory had returned home, and it was the same kind of clear, windy day as the one when they had closed in on Yora. He remembered thinking how it was all going to be different this time. It was almost enough to make him laugh.

Now Yora had gone the way of Vill and Crent and Bute. It was the bargain he had made by turning north instead of south. He thought of the iron stove in Strobe's home, and the dock where the old men sat and smoked, and the mantelpiece where Goth had kept his soulstone—all rubble and Inning bootmarks by now. And all those close-knit, close-minded people of Yorabay—where were they? Scattered to a dozen islands? Had they been able to take their dogs?

He tried to force himself to stop thinking about it. It was gone; there was nothing to do. The home he had spent years trying to get back to, and another year fighting for, no longer existed. His thoughts strayed back to other places he had been, yet he couldn't think of a single one where he belonged. His entire past was like a landscape of smoking ruins, as if he had passed through life using up and discarding everything. All of it consumed, nothing to turn back to.

For a moment he thought of sailing randomly west, of losing himself somewhere in the Widewater and never coming back. Just running toward the sun till he ran out of sea. It would be so simple.

And yet there was that heavy feeling in his gut, that feeling of responsibility. He had no choice, really. It felt as if all of this had been decided long before he was born, by forces greater than himself.

On the day they drew near to Lashnish, the sun was low in the west, and bright salmon streamers of cloud arched overhead. "We'll be at anchor in a quarter of an hour," Katri said to him.

"Good," he said automatically. Ahead, there was a string of buoys across the bay entrance, marking a log-and-chain boom; one of the frigates they had left with Tiarch was anchored on guard. On one of the heights above the harbour the forest had been cleared, and a wooden lookout tower stood, facing south.

Lashnish looked very different. Its clear air was hazed from the smoke of hundreds of campfires burning along the waterfront. All down the coast the refugee camps had multiplied. There had to be thousands of people in them by now.

The harbourmaster's boat had already set out from the dock by the time they were casting anchor in the harbour. "If she sends Joffrey to talk to me, I'll tip him in the bay," Harg said to Katri.

It wasn't Joffrey in the boat; it was Tiarch herself, as if to make up for lukewarm welcomes of the past. Along with her in the boat—Harg looked again in surprise—was Tway. He thought briefly of lining the gunners up to give the Governor a salute; but it was just the sort of thing the Innings would do. As she heaved herself on board, muttering irritably at the sailors who tried to help her, Harg was struck by how much she had aged. Her iron-grey hair was shot through with white, and her face looked worn and weary.

But the impression disappeared as soon as she saw him. She came forward, looking him over with a curious mix of pride and apprehension. "Congratulations," she said. "One of these days you ought to consider failing at something, just for the variety. But not right away, please."

Her eyes were travelling over his face, measuring him. She was trying to appraise how they stood. He only realized then how completely their roles had reversed. "We saved your palace in Tornabay for you," he said. "You can go back whenever you want."

She smiled, though the questions weren't gone from her face. "It's still there, is it?"

So she knew it hadn't been a clean victory. He felt relieved not to have to tell her.

"We did what we could," he said, then gestured toward the great cabin. "We can talk inside."

As Tiarch turned to go below, Harg's eyes met Tway's. Remembering how they had parted last, he grasped her hand and said, "I'm glad you're still here." Old friends seemed too rare and precious to lose these days.

She squeezed his hand and said, "You're the best show in town, Harg."

"Come with us," he said, turning to the gangway.

"Did you see Joffrey?" Tiarch asked as she settled into a chair in the aft cabin.

"No, should I have?"

"He was going to Tornabay with the payroll."

"Well, they'll be glad to see him, then."

He told Tiarch the neutral facts of what had happened at Tornabay. Stated that way, the outcome sounded completely inevitable. His luck had been so steady.

"It's a pity we haven't got time to let the Innings blunder themselves into extinction," Tiarch said.

"I wasn't dealing with Talley," Harg said.

"True." The name made Tiarch's face go grim.

"What's happened?" he said.

"He's in Harbourdown now, you know. He's issued a proclamation that the land and property of all Adaina who have resisted is forfeit, and will be parcelled out to Torna claimants. It's caused quite a sensation. You can imagine, the Adaina are calling the Torna collaborators, and things worse than that."

It was fiendishly clever. Talley was driving a wedge into the racial rift in the alliance against him. Harg said, "The Tornas would have to be dogs to accept such rewards."

"No," Tiarch said wearily, "they would just have to be human."

There would be a rush of Tornas into the South Chain now, trying to stake claim to the best property. The ruined towns, the empty farmland—it would all become Torna soon, unless something were done.

"That bastard hasn't won a single battle, and he's still beating us," Harg said bitterly.

"He's got greed and ruthlessness on his side."

It made Harg feel like he had bet on the wrong dog in the race. He had put his stakes behind balance and honour. He looked back at Tiarch. "What do you think he'll do next?"

She shrugged. "The next logical target is Lashnish."

She was right; Harg knew it. It was what he would do.

"We can't let him have it," he said. It was that simple. Their backs were against the wall. It almost gave him a feeling of relief, to know exactly what he had to do. He would have to draw Talley into a confrontation and settle the matter, once and for all.

"We won't lose this one," he said. "The forces of mora won't let it happen."

When they came back on deck evening had fallen, and a thousand campfires glimmered redly all along the shore. After seeing Tiarch off, Harg went to the foredeck and sat on one of bow chasers, staring out at the fires. They were watching him, like the eyes of children, trusting him to protect them. In the evening quiet he could feel the isles themselves, watching him.

Tway sat down beside him quietly. He waited for her to speak. For once, it seemed to be coming hard for her.

"You seem better," she said. "Are you?"

He felt changed. He wasn't sure he would call it better. "Have you heard anything about Spaeth?" he asked.

She shook her head. He looked away, realizing why he had asked. If Spaeth had been here, he would have been ready to surrender, and become Ison in truth as well as seeming.

"There is something you have to know, Harg," Tway said at last. "Tiarch doesn't need to know it, but you do."

She paused. Surprised into silence, he waited.

"Harg, she isn't really the Heir of Gilgen," she said, barely loud enough for him to hear. "Goth didn't give her the Emerald Tablet."

Harg sat immobile, thunderstruck.

"She said she was," he said.

"I know. It wasn't true."

"Then it was all a charade," he said. "The dhota-nur. I'm not Ison, and can't ever be."

It suddenly struck him as impossibly funny. Everything he had taken on—the ceremony, the reverence, the responsibility—it was all a fraud. He wasn't the one chosen to set the balances right; he was just a plain human being.

He started to laugh, and couldn't stop. Tway grasped his hand, distressed. "Harg," she said, "you can't stop being Ison now. Why do you think she did it in the first place? Yes, it's a lie, but it's a lie we need."

The laughter wouldn't let him go. Distraught, she said, "You can't let this change anything, Harg! The Emerald Tablet doesn't matter. The Isles do."

His laughter died down. His stomach ached. "Why did she tell you, and not me?"

"She didn't. I found out from the Grey Folk. They've known all along."

So they had duped him into walking into this trap. Oddly enough, he didn't blame Spaeth. It was too likely that she had only been manipulated, as well—manipulated into doing what Goth would never have done. Something, *someone* had needed Harg to put his foot so firmly into the snare that he could never wriggle out again.

He looked out at the campfires again. So he had been wrong; the Isles weren't watching him. There was no mora here, no fate, no balance.

"We'll still do it," he said softly. "We don't need the Grey Folks' power. We'll do it, even if we're just ordinary people, muddling along."

"That's the Harg I know," Tway said.

They sat side by side, their arms entwined, looking out at the city. It seemed to Harg as if all he saw was doomed.

The island of Roah was shaped like a hairpin or a tuning fork; it had two long arms outstretched to the west. At their base, Lashnish lay, ringed behind with mountains. From the top of the ridge that formed the island's southern arm, Harg could see the city on one side, nestled down in its watery cleft, the mist still hanging over it. On the other side he saw all the south coast of Roah. Everywhere along that coast were little bays with sandy beaches—perfect landing spots for an invading army.

It hadn't come to Harg all at once, in a flash—just in small increments, tiny details that added up to one damning conclusion: Lashnish would have been superbly defensible with an army large enough to man all the heights, but he had no such army. As it was, his forces would be spread dangerously thin. There were just too many potential routes of attack.

Around him was a scene of manic activity. They had spent the last four days clearing trees along the ridgetop, and now were building ramparts and timber parapets to mount the big guns to be taken from the ships, when they arrived from Tornabay. Half the population of Lashnish had turned out to help, it seemed: stocky Torna shopkeepers, pimpled apprentices, maids, dockhands. The city must be deserted. A wagon was bumping up a makeshift road, piled with bread fresh from the ovens, and some elderly women were cooking up a huge pot of stew nearby. The dark forest soil had turned into a slippery mud with last night's rain, and everyone was covered with it.

The activity gave the townsfolk a sense of purposeful progress, but to Harg's eyes it was inadequate. Admiral Talley might land anywhere along a six-mile coast, or he might attack from the west, by sea. Or worst of all, from the north, which was wholly undefended. The islanders' artillery would be spread out in a perilously thin line, their firearms so scarce they would have to use old shotguns, their ships depleted of armaments. When the ships finally arrived. He turned west to scan the entrance to Roslip Firth, where the fleet would be stationed. He had been expecting them all week. It would leave Jearl with almost no force to keep Tornabay under control.

If there had been nothing but tactics to consider, Harg would have retreated, then recaptured Lashnish as soon as Talley left it. But when he looked down on the city, where the campfires of the refugee town were beginning to haze the air, he knew that was impossible. To retreat was to leave all those people at Talley's mercy. No Ison would do such a thing, and Harg couldn't either.

A ship was warping out of the harbour below. Harg squinted at it, then called Gill over. Gill had been unusually quiet since seeing his family, and Harg constantly felt he was bringing him back from other thoughts. "What ship is that, Gill?" he asked.

"It's that Rothur ship," Gill said.

"Leaving, rot them," Harg said. The Rothurs had been so full of promises and encouragement, so totally lacking in concrete support. The ambassador bowed and smiled and said that all the islanders had to do was demonstrate resolve, and there would be arms, there would be ships—only the arms and ships never arrived. Just more promises.

"I'm going down to talk to Tiarch," Harg said. "You keep things moving here, all right?"

"All right," Gill said, but his mind already seemed far away.

Harg looked at him closely. "Gill? You all right?"

With an effort, Gill smiled at him. "Don't worry, Harg. I'll keep them moving."

"That's not what I asked."

"It's nothing you can help, Harg. It's not your fault, it's mine."

Harg did not feel reassured.

When he entered Tiarch's office, the Governor was with her secretary, sorting papers and packing them in boxes. "Going somewhere?" Harg said.

"There are a lot of names in these records I wouldn't care to have the world see," Tiarch said. She shooed the secretary away then, and closed the door. "How are the defences coming?"

Harg looked at her broad, aging face and thought that they really made a remarkable team. Their minds worked at exactly the same speed, and in the same direction. When she said something would get done, it got done. Harg hadn't always trusted her, but at least they had never lied to each other.

"The defences are a joke," he said. "Oh, we'll be able to slow them down. We might even turn them back, if Talley's afraid to take heavy casualties."

"Right," Tiarch said. "Talley, afraid to take casualties. The kindest heart in all the Widewater."

Harg didn't need to answer. "I saw your Rothur friends abandoning us just now," he said.

"Practical folk, the Rothurs."

"I'm glad you like them. They never gave us a firecracker or an old bullet, did they?"

Tiarch hesitated. "Actually, they *have* given us something."

"Oh?"

"The ship wasn't leaving. It was moving around the coast to wait. The Rothurs have agreed to give us both refuge, if we want it."

Trust Tiarch to have her escape all planned out. It might have seemed funny to Harg, if there hadn't been a whole city full of people out there who had no escape and no Rothur friends.

The Governor was watching him sadly, as if she knew what he was thinking and wished she didn't. "I haven't given up yet, Harg. But there's one thing we need to think of."

"What's that?"

"We don't know Talley's terms for surrender. They might be better than you would think. We're in a stronger position than I ever thought we'd be. We've got Tornabay. It's a powerful bargaining chip."

Harg had thought it was much more. How could they trade it back, as if it were just a shipment of oysters? And trade it for what? A South Chain depopulated by war? A marred and servile future?

"We're never going to have a whole victory," Tiarch said. "We've got to settle for half of one. But we've got to do it now. Talley doesn't know yet what we're up against. If he can avoid a faceoff, he'll deal."

Harg shook his head. "Talley *wants* a faceoff."

"You don't know that."

"Yes, I do. I know him." He had begun to feel superstitious about it.

"He still might bargain. Let me try, at least."

At last, slowly, he said, "It can't do any harm, I suppose."

"Just leave this part to me," Tiarch answered.

The next day the fleet still hadn't arrived from Tornabay, so Harg sent a sloop out looking for them, to hurry them on. Up to now their absence hadn't worried him; adverse winds could easily account for the delay. But he had begun to feel nervous about the Innings' arrival. As he headed back up to the ridge to check on the defences, he saw the messenger boat heading out, and wished he could be on it. It was impossible; if he had left at this juncture, the morale of Lashnish would have left with him.

At sunset the volunteers from the city began to go home, leaving the ridge to the professionals, who would work on into the night by bonfire and torchlight. They took a break as the stars began to come out, sitting around fires strung out along the ridge. Harg found himself with a group from the *Windemon* that had been with him throughout the campaign. He knew most of their faces, but not names. Weary, he stretched out his legs toward the fire and lay back, smelling the sweet tang of dreamweed on the cool air. Above him the stars looked like jewels scattered on velvet. The air was perfectly still except for the distant sound of breakers on the shore. It was a beautiful, peaceful evening; looking around the circle, he could see the awareness on all their faces that there might not be another one for them.

They were talking, but not about the war. The conversation ran toward the past, particularly the good times—holiday dinners, what the children of their villages did on the rare occasions when it snowed. Listening, silent, Harg knew that many of the homes they spoke of no longer existed.

He thought of Gill. After all the effort, and all the fighting, Gill had realized that his family was really the most important thing to him. And there was no way to get it back now the way it had been.

The mood had changed since they had begun to fight. There was an odd calmness around the campfire now. Harg said, "Isn't anyone scared?"

There was a pause. "Why should I be?" one man said. "My home is gone, I don't know where my family is. What's left to be afraid for?"

"You know what I've figured out?" a woman said, knocking the ash from her pipe. "When I die, nothing is going to change. People who have known me will just pick up and turn back to whatever they were doing, the way I did when friends of mine died. They'll marry and have kids, and forget. There will be a whole future without me, and the fact that I lived will make no difference."

There were nods all around the campfire. No one spoke for a long time.

Looking at their firelit faces, it came to Harg that he had lost his taste for fighting. Not that he would stop; it was almost automatic now, he'd been at it so long. But it no longer brought him a sense of accomplishment. He had lost his faith that it was possible to win.

When they spotted the Inning fleet two days later, their own ships still hadn't arrived. Harg stood on the fresh plank floor of one of the gunless gun towers, a spyglass pressed to his eye, counting ships. Every time he thought he'd gotten them all, another one appeared. Talley was holding nothing back now; he had his quarry cornered, and was going for the kill.

Harg looked down at the entrance to Roslip Firth, where the missing warships would have guarded the city from the sea. There were four ships there—one that had fled here from Harbourdown, the two stationed here, and the one he had arrived in, the *Windemon*. There was also a collection of merchant ships and fishing cogs crewed by townsfolk with muskets and grenades. Talley would cut through them like a hot knife.

All down the ridge the defenders were stationed and ready. Their faces looked grim as they, too, counted the odds. The cannons they had relied on were mostly on the ships. They would have to make do with a peculiar assortment of mortars, swivel-guns, and small arms.

He watched tensely as the Inning armada came into the lee of the island, wondering which way they were going to go—by land, by sea, or the most likely, both. A small cutter with brown sails broke off from the rest of the fleet, tacking round the headland to the firth entrance. The warships were preparing to cast anchor.

"By the horns," Harg whispered. "They're going to negotiate." He had been wrong, Tiarch had been right. He handed his spyglass to Gill and said, "Send a messenger if there's any change. I'll be with Tiarch."

When Harg reached the Isonsquare, he looked down the Stonepath to the harbour. One of their own boats was landing, doubtless bearing some news or person exchanged at the blockade. Tiarch was already alert to the new development when he entered her office. "If he's sent an Inning, let me do the talking," she said.

But when the three-man delegation from Admiral Talley arrived, all of them starched and pressed in their shining uniforms, the person at its head was not an Inning. It was Joffrey.

Harg and Tiarch stood side by side as he entered the office, and neither of them could utter a word.

Joffrey did not open with diplomatic pleasantries. "First, I need to inform you that your fleet will not be arriving tomorrow, or any time soon, at least not if Jearl has obeyed my orders, as he said he would."

Harg looked at Tiarch. Her face looked like it was made of stone.

"However," he went on, "Admiral Talley is prepared to be generous in his terms of surrender."

He laid it out then: all combatants were to cease hostilities at noon the next day. The Innings would occupy the city peacefully, and no civilians would be harmed. The only requirement was that Tiarch and Harg personally surrender to Admiral Talley aboard his flagship at noon, and become his prisoners.

"To be tried, I suppose?" Tiarch asked. For the first time since he had known her, Harg saw a flicker of fear in her eyes.

"That's not included in the terms," Joffrey answered. He waited a few moments, then said, "Shall I take back your answer?"

"No," Harg said. "We'll send someone with our answer. Someone we trust."

Joffrey gave them both a cool, condescending look, then left.

For a while, they said nothing to each other. Harg stood at the window, watching the Inning delegation leave. There was a group of people gathered outside, watching the door anxiously for news. Across the square the Pavilion gate stood open; beyond it the Isonstone lay, inert. Even it existed in an Inning world, now.

At last Tiarch sighed and said, "Well, you were right about him."

"He was bluffing about the fleet," Harg said. "Jearl would never turn traitor. I know him too well."

Tiarch gave a fatalistic shrug. "When Joffrey left here, he had with him enough money to pay the whole fleet." She left the implications unspoken. It was just as well, for Harg would have bristled if she had said the word "bribe" aloud.

"He must have used deceit to delay them," Harg said.

"Well, it doesn't matter now."

Harg tried to think of his options. He pictured all the refugees out there, all the townsfolk, all the people on the ridge and aboard the ships preparing to fight a hopeless defence with little better than kitchen knives, whose lives he could save simply by giving himself up. He looked at Tiarch. "What do you think?"

"If we choose to fight, will we be any better off?" she said.

He almost laughed. Was anyone ever better off for choosing to fight? He'd thought he knew the answer to that, once.

"We can't just accept his terms," he said. "At the least, there's got to be a general amnesty. No reprisals. And he's got to rescind his declaration about Adaina lands. Property rights in the South Chain stay unchanged."

Tiarch said, "We could ask him to pledge us a civilian peace commission to determine the governance of the Isles after military law is lifted."

"With both Torna and Adaina representation," Harg added.

They went on for the better part of an hour, cobbling together a list of counterproposals. There was a weird unreality to it—just the two of them, sketching out a visionary blueprint for peace.

At last, just before Tiarch was about to send for her secretary to write up their demands, Harg said, "Are we going to agree to his main condition?"

They looked at each other. "Let's just send him our proposals and see how he reacts," Tiarch said. "We won't promise or deny anything yet."

How canny she was.

After the messenger left, Harg went back up to the ridge to wait for Talley's reply. People gathered around him eagerly to learn what was going on, but all he would say was, "We're negotiating." He watched those words pass down the line like wind, raising ripples of hope wherever they went. As evening fell he walked from campfire to campfire, and the talk was animated again. He found Gill conscientiously overseeing things, but looking as if he was making mental lists of things to do before heading home.

"What are we going to have to give up to get peace?" Gill asked him. When Harg didn't answer, Gill said, "We all know it won't come free. That's not how these things work."

"We're trying to make it as cheap as possible," Harg said.

The response didn't come until dawn. Harg saw the cutter rounding the headland and commandeered a wagon to take him back to the city. He arrived before Tiarch had even risen from bed, and was waiting in her office when Joffrey came in. Harg sent a servant to tell the Governor, then turned to face Joffrey. "Well?" he said.

With a stiff formality, Joffrey said, "Admiral Talley gives his word that all his actions will be regulated by justice, but he will agree to no specific terms or conditions. This is his final response. He requires an answer by noon, or the attack goes forward."

"He thinks we're just stalling?" Harg asked.

"Aren't you?" Joffrey said.

Harg gave him a look that would have made most men flinch. "Well, Tiarch and I will have to talk it over." He looked to the door, wondering what was taking her so long.

Joffrey had already left when the servant who had gone to find the Governor came back.

"Sir, she's not in her chamber," the girl said. "I can't find her anywhere. Her secretary's gone, too."

Something cold seemed to have taken Harg by the throat. "Was her bed slept in?" he asked.

"No, sir."

He stood motionless, scarcely able to believe it. All the lives in Lashnish depending on her, and she had slipped away to safety in the night.

He sat down at Tiarch's desk and pulled out a drawer, but it was cleaned out. He leaned back, thinking. There might still be time for him to make it to the Rothur ship as well, if he left quickly. They might wait to see if he was coming.

He thought of taking the first step, but something seemed to be weighting his feet. It was the Isonstone, he thought—tied around his feet, dragging him down.

It was an hour before Harg stirred again. He called in an aide to send a series of messages to Gill, Katri, and his other captains. Then he went to change his clothes. Something plain and utilitarian, he decided. Something unlike what an Inning would wear.

There was a crowd gathered at the wharf by the time he got there, all anxious to know the news. He avoided their gazes. Gill met him at the dock, frowning darkly. When they climbed into the launch together, Gill said in an undertone, "Is this your idea of a cheap bargain?"

"Don't say a word, Gill," Harg warned.

They drew up to the *Windemon* on the blockade line at the mouth of the firth. "This isn't right, Harg," was the first thing Katri said as they clambered aboard. "I know we can beat them."

"You can't see their fleet from here," Harg said.

"I don't have to. I know you'll think of something. You always do."

"Right. This is what I've thought of," Harg said.

She subsided into a discontented silence.

Harg didn't look back as the *Windemon* pulled away from the other ships. He didn't think of past or future. All he had to do in life was get through the next hour, and then it would be over.

They passed the westernmost lookout tower, then rounded the headland to the south. When the Inning fleet came in view he watched Katri take it in, as he had done from the ridge. She still had a defiant look, but it was a hopeless defiance.

Several ships had guns trained on them as they approached the flagship, as if expecting some suicidal gesture. When they cast anchor a stone's throw away, Harg took out his watch and checked to make sure it was still before noon. He turned to Gill. "Go over and make sure Talley's there," he said. "I'm not talking to any of his minions. Particularly not Joffrey."

Presently they heard the shrilling of a fife and the drumming of feet on wood as, on the other ship, the seamen and soldiers paraded onto deck and assembled in lines to witness. At last the rowboat returned, and Gill swung himself back on deck. "They're ready."

"Is Talley there?" Harg asked.

"Yes. Horns, but he's a cold fish."

Harg gestured Gill and Katri to come with him. The oarsmen rowed them over, and they climbed the rope and board ladder the warship had slung overside. When he stood on the warship's deck, Harg paused to take in the lines of silent marines and sailors, the wind tugging at their uniforms, snapping their flags. The officers were gathered on the quarterdeck, waiting. Harg forced his face into an air of impassivity as he walked down the double line of armed marines to mount the gangway.

A group of Inning officers faced him; he scanned them to pick out the slight, fair-haired man he remembered, who bore himself as if shelled in armour, impervious and perfect. When Harg saw his eyes, they were not cold, as Gill had said; they were burning with an interior fire. Harg walked up to him, stopping several feet away.

"Harg Ismol," Talley said, searching his face.

"Admiral."

"You have come to accept my offer?"

"Yes."

It seemed to take an effort for Talley to drag his eyes off Harg's face. He glanced around. "Where is Governor Tiarch?"

Harg tried to sound unmoved, but it came out bitter anyway. "Fled. She has taken refuge with the Rothurs."

Talley's expression changed. "This is not the bargain I agreed to."

"It's all I can give you," Harg said. "I can no more fetch her back from Rothur than you can."

There was a hard expression in Talley's eyes, and alarm twisted in Harg's stomach. It was perfectly possible for the man to go back on his word—take them all prisoner and destroy Lashnish anyway. He said quickly, "She can do you no harm from Rothur. You don't need a hostage to guarantee the good behaviour of the Torna; and if what you want is an example, I should do."

Talley's eyes narrowed. "You should. You should indeed."

Something was about to go wrong; Harg could feel it. He caught Talley's eye and said, "I've kept my end of the bargain. It would be unjust for you to go back on your word now."

Talley was silent for several moments. Then he said, "You have betrayed your nation and you have betrayed me. I have no obligation to honour any agreement with you. But I am a just man, and so I will." He raised his voice so all the waiting troops could hear. "I hereby take you into the custody of the court, to be tried for your crimes by law."

Before anyone could move, Harg turned to Katri and Gill and said, also in a loud voice, "See that all my commanders keep our agreement with the strictest honour. All ships are to be surrendered, all arms laid down. The Inning forces must be allowed peaceful entrance to the city." He looked at them each in turn, till he was sure they understood: any pretext could bring the whole agreement tumbling down, and waste whatever good his surrender might do.

"You may go now," Talley said to Katri and Gill, in the voice of a commanding officer. "We will wait one hour before following you."

They turned and walked away then, down the row of soldiers to their own ship. Everyone watched them, motionless, till they cast off. Then a breath of wind blew past, and a stir passed through the waiting soldiers.

"Take him to the brig," Talley ordered. The Torna guards who stepped forward did not touch Harg, but fell in, one on either side and one in front. A seagull laughed as Harg followed them, but it was the only sound.

15
JUSTICE

The warship *Pragmatic* came into Tornabay at dawn. In the near-total gloom of the hole where they had him confined, Harg had managed to find a pinhole where the caulking had shrunk. When he pressed his eye to it he saw for a moment the city rising up the mountainside, still scarred by the fires. It looked quiet, as if exhausted. Even the mountain was no longer smoking. Then the ship came about, till all he could see was headland and sky. Voices conferred on the deck above, and a scow bumped against the hull. He rose, nervous with the expectation that something would happen now, but nothing did. That was the way these days; his life was one galling anticlimax after another.

For days he had been blocking off the part of his mind that thought about the future, forcing himself to live one moment at a time. Once in Tornabay, he expected Inning justice to be swift and summary. There would be no time then for reflection.

It was mid-morning before the marine guard came to get him. Coming up onto the open deck, he squinted in the bright sun. He moved stiffly, not just from lack of exercise; they had given him Inning clothes, and they fit oddly, making him feel restricted and uncomfortable.

Alongside the warship a six-oared skiff was waiting. As he climbed down into it, he noticed the furtive, guilty stares of the Adaina boatmen, and wondered if they knew something he didn't.

"We bound for the palace?" he asked his guard. The man looked away.

Harg said drily, "A secret, eh?"

"A secret the whole city knows," one of the boatmen muttered. The Torna shot him an angry glance.

As the boat approached the shore, Harg saw that the dock was lined with troops in bright dress uniform, forming up to march. It looked like there was going to be a parade.

Waiting on the dock was a mule-drawn wagon. A Torna sergeant curtly ordered Harg to stand in the bed, then brought some iron manacles to clamp on his wrists and ankles. It was then Harg realized he was in the midst of a performance, a piece of theatre staged to demonstrate his abject defeat to the populace of Tornabay. Talley was surely behind this; he wanted the islanders to see their Ison carted through the streets in chains.

That thought stiffened his back and cleared his mind. It was not Harg Ismol being treated this way; it was Ison Harg, and by implication everyone who had fought against Inning. If this was theatre, then he knew how to play his part. *There is one thing Talley doesn't know: if the Adaina are good at anything, we are good at defeat.*

A fife signalled, and the soldiers formed up. The wagon lurched into motion, nearly knocking over Harg and the two Torna guards stationed on either side of him. "I hope you get a bonus for this," Harg said to one of them. The man looked stonily forward.

The route of the procession ran through the Harbourmarket, as if deliberately to retrace the way Harg had come as conqueror barely more than a month ago. The square was packed with people; even the upper-storey windows had children leaning out, their mothers pointing and explaining why the man was being punished. Below, the shopkeepers had come to their doors to witness the last Ison any of them was likely to see.

Harg tried to keep his head up and look out at them, as Ison Harg would; but every set of eyes wore a little more of the part away, and plain Harg began to show through in patches. He tried to wet his lips, but his mouth was dry. The crowds were strangely quiet as he passed, a thousand eyes just watching. He couldn't tell if it were pity, contempt, or something else behind them.

The procession plunged into the steep, narrow streets winding up to the Gallowmarket. Here there were fewer witnesses, and Harg allowed himself to look at his feet awhile. His shoulders ached from the effort of holding his head up.

The Gallowmarket was teeming when they emerged into it. The impaling stake had been set up again, and for a panic-stricken moment Harg thought they were going to execute him then and there. He clung to the memory that Talley had mentioned a trial.

Across the square the palace gates opened and another line of soldiers marched out to form a double row. They presented their arms, and then from the gates Provost Minicleer emerged, resplendent in official dress, to meet the approaching column. The cart carrying Harg, and the troop of soldiers around it, drew aside and came to a halt just under the execution stand, so that Harg stood with the stake at his back. The rest of the military procession came to a halt before the gates of the palace. A fife and drum corps shrilled a stirring tune. Then, bringing up the rear of the column, came an open carriage draped with flags and carrying the Admiral. Two people sat beside him: Spaeth, wearing a midnight-blue Inning gown and a jewelled silver necklace that echoed the coils of her hair; and Goth, so frail and wasted he barely seemed alive.

The crowd hushed at the sight of the two Lashnurai riding with the Inning conqueror. The carriage passed through the square, then came to a halt just outside the gate. Minicleer walked forward to meet it. The drums rolled as Talley descended from the carriage to exchange some ceremonial words with the Provost, who then presented him with a red velvet-wrapped dowel with gold tassels on either end. Talley mounted into the carriage again and held the symbolic stick over his head. The people in the front of the crowd began to cheer. The Admiral acknowledged them with a wave, then turned to Spaeth and took her hand. She rose to stand beside him, breathtakingly beautiful, yet another Inning possession.

Harg stood watching stonily. It was a cynical, manipulative show, but very clever. Talley seemed to be signalling that he would not denigrate the most sacred symbols of the Isles; he would appropriate them.

As the honour guard saluted and the cheering grew, Spaeth looked out over the crowd and her eyes fell on Harg. The involuntary flinch she gave was more eloquent than a thousand speeches. At that moment, some Adainas at the back of the crowd began to chant softly. At first Harg couldn't hear the words; but as the volume rose he realized the chant was "I-son, I-son." When he looked in their direction they responded, even louder. The guards at his side moved closer, tense; one took hold of his chain. The chant had reached the Innings' ears now, and some soldiers started out across the market square toward the offenders, but they scattered before anyone could reach them.

The procession started up again. Talley's carriage passed on into the palace, and Harg faced forward as the fortress gaped to swallow him. The unruly gang had upstaged Talley's victory ceremony, and there would be repercussions. Talley had misjudged the Adaina. Defeat was nothing new to them; in fact, a defeated Ison might be even more fully theirs than a successful one. And a dead one might be the most potent of all.

～

It was three weeks after arriving in Tornabay that Nathaway Talley got the first intimation that his situation was about to change.

He had been unwell ever since Harbourdown. The effects of the flogging had healed slowly, but left him susceptible to a series of infections, the latest of which was a painful bronchitis that made him chronically short of breath. At the same time, his nerves were corroded by the knowledge that at any moment it might happen all over again.

Hope finally came in the form of a round, energetic man with a wild frizz of curly blond hair that ringed his bald skull from ear to ear. His name was Wabin Bartelso. *The* Wabin Bartelso, as they said in Fluminos—crusading defence attorney, champion of lost causes, grandstander extraordinaire. Nathaway had known him since childhood. He didn't always win, but he had a knack for making even his defeats spectacularly public. There was no one who struck more fear into the hearts of prosecutors.

Nathaway didn't even know he had an advocate until the day they brought him to a courtroom for a perfunctory hearing before a military judge. It was held in the strictest privacy. At first, he and the sergeant guarding him were the only ones in the courtroom, and he stood waiting, unable to find out what he was there for. But when the lawyers entered the room and he recognized Bartelso, he felt such a painful surge of hope that his throat ached and he had to wipe away the tears that started to his eyes.

They were not able to exchange any words before the judge entered—a Navy officer Nathaway had never seen. As soon as he was seated he called the attorneys to his bench for a low-toned conference and an exchange of paperwork. When this was accomplished, the judge brought down his gavel and announced, "Prisoner, you are free on bond. You will keep the court apprised of your whereabouts while your petition for change of venue is being considered." He then rose and left.

That was it. Nathaway stood stunned, his legs feeling too shaky to move, till Bartelso came over to him. "I'm free?" Nathaway said to him.

"On a pretty pricey bond, so don't go skipping off," the lawyer said.

It was not just the thought of being free; it was the thought that someone had actually helped him that collapsed Nathaway's shaky control. This time, he broke down and wept, putting his arms around Bartelso in inarticulate gratitude. When he was able to get control of himself, the lawyer handed him a handkerchief and said, "Nat, my boy, you look perfectly shocking. It's a good thing your dear mother can't see you. Can you make it to the gate?"

Nathaway nodded, wanting to escape before someone changed their mind. He had always felt safe and at home in courtrooms, but not this one.

Before they reached the door, Bartelso stopped him and said, "You need to know, there will be some gentlemen of the press outside. I don't want you talking to them in this state, but they need to see you. All right?"

Nathaway nodded.

It felt unreal, dreamlike, to be out on a busy, sunlit street, where people were going about their business as if it were a normal day. Bartelso had a cab waiting, and swept him toward it past the curious stares of the onlookers. With Nathaway safely stowed inside the carriage, the lawyer turned back to talk to the newspaper men. Nathaway could hear his tone of shock and outrage, but not the words.

When Bartelso joined him in the cab, he said, "I've promised an interview to the *Intelligencer*, once you feel up to it."

Nathaway's brain felt full of cotton balls. "What do they want to interview me about?"

"Those prison walls must have been pretty thick if they could keep out all the controversy you set off."

"Controversy?"

Bartelso assessed him as if to be sure he could handle the news. "Well, in a nutshell, what the Navy did to you sent the most frightful shock through the land. It was one thing to hear of a hundred cruel atrocities perpetrated against the natives—but a single injustice against an Inning, why, that was too much. And not just any Inning, either. It finally made everyone realize that what your brother did in the Forsakens today, he could do to them tomorrow. What's more, he would."

"That should have been obvious for months," Nathaway said bitterly.

"Ah, but there's nothing like a little sympathy to change the landscape. The natives who suffered were ciphers. You, they knew. They remembered you as an appealing child. They'd watched you grow up. And those letters of yours—well, they made you friends you'll never know. It's going to be a pleasure to defend someone popular for a change."

So, popular or not, they were still going to try him. "When is the trial?" he said.

"Not set yet. I've petitioned to get it moved to Fluminos, where there's not this absurdity of martial law to contend with."

"No," said Nathaway.

"What's that?"

"I'm not leaving the Forsakens," he said, with a touch of the steely stubbornness that had gotten him into this mess. "Not without Spaeth."

For once, the premier debater of the land declined to argue. "It may not be an issue," he said. "Honestly, Nat, I think there wouldn't be much eagerness to prosecute you, in the Navy or out, if it weren't for your brother. This whole thing has gotten far too hot for the brass to touch, and they would just as soon drop it, if Corbin weren't pursuing it like the moral absolutist he is. There is something vindictive about it. Your father made a devil's bargain, giving up his firstborn to appease the military. I told him he would live to regret it, but he listens to advice about as well as the rest of you."

They soon arrived at the hotel where Bartelso was staying. It was a cozy, family-run place on a secluded street off the Rivermarket. The proprietor, a motherly Torna woman, took one look at Nathaway and decided that he needed pampering. He was soon bundled off to the room adjoining Bartelso's, with a full meal in hot pursuit.

Over the next week, as Bartelso cautiously reintroduced him to the world, Nathaway found that a striking Inningization had come over Tornabay. The war, followed by the arrival of something like peace, had brought an influx of journalists, contractors, and most of all, lawyers from Fluminos. The hotel where they were staying was packed with them, and the adaptable Torna had obviously learned to cater. Nathaway's room was furnished with such studious Inningness that at first he suspected Bartelso of trying to reclaim him from temporary cultural confusion. The shelves were lined with classics, the food was a homey blend of recipes. But he soon concluded it was the Torna themselves doing it, because everywhere he looked it was the same. Inning was simply the fashion of the day.

The courts being closed, the locus of debate and lobbying had shifted to the taverns and coffee houses, where the universal refrain was the iniquity of martial law and the need to reinstate the civilian courts to settle the horrendous questions of land titles, governance, and race relations that the war had created. It was not that the flocks of Inning lawyers were deeply concerned about the Forsakens; the debate was really about the nature of their own country, and whether empire was compatible with liberty. Tornabay was where the fault line between the rule of law and rule of force was exposed in its rawest form—that same fundamental rift that Tennessen Talley had spent a lifetime trying to paper over. The fact that two of his sons were now symbolically facing each other across the divide was too good a metaphor for opinion-makers to miss.

Two biweekly newspapers had sprung up to advocate different policies, and Nathaway could easily have made his views known. But Bartelso coached him not to let slip any comment that could be construed as opposition. "It may be your right, but Corbin is still dictator, and could close down these rags and clap you back in jail any time he took a notion to do it," he warned.

"I think his opposition would love that," Nathaway was forced to observe.

"Maybe so, but we can make our point without it," Bartelso said. He had a fine-tuned talent for implication and innuendo, and made sure that Nathaway's gaunt and pallid condition became a matter of public record. Nathaway often felt like Exhibit A in Corbin's ongoing trial by public opinion. If the journalists realized that they were being manipulated, they seemed eager to cooperate.

One day he and Bartelso sat eating lunch together at a suitably conspicuous table in a restaurant where expatriates could stare at them in scandalized sympathy. Or rather, Nathaway sat pushing some food around a plate while Bartelso sipped a cup of the black concoction that kept him moving sixteen hours a day, not always in pursuit of truth and justice, but in that direction a sufficient portion of the time.

"You will need to put some of that food in your mouth if you want to stop looking like a walking cadaver," Bartelso said.

Nathaway gave up and pushed the plate away. The fact was, nothing Inning seemed appetizing to him any more. Inning boots chafed his feet now, and Inning manners chafed his patience. It all felt alien and artificial.

Everyone around him seemed to be forgetting something: this wasn't all about Inning, it was about the islanders, too. It was about the people he had left in the refugee camp in Lashnish, and the prisoners crammed into the hold of the warships, and the ghosts that now populated Yora. It was about the people even now imprisoned in the dank cells of the palace.

"Wabin," he said hesitantly, "would you consider taking on another case?"

"Mmm," said Bartelso, watching him speculatively. "Whose case do you have in mind?"

"Two of them, actually," Nathaway said, looking at him seriously. "Spaeth Dobrin and Harg Ismol."

Bartelso's eyebrows climbed his forehead. "You must think I love lost causes."

"No, *just* causes."

The lawyer waved at a waiter to bring him another elixir of caffeine. He then settled back, eyeing Nathaway keenly. "I had anticipated your asking about the lady. The other one perplexes me. You realize, we have no reason to thank this young fellow for causing such a ruckus. At the end of the Rothur campaign there was considerable support for disbanding major portions of the Navy. When things flared up in the Forsakens, that died. The court could have made some headway but for this man."

"Not everything that happens is about Inning," Nathaway said in some frustration. "These people just wanted what we all want, some autonomy and self-control. You would have fought, too, if that was all you knew how to do."

"Perhaps. But for our purposes, the best thing might be to let your brother and his cronies kill the poor bastard in some suitably gruesome way, in order to shock the waverers back home."

Nathaway sat forward, staring at Bartelso's fatherly face. "You can't mean that," he said.

"Why not?"

"It's *unjust*."

"No, dear boy, it's only politics."

The waiter arrived with his coffee, and he paused to tip the man. When he turned back to find Nathaway still staring at him in deep disillusion, he grumbled, "You and your brother are two of a kind, you know that? Both of you amateur ethicists. I swear, the two of you could turn the world over, if you could just heave on the same side."

"So you won't do it?" Nathaway said.

"I didn't say that. I'll look into it if it would give you pleasure, Nat. But I cannot hold out much hope. I must say, it perplexes me why you should wish the man well. If I'm not mistaken, he was your rival for the affections of the young lady, true?"

First, Nathaway sat thinking of how to explain the difference between lover and bandhota; then he sat wondering when he had started to understand the difference himself. At last he shook his head. "It's complicated," he said.

"Evidently." Bartelso paused to spoon sugar into his coffee until the sight made Nathaway queasy. "The young lady, now. I am ahead of you there. I have been checking into her status, and—" he gave Nathaway a furtive glance— "well, what I found may influence your decision whether to go ahead."

Unable to imagine anything that could induce him to change his mind, Nathaway said, "Go on."

"Well, to begin with, she hasn't yet been charged with any crime, and it's a little difficult to imagine what crime they *would* charge her with. We stopped prosecuting people for witchcraft quite some time ago, and sleeping with the enemy is not illegal. Since your brother has apparently decided not to charge her for attempted assassination, we—"

"Assassination?" Nathaway interrupted.

"Yes. The story is, she broke into the Admiral's room at night; the guards found her standing over him with a razor. But the only blood shed was her own. She had—what is it, my boy? You know something?"

Nathaway felt as if his stomach had dropped through the floor. "Oh, my god," he said. "She tried to give him dhota."

"That's bad, is it?" Bartelso said.

"It's terrible." The thought was like a hot poker twisting in his vitals. How could she have done it? Corbin, of all people. "Do you know any more?" he said urgently. He had to know how far it had gotten.

"Well, they concluded that it was some sort of native sorcery. But, unlikely as it sounds, it appears to have worked. Among the inner staff, the whisper is that he is quite besotted with her. She is lodged, along with the old man, in the chambers adjoining the Admiral's, where he can visit her at all hours. The officers say he is distracted and impatient with details, generally quite unlike himself. They all assume she has seduced him."

Nathaway was in torment. Had they made love? Had he fed her the psychic poison of his mind? Was she suffering for him as she had done for Harg? Or did she love that repellent man with all the helpless instinct of the dhotamar? "Wabin," he said, "you've got to find some way I can get in to see her."

"Don't push your luck, son," the lawyer said. "This is no time to inject a quarrel about a woman into all the other problems you're facing."

"That's not what I want," he said desperately. "I want to marry her."

If only it had been as simple as seduction.

It was true, Spaeth and Goth were luxuriously housed in a suite of rooms adjoining the Admiral's in Tornabay Palace, with a private door connecting them. It was a lovely setting—tall, airy windows opening onto a garden just budding out with spring, thick carpeting, furniture inlaid with tropical woods. It was lodging fit for the sovereign's consort, perhaps even designed for that purpose. And he came to see her frequently, at least once a day. Lately, he had started eating dinner with her every night when he didn't have a social engagement. Sometimes Goth joined them; more often they were alone. But despite what was universally assumed, they had touched one another only in rare, charged moments.

It had been going on ever since that night in Harbourdown. His orders exiling her from his presence had lasted less than a day. Then he had come to see her, restless as a maddened animal, demanding to know what she had done to him. At first he didn't believe her. Over the following days he probed and questioned, argued, gathered evidence, discarded several alternative theories, and at last was convinced that what she claimed to have done was real.

For a while then he was deeply angry, to have had his innermost soul violated as she had done, against his will. During this stage he had shunned her and thrown himself into his work. It was not until after the surrender of Lashnish that he had returned, and then it was as if something had changed. The idea that another person had shared his secrets had started to have a hold on his mind. It was terrifying and abhorrent to him—and yet it fascinated him, drew him to her. Gradually she had begun to see in furtive moments the pleasure he got from the thought. For the first time in his life, he entertained the notion that someone knew him, truly knew him, without any barriers of self-interest or delusion, and still did not recoil, still wanted to touch him, still would give him as much of her as he would take, and take as much of himself as he would give.

By the time they came to Tornabay, he was so explosive with pent-up desire that even the Innings around him could see it. They all assumed it was sexual, and they were right; but it was far more than that. He was preoccupied by the strange temptation to see himself as he never had before, as the sort of man who could inspire love.

Still, he fought it. One night, as they were dining together, he said abruptly, "You know, some men take native concubines. I've never thought of myself as the type."

"Is that what you think is going on?" she said.

He hesitated, and she realized he was trying to classify what was going on into some category he knew. "That's what the world would think," he said.

"The world would be wrong."

"You're right," he said. "Fuck the world."

And yet, that night he returned to his own room and locked the door between them.

That locked door became a symbol of the contest of wills that was going on.

Every night she tried the door to see if he had finally left it open for her. He knew she tried it. Sometimes she could feel him standing on the other side of it, inches away, debating whether to let her in, forcing himself not to.

It was testing every fibre of Spaeth's self-discipline. If it had only been sexual, it would have been simpler; they both desired it more with every passing day. The thing he feared was what sexual abandon might lead to, the chance that in a vulnerable moment she would take from him something he was not yet ready to surrender. Until he was prepared to put himself at risk, there was nothing she could do but wait.

In the end, the only person who could really seduce him was himself.

The thing that cinched the bond between them was Goth. Together they watched him decline till he could barely move from his bed, and his mind was absent most of the time. It seemed almost impossible that he could still be hanging tenaciously to a thread of life. Their shared grief over Goth brought Spaeth and Corbin together in a way that even dhota couldn't. It was a simple comfort to both of them not to have to watch him die alone.

Gradually, Corbin began to confide in her some of what was on his mind, so she heard about the political firestorms his victory had set off.

"Now that I have done exactly what they asked me to do, they have decided perhaps it wasn't what they wanted, or they don't like the way I did it," he told her. "When we were at war, no severity was too harsh. Now that I've secured peace for them, everyone is racked with conscience. To hell with them all. How did they expect me to fight an *ethical* war?"

He was at the pinnacle of power. No one in the Forsakens could oppose him, and yet he felt more isolated and embattled every day. "It's just as well that I didn't take it seriously when they were all idolizing me," he said with a cynical, dismissive humour. "At least now that they're demonizing me it's not such a shock." And yet, whatever he said, she knew that he *had* taken the adulation seriously, or at least enjoyed it enough that its sudden withdrawal felt like a galling injustice.

"I don't need to put up with this," he told her more than once. "I'm going to resign. All I have to do is hang on long enough to finish what I started here, so I don't leave things worse off than when I arrived."

"Then what will you do?" she asked. He only sat staring ahead of him, unable to answer.

At last one evening he came in with a stern and rigid face. He sat down on a settee, and she sat down next to him, curling her bare feet under her. When he didn't tell her at once what was wrong, she cautiously took his hand in hers.

"My mother's lawyer has filed a writ of habeas corpus on your behalf," he said.

"What does that mean?"

"It means my family is going to mount a legal battle to get me to turn you over."

"Oh," she said.

"I'm not sure I can win it. I cannot defy the law outright. I am supposed to be upholding it." He stared stonily ahead, hiding from her. "The attorney is demanding to be allowed to see you. I have very few grounds to refuse him."

"All right," she said.

He turned to look at her then, his eyes challenging. "Is that what you prefer? To get away from here, and go back to my brother?"

She saw then what this was about. She drew back a little; his jealousy was radiating hot enough to scorch her. "Nathaway is my bandhota," she said. "You could be, but you won't. It's what you've chosen."

His jaw clenched. He said, "I hope Nathaway rots in hell."

She still had hold of his hand, and now she tightened her grip. "No, you don't," she said. "The only reason you resent him is because he was allowed to have the life you wanted to live."

His eyes on her widened for a moment; then he stood up and turned away. "I have to dress for dinner," he said, his voice harshly controlled. "I have an important meeting tonight." He left then, through the door into his own room. But whether from oversight or intention, he didn't lock it after him.

Spaeth waited a while, listening. At last she heard him moving around in the next room, and went silently to the door. When she let herself in, he was standing before the mirror in a silk dressing-gown. His hair was still damp from his bath. He saw her in the mirror and stiffened, but didn't turn. Then she knew the unlocked door had been an invitation.

Slowly she came forward till she could see his face in the mirror. His mood had changed; he wasn't angry any more. "What are you thinking?" she said.

He gave a slight, remorseful smile. "I was thinking that I'm not entirely decrepit. There are still parts of me reasonably intact."

She put her hands on his shoulders, then ran them down his back. She could feel the sharp shoulder bones under the thin fabric. He was more than just intact; he was taut, lean, and charged. Nathaway she had loved because she felt perfectly safe with him; Corbin was thrillingly dangerous.

He turned around to look at her with an expression of painful conflict. "Would you be willing to sit for an artist?" he asked. "I would like to have a picture of you, before . . ." Hesitantly, lightly, he touched her face.

"You don't need to settle for a picture," she said.

She could feel all his discipline singing with tension. It was maddeningly attractive. The desire was building in him, fuelled by impending loss, swelling till it became unbearable.

"For weeks I've felt like I have bees under my skin," he whispered. "I can't get rid of it. I can't sleep, I can't think of anything but being with you."

"You have to let me help you," she said. "You have to give in."

He had been trained to seize and overpower things, and it had always worked, up to now. She knew every cranny of his damaged, difficult soul; what she needed to do was teach him to surrender.

Slowly she reached out to unfasten the sash of his robe. He watched her, fascinated, paralyzed by anticipation. She pushed aside the garment and pressed her hands against his naked chest. He breathed in sharply. Then their bodies came together, pressed against each other. His lips were hard and demanding against hers. She ran her hands down his back, feeling the skin quiver. He was nearly mad with excitement. She would have to find something to cut herself, to draw the blood that would make his mind as open as his body.

There was a knock on the door. He stopped, suspended agonizingly just on the edge of acting.

"Sir? Admiral Talley?" a voice called.

"Don't answer," Spaeth whispered in his ear.

He whispered a curse, then called out, "What is it?"

"Vice-Admiral Joffrey needs to speak to you before you leave. I'm sorry, he said it was urgent. Also, your carriage is waiting."

"All right, thank you," he said.

She felt his body shiver with thwarted desire. He pulled away, then sat down in a chair, trying to collect his control. "I'm sorry," he said. "I can't cancel this. There are fifty people waiting for me; we've been trying to get them together for weeks."

"You're the ruler of the Isles!" she said. "You can do what you want."

He drew in a shaky breath. "I wish it were true." He looked up at her, and then suddenly they were kissing again, lost in the sensation of mingling breath and boundaries broken. Then he pushed her away. "Get out of here. I can't think with you nearby."

"Promise you'll come to me when you get back," she said.

"I will," he said.

She waited for him on the settee in her room, but the sky was growing light and he still had not returned by the time she fell asleep. When she woke, the sun was streaming in the window, and the door between their rooms was locked again.

৯৹

Two days later, the attorney came to see her.

He arrived in the morning, a time of day when Corbin was invariably gone; but the staff had apparently been expecting him, because an adjutant accompanied him and his clerk, showing them into her room and withdrawing only when the lawyer gestured him peremptorily to leave. He then turned to beam benignly at her; but she barely saw him. Her eyes were on the tall scarecrow clerk in his broad-brimmed hat and shabby black coat. The instant the door was closed, she crossed the room like a gust of wind and threw her arms around him. He held her desperately tight against him. They exchanged a long, passionate kiss. She had forgotten how ardent he was. Just like his brother.

"Oh, Nat," she breathed. "Come to bed with me, now."

The lawyer gave a little, self-conscious cough. Nathaway glanced at him and said, "Later, Spaeth. We have business right now."

His face had changed. He was very thin, and there were creases under his eyes that gave him a strained, sad look. There was an air of uncured pain in him that teased her senses. "You've been hurt," she said, refusing to let him go. "I can't let you be ill. You need to be happy. Let me help."

"Later, I promise. The instant we can get you free."

"I don't have to be free. I'll do it now."

"Excuse me," the lawyer said, "This is very touching, but we really are under some time pressure."

Nathaway's eyes searched the room and stopped on the door into the adjoining bedchamber. Seeing where he was looking, Spaeth said, "He isn't here this time of day."

A chill seemed to pass through Nathaway's body; it was like he was freezing in her arms. He looked at her and said, "What has he done to you?"

"Nothing. Don't worry." She stroked his arm to thaw him.

It wasn't, of course, true; Corbin had nearly driven her mad, withholding himself. Nathaway seemed to sense she was lying, but not what she was lying about. He looked up to the lawyer and said, "Let's get it done. Now."

"Well then, hand me the document case."

Nathaway picked up the long, tubular tin box that he had carried in, and handed it to the lawyer, who opened it and extracted several elaborately written pieces of paper. He spread the first one on a table and took an inkpot and quill from his pocket, then beckoned them over. "Wabin Bartelso at your service, madam," he said, gallantly pressing Spaeth's hand between his and bowing. "Nat has told me a great deal about you, and I must admit, reality exceeds expectation."

"Who are you?" she said. She had never seen an Inning so odd-looking. His hair looked like a bird's nest.

"A very pertinent question. This first document defines who I am. If you sign it, I will be your advocate and attorney."

"What's that?" she said.

Nathaway was standing close behind her. He put his hands on her shoulders and said, "Sign the paper, Spaeth. He's on our side."

Spaeth had often seen people using pens, but had never actually held one herself. Nathaway had to show her how to place it between her thumb and forefinger, resting against her middle finger. It felt awkward, and she didn't know what to do next, so Nathaway held her hand in his, dipping the pen in the ink and then guiding it to make some signs on the paper. "Is that my name?" she asked when they were done.

"Yes," Nathaway told her. "At least, close enough."

The lawyer took away the first sheet. There was another underneath, even more elaborate with scrolls and calligraphy. "Now, this is the marriage license, but it can't be signed till we have finalized the contract. Nat, my boy, perhaps you'd better ask her. Be quick about it."

Nathaway took both of her hands in his and faced her earnestly. "Spaeth, will you marry me?" he said.

"What for?" she said.

He looked a little taken aback by the question. "Well, it will give you some legal protection, and certain rights. You will become one of my family, and your children will be my heirs."

"Do you want children, Nat?" Spaeth said. It was a novel thought, but it rather pleased her.

"Maybe. Someday," he said.

"Glad to see you young people have thought this through," Bartelso muttered.

"Besides," Nathaway went on, "when you get out of here, we'll be able to cohabit without getting arrested for lewd behaviour."

"Oh, this is the license to have sex!" she said, understanding at last.

"Yes. Please say yes, Spaeth. It's important to me."

"But we've been having sex for months."

With an embarrassed glance at the lawyer, Nathaway said, "It hasn't been legally binding. The marriage is like a public declaration—"

"You want to publicly declare we're having sex?"

"No," he said desperately, "that we have a commitment to one another."

"Nat," the lawyer interrupted, "might I have a word with you?" He put a fatherly arm around Nathaway's shoulder and drew him off to one side. Spaeth sat down at the table, listening to them talk.

"My dear boy," Bartelso said in a low voice, "your parents would never forgive me if I didn't ask whether this is truly the wisest course for you to take. I know, I know, your intentions are honourable. But think about your future, and all the possibilities you might foreclose. There are other ways to provide for her and fulfill any obligations your conscience may require."

"I'm not doing this out of guilt, Wabin," Nathaway said. "I'm doing it for love."

"I don't doubt that, son. But the young lady doesn't even understand the concept of marriage. No one would expect you to formalize a liaison like this, or think worse of you for not doing it."

"It's not a liaison," he said stiffly. "She's the person I want to spend my life with."

The gravity of their tone made Spaeth realize that this was more important than the licenses to fish or trade that the Innings were so fond of. The two men seemed to regard it as one of their great law-spells. It was something perilous and life-changing for them.

When they returned, she said seriously, "Nat, if it's important, I'll do whatever you want."

"It is," he said.

"Then yes, I'll marry you."

Bartelso sighed, outnumbered. "Well then, sit down, both of you," he instructed. They sat at the table, side by side, and he sat facing them. He had a sheaf of pre-printed papers and began reading hastily through them. "Sorry, I don't do this often. This part is all standard boilerplate—joining in a state of legal matrimony, etcetera, etcetera . . . ah, here's the first important bit. Spaeth Dobrin, do you have any property to reserve to yourself or to bring to this union in common?"

"Property?" Spaeth said, looking at Nathaway.

"Did Goth leave you anything?" he asked. "The house in Yorabay?"

"They burned it," she said.

Nathaway said to the lawyer, "She still might have a land claim."

"Is there a deed?"

"No."

"She needs to tell me herself."

"Tell him no, Spaeth."

"No," she said.

Bartelso looked at them dubiously, but finally turned to Nathaway. "What about you, Nat?"

"I think there is a trust fund, in bonds. Plus whatever share I have in my parents' estate. If they don't disown me for this."

"Not to mention disbarring me," the lawyer muttered, then said, "Do you want it to go to her children?"

"Yes," he said.

"Next question. Do you, Spaeth, swear to hold yourself inviolate for Nathaway, forswearing all other unions?"

"No," she said.

"Say yes, Spaeth," Nathaway coached her.

"How can I?" she protested. "I have bandhotai. What about Harg? What about—"

Nathaway's cheeks and ears had turned red. "Please, we'll talk about it later. For now, just pretend, and say yes."

Against her better instincts, she said, "Yes."

Bartelso shook his head and made a mark on the paper. "Do you attest that this is your first union?"

"No," she said. "There was Goth, and Harg, and now Corbin."

"Bandhotai don't count," Nathaway said. "You weren't legally married to them."

"Oh," she said, "then yes."

"Do you have any children?"

"No."

Bartelso turned the paper around and held out the pen. "Sign at the bottom, please."

Again Nathaway guided her hand in a signature, then took the contract and signed his own name. Then they held hands and said some ritual words, and both signed the license paper. Bartelso signed as witness.

"Congratulations," he said. "You are now husband and wife." He took out his watch. "And just in time. We have to leave, Nat."

"No!" Spaeth said, holding onto Nathaway's hand. They had wasted all their time together.

Nathaway was looking nervously at the door to Corbin's room. "I'm sorry, Spaeth, we were only given a short time window. But this will make it easier to get you free."

"I can't leave here," she said. There was Goth, and Corbin, and somewhere in the building, Harg. Her ties to them outbalanced any to Nathaway.

"You two are going to have to work this out some other time," Bartelso said. "I will take care of getting this marriage registered and published. You'd better be prepared for a reaction. People are going to notice it." He finished putting the papers back into the case and took Nathaway firmly by the arm. "Come along, Nat. Look clerkish."

Reluctantly, he rose. Spaeth followed them to the door, and she and Nathaway exchanged one last, long kiss before Bartelso pushed Nathaway out ahead of him.

"A pleasure to make your acquaintance, Mrs. Talley," the attorney said, and closed the door behind him.

❦

In alternate moments Harg wished it would all end, and daydreamed that it never would. He had lost the battle to keep his brain quiet, and found himself weaving elaborate scenarios. Every sound brought him tensely to his feet, and yet he was nearly mad with boredom.

The prison cell they had put him in was in a block of five, arranged in a row along a corridor with only bars on one side, like zoo cages. The others were empty. His cell was a primitive affair with just a cot and ceramic commode. By the height of the tiny window and the damp smell, he judged it to be below ground. It rained the second night, and he found that it flooded an inch deep. He lay on his cot in the blackness listening to something moving in the water, his mind on rats. The next day he asked for a light, but the guard ignored him.

The guards obviously had orders not to speak to him. Every attempt to draw them out brought silence. He began devising ways to keep his mind away from the future, or worse, the past: reciting old songs, trying to remember the names of all the cities on the Rothur coast, just pacing to quiet his thoughts.

Back in Lashnish, when he had been Ison Harg in everyone's eyes but his own, nobility had come easily; but as isolation slowly stripped the Ison part away, leaving just himself, he realized he didn't want to pay the price. There were still a thousand things he wanted to know and do and see. He had never seen the Outer Chain or learned to play a fiddle or seen a woman smile at him across the breakfast table. He had never taught a son to handle a boat. He wanted all those things now; he wanted another chance to be a different person. All his life he had wasted time on inessential things, and never done the things that might, just might, have made him content to leave the world.

Death shouldn't come like this, he thought, to someone who hadn't finished with life. It should come after he had grown weary, when the ripples of his death would not spread far. When he had seen all he wanted of the world, all the sights and mysteries he would never know now.

He was dozing when they came to get him. The soldiers led him down a smoke-stained tunnel to a room that held only a large plank table with a lamp hanging over it, and left him there alone. He waited, noticing all the details—the worn spots on the table legs where it looked like straps had been attached, the stains on its well-scrubbed surface, the iron hooks high on the walls. There was a murmur of voices in the adjoining room, barely audible, then the clink of metal. Soon he heard the voices raised in argument, and crept over to listen at the door; but the low murmur had resumed. After half an hour there was silence; then the guard came and led him back to his cell.

The second time they came for him, it was the dead of night. A tense young Torna colonel gave him a heavy cloak to put on, then tied a blindfold over his eyes and pulled the hood over his head. They led him down steps, across what seemed like an open courtyard, past a place that smelled of garbage, then into another building. They left him in a wood-panelled room with a carpet, a table, and a couch. He waited, expecting someone else to appear, but no one did. At last he lay down on the couch, not particularly caring whose it was. When he woke up with sunlight filtering through the louvres in the shutters, it occurred to him that perhaps it was his.

Twice in one day, he heard loud arguments in the hall outside, and the guards apparently refusing someone entrance to his room. That evening, after bringing in his food, the guard suddenly came back in and snatched the tray away again before Harg could touch it.

Was someone trying to poison him? With nothing else to think of, the idea became an obsession; yet it made no sense. Why should the Innings want to kill him in such a private way, when every other method was at their disposal? The chilling notion struck him, that perhaps it was his friends trying to kill him kindly, in order to spare him a worse death. Had he already been condemned without trial? Would the guards show up some morning to take him to execution without warning?

It was evening when the guards showed up. He had scarcely slept the night before, full of premonitions. This time they led him openly into another wing of the palace, into yet another room, this one a stone-walled bedroom with a jute rug on the floor, a table, and a cold fireplace. When he stood by the door he could hear the distant sound of music.

A few minutes later the guard unbolted the door and a man bustled in, carrying a lamp and a sheaf of papers. He said, "We haven't got much time. Take a seat, my boy, and we'll get to business."

Wild theories flashed through Harg's brain. The visitor was a round man with a blank, domed skull protruding from a fringe of curly hair. "Are you an Inning?" Harg asked suspiciously.

"Inning and in practice, as the saying goes." He held out a hand. "Wabin Bartelso, Advocate. I'm your legal advisor."

Harg crossed his arms and stepped back. The man was obviously a clown sent to suit the letter of the Inning law, so it would appear as if they had treated him fairly.

The lawyer took in Harg's hostile stance, then lowered his hand. "Ah. I see there's going to have to be a leap of faith here. Unfortunately, the first thing I need you to sign is a paper appointing me your counsel so I can represent you at the trial."

"What trial?" Harg said.

"You don't know? You are probably the only one in Tornabay, then. There has been quite the controversy over it." He brought out a sheet, densely written with large calligraphy at the top, and laid it on the wood table. He then took a pen from the frizz of hair behind his ear, and an inkpot from one of many pockets in his voluminous overcoat. "Right there, if you please," he said, indicating a place for Harg to sign.

Harg didn't move. "How do I know what it says?"

Bartelso took out a pocket watch and glanced at it. In a voice of strained patience he said, "Unfortunately, the Admiral has only allowed me half an hour with you, and we've got a lot to cover. But do read it, if you must."

Harg wasn't sure whether the man meant to mock him or was merely an idiot who thought Adaina fishermen learned to read legal documents, so he just stared at him in silence.

After a few beats Bartelso said, "Ah. Not yet, eh? Well, we can take care of that later, then." He whisked the document away and sat down at the table, putting on a pair of reading glasses and arranging his papers before him. "Have a seat, my boy. You make me nervous, standing there with murder in your eyes."

"I'm not your boy," Harg said.

Bartelso, who had up to now been in a constant flurry of motion, suddenly came to a stop. He took off his glasses, studying Harg seriously. "No, of course not," he said. "An unfortunate figure of speech. I do beg your pardon."

It was so startling to have an Inning apologize to him that Harg sank down on the edge of a chair. Outside the door, the music had grown louder. It was a waltz.

"Who sent you?" he said.

"A friend of yours. Nathaway Talley."

Harg was not the slightest bit sure that Nathaway really was his friend.

"What are they charging me with?" he said.

"Only two things," Bartelso answered. "Unfortunately, they're assassination and treason. Either way, the penalty is death."

It was no more than Harg had expected. He was silent.

"Now here's the important part," the lawyer said. "Because of the political situation, the Admiral needs to try you in public, as a civilian. It's a demonstration of impartial Inning justice, you see."

"You mean it will be fair?" Harg said sceptically.

"Goodness, no. It's just better than a military trial would be. But what he has in mind is to try you on the block. Trust me, you don't want that."

"Why not?"

"What they would do is chain you down to a block of wood throughout the trial. You couldn't see the judges, or the witnesses, or face the court. It's meant to intimidate and humiliate, and it's very effective."

It sounded like something Talley would want for him. Harg's stomach ached with tension.

"Don't worry, I can get you out of it," Bartelso said. "The block is only intended for cases where the defendant's own testimony is likely to incriminate him. By robbing a person of dignity, you can rob him of caution and guile as well. What I will do is declare that you are going to renounce your right to testify in your own behalf."

Harg stared at him, wondering whether this was a ruse to gag him.

"Now, listen," Bartelso said, leaning close. "When you enter the court, you must not utter a word. There's a legal reason it's too complicated to explain right now. Believe me, though, you have to leave the talking to me, even when they ask you directly to reply."

"I can't justify myself?" Harg said.

"Holy blazes! That's the last thing you should try to do."

He had thought at least he would be able to put forward his arguments, his reasons. Without that, his execution would be senseless. "If I say a word, they'll put me on the block?" he said.

"Not exactly," Bartelso said. "You can avoid the block as long as you don't testify. No, it's a jurisdictional argument I'm going to make. If you utter a word, you acknowledge the court's jurisdiction over you."

It sounded ridiculously arcane. All Harg wanted to know was the basics. "They're going to execute me anyway," he said, looking at the Inning to see if he would be honest.

Bartelso's eyes held a glint of sympathy. "I wouldn't say you had a good chance. I'm professionally obligated to say you have a chance. But you're in a heap of trouble, son."

Hesitantly, Harg said, "Is there any way you could get them to hang me, instead of . . ."

Bartelso interrupted hastily. He looked embarrassed. "That's another step. Don't worry about that yet. If there's one thing I'm sure of, it's that I can delay things."

Harg wasn't sure that was what he wanted. He never got to say so, for the guard opened the door and gestured Bartelso to leave.

"It hasn't been half an hour!" the lawyer protested, snatching out his watch.

"That's all you get," the guard said implacably.

Bartelso shoved the contract at Harg again. "Sign it," he said. "Don't worry about the bills; the Talleys will pay."

Harg might have reached for the pen, but with that statement he pulled back, reminded that he had no idea who to trust, and no idea what the paper said.

"Come along, sir," the guard said.

"I'll leave it with you," Bartelso said. "Bring it to the courthouse." He tucked his other papers under his arm and held out his hand. "Good to meet you, sir."

Harg stared at him motionless, so uncertain what to think that he could not act, till Bartelso threw up his hands up in a helpless shrug and left.

THE TRIAL OF
HARG ISMOL

Even though Bartelso had told her to expect it, Spaeth was not prepared for Corbin's reaction when the marriage notice was finally published.

She sensed something when she heard swift, booted footsteps approaching down the hall, and the guard's salute. He entered her chamber not through the private door, but from the hallway. It was late in the evening; he had left for a banquet hours ago, and now he was dressed in full uniform. With a coldly controlled motion, he threw down a printed sheet on the table before her. "Explain this, if you please," he said.

She looked at the broadside. "What is it?"

"It is a wedding announcement."

Spaeth didn't know what he wanted her to say. He was pale as ice.

"For the past three hours I have been fending off questions about it," he said.

"What do you want to know?" she asked.

"You might start with whether is it true. No, don't bother. I sent someone to check, and it has been registered."

"Then you know all I do."

"I don't know why you did it. I don't know what I have done to make you betray me."

Astonished at this reaction, she searched his face. He was being perfectly honest; the uppermost thing in his mind was betrayal. It was the thing in life he feared and despised above all, and it had happened to him over and over again, from childhood on. "I didn't betray you," she said seriously. "It had nothing to do with you. It was a private thing between me and Nat. He wanted it; I didn't see any harm."

He was speechless for a moment, then said acidly, "You can't play the naive native with me. I know you, remember. At least, I thought I did. I thought—" He stopped, looking away from her, unable now to say what he had thought.

Spaeth rose and tried to take his hand. He stepped back. "It doesn't matter!" she pleaded urgently. "It has nothing to do with you and me. We're bandhotai, or could be. There's nothing more important than that."

"You're joking," he said.

"I'll marry you, too, if you want," she said desperately.

He stared at her for a few moments, rage and infatuation warring in his eyes. Then he turned and went to the hall door. When he opened it, the soldier just outside came to attention. "Take this woman down and put her in a cell with the rest of the prisoners," he said.

"Yes sir!" said the guard.

Corbin turned back to Spaeth. "You have elected to be my enemy. Very well, you will be treated that way."

᪤

Bartelso's visit had left Harg in a state of terrible unease. He felt as if his life were being used as a shuttlecock in a game where he didn't know the rules, or even the point. Yet none of the other players was going to be dead at the end.

On the night before the trial, they transferred him back down to the dank row of cells in the basement where he had started out. As before, they left him without a light, so as evening came there was absolutely nothing to do but sleep, and that he could not do. He lay down, thinking he needed rest to be alert tomorrow; but his heartbeat was so loud in his ears he felt his neck-veins would burst. Every slight sound—the scrape of a foot outside his door, a dog's bark outside—made him start, skin tingling. As he stared into the dark, scenes from his life started playing in his mind like tormenting insects, stinging. Why, on this of all nights, was he harried with horrors and mistakes? Why could he remember no *good* things?

He could time his nights by the change of guards an hour before midnight. He heard it too soon and sat up, despairing of ever getting rest. Minutes after, the heavy door at the end of the row of cells banged open. There were footsteps, men's voices, and a light. He came to his feet, alarmed that they had come already to take him to trial.

But they were only bringing in another prisoner. He stood at the iron gate of his cell, watching. At first he thought he was hallucinating from lack of sleep. It was a woman, wearing an elegant dressing gown hastily thrown over nightclothes. When the guard raised the lamp over her head, he saw her clearly—silver hair tied back from her face, grey eyes lined with worry. "Spaeth?" he whispered, disbelieving his own lips.

She saw him then, and her lips formed his name. As the Torna guard pushed her past, he reached out through the bars, and their hands touched. Her eyes on him were hungry as a starved dog's.

"Get your hands off the Admiral's woman, you stinking pile of brown," the guard said. He shoved Spaeth on and let her into the cell next to Harg's, locking the gate.

When the cell block door boomed shut and silence fell, Harg whispered, "Spaeth? What are you doing here? I thought . . ." He thought of how he had seen her last, standing next to Corbin Talley, lending him her mystery. The guard's words were still ringing in his mind.

"He is angry at me," she said simply.

He tried to keep from imagining what sort of lover's quarrel had landed her here. Or what sort of lover Corbin Talley must be. He tried not to think of how she had been touched with those ice-cold hands, used to ease his bodily desires, made into his possession like the rest of the Isles.

"Harg?" she said.

Why was he tormenting himself? He had no claim on her. He had had his chance, and let it pass. Talley had just taken what he had not had the courage to.

"Harg?" she said again.

"Yes. I heard. He's angry at you. Me, too." He gave a strangled laugh.

"Hold your hand out," she said.

There was only a stone wall separating them. He reached out between the bars. When he stretched as far as he could, his fingertips brushed hers. The bare touch brought the rest of her vividly to mind. He could almost feel her, pressed against the other side of the cell wall, just as he was pressed to his side.

"They're going to try me tomorrow," he said.

"What does that mean?"

"It's just the show before the execution."

She was silent then. "Touch me again," she said at last.

Their fingertips brushed. All the lost chances in his life were aching.

"Spaeth," he said, hesitantly.

"Yes?"

"The guard this time of night is Adaina. He comes through around midnight. He's been ordered not to talk to me, but he might listen to you."

She didn't answer, but he knew she understood.

When the guard came through and shone his light into Harg's cell, Harg was lying on his cot as if asleep. He listened intently, and heard the man's steps pause at the next cell. There was a whispered exchange; he couldn't hear the words until Spaeth said, almost aloud, "Please." Then the guard moved on.

When he came back down the row of cells, there was another whispered conversation. At first the guard started to leave, then went back. That was when Harg knew she had persuaded him. He forced himself not to move as he heard the soft sound of the key in the lock. The light came opposite his cell, and he turned to look as the guard opened the gate and Spaeth slipped inside. The man locked it after her, then left.

Without the guard's light it was pitch dark, but Harg knew exactly where she was, for she radiated longing like a banked fire. All the things she had once stirred up in him were aching again, brought to life by her presence. He was almost afraid to touch her.

"I didn't think I'd ever see you again," she said softly. "I thought you would go to your grave unhealed, and I was going to have to carry your pain around in me forever."

"I'm sorry, Spaeth," he said. "I was a damned fool."

"Is he truly going to kill you?"

"Yes."

"Then there is nothing I can do but help you go without pain."

His mouth felt dry. He tried to laugh, but it sounded macabre. "I don't think that's what Talley has in mind."

"Your past pain, I mean," she said.

"I know what you mean."

It seemed like a very different offer now that there was only a day or two left of his life. For that little time he could be free of the entrapment of the past. He could walk into tomorrow healed. The only price would be himself—a worthless currency.

"I still wouldn't be Ison," he said.

"No. You didn't need any help to become Ison, Harg. You fought the Mundua and won, all by yourself. In the end, they couldn't control you."

"They came damned close."

"Then perhaps I did help you, a little."

"You did." He took her hand then, savouring that unconditional Lashnura forgiveness. No matter what he had become, she would still love him.

A shiver passed through her body when he touched her. Feeling it, he tensed, his mind alive with memories. "Will it be like last time?" he whispered.

"No," she said. "You have done the hard part. Now all you need to do is let go."

"You won't take away the memories?"

"No, only their pain. And I can't take anything but what you give me."

She was trying to hide the longing in her voice. He sat down on the bed, trying to calm his nerves, and she sat beside him.

"I need something to draw blood," she said.

"They don't let us have knives down here."

"I know! He gave me a brooch."

He waited while she unpinned it. He felt the swift little motion as she stabbed herself with the pin; then she touched his temple, and her finger was wet. Almost instantly he felt a dizzy, euphoric openness, as if his consciousness were a spreading pool. He thought, this was the way it was supposed to feel.

She touched the other temple, then his forehead and throat. Then she raised a hand to his face and gently pushed the patch away from his eye. Where her fingers touched the knotted skin, an electric tingling woke his senses into excruciating clarity.

"Close your eyes," she said. "Do you see the wound?"

He did. It was still festering in his face, rooted with fishhook feet in his brain. How had he managed to ignore it?

Her cheek was cool against his face. He felt her lips move lightly against the blind, burning socket. The scar's roots were relaxing their hold; deep in his brain the barbs grew slack. It was an alien thing, he realized, not part of himself. He had grown twisted around it till he mirrored it, like a mould; but it wasn't him.

"Let it go," she said.

Slowly, like a gentle surgeon, she drew it from his flesh. As its deep-buried roots pulled free, he felt wholesome blood rush into its place. Suddenly released from a pain to which he had grown so accustomed he had not even felt it, he laughed. He felt giddy and light.

Spaeth's body had gone stiff. Her indrawn breath hissed through teeth bared in a silent grimace. He touched her face; her eye was closed and watering. He took her in his arms, feeling an intense tenderness.

"Don't worry," she said distractedly. "It will pass. We can't stop now."

She opened his shirt to touch him just under the ribcage, where his body carried the invisible wound he had inflicted on Goth. When he closed his eye he saw it: a bleeding gap where something had been cut from inside him. He groaned, barely able to breathe from the pain. Quickly, Spaeth threw off the dressing gown she wore and pressed her body against his so that he felt the breath under her skin. And then her breath was inside his skin, and the pain was flowing into her, leaving him free.

Again and again she returned to find the parasite wounds embedded in him. The cell around them receded as he grew lightheaded with curing energy. He no longer wanted to hold back; he wanted to pour everything into her, to feel that delicious surge of painlessness. Each cure became a consummation.

Hours later he drifted up out of a healing sleep. There was a hint of grey light at the window. His body felt more utterly relaxed than it had been in months— no, years. He savoured the feeling of just resting, unencumbered.

Spaeth's head was nestled against his shoulder, her arm across his chest. Her bare skin felt hot against his. Looking down at her, he saw a resemblance to Goth in her face. It was that feverish glow of disease that wasn't hers. The thought didn't produce the familiar wrench that accompanied all his thoughts of Goth. He turned his head to kiss her rumpled hair, and thought, *What a strange feeling*. He felt light, and marvellously simple, yet not unlike himself. In fact, what was left in him was more truly *him* than what was gone.

He tried to gently draw away from Spaeth in order to sit up; but even in sleep she instinctively clutched at him. When he lifted away her arm, she woke.

"Go back to sleep," he said. "You need it."

She shielded her eyes from the dim light; the left eye was bloodshot and tearing. There were, in fact, shadow-scars all over her. He bent down to kiss one. Her grey skin was velvety smooth, and quivered under his lips. Her body was half his now, and intensely precious to him. He wanted more than anything to start touching it all over again. She lay there gazing at him as if he were all she wanted in the world. It made him feel euphoric.

"Harg," Spaeth said, "do you want to have children?"

The question, so out of context, didn't jar him as it should have. He had fantasized about being granted a normal existence; but would he really do it? "I don't know," he said.

"Why not?"

"I've never wanted to be responsible for a child."

She picked up his hand from where it rested on the blanket and meshed her fingers in his. "You sound just like Goth."

With a shock, he realized she was right. What he felt was exactly what Goth must have felt, what had stood between them all these years. *I am no better than he is*, Harg thought; and then, an even stranger revelation: *He is no better than me.* Goth was just a fallible person caught between his intentions and his actions. Trapped and floundering, like everyone else.

Spaeth put a hand on his arm. "What is it?" she asked.

"Nothing," he said. "It doesn't matter." And while the first part wasn't true, he slowly realized that the second part was.

 споро

The guards that came to fetch him were dressed in red and black uniforms Harg had never seen. Two of them trooped heavily into the room a little after sunrise, rousing Harg and Spaeth from a doze. The younger one laughed hilariously to find the prisoner naked in bed with a woman; the older one was angry at the lapse in security. He ordered Spaeth out of the bed, and when she moved sluggishly he yanked her by the arm and thrust the dressing-gown at her. "Have a care!" Harg said angrily. "She's ill, you dolt." With a glare at him, the guard pushed Spaeth out into the corridor half dressed.

"He's just jealous," the younger guard said with a wink. "They say the grey ones are insatiable." It took all Harg's control not to flatten his face.

They had brought him a new set of clothes, of a nasty dried blood colour, and a basin to wash in. There was a short argument among the guards whether to let in a barber who had come to shave him, apparently at Bartelso's request. After that another argument ensued, this one between Harg and the barber, as to whether he ought to go into court well groomed by Inning standards or Adaina ones. Harg won. The Innings had already made up their minds, he said, and one beard more or less was not going to sway them.

When he looked at himself newly trimmed in the barber's mirror, he saw that the scar on his face was already healing; the pale, dead skin was flushed, and even the eye socket looked pink where the new eye would soon begin to grow in. He put his old patch on nonetheless; it had become something of a symbol by now.

The bells outside were ringing when he left his cell accompanied by the two court guards. He felt an unaccountable optimism about the new day, a desire to take it on and live it out. He hadn't felt so full of life in months.

When they brought him into the courtroom, the tall, vaulted hall was filled with the hum of voices. His entry by a door at the front end caused a stir. The guards, suddenly grave and formal, led him up two steps to a platform bordered by a railing, and stood flanking him. He scanned the scene.

The room seemed designed for a performance. It was long and narrow, the west end filled with benches where well-dressed Tornas and a smattering of Innings sat watching. Some of them were snacking from bags; others had brought their children, who squirmed in formal clothes. On the front bench, a middle-aged Inning with a sketchpad was gazing at him intently and drawing with a pencil. At the back of the room was a space without seats, and here a horde of Adainas were packed in elbow to elbow, jostling for a better view.

At the front of the room Harg's eye stopped on a round window leaded in the shape of a spider's web. Under it stood a tall wooden lectern like an altar, unoccupied at the moment, with two other lecterns flanking it. The dais where Harg stood was below the lecterns and to one side; on the other side, facing him, sat three Innings dressed in red. One was Bartelso. He was speaking urgently to a guard, glancing at Harg. Directly below the tallest lectern, in the centre of the room, was the block.

Harg scarcely had time to get his bearings before the performance began. A bailiff gestured the audience to rise. As silence fell, an usher came down the central aisle, ceremoniously carrying a grey cat at arm's length, its hind legs swinging. He was followed by another usher with what looked like a wooden carving of a sprouting potato. When the cat and the potato had left the room, silence fell. The head usher stood before the block and recited something in a language Harg had never heard, made up of repetitive syllables like ba-ba and mook-mook. People in the audience began to titter, and were glared at by neighbours attempting to look respectful of ancient Inning customs.

When the recital ended, a side door opened and three judges entered. The first two, who took their seats at the lower lecterns, were dressed in robes and bulbous hats like onions. The last judge, who mounted to the tallest seat, was Corbin Talley, in his dress uniform.

In a solemn voice, Talley opened the trial. "Has the cat come in?" he asked. "Sir, it has," the head usher replied. Everyone was then allowed to sit. Since they had provided him no chair, Harg remained standing.

Talley began with a homily on justice. He expounded in a statesmanlike tone on how the law was the greatest gift Inning had to give the Forsaken Islands. All of Inning's great achievements, he said, were based on the impartiality of the courts. "This trial," he said, "will demonstrate how the law operates to preserve peace and an orderly society, despite those who seek to disrupt it."

Across the room, Bartelso was slumped in his chair, head back in an attitude that indicated either deep sleep or intent study of the ceiling. As the sermon ended he started upright and blew his nose loudly with a handkerchief. Talley turned to the lawyers' bench. "Advocates, you may approach me."

In a ceremonious line they each went up to the lectern, bowed, and handed him a roll of paper. He glanced at the first two and set them aside, but scrutinized Bartelso's. "Mr. Bartelso," he said, "your papers are not in order. I can find no verification that the prisoner has in fact appointed you his advocate."

Bowing, Bartelso said, "Your honour, if your diligent guards would allow me to walk across the room and give him that paper, you would have your verification."

"The court already allowed you time to consult with the prisoner. Since you neglected to make use of it, your request is denied. The court will appoint a disinterested advocate to act on the prisoner's behalf." He gestured to one of the other two lawyers, who gathered his papers and crossed the room to stand on Harg's side.

So Bartelso *was* on his side, Harg thought; Talley's measures to thwart him proved it.

"Sir, I must protest," Bartelso said. "This procedure is highly prejudicial."

Talley leaned over and consulted in a whisper with the judge on his left—his legal advisor, Harg guessed. Soon he announced, "Our procedures are within judicial guidelines, Mr. Bartelso. Please be seated." He turned to look at Harg for the first time then. "Prisoner, are you Harg Ismol of Yora?"

Bartelso had told him not to say a word; but whatever legal advantage there was in it was gone with Bartelso. Harg glanced at his appointed advocate, but the man was inert; he then glanced across the room, where Bartelso had retreated, fuming, to the advocates' dais. He was shaking his head in a warning "no." Harg stared in front of him, silent.

Talley repeated the question, then asked impatiently, "Is there anyone who can identify the prisoner?"

"I have a witness who can, sir," the prosecuting advocate said. He was a lean, dour man whose long face looked like a drooping dishrag.

"Please oblige us, Mr. Gaveril," Talley said.

They brought in Minicleer then, who pointed Harg out. For a moment their eyes met, and Harg saw a cruel triumph in Minicleer's face.

"Chain him to the block," Talley ordered dispassionately. The guards moved to lead Harg forward. Bartelso was signalling him to submit, apparently thinking it was better to endure the block than to give up the advantage of silence. Harg only hesitated a second. He then said loudly, "Sir, I wish to renounce my right to testify on my own behalf."

His words brought the proceedings to a confused halt. Talley leaned over to talk with his legal advisor, a consultation that turned into a whispered argument. The guards stood waiting. The audience hummed with speculation. Bartelso bowed his head on his knuckles, shaking it as if all were lost.

At last Talley turned back to him. "Prisoner, are you aware that giving up your right of testimony could be detrimental to your case?"

Wary of being trapped by answering either yes or no, Harg simply said, "Sir, I wish to repeat my statement."

Looking vexed, Talley said, "Very well. We shall proceed." The guards backed away.

One of the judges read an elaborately worded set of charges, then the prosecutor gave a speech expounding on the malicious and savage nature of Harg's crimes against civil order. When they gave Harg's advocate a chance to speak he said only, "My client maintains his innocence." He never even glanced at Harg.

Harg watched the audience. Were they seeing what a travesty this was, or were they fooled by the ceremony and rhetoric? He wondered if Bartelso had been right, and he should have let them humiliate him as well, just to make the point clearer. The thought made his stomach knot.

They began bringing out witnesses to testify to the first charge, which was the murder of Proctor Fullabeau at Harbourdown. The first witness, an Inning lieutenant, gave a convincing account of how, during the natives' treacherous attack on the Redoubt, the heroic commander had fled to the tower to signal the warships; but Harg had followed and, in a cowardly attack, pushed him to his death.

They seemed about to let the man leave. Harg, unable to contain himself any longer, said, "Sir, may I question the witness?"

The judges' bench was again thrown into a whispered consultation. At last Talley turned back to him and said, "Prisoner, you have an advocate to speak for you. It would be to your advantage to allow him to do so."

The advocate assigned to Harg rose and said, "I have no questions, your honour."

There had been something about this in the Inning law book Nathaway had read to him back in Harbourdown. Harg glanced at Bartelso. He was giving a half-hidden thumbs-up sign. "Sir," Harg said, "I believe the law guarantees the right of any man to confront his accusers. I wish to exercise that right."

Up to now, Talley had maintained a calm, detached air. Now his eyes on Harg were icy. "Very well," he said, "this court will grant you every advantage that is your right under law. But remember that you have renounced your right to testify. Questions only."

"Thank you, Admiral Talley," Harg said. "I am grateful that even humble Adainas like myself have rights under Inning law." He sensed a stir in the audience. Perhaps they had imagined a tiny bit of sarcasm in his tone.

He turned to the witness, who was trying to hide his nervousness under a stoic, military air. "Where were you at the time Proctor Fullabeau was killed, Lieutenant?" he said.

With a slight hesitation, the man said, "I was imprisoned in the armoury. The fort had been overrun—"

"Did you actually see his death?" Harg cut him off.

"No."

"Then how do you know how it happened?"

"It was common knowledge."

"Hearsay, you mean?"

Talley interrupted coldly, "That is not a question, prisoner. That is a prompt."

"Your pardon, Admiral," Harg said. "I am just getting the hang of this 'law' business."

There was a titter from the audience. "Silence!" Talley ordered.

"Did you ever hear me describe how Proctor Fullabeau's death occurred?" Harg asked the witness.

"No."

"Did you ever hear a single eyewitness describe how it occurred?" There had been no eyewitness but a man named Gibbon; and the gods alone knew where he was.

The Inning shifted in his chair, and Harg thought, *He is going to lie.* But to his surprise, the officer said, "No."

They tell the truth in court, Harg thought. *The damned cat and potato are like their Emerald Tablets—the things they respect even at their own cost.*

"Are you done?" Talley said.

"Yes, thank you, Admiral," Harg said.

"You may go," Talley said to the witness. There was a rustling from the audience, and Talley had to speak sharply to them again. Harg looked over to Bartelso. The lawyer was nodding with the look of a man who delights in mischief.

There were two other witnesses to the murder charge, both with similarly third-hand accounts full of conflicting details. With every question Harg expected Talley to stop him, but apparently he had hit upon some sacred quirk in Inning law that not even Talley could override.

The court then turned to consideration of Harg's role in the assault on Harbourdown Redoubt. The lieutenant came back in to describe the deceitful attack that allowed the natives to overrun the fort. Listening, Harg considered his strategy. It was no use denying that he had led the attack; hundreds of people knew it, and he had no desire to deny it anyway. Somehow, he had to change the focus. When the time came for him to question the witness, he said, "Lieutenant, why had the Inning Navy occupied the Redoubt at Harbourdown?"

The Inning looked to Talley. "Do I have to answer that, sir?"

Talley said, "Please do. We have nothing to hide."

With the air of someone reciting orders, the lieutenant said, "We had come to take possession of the island and establish order in preparation for introducing law and a civil government."

"At the time you arrived, how was Thimish ruled?"

"It wasn't ruled at all. It was in the hands of a type of criminal brotherhood."

"Were there any courts?"

"No."

"It was completely lawless?"

Annoyed, the man said, "That is correct."

"If there was no law in Harbourdown, how could I have broken it?"

Talley interrupted, "That's a specious question, and it has no bearing on this case."

Harg turned to him. "Sir, it seems to me I am being tried for breaking the laws of a country that had no sovereignty at the time and place I acted. You might as well try me for breaking Rothur law."

There was a hum of comment from the audience. Talley's voice cut through the noise like an axe. "Prisoner, if you wish to testify you will do so from the block."

"Your pardon, sir," Harg said. "I have no testimony. I was merely seeking clarification."

Talley looked out at the audience, which sounded unsettled as a cloud of gnats. He said, "This court will take an hour's recess." Without another word, he left the room. The other two judges followed.

As the guards were leading Harg back along the corridor to his prison cell, Bartelso popped out of a side hall and started walking along beside them. Across one of the guards he said, "I had you pegged for a sullen chap without many cards to play. You're a different person in front of a crowd, do you know that? You ought to think of taking up law someday, when you give up insurrection."

"Am I doing all right, then?" Harg said.

"Terrible!" Bartelso exclaimed. "It's a disaster. I never gave anyone better advice than when I told you to keep your mouth shut. Every time you open it, you dig yourself in deeper."

Harg scowled, uncertain how to take that. "I'm landing some hits, though," he said.

"From the crowd's point of view. But they're not going to decide your fate."

Harg retorted, "If I'd taken your advice, then this would all be over, and I'd be condemned."

"But we would have had grounds for appeal."

"What's appeal?" Harg said.

Bartelso groaned. "Dear boy, this is why you ought to let professionals handle your affairs."

One of the guards finally said to Bartelso, "Sir, are you authorized to talk to the prisoner?"

"Of course I am," Bartelso said. "Don't be absurd."

"If I'm doing so badly," Harg said, "why are you sitting across from me looking like the cat that got the bird?"

"There are always two courts to consider: the legal one, and the court of public opinion. You're condemning yourself in the first, but you're doing all right in the second. I couldn't have played to the crowd so well, because I would have had a small professional obligation to save your life."

They were nearing the guardroom door, and he knew they wouldn't let Bartelso in. He said, "Can Talley shut me up?"

"Certainly, if you cross the line. You were risking it, there at the end. He's leaning over to obey the forms, because of the Innings in the audience. He's facing a lot of criticism."

They were at the door then, and the other ninety-nine questions he had for Bartelso stayed unasked. When they shoved him back into his cell, there was no sign of Spaeth anywhere in the cell block. He spent the time alone eating the sparse lunch they brought him and thinking feverishly about strategy.

When the court reconvened, word had apparently spread that the trial was not the tedious, perfunctory ritual everyone had assumed. The room was packed now. Some people had even climbed up to the struts supporting the rafters. It was noisier than before. In the stir that met his entrance, Harg even heard a muffled shout of "Ison!" When Talley entered, he stood for a long time regarding them coldly. When he took his seat he gestured for a bailiff, and gave some whispered instructions.

The prosecutor's star witness was the first one called into the court. When Harg saw him enter in a spotless Inning uniform, he thought that this was how Joffrey should have looked all along. When he identified himself as Governor Joffrey, Harg realized that he had taken Tiarch's place as the Innings' puppet ruler in the Forsakens.

Joffrey's testimony was lengthy, detailed, and scrupulously accurate. It was also exquisitely damning. He could cite dates and specifics. From time to time he referred to a little notebook to give the exact words Harg had spoken. The courtroom had fallen totally silent, listening to his meticulous story. When he finished, there was something like a collective sigh as people turned to look at Harg, wondering how he could hope to refute this.

"Vice-Admiral Joffrey," Harg started.

"Governor," Joffrey corrected. His black eyes gleamed with the old animosity, but only Harg could see it.

"Congratulations," Harg said.

"Thank you," Joffrey replied.

"Tell me, who were you working for at the time you made all these observations?"

With a slight hesitation, Joffrey said, "For Admiral Talley."

I knew it, Harg thought. "Was Governor Tiarch aware of that fact?"

"I cannot speculate as to what Governor Tiarch was aware of," Joffrey said.

He was a slippery one, more intelligent than all of the Innings and their pedigrees combined. "What was the nature of your work for Admiral Talley?"

"I provided him with information."

"Is that the same as spying?"

Talley interrupted, "Stop badgering the witness and get to the point."

"Yes, sir," Harg said. "Governor, would you say that your job required you to be an expert at deceit?"

Before Talley could interrupt again, Joffrey replied smoothly, "Every job that involves the management of people requires a certain amount of judicious deceit."

"So you could, for example, deceive these people?" Harg gestured to the audience.

"Not in court," Joffrey answered. "I have far too much respect for the sanctity of the law."

This was going nowhere. Joffrey was too clever.

Harg abruptly changed the subject. "What is the definition of treason?"

Joffrey looked wary. "I am not a lawyer; I couldn't give you a legal definition."

"Can you give us your definition as the Governor of the Forsakens, sworn to enforce the laws of Inning?"

Flushing slightly, Joffrey said, "I believe it refers to illegal actions aimed at overthrowing one's government."

"Could a Rothur be charged with treason against Inning?" Harg was genuinely fishing for information now, and it wasn't Joffrey he wanted it from. He glanced at Bartelso, who had understood, and was subtly shaking his head.

"I don't believe so," Joffrey said. "Rothurs are not subjects of Inning."

Talley said, "Mr. Bartelso, is something troubling you?"

Bartelso stood and said, "It's a tic, your honour. Very troubling. Affects my head." There was a ripple of laughter through the audience as he sat down.

"Keep it under control," Talley said.

Harg turned back to Joffrey. "Are you a citizen of Inning, Governor?"

"No," Joffrey replied, "but I hope to achieve that honour someday soon."

"How is it that, despite such faithful service, you are not a citizen?"

"Citizenship is granted to non-natives only by the High Court."

Feigning surprise, Harg gestured to the audience. "Then what are all these people?"

Joffrey shifted in his seat. "Technically, wards of the court." There was a buzz of comment from the audience.

"And if one of them disagrees with an Inning citizen in authority, what recourse does he have?"

"He can sue in regional court."

"Represented, as I am, by an Inning lawyer?" Harg gestured to his inert advocate. There was a wry laugh from the audience.

Coldly, Joffrey replied, "That would be to his advantage."

"And the Adaina of the South Chain? What rights do they have?"

"The same, until they achieve a level of civilization consistent with citizenship."

"So I am not a citizen of Inning?"

"No, not technically."

"If I'm not a citizen, how can I be accused of treason? Isn't that like accusing a Rothur of treason?"

Talley interrupted impatiently, "The appropriateness of the charges is to be decided by the judges, who are learned in the law."

"Oh, so the law need not make common sense?" Harg shot back. There was an audible gasp from the audience.

"That is an insubordinate question," Talley snapped.

"Then I withdraw it," Harg said mildly. "I am just a savage trying to understand the subtleties of Inning civilization." A nervous laugh bubbled up around the room. Harg could tell the audience was his now.

Talley said tensely, "I am tolerating you, prisoner, in hopes of demonstrating our fairness. Your questions are irrelevant and are wasting this court's time. Only matters of fact are being judged here. Please confine your questions to them."

"Yes, sir. I have no more questions."

As Joffrey left the room, over the animated hum of conversation, there was a loud hiss from the back of the audience. Talley heard it and rose to his feet, trying to locate the perpetrator. *He has lost them*, Harg thought, *and he knows it*. For a moment Talley looked down at Harg, a virulence in his eyes that almost shook Harg's nerve. Then Talley announced loudly, "This court is adjourned. We will reconvene at eight o'clock tomorrow morning."

A strategic retreat, Harg thought. Then the guards were hustling him away before any more ground could be lost.

That evening, from the window of his cell, Harg could see firelight reflected on the low undersides of the clouds. When the guard came to give him dinner, he asked, "There's no rioting in the city, is there?"

The guards' discipline must have relaxed a little, because the young man actually answered, "No. Those are just bonfires in the Gallowmarket. People are camping out for good seats tomorrow."

For the first time in weeks, Harg slept soundly that night.

If the courtroom had seemed full the first day, it was nothing compared to the second. People were not only packed into every inch of space; they were on the window ledges and massed in the square outside. Talley had increased security, but not enough to match the increase in the crowd. Harg felt a volatile tang in the air.

The day started with more testimony, this time from Minicleer, covering the attack on Tornabay. The substance of it was incriminating enough, but the Inning spoke in a condescending sneer that set Harg's teeth on edge. Scanning the audience, he saw he was not the only one.

When it came his turn to speak, Harg paused a long time, looking out at the audience, trying to catch as many eyes as he could. *They must feel like participants,* he thought. *They cannot feel this is someone else's business, someone else's responsibility.*

"Provost, before you were appointed to your present position, what was your profession?" Harg asked Minicleer.

"I was an officer of the Inning Navy," Minicleer said, as if it irked him to have to answer.

"Tell me, have you ever been responsible for men being killed in battle?" Minicleer glared at him. "Yes."

"Are you concerned that you will be tried in court for it?"

"Don't be ridiculous."

With an air of surprise, Harg said, "Oh, is it not a crime in Inning law to kill a man in combat?"

"No."

"Is it a crime to fire a gun on the enemy?"

"No."

"Is it a crime to liberate a city occupied by the enemy?"

"Of course not!"

"Then why do you think I am standing here, and you are not?"

At last Minicleer saw where Harg's questions had been leading. He flushed angrily and looked to Talley for support. Impatiently, the Admiral said, "Prisoner, there is a difference between war and insurrection. You owed allegiance to Inning, both as an officer and as a subject. We were your rightful and legally constituted rulers."

"Pardon my confusion, Admiral," Harg said. "No one has ever explained that to me clearly before."

He turned back to Minicleer. "Tell me, Provost, by what right did Inning assume rule over the Forsaken Islands?"

Minicleer said in a venomous voice, "By right of conquest."

"Did the people of the Isles give their consent?"

"I don't know how we could have found that out. You can't visit every flea-ridden hovel."

There was a stir in the audience. Harg wondered why Talley wasn't breaking in. It came to him in a flash, that Talley was giving them both enough rope to hang themselves. Well, best to sail while the wind was blowing.

"Did your authorities ever consult the existing government of the Forsakens?" Harg pressed on.

With a slight laugh, Minicleer said, "There was none."

"Have you ever heard the word 'Ison'?"

"I heard it when you started going by that name."

"Have you ever heard of the Heir of Gilgen?"

"I've heard some myths and legends."

Raising his voice, Harg said, "Is it possible these offices constitute a government you did not consult before invading and waging war on us? Is it possible we were a nation with a right to our own sovereignty?"

The courtroom had been buzzing, and this question threw it into a tumult. Talley rose and gestured the guards to restore order. In a red and black line they passed into the crowd and began to wrestle some of the louder members out the door. Harg heard clubs come down on flesh.

Talley's voice rang out over the hubbub, "Prisoner, you are perverting the privilege of question which we have generously granted you. You are using this court as a forum for sedition and rebellion. You only make the blackness of your guilt more apparent."

Harg shouted, "What's apparent is the sham you call 'justice.'"

"Put him on the block," Talley ordered. The guards seized Harg's arms and nearly dragged him off his feet as they hurried him roughly to the centre of the floor. They forced him down on the block, face up, and wrenched his arms back to chain him down.

New shouts of protest went up. *At last*, Harg thought, *they see that I am them*. Shouts of "Ison! Ison!" had started up at the back of the room, where the Adaina were. The guard clamped a metal collar around Harg's neck, choking tight. He struggled to breathe.

The noise did not die down. There was a sound of scuffling, and a woman's angry cry. Harg heard Talley giving some hasty orders, then suddenly the guards were releasing him again. Before he could look around, they were dragging him at a near-run from the courtroom. Two more guards followed; Harg saw that they had guns.

They rushed him down the corridor, past some soldiers running the other way, and down the stairs into his basement cell again. Outside the tiny window, in the Gallowmarket, there was shouting and the sound of marching troops. Harg tried to climb on the cot to see out, but the window was too high. He sat there listening, half excited, half terrified by what he had done.

Not the Mundua nor all the lawyers in the world could save him now.

A bird was singing in the garden outside Spaeth's window. The sound ripped through her brain like a saw, its teeth shredding nerve fibres as if they were so much soft wood.

After they had taken Harg away, the guards had come back to move her to a new room, plainly furnished but above ground. For the first few hours she had paced restlessly, as if by moving she could stay ahead of the pain. By noon her eye had swollen shut and the whole side of her face was purple-bruised. A knife was stabbing her side with every breath. At last her joints became so painful she could no longer move, though the bed felt uncomfortable as a rocky beach, every crease in the fabric digging into her flesh.

By the next morning she was drifting deliriously in and out of this circle, in and out of the past. She kept seeing Harg asleep in the bed beside her, newly cured. His skin was warm and dry against her body, gently shifting with his breath.

How whole he was! She felt intensely proud. It was as if she had reknit him with her own tendons, filled him with her blood, created him anew. He was perfect now, a masterpiece; and yet, the instant he went out into the world something new would harm him. She wanted to spend the rest of her life as they had spent the one night, trying to get closer than the barriers of skin would permit—one person, and yet miraculously two. But in the intervals when she came awake, and found herself alone, she knew she had seen him for the last time.

At other times it seemed to her that Ridwit crouched at the foot of her bed, black fur sleek, the tip of her tail wrapped around her feet, twitching.

There were fires outside her window that night; their light made sinister patterns against the ceiling. Now, as waves of nausea passed through her, she realized what had happened: she had taken on too much. If she had been perfectly healthy, she could have survived such a dhota. But she had been weak to begin with, and Harg had poured a whole lifetime of hurts into her. It was more than even a Lashnura body could bear.

Someone was standing over her—a real person this time, looking down on her with a lantern. She tried to turn away to shield her eye from the light, whimpering a little; lifting her hand was too much effort.

"What did he do, beat you?" a sharp voice said.

She realized who it was then, on a primitive, instinctual level: her other bandhota. The thought that she might drink from him as well sent a shiver of desire through her. Though she knew it would poison her beyond cure, she still wanted him. It gave her enough energy to struggle awake.

Corbin was holding the light to inspect her bruised face, a strange mix of emotions radiating from him, tugging at her. She reached out to touch his hand. There were little blond hairs on the back of it. He wore a uniform with starched cuffs that made him look cased in authority. She loved him deliriously.

"Don't worry," he said, his hand closing over hers possessively; "he'll pay for this."

"He didn't touch me, except in love," she said.

His hand stiffened as if the words had stung him.

Still clutching his hand, she said, "These are his hurts on my body. I took them so he could be free. He is cured now. There is no pain left in him. In two weeks he will have a new eye, just as good as the old one."

Corbin sat on the edge of the bed then, setting the lamp down. His eyes were searching her face, her body, as if it had occurred to him, against every instinct, to believe her. He reached out to touch her swollen eye, very gently. "Why did you do this?" he said.

"Because dhota is the only solution I have," she said. "I thought otherwise for a long time, but now I know it's true."

"Dhota," he said flatly. "You and your father." He was looking past her now, with a haunted expression.

She realized he was speaking of Goth. She pressed his hand against her cheek. "Is he all right?"

"It depends on your definition," he said.

He looked like a man who had destroyed a thing he loved. His pain was so sharp, Spaeth said, "Let me heal you."

He looked down at her and said harshly, "You're dying."

"I know," she said.

"To cure me would kill you. I'm not going to kill another of you."

"It would be a beautiful death," she said, smiling crazily. Rainbows of desire were dancing before her eyes; she realized she couldn't hold on much longer. "Please," she said.

"No!" he said, and meant it.

She closed her eyes then, and despair seeped into her. It was Harg's despair, she realized indistinctly; but now it was hers as well. Its blackness pervaded everything.

Corbin was gathering her in his arms, picking her up. She clutched his neck, her head against his shoulder, the sharp epaulette digging into her cheek. His closeness fed her, sustained her. She savoured his texture, his smell.

Then they were in another room. He laid her gently on a bed, and kissed her forehead, stroking back the hair. There was a whole wall of windows beside her, looking out on a garden. There was no moon.

Orbs of light drifted before her eyes. The pain was still there, but far away. Corbin was no longer holding her hand, but someone else was. She watched the light drift before her like glowing smoke, till it formed an insubstantial face.

"Goth," she said. She wondered if they had entered another circle together.

"Spaeth," he said. He looked like a man dead for centuries, just a skeleton with a little grey skin stretched over it. His voice was breathy and faint. "What has happened? Whose hurts are these you are carrying?"

A year ago, he would have known. A year ago, he had been the Goth she had known all her life. "I was afraid you would die without me," she said.

"I would have," he said, "but for unfinished business."

She tried to smile, but it hurt. "You can go now. I have finished it for you."

Wondering, Goth reached out to touch her face. Suddenly, his eyes fired. "Harg! You have cured him," he said; then, with alarm, "Spaeth, you will die."

"I know," she said, smiling.

"Was all my teaching worthless? Couldn't you hold back?"

"No," she said. "There will be no other chance. He will die before he heals."

Goth realized what she meant. With a terrible grief, he said, "Talley?"

Spaeth nodded. "I couldn't cure him. He is too devoted to his pain."

"I know," Goth said. "If only . . ." He was stroking her forehead with a papery hand. "Spaeth, would you do the only thing in the world that could make me happy now?"

"Of course," she said.

"Give me the pain you took from Harg."

She drew back, horrified. "No! It's mine."

"Please," he said, his voice shaking. "You don't know how much of that pain is mine."

"Yes, I do," she said.

"Please let me set it right."

"But I want it!" she said weakly.

"Please. He would never even let me touch him. Not even a touch." His eyes were glistening with tears. Wondering that such a dry and brittle body still could weep, she reached out and touched the corner of his eye, to feel the tear on her finger.

"I love you, Goth," she said.

She never had to say she had changed her mind. They both just knew it.

It didn't even take blood; just that one teardrop, touched to her forehead, made their minds blend seamlessly. With all the gentleness she remembered, he began to draw from her the wounds that had poisoned her body. His spine arched and his head fell back as the pain entered him; but still he stopped to savour each one, to feel it fully. He had been waiting two decades and more for some of them.

As the night stretched on, he grew so weak he could no longer sit up, so he lay down on the bed and Spaeth cradled him in her arms, her vitality returning as his ebbed. Still he came back for more, till his breath was dry and ragged and his eyes stared sightless into the dark. She could feel the tremors passing through his body, and kissed him, stroking his drug-pocked arm.

He lasted till there was only one hurt left in her; then quietly, without a word, his limbs grew stiff in her arms. She lay there holding him till dawn grew light in the windows.

17
THE VICTOR AND THE VICTIM

Harg's second trial was much different from his first. It was a military court this time, and private. Evidently, Talley had concluded that the risks of convicting him in public outweighed the advantages. The change of venue was a tacit admission of defeat.

There were exactly five people in the courtroom, other than Harg: three officers sitting as judges and two advocates, one for each side. Neither said a word through the whole proceeding. There were no witnesses this time, the testimony having been given in advance, in writing. They made Harg stand before the judges to hear the charges, then to hear the verdicts: guilty, guilty. Talley gave the sentence in a dry, mechanical tone: "Three days hence you will be taken to the public square and there impaled upon a stake and left in public view until you die, as a warning and a lesson to all."

Harg had always known what the penalty would be; he had known he was courting it. Still, its proximity and inevitability completely unnerved him. Three days hence. As long as there had been no date set, it had been unreal, somewhere in the future, possible to dodge, like a bullet not yet fired. He stood staring stupidly at the judges till they told him to leave. He managed to make his legs take him from the courtroom; but once out, he stumbled like a drunkard.

The next day they took him again to the room where he had originally met Bartelso. At first he thought his jailors, at last showing a spark of humanity, meant to improve what was left of his life, but he was mistaken. Soon the sound of footsteps and voices in the hall told him it was only that he had been granted another visit.

There were two of them this time: Bartelso and another Inning, the weathered man with scanty, unkempt hair that Harg had seen drawing sketches in the courtroom. He came in with an armload of equipment, which he leaned up against a wall, then turned to survey Harg with an unnervingly concentrated gaze. In the meantime, Bartelso shook Harg's hand and said, "A thousand apologies for imposing on you, but would you mind if Mr. Mattingly here took your likeness? There is the most acute curiosity about you in Fluminos, and a picture would help immensely."

The idea made him uncomfortable, but he tried not to show it. Mattingly, the artist, came forward and said, "We have the masterful portrait of Admiral Talley by Roland that was exhibited at the Academy last summer, but his opponent is a blank to most of the nation. A companion portrait would capture the contrast as no mere words could do."

Harg glanced at Bartelso. "Do it. Think of your legacy," the attorney said, squeezing his shoulder.

And so Harg allowed himself to be seated self-consciously in a chair opposite the window while the artist set up an easel and canvas and began mixing paints. It was a little unreal. These men were so busily caught up in the concerns of the world that they seemed oblivious to the fact that he was about to quit it.

"Keep talking," the artist instructed. "Your face is more animated when you talk."

Bartelso drew up a chair and handed him a sheaf of newspapers. "I brought the accounts of your trial," he said. "Your performance was immensely popular with the press. You gave them a lot to shoot at each other about." He paged through one newssheet and read out, "'Nothing could have been more poignant than the sight of this man vainly defying the implacable force of law arrayed against him. On the bench was all that was disciplined, refined, and cerebral. In the dock, all that was instinctive, natural, and vanquished. With all his power he had fought an unequal war against the spread of empire; but now the knowledge of his doom was clearly written in his face.' That's the most favourable one. The negative ones are less edifying."

"I'm glad they were entertained," Harg said, rankled at being reduced to a man of nature. He imagined all the Innings in their comfortable parlours who would thrill to the fiction of a noble warrior unable to defy their empire. It would simultaneously assure them of the worthiness of the opposition, and their own unassailable right of conquest.

Briskly, Bartelso said, "Now, as to business. I have taken the liberty of appealing your case to the High Court."

Harg looked up at him. "Is there any hope . . .?"

"No, not really. The Court might well review the case, but the Admiral is in such an unseemly hurry to carry out the sentence that by the time we receive word, it will all be moot. In view of that, I also petitioned the Admiral to stay the sentence till the High Court could respond, but he denied it. So I petitioned him for clemency. It's really the last hope."

Clemency. From Corbin Talley. Harg said, "Why are you still bothering?"

"Apart from the fact that you deserve a defender, you mean?" Bartelso's eyes had an expression Harg had never seen on an Inning face: a mix of regret, admiration, and paternal concern. "To be honest, this case has been a scandalous travesty. I expected there to be a pretense of impartiality; our system is supposed to guarantee that, at least. We haven't just failed you. We have failed ourselves."

But none of them was going to die.

His expression must have said it, because Bartelso cleared his throat and said, "Pardon me for asking, Harg, but have you made out a will?"

At last, they had come down to reality. Harg shook his head. "I don't have anything to leave, and no one to leave it to."

"Nothing at all?" The Inning looked a little unwilling to believe it. Harg tried to think.

"Nothing," he said. "Only my story." He looked down at the newspapers and realized, not even that. His story was not his own now. There was another Harg springing to life in the Inning mind, one that served their purposes and not his. He looked up at Bartelso. "Would you take it down, if I told it to you? Do we have time?"

Bartelso said, "They didn't give me a limit this time. There is no more mischief we can get into."

"Did you bring paper and pen?"

"Of course."

"Then take this down."

And so he spent the afternoon dictating his story to the lawyer, while the artist worked silently. He wanted to leave something behind that was really his, and this was all he had. The story told his way, not the way the Innings would reshape it and make it their own.

The light was fading from the window by the time Mattingly laid down his brushes and Harg fell silent. He hadn't said all he wanted to, but he might never figure out everything he ought to say. Bartelso put down his pen, flexing his wrist, then got up to view the canvas. Harg did the same.

At first, Harg barely recognized himself. The features were his, but the tragic expression, the mortality-haunted gaze seemed to belong to someone greater. In the painting, his shirt was unbuttoned to show a glimpse of muscled chest, vulnerably exposed.

"I needed to signal the radiant life-force and vitality," the artist explained. "This portrait shows your heart. It's an answer to Roland's, which shows only intellect."

So this was the Harg the Innings saw. This was what they wanted—no, *needed*—him to be. And this was the person they had to kill. He shook his head slowly. "I'll never understand you," he said.

After the two Innings left, the guards took Harg back to his cell and left him, as usual, without a light. As night fell he sat on his cot, thinking about the person in the painting. It was almost as if the Innings longed for an Ison Harg as much as the islanders did—not to lead them, but to die at their hands.

He heard the guard change an hour before midnight, but he felt no desire to sleep. A feeling of purpose had taken hold of his mind, and with it a mood of peace. What lay ahead for him was a kind of dhota, without which the war would never end. The Innings needed to pour all their rage and revenge into a final, vicious act that would purge them of their pain. If they could not kill him, they would never be cured, and would continue to damage the world. An Ison, he realized, was like the dhotamar to a nation; but it was not his own nation he needed to cure. It was Inning.

He fell asleep at last, resting in resignation, and did not dream.

The next day, they took him to see the stake that was being prepared for him, and to get a briefing from the Inning technician who would supervise his execution. In a cool, dispassionate tone, the man explained the anatomical discoveries that had made it possible for them to thrust a stake up a man's spine without killing him, and all the technical improvements they employed to prolong the process of dying. He learned each step that would happen to him the following day, and viewed the preparations in the Gallowmarket. He managed to stay in control till they brought him back to his cell, and then he vomited convulsively.

It had been their purpose to fill his mind with grisly visions, and rob him of any courage or dignity. He knew it, and yet it worked. For the rest of the day, as he listened to the hammering as they constructed grandstands outside his window, his senses seemed unnaturally acute. He was vividly aware of his own body. It was a sacred symbol of the Isles, Agave had said. It was also the thing that gave the Innings power to drag him down and bestialize him. There would be nothing heroic or noble about his death. No one would see Harg in the naked, soiled form writhing on the stake tomorrow. By the time he died, he would barely be human.

The remaining hours of the day flew by. He paced, struggling to regain his mood from the night before, but his mind was too full of horrific details. His own imagination had reduced him to quivering, hyperactive reflexes.

As night fell, he begged the guards again to give him a light, but they refused even such a petty request. As the darkness in his cell grew impenetrable, his fear expanded to fill all the spaces he couldn't see. It was a debilitating terror that made him sweaty and weak-bowelled, that left him crouching on the floor, his back against the wall, knees drawn up, waves of useless panic coursing through him.

Just after midnight, there was a noise at the cellblock door. As he heard the key in the lock he thought he ought to move, or they would find him like this, cowering against the wall almost senseless with fear; but somehow his body was unable to move. As he waited, slow footsteps and a light approached down the corridor, till at last they came to a halt outside his cell.

It was Corbin Talley, alone.

He stood there a while, just watching, and neither of them said a word. He raised the lamp a little to study Harg's face, taking in his terror without any sign of pleasure. At last Harg managed to make his voice say, "What do you want?"

"Just to see you," Talley said. He set down the lamp then, and took out a key. He unlocked the cell door and let himself in, drawing the gate closed again behind him. There was not a guard in sight. Harg wondered if it were some sort of test of courage, like entering the cage of an animal. He stood up, his back still against the wall.

Talley walked forward till he stood directly in front of Harg. Slowly, as if not to startle him, the Admiral raised a hand to the patch on his eye, then carefully removed it. He studied the wound with fascination. Harg realized he could sense light a little on that side.

"So she told the truth," Talley said. "She did cure you."

"Yes," Harg said.

"What a waste," Talley said.

There was a sharp regret in his tone. It made Harg say, "Why? Is she all right?"

"She will recover," Talley said. "But Goran, son of Listor, is dead."

Goth dead. Somehow, with so little left of his own life, it didn't seem as final as it would have otherwise. "I wish I could have seen him," Harg said.

"I regret what happened to him," Talley said. "We became rather like friends at the end."

With a little wonder, Harg realized it was grief in Talley's voice.

"I've been trying to see something of him in you, but I can't," Talley said. "There's not a speck of resemblance."

"No," Harg said. "There never was, on the surface."

Talley turned away then, as if he didn't want Harg to see his face. With his back turned, he said, "I have been thinking. Every now and then, a man should be entitled to act for himself, and not for his country."

He turned back then. He had unbuttoned his coat, and Harg saw that he was wearing a pearl-handled pistol in a holster on his belt. He took it out, and for an instant Harg stiffened, thinking the Admiral had decided to take his revenge personally rather than allowing the law to take its course. His next thought was that it would be an act of uncommon mercy.

There was a slight smile on Talley's face, as if he had followed each succeeding thought in Harg's mind. Then he confounded them all by turning the gun around and offering the handle to Harg.

At first Harg didn't move. "Go ahead, take it," Talley said.

Harg took the gun and checked to see that it was loaded. Then he looked up at Talley's face, wondering if he should thank him. There was a look of cool speculation in the Inning's eyes. Not until then did it occur to Harg that Talley was standing there unarmed now, close to touch—the butcher who had turned the South Chain into a lifeless waste.

Slowly, he cocked the gun and turned it around till it pointed at the Inning. Talley stiffened with tension, but didn't move, and his eyes never left Harg's face. Harg pressed the muzzle to Talley's chest, just over his heart. He could feel the man's pulse in his hand, through the butt of the pistol, through his finger on the trigger. It was a curiously intimate moment, only the two of them in the cell, Harg standing with his enemy's heart in his hand.

"Only one ball, I suppose?" Harg said.

Talley nodded. Suddenly, he was the one unable to speak.

Harg lowered the gun and uncocked it. "Then I think I'll save it."

The blood rushed back into Talley's face. He stepped back, drew a breath, then said, "You would have been a hero, you know. We could both have been heroes—you for your people, I for mine."

So he really hadn't expected to walk out alive. Harg thrust the pistol into his belt and crossed his arms, glad not to have obliged him.

For a moment Talley stood there trying to gather his thoughts. He looked a little unnerved now. At last he seemed to reach a resolution, and went to the cell door. But instead of leaving, he said, "Come with me."

Suspicious of a ruse to get the gun and its precious ball away from him, Harg for an instant considered using it then and there. "I'm not giving it back," he said.

"I'm not asking you to," Talley answered. He held the cell gate open, and at last Harg followed him.

Outside the cell block was a guard's room where two Torna soldiers sat playing cards. They both rose to attention as the Admiral entered. "One of you, come with us," Talley said curtly. The guard, looking at Harg, moved to take a set of manacles down from the wall, but Talley said, "Leave those. We won't need them."

With the guard at Harg's back, Talley led him up a flight of stairs and through a tall, unlit hall. Harg had his bearings now; they were making for the Gallowmarket gate. He thought he knew what this was all about.

The soldiers at the gate challenged them, but Talley's curt order got them through. They emerged from the palace together, and Harg saw the site of next morning's spectacle, lit by the rising moon. The wooden grandstands stood on one side, draped with bunting, and there was space for a huge audience on the other. On the execution platform below the palace walls, the stake was waiting, set horizontally on trestles. It gleamed in the moonlight, as if greased. Harg's knees suddenly felt weak.

Talley paused, scanning the empty plaza. "We had to clear the square forcibly at sunset," he said. "There were crowds camped out. Your countrymen are ghouls."

"No, you're wrong," Harg said, his voice faint. "They know the power in what you're about to do. Unwitnessed, it would have no sanctity or meaning."

"Sanctity!" Talley exclaimed in disgust.

"For us, suffering consecrates and heals."

He could feel the gun in his belt, pressing hard against his flesh. His escape. The way out that would leave things forever unresolved. There would be no catharsis, no cure, no significance to a banal death by his own hand. He needed to give the gun back. He needed to do it for the Isles, and for Inning. He tried to make his hand move to grasp the butt, and couldn't do it. He was too much of a coward.

A wave of dizziness passed through him, and he swayed. Talley gripped his arm to keep him upright. "This way," the Inning said. "Don't make us carry you."

A covered carriage drawn by two horses was parked under the shadow of the palace walls. Talley pushed Harg into it, then climbed in himself, sitting in the facing seat, and dismissed the guard. He rapped on the ceiling and the carriage lurched into motion. Harg no longer thought he knew what was going on.

They clattered through dark streets, weaving around corners, often climbing, till Harg was thoroughly lost. He tried to divine something from Talley's manner, but the Admiral was like a mechanical man now, acting automatically. At last, from the sound of the wheels, Harg could tell they were on a dirt road. He leaned over to look out the window, and saw only fields and roadside bushes. "Where are we going?" he finally said.

"Croom," Talley answered, his voice neutral. "There will be some friends of yours waiting there with a boat. The only promise you must give me is to leave the Forsakens by the shortest route. Otherwise you will be hunted down."

Harg saw the gleam of Talley's teeth as he gave a joyless smile. "You understand, this is not a bargain Inning will honour. This is strictly a private matter between you and me. My orders were to carry out your execution tomorrow, so that the High Court in Fluminos could act suitably shocked by my severity, and disavow responsibility. They weren't sure of the repercussions, you see, and wanted to be able to pin the blame on someone else. It is always handy to have a monster to hold over people's heads."

His voice was unemotional. Harg stared at him, still disbelieving. "Are you acting against orders, then?" he asked.

Talley smiled thinly at him. "You could say that. I have just broken the law and helped a condemned fugitive to escape. Not even my family will be able to cover this up, not that they would try. I'll be the one accused of treason now." His smile was like a black glass knife.

"You deserve worse," Harg said, thinking of all Talley had done.

Looking out the window, Talley said, "Justice is more elusive than our law implies. And mercy is nearly driven from the land."

The racket of the wheels filled the silence between them. "What if I had used the gun and shot you back there?" Harg said.

"Then, obviously, I wouldn't have been able to carry this plan out."

It had been some sort of strange, twisted test. Another trial, this one of Talley's own devising.

The carriage stopped at the head of the cliff, where the road plunged in steep switchbacks down to the sea. "You will have to walk from here," Talley said. "The road is too dangerous for a vehicle at night. Go to a tavern called the Sunken City, on the main street. Your friends are waiting there."

Harg sat staring at him for a second.

"Go on! Get out of here!" Talley said.

On a sudden impulse, Harg reached across and grasped Talley's hand. For an instant, it was as if he touched the Inning's mind; it was all laid bare, as in dhota. Harg felt a compassion that terrified him. "Let her cure you," he said, then dived out the carriage door.

He ran the first hundred yards or so, partly out of sheer exuberance in his freedom, partly out of fear that it was all a trick, and soldiers would come out of the shadows to arrest him. On the second switchback he slowed to a walk, panting, able to see by moonlight before and behind, and no one was waiting in ambush. It was a clear, chilly night. Below, he could see the lights of Croom, and the moon cast a shiny trail on the sea, as if someone had newly buffed the waves.

The Sunken City showed signs of having been a popular place earlier in the evening. Now the crowds were gone and the staff was clearing up. He stood at the door, looking around, feeling conspicuous. Two people were still drinking at a table in the shadows; they saw him and started up. He almost dodged out the door before he recognized Katri and Tway.

They each hugged him wordlessly; no names were uttered. Katri tugged him by the arm into a shadowy alcove, whispering, "Horns, am I glad to see you whole."

"There's going to be some disappointed people when they have to cancel the show tomorrow," he said. He was still trembling with the thought that he'd escaped it.

"I've got two boats," Katri said. "Talley gave me my freedom on condition I get you safely to Rothur, so they'll think you're with me. But you won't be. My boat will be the decoy, and the other's yours. She's all stocked so you won't have to lay in to port till you reach Rothur. Want to see her?"

"Yes!"

They left the inn and headed for the dock. The boat was a sloop fitted for single-handed sailing. Harg jumped on board and began checking out the sails and lines. Katri's boat was moored alongside. She said, "I'll make straight south, as if to Rothur; you go west, as if to Lashnish. If anyone gives chase, they'll follow me." She leaped aboard her boat and disappeared below.

Tway was standing on the dock, watching. "Want a crew?" she said.

He couldn't imagine she meant it. "I'm leaving the Isles, Tway. Only the Ashwin know if I'll ever be back."

"Do you think I'm as dumb as that knot you're tying?" she said impatiently. Then, conversationally, "You're doing it backwards."

He looked down, found she was right, and unravelled it. He said, "You don't know what you're asking. The Rothurs are beasts. They make their wives live in separate houses."

"You think I want to marry one?" Tway said.

He tried to picture Tway in Rothur—Tway, with her tart tongue and her practical grasp of what mattered. He almost laughed. It would serve the Rothurs right.

"Is that a yes or a no?" she demanded.

"You got any skills?" he said, to tease her.

She said, "I can tie knots in places you've never even imagined."

"You're hired," he said.

She jumped aboard and quickly set about loosing the mainsail.

She was everything he came from, familiar as his own past. A part of his past he could still salvage, that he hadn't destroyed beyond recall.

"Tway," he said seriously, resting his arms on the transom of the cockpit, "you can find someone better than me."

She paused to look at him over the boom. "Oh, I think you'll do for now," she said.

There was a good east wind, and they set course down the channel north of Rusk with the sails splayed wide. Sitting with his feet braced against the edge of the cockpit, with Tway sitting warm beside him, Harg looked up at the stars and nearly shouted in joy at his freedom.

Tornabay was finally getting back to normal. The mongers were back haggling in their stalls, the insurance offices were doing a brisk business, and Torna developers were looking with interest at all the real estate fortuitously cleared by the fires. Even the Adainas camping in the ruins had a new look of solidarity, as if each of them personally had outwitted Inning justice. Though the entire year of conflict had netted them precisely nothing, when they met on the street they looked like they were exchanging secret handshakes with their eyes.

"Don't they know they've lost?" Nathaway said to Spaeth. "They're so complacent to be victims."

They stood on the balcony outside his hotel room, which looked out on the Rivermarket. She was wrapped in a woollen man's coat that nearly reached her ankles, for the east wind was chilly. Her hair was braided and coiled on her head again, the way she liked it.

It was two days since she had told him she was pregnant. The news had staggered him. The first words out of his mouth had been, "Whose is it?"

"What do you mean? It's mine," she said.

"I mean, who's the father?"

"You can be, if you want."

He had still tried to probe, to suit his Inning notion of paternity, but it was useless. She didn't know and didn't care.

He was getting used to the idea now. Though it still made him jumpy, and he sometimes looked at her like a man doomed in court to a life sentence, she could tell he was already falling in love with the child, sight unseen.

Pregnancy was a lovely consolation, but there was still a hungry, empty space inside her—and would be, as long as Harg and Corbin were alive, and Corbin uncured. Her two complicated bandhotai, carrying all the cares of two incompatible worlds. She leaned against Nathaway, enjoying the simplicity of her feelings for him. He was in his usual state of unfocused dissatisfaction with the world. Nothing ever quite lived up to his expectations.

"They're just going to fall back into that Adaina stoicism," he said. "The Governor's already reneging on his promises about the land, and no one will fight him."

Spaeth squeezed his hand. "Fighting doesn't work. What we need is dhota."

"There's not enough Grey People alive to do the curing the Isles need," he said.

That was why the Emerald Tablet had passed on, she thought. She looked at Nathaway, and thought with a quirk of inner laughter that dhota had worked on him, and no dhotamar had ever touched blood to him. It had been the dhota of the ordinary Adaina that had captured him. He had absorbed the memory of them into his pores, and nothing could ever get it out of him. Perhaps the Inning empire would be the same. "They should have a care who they conquer," she said. "They say the victor always becomes the victim."

"Is that another of your Lashnura proverbs?"

"Yes."

She put her arms around him, and he held her close. She said, "You think the war is over. It's not. We're going to beat the Innings yet, but not their way. We'll have to do it our way, with mora. The more they make us sacrifice, the more power we will have."

"That's outrageous!" Nathaway said. "It's totally unjust."

There was a minor commotion behind them, back in the room; Bartelso had arrived. He joined them on the balcony, breathless from climbing the stairs. "My dear boy," he said, seizing Nathaway's hand, "I just heard the good news, that your lovely wife is adding another Talley to the world." He turned to Spaeth, beaming. "Well done, my dear. Now I'll get congratulated for having had the foresight to marry the two of you in time."

Spaeth had no idea what he was talking about, but it seemed well intentioned, so she smiled. Nathaway was looking awkward. Bartelso clapped him on the back. "I dare say your mother never suspected you would be the first one to present her with a grandchild, but she will be very pleased."

"You think so?" Nathaway said anxiously.

"I know it." His face changed, and grew more serious. "It will soften the bad news." He took a newspaper from his pocket and handed it to Nathaway. "They're not going to let the Navy handle Corbin's case. They're going to try him before the court in Fluminos," he said. "It's going to become a political lynching."

Spaeth felt a cold dread at the news. She looked up at Nathaway. They both knew what it meant. She had to follow her bandhota.

"Then we'll go," Nathaway said, squeezing her hand.

"You'll love it, my dear!" Bartelso said. "It's the most exciting city in the world. You know, if you spit from a rooftop anywhere between the Knob and Holton Street, you're sure to hit a lawyer."

"We'll make an effort to try," Nathaway said.

Bartelso looked at the two of them, sizing them up. "You'll definitely liven the place up. Yes, indeed."

After he had bustled off, Spaeth stood trying to convince herself that he was right, and she could be happy outside the Isles.

Nathaway put his hands on her shoulders. "You *will* like it, Spaeth," he said. "I promise. Some night I'll take you up onto the hills overlooking the city, and you'll see the whole valley sparkling like a thousand stars. You'll say there is magic in us, too."

"I have walked other circles," she said. "I suppose I can walk Holton Street."

Seriously, he said, "Isn't there any way to free you from my brother?"

She shook her head. "No way at all. I must cure him some day. When that happens, he will love me, and I will love him more than anything in the world. But it won't change the way I love you." She could see that it troubled him, but there was nothing she could do about it. Her ancestors had seen to that.

Later that day, when Nathaway was out booking passage on a ship to Fluminos, she returned to the balcony, a terrible ache of homesickness already in her heart. No Lashnura was meant to leave the islands for the lands outside, where the earth was inert and unfeeling. She thought of the words she had spoken, about sacrifice, and felt that it wasn't over for her.

She had no illusion that the Innings would be kind to her, no more than they would be to the Isles. She thought, *We are their past they have lost. They need us, and therefore hate us. They want to destroy us because we are their salvation.*

The rooftops by her balcony came together in a complex mesh of angles, slate and clay and cedar shingle all mossy with age. In one of the rooftops was a gable window standing open, where a black housecat with yellow eyes was watching her. Tensing, she leaned over the railing toward it. "Ridwit?" she whispered.

The cat blinked slowly, but said nothing.

How the panther would ridicule her for what she had become—just another dhotamar enslaved to her bandhota. And yet it was only through dhota that she had achieved any justice. Only by giving up control had she found control.

"Ridwit, am I doing the right thing?" she said.

The cat didn't answer.

ABOUT THE AUTHOR

Carolyn Ives Gilman writes both fiction and nonfiction about frontiers. Growing up close to the U.S.-Canada boundary, she became a historian of borders between nations, races, and cultures, and a writer of fiction about even more exotic worlds than ours.

Carolyn Ives Gilman's most recent novel, *Isles of the Forsaken*, starts the story concluded in *Ison of the Isles*; it has been compared to the works of Mary Doria Russell and Ursula K. LeGuin. Her first novel, *Halfway Human*, was called "one of the most compelling explorations of gender and power in recent SF" by *Locus* magazine. Her short fiction has appeared in *Fantasy and Science Fiction*, *The Year's Best Science Fiction*, *Bending the Landscape*, *Interzone*, *Universe*, *Full Spectrum*, *Realms of Fantasy*, and others, and she has a collection of short fiction, *Aliens of the Heart*, from Aqueduct Press. Her work has been translated and reprinted in Russia, Romania, the Czech Republic, Sweden, Poland, and Germany. She has twice been a finalist for the Nebula Award.

In her professional career, Gilman is a historian specializing in 18th- and early 19th-century North American history, particularly frontier and Native history. Her latest nonfiction book, *Lewis and Clark: Across the Divide*, was featured by the History Book Club and Book of the Month Club. Her history books have won the Missouri Governor's Humanities Award, the Missouri Conference on History Best Book Award, the Northeastern Minnesota Book Award, and the Outstanding Academic Book of the Year award from *Choice* magazine. She has been interviewed on *All Things Considered*, *Talk of the Nation*, *History Detectives*, and the *History Channel*. She is currently working on a history of the American Revolution on the frontier.

Carolyn Ives Gilman is a native of Minnesota who now lives in St. Louis and works for the Missouri History Museum.

COMING IN SPRING FROM
WORLD FANTASY AWARD-
NOMINATED PRESS

ChiZine Publications

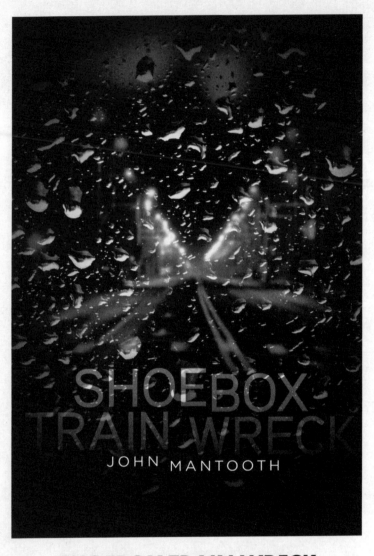

SHOEBOX TRAIN WRECK

JOHN MANTOOTH

AVAILABLE MARCH 2012
FROM CHIZINE PUBLICATIONS

978-1-926851-54-9

ALSO AVAILABLE FROM CHIZINE PUBLICATIONS

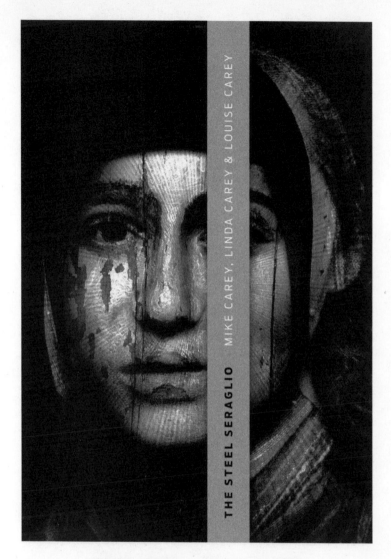

THE STEEL SERAGLIO

MIKE CAREY, LINDA CAREY & LOUISE CAREY

AVAILABLE MARCH 2012
FROM CHIZINE PUBLICATIONS

978-1-926851-53-2

WESTLAKE SOUL

RIO YOUERS

AVAILABLE APRIL 2012
FROM CHIZINE PUBLICATIONS

978-1-926851-55-6

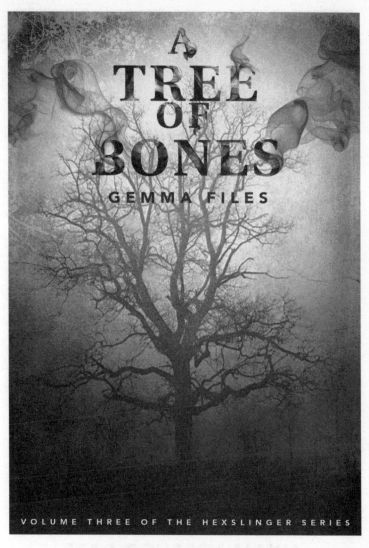

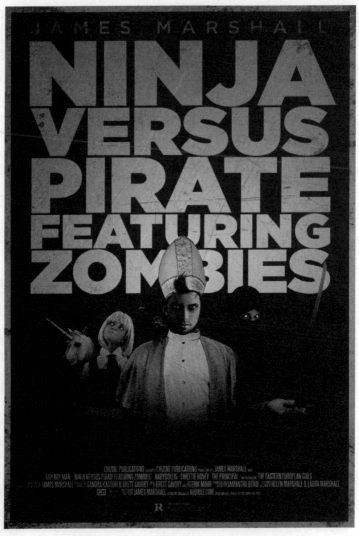

NINJA VERSUS PIRATE
FEATURING ZOMBIES

JAMES MARSHALL

AVAILABLE MAY 2012
FROM CHIZINE PUBLICATIONS

978-1-926851-58-7

ALSO AVAILABLE FROM CHIZINE PUBLICATIONS

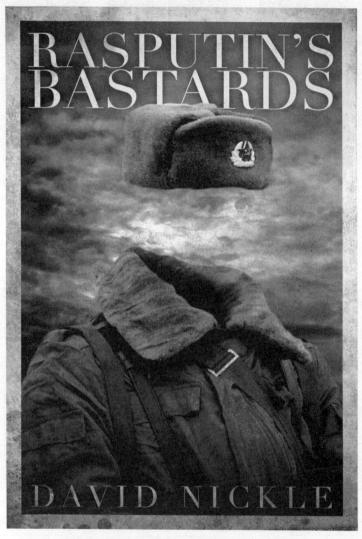

RASPUTIN'S BASTARDS

DAVID NICKLE

AVAILABLE JUNE 2012
FROM CHIZINE PUBLICATIONS

978-1-926851-59-4

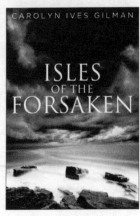

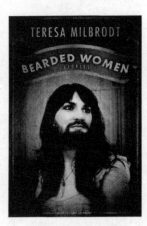
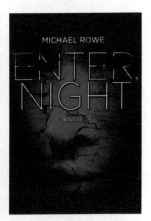

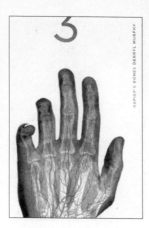

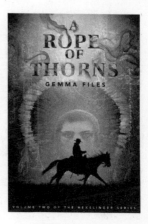

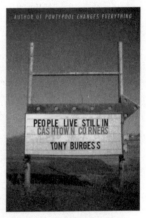

978-0-9812978-9-7

TIM LEBBON

**THE THIEF OF
BROKEN TOYS**

978-0-9812978-8-0

PHILIP NUTMAN

CITIES OF NIGHT

978-0-9812978-7-3

SIMON LOGAN

*KATJA FROM THE
PUNK BAND*

978-0-9812978-6-6

GEMMA FILES

**A BOOK OF
TONGUES**

978-0-9812978-5-9

DOUGLAS SMITH

CHIMERASCOPE

978-0-9812978-4-2

NICHOLAS KAUFMANN

*CHASING THE
DRAGON*

"IF YOUR TASTE IN FICTION RUNS TO THE DISTURBING, DARK, AND AT LEAST PARTIALLY WEIRD, CHANCES ARE YOU'VE HEARD OF CHIZINE PUBLICATIONS—CZP—A YOUNG IMPRINT THAT IS NONETHELESS PRODUCING STARTLINGLY BEAUTIFUL BOOKS OF STARKLY, DARKLY LITERARY QUALITY."
—DAVID MIDDLETON, *JANUARY MAGAZINE*

978-0-9809410-9-8

ROBERT J. WIERSEMA

**THE WORLD MORE
FULL OF WEEPING**

978-0-9812978-2-8

CLAUDE LALUMIÈRE

**OBJECTS OF
WORSHIP**

978-0-9809410-7-4

DANIEL A. RABUZZI

THE CHOIR BOATS

978-0-9809410-5-0

LAVIE TIDHAR AND NIR YANIV

**THE TEL AVIV
DOSSIER**

978-0-9809410-3-6

ROBERT BOYCZUK

**HORROR STORY
AND OTHER
HORROR STORIES**

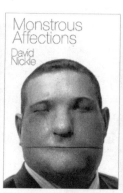

978-0-9812978-3-5

DAVID NICKLE

**MONSTROUS
AFFECTIONS**

978-0-9809410-1-2

BRENT HAYWARD

FILARIA

"CHIZINE PUBLICATIONS REPRESENTS SOMETHING WHICH IS COMMON IN THE
MUSIC INDUSTRY BUT SADLY RARER WITHIN THE PUBLISHING INDUSTRY: THAT A
CLEVER INDEPENDENT CAN RUN RINGS ROUND THE MAJORS IN TERMS OF STYLE
AND CONTENT."

—MARTIN LEWIS, *SF SITE*

ALSO AVAILABLE FROM CHIZINE PUBLICATIONS